PRAISE F[...]
OF THE [...] T0014384

Skin Game

"This is urban fantasy par excellence, with magical action, moral dilemmas, and a wonderful cast."
—*Library Journal* (starred review)

"Jim's characteristic writing skills have made the Dresden Files such a publishing phenomenon. *Skin Game* continues in that rich vein, and if you are a Dresden fan, then you will love it. . . . Epic, simply epic is the adjective I would use to describe *Skin Game*. . . . Jim Butcher is back, boys and girls, and *Skin Game* will have you rejoicing and gallivanting like none other."
—Fantasy Book Critic

"Much of what makes the Dresden Files so phenomenal and addictive is Butcher's ability to bring a level of complexity to his stories and characters that always challenge his readers and leave them guessing . . . exhilarating and intense." —*RT Book Reviews* (top pick, starred review)

"Butcher's style is an addictive and clever one; his approach is warm and easy, but he loves to toy with the reader, adding twist after twist." —*Starburst*

"The prose, editing, pacing, and plotting are all top-notch. It was tightly knit from beginning to end, and I could not put it down. . . . *Skin Game* is another fantastic addition to the Dresden Files that will certainly satisfy longtime readers." —Kings River Life Magazne

continued . . .

"Jim Butcher isn't lacking in the original-ideas department. To add to this, his writing is still frighteningly sharp, considering the series' impressive length. . . . The pace is still quick, the action is still impressive, and the series' increasingly epic feel retains its shine. In addition, Butcher is still able to masterfully tug at the heartstrings when necessary through his strong characterization."

—Fantasy Faction

"Harry is easily one of the best characters in fantasy literature today. He's powerful, wise, fallible, kindhearted, and can always find humor in the darkest of hours. This latest installment is fast-paced and full of adventure, suspense, thrills, and more great characters. This solid series never disappoints and always entertains."

—SciFiChick.com

PRAISE FOR THE OTHER NOVELS OF THE DRESDEN FILES

"Jim Butcher easily proves that he's still the master, and when it comes to conjuring literary magic, he's as talented if not better than any wizard known to mankind."

—Fantasy Book Critic

"Think *Buffy the Vampire Slayer* starring Philip Marlowe . . . a fast and furious adventure with winking nods to Bugs Bunny and John Carpenter."

—*Entertainment Weekly*

"One of the most enjoyable marriages of the fantasy and mystery genres on the shelves."   —*Cinescape*

JIM BUTCHER

SKIN GAME

A NOVEL OF THE DRESDEN FILES

ACE
New York

ACE
Published by Berkley
An imprint of Penguin Random House LLC
penguinrandomhouse.com

Copyright © 2014 by Jim Butcher
Penguin Random House supports copyright. Copyright fuels creativity, encourages
diverse voices, promotes free speech, and creates a vibrant culture. Thank you for buying
an authorized edition of this book and for complying with copyright laws by not
reproducing, scanning, or distributing any part of it in any form without permission.
You are supporting writers and allowing Penguin Random House to continue to
publish books for every reader.

ACE is a registered trademark and the A colophon is a
trademark of Penguin Random House LLC.

ISBN: 9780451470041

Roc hardcover edition / May 2014
Roc premium edition / March 2015
Ace premium edition / January 2024

Printed in the United States of America
14   16   17   15   13

For Lori, Julie, and Mom.
You guys really came through for me. Thank you.

Chapter
One

There was a ticking time bomb inside my head and the one person I trusted to go in and get it out hadn't shown up or spoken to me for more than a year.

That's a lot of time to start asking yourself questions. *Who am I? What have I done with my life?*

Who can I trust?

That last one is a doozy. It haunts you in moments of doubt. Sometimes when you wake up at night, you wonder if you've put your faith in the right people. Sometimes when you find yourself alone, for whatever reason, you review every little thing you know about someone, searching your memory for small, subtle things that you may have missed about them.

It makes you scared. It makes you think that maybe you've made some horrible mistakes lately. It drives you to *do* something, to act—only when you're stuck on an island in the middle of Lake Michigan, you're kind of limited in your choices of exactly what you can do to blow off steam.

I'd gone with my usual option. I was running through

long tunnels filled with demons and monsters and nightmares, because it was easier than going to the gym.

The tunnels were big, the size of some of the substreets beneath the city of Chicago, their walls made of earth and stone, wound through with things that looked like roots but could not possibly belong to any tree this deep in the earth. Every few yards, more or less at random, there was a mound of luminous pale green quartz crystals. Inside every crystal mound was a recumbent, shadowy form. Some of the mounds held figures no larger than a medium-sized dog. Some of them were the size of houses.

I had just finished climbing over one of the huge mounds and was sprinting toward the next, the first in a series of three mounds more or less the size of my deceased Volkswagen.

"Parkour!" I shouted, and leapt, hitting the top of the mound with my hands and vaulting over it. I landed on the far side, dropped into a forward roll over one shoulder, and came up running.

"Parkour!" I shouted at the next mound, putting one hand down as I leapt, using it to guide my body up to the horizontal at the same level as my head, clearing the next mound, landing, and staying on the move.

"Parkour!" I screamed again at the third, and simply dove over it in a long arc. The idea was to clear it, land on my hands, drop into a smooth roll, and come up running again, but it didn't work out that way. I misjudged the dive, my foot caught a crystal, and I belly flopped and planted my face in the dirt on the far side of the mound.

I lay there on the ground for a moment, getting back the wind I'd knocked out of myself. Taking a fall wasn't a big deal. God knows, I've done it enough. I rolled over onto my back and groaned. "Harry, you've got way too much time on your hands."

My voice echoed through the tunnel, number seven of thirteen.

"Parkour," said a distant echo.

I shook my head, pushed myself up, and started walking out. Walking through one of the tunnels beneath the island of Demonreach was always an experience. When I ran, I went by the mounds pretty quick.

When I walked, the prisoners trapped inside them had time to talk to me.

Let me fulfill your every desire, crooned a silken voice in my head as I went by one.

Blood and power, riches and strength, I can give you all that you—promised the next.

One day, mortal, I will be free and suck the marrow from your bones, snarled another.

Bow down in fear and horror before me!

Loathe me, let me devour you, and I will make real your dreams.

Release me or I will destroy you!

Go to sleep. Go to sleep. Sleep and let me inside you . . .

Bloodpaindeathbloodfleshbloodpaindeath . . .

BLARGLE SLORG NOTH HARGHLE FTHAGN!

You know.

The usual.

I skirted around a fairly small mound whose occupant had simply sent me a mental picture that had kept me up for a couple of nights the last time I walked by, and passed one of the last mounds before the exit.

As I walked by, the mound's occupant projected a mental sigh and an unmistakable image of a man rolling his eyes. *Ah. A new one.*

I paused and studied the mound. As a rule, I didn't communicate with the prisoners. If you were locked up under Demonreach, you were a nightmare the likes of which few people could really understand—immortal, savage, and probably foaming-at-the-mouth, hair-on-fire crazy to boot.

But . . . I'd been locked up almost as well as the prisoners for months, trapped on the island and in the caverns beneath. There wasn't a lot of choice. Until I got the thing in my head out again, only the island had the power to keep it in check. I had visitors sometimes, but the winter months were dangerous on Lake Michigan, both because of the weather and because of the ice, and spring had only barely begun to touch the world again. It had been a while since I'd seen anyone.

So I eyed the mound, one about the size of a coffin, and said, "What's your problem?"

You, obviously, replied the occupant. *Do you even know what the word* stasis *means? It means nothing is happening. You standing here, walking by, talking to me, for God's sake, buggers that up entirely, the way you novices always do. What was the phrase? Ah, yes. Piss off.*

I lifted my eyebrows. To date, every single prisoner who had tried to communicate with me had been pretty obviously playing to get out, or else howling nuts. This guy just sounded . . . British.

"Huh," I said.

Did you hear me, Warden? Piss. Off.

I debated taking him literally, just to be a wiseass, but decided that body humor was beneath the dignity of a Wizard of the White Council and the Warden of Demonreach, thus disproving everyone who says I am nothing but an overgrown juvenile delinquent.

"Who are you?" I asked instead.

There was a long moment of silence. And then a thought filled with a terrible weariness and purely emotional anguish, like something I'd experienced only at the very lowest moments of my life, flowed into me—but for this being, such pain wasn't a low point. It was a constant state. *Someone who needs to be here. Go away, boy.*

A rolling wave of nausea went through me. The air was suddenly too bright, the gentle glow of the crystals too piercing. I found myself taking several steps back from the mound, until that awful tide of feeling had receded, but the headache those emotions had triggered found me nonetheless, and I was abruptly in too much pain to keep my feet.

I dropped to one knee, clenching my teeth on a scream. The headaches had gotten steadily worse, and despite a lifetime of learning to cope with pain, despite the power of the mantle of the Winter Knight, they had begun kicking my ass thoroughly a few weeks before.

For a while, there was simply pain, and aching, racking nausea.

Eventually, that began to grow slowly less, and I looked up to see a hulking form in a dark cloak standing over me. It was ten or twelve feet tall, and built on the same scale as a massively muscled human, though I never really seemed to see much of the being beneath the cloak.

It stared down at me, a pair of pinpoints of green, fiery light serving as eyes within the depths of its hood.

"WARDEN," it said, its voice a deep rumble, "I HAVE SUPPRESSED THE PARASITE FOR NOW."

"'Bout time, Alfred," I muttered. I sat up and took stock of myself. I'd been lying there for a while. The sweat on my skin had dried. That was bad. The ancient spirit of the island had been keeping the thing in my skull from killing me for a year. Until a few weeks ago, when my head started hurting, all it had to do was show up, speak a word, and the pain would go away.

This time it had taken more than an hour.

Whatever was in my head, some kind of psychic or spiritual creature that was using me to grow, was getting ready to kill me.

"ALFRED," the spirit said soberly. "IS THIS TO BE MY NEW NAME?"

"Let's stick with Demonreach," I said.

The enormous spirit considered that. "I AM THE IS-LAND."

"Well, yes," I said, gathering myself to my feet. "Its spirit. Its genius loci."

"AND I AM ALSO SEPARATE FROM THE IS-LAND. A VESSEL."

I eyed the spirit. "You know the name 'Alfred' is a joke, right?"

It stared at me. A wind that didn't exist stirred the hem of its cloak.

I raised my hands in surrender and said, "All right. I guess you need a first name, too. Alfred Demonreach it is."

Its eyes flickered brighter for a moment and it inclined its head to me within the hood. Then it said, "SHE IS HERE."

I jerked my head up, my heart suddenly speeding. It made little echoes of pain go through my head. Had she finally responded to my messages? "Molly?"

"NOT GRASSHOPPER. GRASSHOPPER'S NEW MOTHER."

I felt tension slide into my shoulders and neck. "Mab," I said in a low, hard voice.

"YES."

"Fantastic," I muttered. Mab, the Queen of Air and Darkness, Monarch of the Winter Court of the Sidhe, mistress and mentor of every wicked being in Faerie—my boss—had been ignoring me for months. I'd been sending her messengers on an increasingly regular basis to no avail. At least, not until today.

But why now? Why show up now, after all those months of silence?

"Because, dummy," I muttered to myself, "she wants something." I turned to Demonreach. "Okay, Alfred. Where?"

"DOCK."

Which was smart. Demonreach, like practically every prison ever, was just as well suited to keeping visitors out as it was to keeping them in. When a freaking Walker of the Outside and his posse had shown up to perform a massive jailbreak on the island's prisoners, they had been beaten back, thanks to the efforts of the island's defenses and several key allies.

I'd spent the last year acquainting myself with the island's secrets, with the defenses that I hadn't even known existed—defenses that could be activated only by the Warden. If the Walker tried that play again, I could shut him down single-handed. Even Mab, as powerful as she was, would be well-advised to be cautious if she decided to start trouble on Demonreach's soil.

Which was why she was standing on the dock.

She expected me to be upset. Definitely, she wanted something.

In my experience, when the Queen of Air and Darkness decides she wants something from you, it's a good time to crawl in a hole and pull it in after you.

But my head pulsed with little twinges of pain. My headaches had slowly gotten worse and worse over several years, and I had only recently discovered their cause—I had a condition that had to be taken care of before whatever was hanging out in my noggin decided to burst its way out of my skull. I didn't dare leave the island until that happened, and if Mab had finally decided to respond to my messages, I had little choice but to meet with her.

Which was probably why she *hadn't* shown up to talk to me—until now.

"Freaking manipulative faeries," I muttered under my breath. Then I headed for the stairs leading out of the Well and up to the island's surface. "Stay nearby and pay attention," I told Demonreach.

"DO YOU SUSPECT SHE MEANS YOU HARM?"

"Heh," I said, starting up the stairs. "One way or another. Let's go."

Chapter

Two

My brother and I had built the Whatsup Dock
down at the shore at one of Demonreach's three
little beaches, the one nearest the opening in the stone
reefs surrounding the island. There had been a town on
the hillside up above the beach maybe a century before,
but it had been abandoned after its residents had apparently
been driven slowly bonkers by all the dark energy
around the hideous things imprisoned below the island.

The ruins of the town were still there, half swallowed by
the forest, a corpse being slowly devoured by fungus and
moss. I sometimes wondered how long I could stay on the
damned island before I was bonkers, too.

There was an expensive motored yacht tied to the
dock, as out of place as a Ferrari in a cattle yard, white
with a lot of frosty blue chrome. There were a couple of
hands in sight, and they weren't dressed in sailing clothes
so much as they were in sailing costumes. The creases
were too straight, the clothes too clean, the fit too perfect.
Watching them move, I had no doubt they were
carrying weapons, and practiced in killing. They were

Sidhe, the lords of Faerie, tall and beautiful and dangerous. They didn't impress me.

Mostly because they weren't nearly as pretty or dangerous as the woman standing at the very end of my
dock, the tips of her expensive shoes half an inch from
Demonreach's shore. When there's a Great White Shark
in the water with you, it's tough to be worried about a
couple of barracuda swimming along behind her.

Mab, the Queen of Air and Darkness, was wearing a
tailored business suit somewhere between the color of
smeared charcoal on newsprint and frozen periwinkles.
The blouse beneath was snow-white, like her hair, which
was bound up in an elaborate do that belonged in the
forties. Opals flashed on her ears and at her throat, deep
colors of green and blue, matching the shifting hues of
her cold, flat eyes. She was pale, beautiful on a scale that
beggared simple description, and I harbored a healthy
and rational terror of her.

I came down the old stone steps in the hillside to the
dock, and stopped an arm's length away from Mab. I didn't
bow to her, but I inclined my head formally. There were
other Sidhe there, on the boat, witnessing the meeting, and
I had worked out a while ago that though I was no danger
to Mab's pride, she would not tolerate disrespect to her
office. I was pretty sure that if the Winter Knight openly
defied her in front of her Court, it would basically be a
declaration of war, and despite what I now knew about the
island, I wanted nothing of the sort with Mab.

"My Queen," I said pleasantly. "How's tricks?"

"Functioning flawlessly, my Knight," she replied. "As
ever. Get on the boat."

"Why?" I asked.

Her mouth turned down into a slight frown, but it was belied by the sudden pleased light in her eyes.

"I'm predictable, aren't I?" I asked her.

"In many ways," she replied. "Shall I answer you literally?"

"I'd like that."

Mab nodded. Then she leaned forward, very slightly, her eyes growing deep, and said in a voice colder and harder than frozen stone, "Because I told you to do so."

I swallowed, and my stomach did this little roller-coaster number on me. "What happens if I won't?" I asked.

"You have already made clear to me that you will resist me if I attempt to compel you directly to obey my commands," Mab said. "Such a thing would render you useless to me, and for the moment, I would find it inconvenient to train a replacement. I would therefore do nothing."

I blinked at that. "Nothing? I could deny you, and you'd just . . . go?"

"Indeed," Mab said, turning. "You will be dead in three days, by which time I should have made arrangements to replace you."

"Uh," I said. "What?"

Mab paused and looked over her shoulder. "The parasite within you will emerge in that time. Surely you have noticed the pains growing worse."

Boy, had I. And it added up.

"Dammit," I snarled, keeping my voice too low to be heard by the goons on the boat. "You set me up."

Mab turned to face me and gave me a very small smile.

"I've been sending out Toot and Lacuna with messages for you and Molly every damned day. None of them got through, did they?"

"They are faeries," Mab said. "I am a Queen of Faerie."

"And my sendings to Molly?"

"I wove nets to catch any spells leaving this island the moment I bade you farewell, my Knight," she said. "And the messages you sent to her through your friends were altered to suit my needs. I find it useful how the tiniest amount of distrust creates so much opportunity for miscommunication. Your friends have been trying to visit you for several weeks, but the lake ice has held unusually long this year. Alas."

I ground my teeth. "You knew I needed her help."

"And," she said, biting the words off crisply, "you still do."

Three days.

Hell's bells.

"Have you ever considered just asking me for my help?" I asked her. "Maybe even saying 'please'?"

She arched a pale eyebrow at me. "I am not your client."

"So you just go straight to extortion?"

"I cannot compel you," she said in a reasonable tone. "I must therefore see to it that circumstance does. You cannot leave the island without being incapacitated by pain. You cannot send for help unless I allow it. Your time has all but run out, my Knight."

I found myself speaking through clenched teeth. "Why? Why would you put me in a corner like this?"

"Perhaps because it is necessary. Perhaps it is to protect you from yourself." Her eyes flashed with the distant fury of a thunderstorm on the horizon. "Or perhaps it is simply because I *can*. In the end, it does not matter why. All that matters is what is."

I inhaled and exhaled a few times, to keep the anger from boiling out into my voice. Given what she had to manage, it was entirely possible that manipulating me and threatening me with death this way *was* asking politely—by the standards of Mab, anyway. But that didn't mean I had to like it.

Besides. She was right. If Mab said I had three days to live, she meant it. She had neither the capability nor the need to speak any direct lies. And if that was true, which I felt depressingly confident it was, then she had me over a barrel.

"What do you want?" I asked. I almost sounded polite.

The question brought a pleased smile to her lips and a nod that looked suspiciously like one of approval. "I wish for you to perform a task for me."

"This task," I said. "Would it happen to be off the island?"

"Obviously."

I pointed a finger at my temple. "Then we have an issue with the incapacitated-by-pain thing. You'll have to fix me first."

"If I did, you'd never agree to it," Mab said calmly. "And I would then be obliged to replace you. For your own health and safety, therefore, you will wear this instead." She lifted her hand and held it out to me, palm up.

There was a small stone in her palm, a deep blue opal. I leaned a little closer, eyeing it. It was set on a silver stud—an earring.

"It should suffice to contain the parasite for what time remains," Mab said. "Put it on."

"My ears aren't pierced," I objected.

Mab arched an eyebrow. "Are you the Winter Knight or some sort of puling child?"

I scowled at her. "Come over here and say that."

At that, Mab calmly stepped onto the shore of Demonreach, until her toes were almost touching mine. She was several inches over six feet tall, and barely had to reach up to take my earlobe in her fingers.

"Wait," I said. "Wait."

She paused.

"The left one."

Mab tilted her head. "Why?"

"It's . . . Look, it's a mortal thing. Just do the left one, okay?"

She exhaled briefly through her nose. Then she shook her head and changed ears. There was a pinpoint of red-hot pain in my left earlobe, and then a slow pulse of lazy, almost seductive cold, like the air on an autumn night when you open the bedroom windows and sleep like a rock.

"There," Mab said, fixing the post in place. "Was that such a trial?"

I glowered and reached up to the stone with my left hand. My fingertips confirmed what my ears had reported—it felt physically cold to the touch.

"Now that I've got this to keep me safe off the island," I said very quietly, "what's to stop me from having Alfred drop you into a cell right this second, and solving my problems myself?"

"I am," Mab said. She gave me a very small, very chill smile, and held up her finger. There was a tiny droplet of my blood upon it, scarlet against her pale skin. "The consequences to your mortal world should there be no Mab would be dire. The consequences to yourself, should you try it, even more so. Try me, wizard. I am willing."

For a second, I thought about it. She was stacking up enough leverage on me that whatever it was she wanted me to do, I was sure I was going to hate it. I'd never wanted to be in Mab's ongoing service anyway. The boss couldn't be the boss if I imprisoned her in crystal hundreds of feet beneath the waters of Lake Michigan. And it wasn't like she hadn't earned some time in the cooler. Mab was a serious bad guy.

Except . . . she was *our* serious bad guy. As cruel and as horrible as she could be, she was a guardian who protected the world from things that were even worse. Suddenly removing her from that balance of power could be worse than catastrophic.

And admit it to yourself, at least, Dresden. You're scared. What if you tried to take her down—and missed? Remember what happened to the last guy who betrayed Mab? You've never beaten her. You've never come close.

I didn't let myself shudder. She would have seen it as weakness, and that isn't a wise thing to show any faerie. I just exhaled and looked away from those cold, endless eyes.

Mab inclined her head to me, barely, a victor's acknowledgment. Then she turned and walked back onto the dock. "Bring anything you may need. We leave at once."

Chapter
Three

Mab's yacht took us to Belmont Harbor, where the late-February ice had evidently been broken up by an unseasonably warm morning. My ear throbbed with occasional cold, but my head seemed fine, and when we docked I hopped over the rail and onto the pier with a large duffel bag in one hand and my new wizard's staff in the other.

Mab descended the gangplank with dignity and eyed me.

"Parkour," I explained.

"Appointment," she said, gliding by me.

A limo was waiting for us, complete with two more Sidhe in bodyguard costumes. They swept us into the city proper, down Lake Shore Drive until we hit the Loop, turned, and pulled up in front of the Carbide and Carbon Building, a vast charcoal-colored creation that had always reminded me of the monolith in *2001*, except for all the brassy filigree. I'd always thought it looked particularly baroque and cool, and then it had become the Hard Rock Hotel.

Two additional Sidhe bodyguards were waiting when we pulled up, tall and inhumanly beautiful. Between one step and the next, they all changed from a crowd of cover models into lantern-jawed thugs with buzz cuts and ear-pieces—glamour, the legendary power of faerie illusion. Mab did not bother altering her own appearance, save for donning a pair of designer sunglasses. The four goons fell into a square formation around us as we went in, and we all marched up to an awaiting elevator. The numbers rolled swiftly up to the top floor—and then went one floor up above *that* one.

The doors opened onto an extravagant penthouse loft. Mozart floated in from speakers of such quality that for a moment I assumed that live musicians must be present. Floor-to-fourteen-foot-ceiling windows gave us a sweeping view of the lake and the shoreline south of the hotel. The floors were made of polished hardwood. Tropical trees had been planted throughout the room, along with bright flowering plants that were busy committing the olfactory floral equivalent of aggravated assault. Furniture sets were scattered around the place, some on the floor, and some on platforms sitting at various levels. There was a bar, and a small stage with a sound system, and at the far end of the loft, stairs led up to an elevated platform, which, judging from the bed, must have served as a bedroom.

There were also five goons wearing black suits with matching shotguns waiting for us outside of the elevator doors. As the doors opened, the goons worked the actions on their weapons, but did not precisely raise them to aim at us.

"Ma'am," said one of them, much younger than the others, "please identify yourself."

Mab stared at them impassively through her sunglasses. Then, in a motion so slight that I doubt any of them noticed, she twitched one eyebrow.

I grunted, flicked a hand, and muttered, *"Infriga."*

I didn't put much power into the spell, but it was enough to make the point: A sudden thick layer of rime crackled into being over the lower two-thirds of the goons' bodies, covering their boots and guns and the hands holding them. The men twitched in surprise and let out little hisses of discomfort, but did not relinquish the weapons.

"The lady doesn't do lackeys," I told them, "and you damned well know who she is. Whichever one of you chuckleheads is holding the brain should probably go tell your boss she's here before she starts feeling offended."

The young goon who had spoken staggered away, deeper into the loft, around a screen of trees and flowers, while the others faced us, dispassionate and clearly uncomfortable.

Mab eyed me and said in an intimate whisper, "What was that?"

I answered in kind. "I'm not killing a mortal just to make a point."

"You were willing enough to kill one of my Sidhe for that reason."

"I play on your team," I told her. "I'm not from your town."

She looked up at me over the rims of her sunglasses

and then said, "Squeamishness does not become the Winter Knight."

"It's not about squeam, Mab," I said.

"No," she said. "It is about weakness."

"Yeah, well," I said, facing front again, "I'm only human."

Mab's gaze remained on me, cold and heavy as a blanket of snow. "For now."

I didn't shiver. I get muscle twitches sometimes. That's all.

The goon capable of human speech returned, and was careful not to make eye contact with anyone as he bowed at the waist in Mab's general direction. "Your Majesty. Please proceed. Your four guards may wait here, with these four, and I will show you to him."

Mab did not so much as twitch to acknowledge that the goon had spoken. She just stepped out of the elevator smartly, her heels clicking with metronomic inevitability on the hard floor, and both the goon and I hurried to keep pace with her.

We walked around the screen of shrubbery where the goon had gone a moment before and found an elaborate raised platform with three wide steps leading up to it. The whole thing was thickly surrounded by more plant life, giving it the cozy feel of an alcove. Expensive living room furniture was spaced around it ideally for conversation, and that's where Mab's appointment was waiting for us.

"Sir," the goon said. "Her Majesty, Queen Mab, and the Winter Knight."

"Who needs no introduction," said a man with a deep, resonant voice. I recognized it. That voice had once been smooth and flowing, but now there was a hint of rasp to it, a roughness that wasn't there before, like silk gliding over old gravel.

A man of medium height and build rose from his chair. He was dressed in a black silk suit, a black shirt, and a worn grey tie. He had dark hair threaded with silver and dark eyes, and he moved with the coiled grace of a snake. There was a smile on his mouth, but not in his eyes as he faced me. "Well, well, well. Harry Dresden."

"Nicodemus Archleone." I slurred into a Connery accent. "My cut hash improved your voish."

Something ugly flickered far back in his eyes, and his voice might have grown a little rougher, but his smile never wavered. "You came closer than anyone has in a long, long time."

"Maybe you're starting to slip in your old age," I said. "It's the little things that go first. For instance, you missed taking the tongue out of one of your goons. You're going to make him feel left out if he's the only one who can talk."

That made Nicodemus smile more deeply. I'd met his gang of hangers-on before. They'd all had their tongues cut out.

He turned to Mab and bowed at the waist, the gesture more elegant than anything I could manage, the manners of another time. "Your Majesty."

"Nicodemus," Mab said in a frosty tone. Then, in a more neutral one, "Anduriel."

Nicodemus didn't move, but his freaking shadow inclined its head anyway. No matter how many times I saw that kind of action, it still creeped me out.

Nicodemus was a Knight of the Blackened Denarius, or maybe it was more accurate to say that he was *the* Knight of the Blackened Denarius. He had one of thirty silver coins on him somewhere, one that contained the essence of the Fallen angel, Anduriel. The Denarians were bad news, in a major way—even though angels were sharply curtailed in how they were allowed to use their power, hobbled and bound to a mortal partner, they were as dangerous as anything running around in the shadows, and when they teamed up with world-class lunatics like Nicodemus, they were several shades worse. Nicodemus, as far as I had been able to find out, had been perpetrating outrages for a couple of millennia. He was smart, ruthless and tough, and killing people was almost as significant to him as throwing away an empty beer can.

I'd survived him once. He'd survived me once. Neither of us had been able to put the other away.

Yet.

"I beg your indulgence for a moment," Nicodemus said to Mab. "A minor matter of internal protocol to which I must attend before we continue."

There was a frozen microinstant of displeasure before Mab answered. "Of course."

Nicodemus bowed again, and then walked a few steps away and turned to the goon who had led us over. He beckoned to the man and said, "Brother Jordan, approach."

Jordan came to rigid military attention, swallowed, and then walked formally forward, stopping precisely in front of Nicodemus before bracing to attention again.

"You have completed the trials of the Brotherhood,"

Nicodemus said, his voice warm. "You have the highest recommendation of your fellows. And you have faced a dangerous foe with steadfast courage. It is my judgment that you have demonstrated your loyalty and commitment to our cause beyond the meager bonds of any oath." He reached up and put a hand on the young man's shoulder. "Have you any final words?"

The kid's eyes gleamed with sudden emotion, and his breathing sped. "I thank you, my lord."

"Well said," Nicodemus murmured, smiling. Then he said, "Deirdre."

The second person in the alcove rose from where she had been sitting quietly in the background. She was a young woman in a simple black dress. Her features were lean and severe, her body graced with the same slight, elegant curves as a straight razor. She had long, dark hair to go with black eyes that were a double of Nicodemus's own, and when she approached Jordan, she gave him an almost sisterly smile.

And then she changed.

First her eyes shifted, changing from dark orbs to pits filled with a burning crimson glow. A second set of eyes, these glowing green, blinked open above the first. And then her face contorted, the bones shifting. Her skin seemed to ripple and then hardened, darkening to the ugly deep purple of a fresh bruise, taking on the consistency of thick hide. The dress just seemed to shimmer out of existence, revealing legs that had contorted, her feet lengthening dramatically, until they looked backward-hinged. And her hair changed—it grew, slithering out of her scalp like dozens of writhing serpents, flattening into hard, metallic ribbons of midnight black that rustled and stirred and rippled of their own volition.

As that happened, Nicodemus's shadow simply grew, with no change in the light to prompt it. It stretched out behind him, and then up the wall, growing and growing until it spread over the whole of that side of the huge loft.

"Bear witness," Nicodemus said quietly, "as Brother Jordan becomes Squire Jordan."

The green eyes atop Deirdre's flickered brightly, as Deirdre lifted claw-tipped hands to cup Jordan's face, quite gently. Then she leaned forward and kissed him, lips parted.

My stomach twisted and flipped over. I didn't let it show.

Deirdre's head suddenly snapped forward a little more, and Jordan's body stiffened. A muffled scream escaped the seal of Deirdre's lips, but was quickly choked off. I saw Deirdre's jaws lock, and then she jerked her head away in the sudden, sharp motion of a shark ripping flesh from its prey. Her head fell back in something that looked horribly like ecstasy, and I could see the bloody flesh of Jordan's tongue gripped between her teeth.

Blood fountained from the young man's mouth. He let out a wordless sound and staggered, falling to one knee.

Deirdre's head jerked in swallowing motions, like a seabird downing a fish, and she made a quiet gulping sound. Then she shuddered, and opened her burning eyes slowly. She turned to move deliberately to Nicodemus's side, her purplish lips black with blood, and murmured, "It is done, Father."

Nicodemus kissed her on the mouth. And, my God,

him doing it with tongue *now* was even more unsettling than it had been the *first* time I'd seen it.

He lifted his mouth from Deirdre's a moment later and said, "Rise, Squire Jordan."

The young man staggered to his feet, the lower half of his face a mass of blood, dripping down over his chin and throat.

"Get some ice on that and see the medic, Squire," Nicodemus said. "Congratulations."

Jordan's eyes gleamed again, and his mouth twisted into a macabre smile. Then he turned and hurried away, leaving a dripping trail of blood behind him.

My stomach twisted. One of these days, I'm going to have to learn to keep my mouth shut. Nicodemus had just casually had a young man maimed solely to make a point to me for teasing him about it. I clenched my jaw and resolved to use the incident to remind me exactly the kind of monster I was dealing with here.

"There," Nicodemus said, turning back to Mab. "I apologize for any inconvenience."

"Shall we conclude our business?" Mab said. "My time is valuable."

"Of course," Nicodemus said. "You know why I have approached you."

"Indeed," Mab said. "Anduriel once loaned me the services of his . . . associate. I now repay that debt by loaning you the services of mine."

"Wait. What?" I said.

"Excellent," Nicodemus said. He produced a business card and held it out. "Our little group will meet here at sundown."

Mab reached for the card and nodded. "Done."

I intercepted her hand, taking the card before she could. "*Not* done," I said. "I'm not working with this psychopath."

"Sociopath, actually," Nicodemus said. "Though for practical purposes, the terms are nearly interchangeable."

"You're an ugly piece of work, and I don't trust you any farther than I can kick you, which I'm tempted to see how far I can do," I snapped back. I turned to Mab. "Tell me you aren't serious."

"I," she said in a hard voice, "am perfectly serious. You will go with Archleone. You will render him all aid and assistance until such time as he has completed his objective."

"*What* objective?" I demanded.

Mab looked at him.

Nicodemus smiled at me. "Nothing terribly complex. Difficult, to be sure, but not complicated. We're going to rob a vault."

"You don't need anyone to help you with that," I said. "You could handle any vault in the world."

"True," Nicodemus said. "But this vault is not of this world. It is in fact, of the Underworld."

"Underworld?" I asked.

I was getting a bad feeling about this.

Nicodemus gave me a bland smile.

"Who?" I asked him. "Whose vault are you knocking over?"

"An ancient being of tremendous power," he replied in his roughened voice, his smile widening. "You may know him as Hades, the Lord of the Underworld."

"Hades," I said. "*The* Hades. The Greek god."

"The very same."

I looked slowly from Nicodemus to Mab.

Her face was beautiful and absolute. The chill of the little earring that was keeping me alive pulsed steadily against my skin.

"Oh," I said quietly. "Oh, Hell's bells."

Chapter

Four

My brain shifted into overdrive.

My back might have been against a wall, but that was hardly anything new. One thing I'd learned in long years of spine-to-brick circumstance was that anything you could do to create a little space, time, or support was worth doing.

I met Mab's implacable gaze and said, "It is necessary to set one condition."

Her eyes narrowed. "What condition?"

"Backup," I said. "I want an extra pair of eyes along. Someone of my choosing."

"Why?"

"Because Nicodemus is a murderous murdering murderer," I said. "And if he's picking a crew, they're going to be just as bad. I want another set of eyes along to make sure one of them doesn't shoot me in the back the second I'm not looking—you're loaning out the Winter Knight, after all. You're not throwing him away."

Mab arched an eyebrow. "Mmmm."

"Out of the question, I fear," Nicodemus said. "Plans

have already been made and there is no room for extraneous personnel."

Mab turned her head very slowly to Nicodemus. "As I remember it," she said, her tone arctic, "when you loaned me your service, you brought your spawn with you. I believe this request exhibits symmetry."

Nicodemus narrowed his eyes. Then he inhaled deeply and inclined his head very slightly in agreement. "I do not have explicit authority over everyone involved. I can make no promises as to the safety of either your Knight or his . . . additional associate."

Mab almost smiled. "And I can make none as to yours, Sir Archleone, should you betray an arrangement made in good faith. Shall we agree to an explicit truce until such time as your mission is complete?"

Nicodemus considered that for a moment before nodding his head. "Agreed."

"Done, then," Mab said, and plucked the card from my fingers. "Shall we go, my Knight?"

I stared hard at Nicodemus and his bloody-mouthed daughter for a moment. Deirdre's hair rasped and rustled, slithering against itself like long, curling strips of sheet metal.

Like hell was I gonna help that lunatic.

But this was not the time or place to make that stand.

"Yeah," I said through clenched teeth. "Okay."

And without ever quite turning my back on the Denarians, I followed Mab back to the elevator.

At the bottom of the elevator ride, I turned to Mab's bodyguards and said, "Time for you guys to get out and bring the car around." When none of them moved, I said, "Okay. You guys filled out some kind of paperwork for how you want your remains disposed of, right?"

At that, the Sidhe blinked. They looked at Mab.

Mab stared ahead. I'd seen statues that indicated their desires more strongly.

They got out.

I waited until the elevator doors closed behind them, flicked a finger, and muttered, *"Hexus,"* unleashing a minor effort of will as I did. Mortal wizards and technology don't blend. Just being in proximity to a wizard actively using magic is enough to blow out a lot of electronics. When a wizard is actually *trying* to blow out tech, not much is safe.

The elevator's control panel let out a shower of sparks and went dark. The lightbulbs went out with little pops, along with the emergency lights, and the elevator's interior was suddenly plunged into darkness lit only by a bit of daylight seeping in beneath the door.

"Are you out of your *mind?*" I demanded of Mab.

Quietly.

There was just enough light to show me the glitter of her eyes as she turned them to me.

"I am *not* going to help that dick," I snarled.

"You will perform precisely as instructed."

"I will *not*," I said. "I know how he works. Whatever he's doing, it's nothing but bad news. People are going to get hurt—and I'm not going to be a part of that. I'm not going to help him."

"It is obvious to me that you did not listen to me very carefully," Mab said.

"It is obvious to me that you just don't *get it*," I replied. "There are things you just don't do, Mab. Helping a monster like that get what he wants is one of them."

"Even if refusing costs you your life?" she asked.

I sighed. "Have you even been paying attention the past couple of years? Do *you* have any doubt that I would rather die than become part of something like that?"

Her teeth made a white gleam in the dark. "And yet, here you are."

"Do you really want to push this?" I asked. "Do you want to lose your shiny new Knight already?"

"Hardly a loss if he will not fulfill a simple command," Mab said.

"I'll fulfill commands. I've done it before."

"In your own inept way, yes," Mab said.

"Just not this one."

"You will do precisely as instructed," Mab said. She took a very small step closer to me. "Or there will be consequences."

I swallowed.

The last Knight to anger Mab had wound up begging me to end his life. The poor bastard had been *grateful*.

"What consequences?" I asked.

"The parasite," Mab said. "When it kills you and emerges, it will seek out everyone you know. Everyone you love. And it will utterly destroy them—starting with one child in particular."

Gooseflesh erupted along my arms. She was talking about Maggie. My daughter.

"She's out of this," I said in a whisper. "She's protected."

"Not from this," Mab said, her tone remote. "Not from a being created of your own essence, just as she is. Your death will bring a deadly creature into the world, my Knight—one who knows all that you know of your allies. Lovers. Family."

"No, it won't," I said. "I'll go back to the island. I'll instruct Alfred to imprison it the moment it breaks free."

Mab's smile turned genuine. It was considerably scarier than her glare. "Oh, sweet child." She shook her head. "What makes you think I shall allow you to return?"

I clenched my fists along with my teeth. "You . . . you *bitch*."

Mab slapped me.

Okay, that doesn't convey what happened very well. Her arm moved. Her palm hit my left cheekbone, and an instant later the right side of my skull smashed into the elevator door. My head bounced off it like a Ping-Pong ball, my legs went rubbery, and I got a really, really good look at the marble tile floor of the elevator. The metal rang like a gong, and was still reverberating a couple of minutes later, when I slowly sat up. Or maybe that was just me.

"I welcome your suggestions, questions, thoughts, and arguments, my Knight," Mab said in a calm voice. She moved one foot, gracefully, and rested the tip of her high heel against my throat. She put a very little bit of her weight behind it, and it hurt like hell. "But I am *Mab*, mortal. It is not your place to judge *me*. Do you understand?"

I couldn't talk, with her heel nudging my voice box. I jerked my head in a short nod.

"Defy me if you will," she said. "I cannot prevent you from doing so—if you are willing to pay the price for it."

And with that, she removed her foot from my throat.

I sat up and rubbed at it. "This is not a smart way to maintain a good professional relationship with me," I croaked.

"Do I seem stupid to you, my Knight?" she asked. "Think."

I eyed her. Mab's voice was perfectly calm. After what I'd said to her, the defiance I'd offered her, I hadn't expected that. She had never been shy about showing her outrage when she felt it had been earned. This perfect poise was . . . not out of character, precisely, but I had expected a good deal more intensity than she was displaying. My defiance endangered her plans, and that never left her in a good mood.

Unless . . .

I closed my eyes and ran back through her words in my head.

"Your precise instructions," I said slowly, "were to go with Nicodemus and help him until such time as he completed his objective."

"Indeed," Mab said. "Which he stated was to remove the contents of a vault." She leaned down, took a fistful of my shirt in her hand, and hauled me back to my feet as easily as she might heft a Chihuahua. "I never said what you would do after."

I blinked at that. Several times. "You . . ." I dropped my voice. "You want me to double-cross him?"

"I expect you to repay my debt by fulfilling my instructions," Mab replied. "After that . . ." Her smile returned, smug in the shadows. "I expect you to be yourself."

"Whatever Nicodemus has going this time . . . you want to stop him, too," I breathed.

She tilted her head, very slightly.

"You know he's not going to honor the truce," I said quietly. "He's going to try to take me out somewhere along the line. He's going to betray me."

"Of course," she said. "I expect superior, more creative treachery on your part."

"While still keeping your word and helping him?" I demanded.

Her smile sharpened. "Is it not quite the game?" she asked. "In my younger days, I would have relished such a novel challenge."

"Yeah," I said. "Gee. Thanks."

"Petulance does not become the Winter Knight," Mab said. She turned to the elevator doors, which had an enormous dent in them the same shape as a wizard's noggin. They swept open with a groan of protesting metal. "Do this for me, and I shall ensure the safe removal of the parasite when the task is completed."

"Nicodemus, his daughter, and God knows what else is in his crew," I said. "I'm working with my hands tied, and you expect me to survive this game?"

"If you want to live, if you want your friends and family to live, I expect you to do more than survive it," Mab said, sweeping out. "I expect you to skin them alive."

Chapter Five

"To Mab's credit," Karrin Murphy said, "she *is* sort of asking you to do what you're good at."

I blinked. "What is *that* supposed to mean?"

"You have a tendency to weasel out of these bargains you get yourself into, Harry," she said. "You have a history."

"Like I shouldn't fight them?" I demanded.

"You probably should focus more on not getting into them in the first place," she said, "but that's just one humble ex-cop's opinion."

We were sitting in Karrin's living room, in the little house with the rose garden she'd inherited from her grandmother. She was sipping tea, her spring-muscle body coiled up into a lazy-looking ball at one end of the couch. I sat in the chair across from her. My big grey cat, Mister, was sprawled in my lap, luxuriating and purring while I rubbed his fur.

"You've taken good care of him," I said. "Thank you."

"He's good company," she said. "Though I wonder if he wouldn't like it better with you."

I moved from Mister's back to rubbing behind his ears exactly the way he liked best. His purr sounded like a miniature motorboat. I hadn't realized how much I'd missed the little furball until he'd come running up and thrown his shoulder against my shins. Mister weighed the next best thing to thirty pounds. I wondered how the diminutive Karrin had managed to keep from being knocked down by his affection every time she came home. Maybe she had applied some principle of Aikido out of self-defense.

"He might," I said. "I'm . . . sort of settled now. And there's nothing on the island big enough to take him. But it's cold out there in the winter, and he's getting older."

"We're all getting older," Karrin said. "Besides. Look at him."

Mister rolled onto his back and chewed happily at my fingertips, pawing at my arms and hands with his limbs without extending his claws. Granted, he was a battle-scarred old tomcat with a stub tail and a notched ear, but damn if it wasn't cute, and I suddenly felt my eyes threaten to get blurry.

"Yeah," I said. "He's kind of my buddy, isn't he?"

Karrin's blue eyes smiled at me over the rim of her teacup. Only attitude kept her from being an itty-bitty person. Her golden brown hair was longer than it had been since I could remember offhand, tied back into a ponytail. She wore yoga pants, a tank top, and a flannel shirt and had been practicing martial arts forms of some kind when I arrived.

"Of course," she said, "you could do it the other way, too."

"What do you mean?"

"You could live here," she said. Then added, a beat too quickly, "In Chicago. You could, you know. Move back to town."

I frowned, still playing with my cat. "I don't . . . Look, when the next freak burns down my place, maybe I won't get as lucky as I did last time."

"Last time you wound up with a broken back and working for a monster," Karrin said.

"Exactly," I said. "And it was only because of literal divine intervention that none of my neighbors died." I shook my head. "The island isn't a kind place, but no one is going to come looking for trouble there."

"Except you," she said gently. "I worry about what will happen to you if you stay out there alone too long. That kind of isolation isn't good for you, Harry."

"It's necessary," I said. "It's safer for me. It's safer for everyone around me."

"What a load of crap," she said, without heat. "You're just scared."

"You're damned right," I said. "Scared that some bug-eyed freak is going to come calling and kill innocent people because they happen to be in my havoc radius."

"No," she said. "That isn't what scares you." She waved a hand. "You don't want it to happen, and you'll fight it if it does, but that isn't what scares you."

I frowned down at Mister. "I'm . . . really not comfortable talking about this."

"Get over it," Karrin said, even more gently. "Harry, when the vampires grabbed Maggie . . . they kind of dismantled your life. They took away all the familiar things.

Your office. Your home. Even that ridiculous old clown car."

"The *Blue Beetle* was not a clown car," I said severely. "It was a machine of justice."

I wasn't looking at her, but I heard the smile in her voice—along with something that might have been compassion. "You're a creature of habit, Harry. And they took away all the familiar places and things in your life. They hurt you."

Something dark and furious stirred way down inside me for a moment, threatening to come out. I swallowed it back down.

"So the idea of a fortress, someplace familiar that can't be taken away from you, really appeals to you right now," Karrin said. "Even if it means you cut yourself off from everyone."

"It isn't like that," I said.

It wasn't.

Was it?

"And I'm fine," I added.

"You aren't fine," Karrin said evenly. "You're a long, long way from fine. And you've got to know that."

Mister's fur was soft and very warm beneath my fingers. His paws batted gently at my hands. His teeth were sharp but gentle on my wrist. I'd forgotten how nice it was, the furry beast's simple weight and presence against me.

How could I have forgotten that?

("I'm only human.")

("For now.")

I shook my head slowly. "This is . . . not a good time to get in touch with my feelings."

"I know it isn't," she said. "But it's the first time in months that I've seen you. What if I don't get another chance?" She put the cup of tea down on a coaster on the coffee table and said, "Agreed, there's business to do. But you've got to understand that your friends are worried about you. And that is important, too."

"My friends," I said. "So this is . . . a community project?"

Karrin stared at me for a moment. Then she stood up and moved to stand beside the chair. She considered me for a few breaths, then pushed my hair back from my eyes with one hand, and said, "It's me, Harry."

I felt my eyes close. I leaned in to her touch. Her hand felt feverishly warm, a wild contrast to the brush of Mab's cold digits earlier in the day. We stayed like that for a moment, and Mister's throaty purr buzzed through the room.

There's power in the touch of another person's hand. We acknowledge it in little ways, all the time. There's a reason human beings shake hands, hold hands, slap hands, bump hands.

It comes from our very earliest memories, when we all come into the world blinded by light and color, deafened by riotous sound, flailing in a suddenly cavernous space without any way of orienting ourselves, shuddering with cold, emptied with hunger, and justifiably frightened and confused. And what changes that first horror, that original state of terror?

The touch of another person's hands.

Hands that wrap us in warmth, that hold us close. Hands that guide us to shelter, to comfort, to food.

Hands that hold and touch and reassure us through our very first crisis, and guide us into our very first shelter from pain. The first thing we ever learn is that the touch of someone else's hand can ease pain and make things better.

That's power. That's power so fundamental that most people never even realize it exists.

I leaned my head against Karrin's hand and shivered again. "Okay," I said quietly. "Okay. This is important, too."

"Good," she said. She left her fingers in my hair for another moment, and then withdrew her hand. She picked up my teacup, and hers, and carried them back to the kitchen. "So. Where did you go after you left the Hard Rock?"

"Hmm?" I asked.

Her voice drifted in from the kitchen. "Given what you told me, you left the meeting with Nicodemus about three hours ago. Where have you been since then?"

"Um," I said. "Yeah, about that."

She came back into the room and arched a golden eyebrow at me.

"What if I told you that I needed you to trust me?"

She frowned and tilted her head for a moment before the hint of a smile touched her mouth. "You went digging for information, didn't you?"

"Um," I said. "Let's just say that until I know more about what I'm up against, I'm playing things a lot closer to the chest than usual."

She frowned. "Tell me you aren't doing it for my own protection."

"You'd kick my ass," I said. "I'm doing it for *mine*."

"Thank you," she said. "I think."

"Don't thank me," I said. "I'm still keeping you in the dark. But I believe it's absolutely necessary."

"So you need me to trust you."

"Yeah."

She spread her hands. "Yeah, okay. So what's the play? I assume you want me to assemble the support team and await developments while you and Thomas go play with the bad guys?"

I shook my head. "Hell, no. I want you to go in with me."

That shocked her silent for a moment. Her eyes widened slightly. "With you. To rob a Greek god."

"Burgle, technically," I said. "I'm pretty sure if you pull a gun on Hades, you deserve whatever happens to you."

"Why me?" she asked. "Thomas is the one with the knives and the superstrength."

"I don't need knives and superstrength," I said. "What's the first rule to protecting yourself on the street?"

"Awareness," she replied instantly. "It doesn't matter how badass you are. If you don't see it coming, you can't do anything about it."

"Exactly," I said. "I need you because you *don't* have supernatural abilities. You never have. You've never relied on them. I need extra eyes. I need to see things happening, someone to watch my back, to notice details. You're the detective who could see that the supernatural was real when everyone else was explaining it away. You've squared off against the worst and you're still here to talk about it. You've got the best eyes of anyone I know."

Karrin took that in for a moment and then nodded slowly. "And . . . you think I'm crazy enough to actually do it?"

"I need you," I said simply.

She considered that gravely.

"I'll get my gun," she said.

Chapter

Six

Karrin drove us to the address on the card in her new car, one of those little Japanese SUVs that *Consumer Reports* likes, and we got there about ten minutes before sundown.

"An abandoned slaughterhouse," she said. "Classy."

"I thought the stockyard district had all been knocked down and rebuilt," I said.

She put the car in park and checked the SIG she carried in a shoulder holster. "Almost all of it. A couple of the old wrecks hung on."

The wreck in question was a long, low building, a simple old box frame only a couple of stories high and running the length of the block. It was sagging and dirty and covered in stains and graffiti, an eyesore that had to have been around since before the Second World War. A painted sign on the side of the building was barely legible: SULLIVAN MEAT COMPANY. The buildings around it were updated brownstone business district standard—but I noticed that no one who worked in them, apparently, had elected to park his car on the slaughterhouse's side of the block.

I didn't have to get out of the car to feel the energy around the place—dark, negative stuff, the kind of lingering aura that made people and animals avoid a place without giving much consideration as to why. City traffic seemed to ooze around it in a mindless, Brownian fashion, leaving the block all but deserted. Every city has places like that, where people tend not to go. It's not like people run screaming or anything—they just never seem to find a reason to turn down certain streets, to stop on certain stretches of road. And there's a reason that they don't.

Bad things happen in places like this.

"Go in?" I asked Karrin.

"Let's watch for a bit," she said. "See what happens."

"Aye-aye, Eye-guy," I said.

"I want you to imagine me kicking your ankle right now," Karrin said, "because it is beneath my dignity to actually do it."

"Since when?"

"Since I don't want to get your yucky boy germs on my shoes," she said, watching the street. "So what's Nicodemus after?"

"No clue," I said. "And whatever he says he's after, I think it's a safe bet that he'll be lying."

"Ask the question from the other direction, then," she said. "What's Hades got?"

"That's the thing," I said. "My sources say he's the collector of the supernatural world. He's famous for it. Art, treasure, gems, jewels, antiques, you name it."

"Nicodemus doesn't seem like an antiquer to me."

I snorted. "Depends. There are a lot of kinds of antiques. Old coins. Old swords."

"For example," she said, "you think he's after some kind of magical artifact?"

"Yeah. Something specific. It's the only thing I can think of that he couldn't get somewhere else," I said.

"Could he be trying to make something happen with the act of burglary itself?"

I shrugged. "Like what? Other than pissing off something as big, powerful, and pathologically vengeful as a freaking Greek god. Those guys take things personally."

"Right. What if he's setting it up to make it look like someone else did the crime?"

I grunted. "Worth considering. But it seems like there'd be simpler ways to accomplish the same thing than to break into someone's version of Hell." I frowned. "Ask you something?"

"Sure."

"You planning to bring one of the Swords with you?"

Karrin had two swords that had been forged with nails from the Cross (yeah, *that* Cross) worked into the blades. They were powerful talismans, borne by the Knights of the Cross, the natural foes of Nicodemus and his crew of thirty silver-coined lunatics (yeah, *those* thirty pieces of silver).

She frowned, her eyes scanning the street, and didn't answer for a moment. When she did, I had the impression that she was choosing her words carefully. "You know I have to be careful with them."

"They're weapons, Karrin," I said. "They're not glass figurines. What's the point in having two genuine holy swords with which to fight evil if you don't, you know, fight evil with them occasionally?"

"Swords are funny," she replied. "The most capable muscle-powered tool there is for killing a man. But they're fragile, too. Use them the wrong way, and they'll break like glass."

"The Denarians are on the field," I said. "They're the people the Swords were meant to challenge."

"The things inside the Coins are what the Swords were meant to fight. The ones holding the Coins are the people the Swords were meant to save," she said, her tone gently emphatic. "And that's why I'm not carrying one. I don't want to save those animals, Harry. And it's not enough to use the Swords against the right foe. You have to use them for the right reasons—or they could be lost forever. I won't be the reason that happens."

"So you'll just let them sit and do nothing?" I asked.

"I'll give them to anyone I think will use them wisely and well," she said calmly. "But people like that don't come along every day. Being a keeper of the Swords is a serious job, Harry. You know that."

I sighed. "Yeah. I do. But Nicodemus and his girl are right over there in that building—and we could use every advantage we can get."

Karrin suddenly smiled. It transformed her face, though her eyes never stopped sweeping the street. "You're just going to have to have a little faith, Harry."

"Faith?"

"That if a Knight with a Sword needs to be here, one will be here. For all we know, Sanya will come walking down the street and get in the car with us."

I scowled at that, even though she was probably right. When a Knight of the Sword was meant to show up and intervene, one would damned well make an entrance and intervene, regardless of who or what stood in the way. I'd seen it more than once. But . . . part of me hated to let go of the advantage the Swords would offer.

Of course, that was what faith was all about, wasn't it—letting go and trusting Someone Else.

Maybe wizards just weren't terribly predisposed to surrendering control. I mean, not when they have so much personal power available to them. Once you've had your hands on the primal forces that created the universe, it's a little hard to relax and let them slip through your fingers. It would certainly explain why so few of the wizards I knew were even mildly religious.

Also, it illustrated pretty clearly why I was never, ever going to be a Knight. Aside from the fact that I was working for the queen of the wicked faeries and getting into bed with jerks like Nicodemus, I mean.

Karrin's eyes flicked up to her rearview mirror and sharpened. "Car," she said quietly.

In a spy movie, I would have watched them coolly in the rearview mirror, or perhaps in my specially mirrored sunglasses. But as I am neither cool nor a spy, nor did I feel any particular need for stealth, I twisted my upper body around and peered out the back window of Karrin's car.

A white sedan with a rental agency's bumper sticker on it pulled up to the curb halfway down the block. It was shuddering as it did, as if it could barely get its engine to turn over, even though it was a brand-new vehicle. Before it had entirely stopped moving, the passenger door swung open and a woman stepped out onto the street as though she just couldn't stand to be stuck in one place.

She was striking—rangy and nearly six feet tall, with long and intensely curled dark hair that fell almost to her waist. She wore sunglasses, jeans, and a thick, tight scarlet sweater that she filled out more noticeably than most. Her cowboy boots struck the street decisively in long strides as she crossed it, heading toward the old slaughterhouse. Her sharp chin was thrust forward, her mouth set in a firm line, and she walked as though she felt certain that the way was clear—or had better be.

"Hot," Karrin said, her tone neutral, observational. "Human?"

I wasn't getting any kind of supernatural vibe off of her, but there's more than one way to identify a threat. "Can't be sure," I said. "But I think I know who she is."

"Who?"

"A warlock," I said.

"That's a rogue wizard, right?"

"Yeah. When I was in the Wardens, they used to send out wanted posters for warlocks so the Wardens could recognize them. I didn't hunt warlocks. But I was on the mailing list."

"Why didn't you?" she asked. "Word is that they're dangerous."

"Dangerous children, most of them," I said. "Kids who no one ever taught or trained or told about the Laws of Magic." I nodded toward the woman. "That one's name is Hannah Ascher. She was on the run longer than any other warlock on recent record. She's supposed to have died in a fire in . . . Australia, I think, about six years ago."

"You drowned once. How much pressure did the Council put on you after that?"

"Good point," I said.

"What did she do?" Karrin asked.

"Originally? Ascher burned three men to death from the inside out," I said.

"Jesus."

"Killed one Warden, back before my time. She's put three more in the hospital over the years."

"Wizards trained to hunt rogue wizards, and she took them out?"

"Pretty much. Probably why she doesn't look worried about walking in there right now."

"Neither will we when we go in," Karrin said.

"No, we won't," I said.

"Here comes the driver."

The driver's-side door opened and a bald, blocky man of medium height in an expensive black suit got out. Even before he reached up to take off his sunglasses to reveal eyes like little green agates, I recognized him. Karrin did too, and let out a little growling sound. He put the sunglasses away in a pocket, checked what was probably a gun in a shoulder holster, and hurried to catch up to Ascher, an annoyed expression on his blunt-featured face.

"Binder," she said.

"Ernest Armand Tinwhistle," I said. "Name that goofy, don't blame him for wanting to use an alias."

Though, honestly, he hadn't chosen it. The Wardens had given it to him when they'd realized how he'd somehow managed to bind an entire clan of entities out of the Nevernever into his service. He could whistle up a modest horde of humanoid creatures who apparently felt nothing remotely like pain or fear, and who were willing to sacrifice themselves without hesitation. Binder was a one-man army, and I'd told the little jerk that if I saw him in my town again, I'd end him. I'd *told* him to stay out, and yet here he was.

For about three seconds, I couldn't think about anything *but* ending him. I'd have to make it fast, take him out before he could call up any of his buddies, something quick, like breaking his neck. Open the car door. Call up a flash of light as I got out, something to dazzle his newly unshaded eyes. A dozen sprinting steps to get to him, then grab him by the jaw and the back of the head and twist sharply up and to one side, then bring up a shield around myself in case his brain stayed alive long enough to drop a death curse on me.

"Harry," Karrin said, quiet and sharp.

I realized that I was breathing hard and that my breath was pluming into frost on the exhale as the mantle of power of the Winter Knight had begun informing my instincts in accord with the primal desire to defend my territory against an intruder. The temperature in the car had dropped as if she'd turned the AC up full blast. Water was condensing into droplets on the windows.

I closed my eyes as the Winter rose up in me and I fought it down. I'd done it often enough over the past year on the island that it was almost routine. You can't stave off the howling, primitive *need* for violence that came with the Winter mantle with the usual deep-breathing techniques. There was only one way that I'd found that worked. I had to assert my more rational mind. So I ran through my basic multiplication tables in my head, half a dozen mathematical theorems, which took several seconds, then hammered out ruthless logic against the need to murder Binder in the street.

"One, witnesses," I muttered. "Even deserted, this is still Chicago, and there could be witnesses and that would get their attention. Two, Ascher's out there, and if she takes his side, she could hit me from behind before I could defend myself. Three, if he's savvy enough to avoid the grab, I'd be out there with two of them on either side of me."

The Winter mantle snarled and spat its disappointment, somewhere in my chest, but it receded and flowed back out of my thoughts, leaving me feeling suddenly more tired and fragile than before—but my breathing and body temperature returned to normal.

I watched as Binder broke into a slow jog until he caught up with Ascher. The two spoke quietly to each other as they entered the old slaughterhouse.

"Four," I said quietly, "killing people is wrong."

I became conscious of Karrin's eyes on me. I glanced at her face. Her expression was tough to read.

She put her hand on mine and said, "Harry? Are you all right?"

I didn't move or respond.

"Mab," Karrin said. "This is about Mab, isn't it? This is what she's done to you."

"It's Winter," I said. "It's power, but it's . . . all primitive. Violent. It doesn't think. It's pure instinct, feeling, emotion. And when it's inside you, if you let your emotions control you, it . . ."

"It makes you like Lloyd Slate," Karrin said. "Or that bitch Maeve."

I pulled my hand away from hers and said, "Like I said. This is not the time to get in touch with my feelings."

She regarded me for several seconds before saying, "Well. That is all kinds of fucked-up."

I huffed out half a breath in a little laugh, which threatened to bring some tears to my eyes, which made the recently roused Winter start stirring down inside me again.

I chanced a quick look at Karrin's eyes and said, "I don't want to be like this."

"So get out of it," she said.

"The only way out is feetfirst," I said.

She shook her head. "I don't believe that," she said. "There's always a way out. A way to make things better."

Oh, man.

I wanted to believe that.

Outside, the sun set. Sunset isn't just a star orbiting below the relative horizon of the planet. It's a shift in supernatural energy. Don't believe me? Go out far away from the lights of civilization sometime, and sit down, all by yourself, where there aren't any buildings or cars or telephones or crowds of people. Go sit down, quietly, and wait for the light to fade. Feel the shadows lengthening. Feel the creatures that stay quiet during the day start to stir and come out. Feel that low instinct of nervous trepidation rising up in your gut. That's how your body translates that energy to your senses. To a wizard like me, sundown is like a single beat on some unimaginably enormous drum.

Dark things come out at night.

And I didn't have time, right now, to dither about where I had my feet planted. I had three days to screw over Nicodemus Archleone and his crew and get this thing out of my head, without getting myself or my friend killed while I did it. I had to stay focused on that.

There'd be time to worry about other things after.

"It's time," I said to Karrin, and opened the car door. "Come on. We've got work to do."

Chapter Seven

We got out of Karrin's little SUV and headed toward the creepy old slaughterhouse full of dangerous beings. Which . . . pretty much tells you what kind of day I was having, right there.

You know, sometimes it feels like I don't *have* any other kind of day.

Like, ever.

On the other hand, I'm not sure what I would really do with any other kind of day. I mean, at some point in my life, I had to face it—I was pretty much equipped, by experience and inclination, for mayhem.

"Too bad," Karrin mused.

"Too bad what?"

"We didn't have time to get you an actual haircut," she said. "Seriously, did you do it yourself? Maybe without a mirror?"

I put a hand up to my head self-consciously and said, "I had some help from the General. And, hey, I didn't say anything about your man-shoes."

"They're steel-toed," she said calmly. "In case I need

to plant them in anyone's ass as a result of him calling them man-shoes. And seriously, you let Toot help you with your hair?"

"Sure as hell wasn't going to let Alfred try it. He'd probably scrape it off with a glacier or something."

"Alfred?"

"Demonreach."

Karrin shuddered. "That thing."

"It's not so bad," I said. "Not exactly charming company, but not bad."

"It's a demon that drove an entire town full of people insane to keep them away."

"And it could have done much, much worse," I said. "It's a big, ugly dog. A cop should know about those."

"You're glad it's there when someone breaks into your house," she said, "because then it can drive them so freaking crazy that the city erases all record of the incident."

"Exactly. And then no one remembers your ugly man-shoes."

By then, we'd reached the door. Both of us knew why we were giving each other a hard time. There was nothing mean-spirited in it.

We were both scared.

I would go through the door first. My spell-wrought black leather duster was better armor than the vest Karrin would be wearing beneath her coat. I gripped my new staff and readied my mind to throw up a shield if I needed one. We'd done this dance before: If something was ready to come at us, I'd hold it off, and she would start putting bullets in it.

Karrin folded her arms over her chest, which happened to put her hand near the butt of her gun, and nodded at me. I nodded back, made sure my duster was closed across my front, and opened the door.

Nothing came screaming out of the shadows at us. Nobody started shooting at us. So far, so good.

The door opened onto a long hallway with light at the far end, enough to let us walk by. The interior walls of the building were old and cracked and covered in decades of graffiti. The night had brought a cold wind off the lake and the building creaked and groaned. The air smelled like mildew and something else, something almost beneath the threshold of perception that set my teeth on edge—old, old death.

"These evil freaks," Karrin said. "They always pick the most charming places to hang out."

"Dark energy here," I said. "Keeps people from wandering in and randomly interfering. And it feels homey."

"I know you haven't burned down any buildings in a while," she said, "but if you start feeling the need . . ."

When we reached the end of the hallway, it turned into a flight of stairs. We followed those up, silently, and at the top of them a door opened onto a balcony over a large factory floor two stories high, running three or four hundred feet down the length of the building. The remains of an overhead conveyor line were still there; it had probably once carried sides of beef from the slaughter pen to various processing stations, but the machinery that had been there was all gone. All that was left were the heavy metal frames, empty now, which had once held the machines in place, and a few rusted, lonely old transport dollies that must once have been loaded up with packaged ribs and steaks and ground beef.

In the middle of the floor were a dozen brand-new work lights, blazing away, and an enormous wooden conference table complete with big leather chairs, brightly illuminated in the glow of the lamps. There was a second table loaded with what looked like a catered dinner, covered with dishes, drinks, and a fancy coffee machine. A few feet away from that was a small pen of wire mesh, and inside it were a dozen restless brown-and-tan goats.

Goats. Huh.

Nicodemus was sitting with one hip on the conference table, a Styrofoam coffee cup in his hands, smiling genially. Ascher was just being seated in a chair, which one of Nicodemus's guards held out for her solicitously. Binder sat down in the chair beside her, nodded to Nicodemus, and folded his arms with the air of a man prepared to be patient. Deirdre approached the table in her girl disguise, holding a cup of coffee in each hand, offering them to the new arrivals, smiling pleasantly.

There were half a dozen of Nicodemus's tongueless guards in sight on catwalks above the floor, and Squire Jordan, now all cleaned up, was waiting for us at the far end of the balcony. He had a sidearm, but it was holstered.

"Hi, Jordan," I said. "What's with the goats?"

He gave me a level look and said nothing.

"I don't like having guns above us and all around us," Karrin said. "Screw that."

"Yep," I said. "Go tell your boss we'll come down there when the flunkies go find something else to do."

Jordan looked like he might take umbrage at the re-mark.

"I don't care what you think, Jordan," I said. "Go tell him what I said, or I walk. Good luck explaining to him how you lost him a vital asset."

Jordan's jaw clenched. But he spun stiffly on one heel, descended an old metal stairway to the floor, and crossed to Nicodemus. He wrote something on a small notepad and passed it to his boss.

Nicodemus looked up at me and smiled. Then he handed the notepad back to Jordan, nodded, and said something.

Jordan pursed his lips and let out three piercing whis-tles, which got the instant attention of the guards. Then he waved a finger over his head in a circular motion, and they all descended from the catwalks to join him. They headed out, toward the far end of the floor.

Ascher and Binder turned to regard me as this hap-pened, the former bright-eyed and interested, the latter justifiably apprehensive. Once the guards were out of sight, I started down the stairs, with Karrin walking a step behind me and slightly to one side.

"You've grown more suspicious, Mr. Dresden," Nico-demus said as I approached.

"There's no such thing as too suspicious with you, Nicky," I said.

Nicodemus didn't like the familiar nickname. Irrita-tion flickered over his face and was gone. "I suppose I can't blame you. We've always been adversaries in our previous encounters. We've never worked together as as-sociates."

"That's because you're an asshole," I said. I picked the chair two down from Binder and sat. I gave him a steady look and then said to Nicodemus, "We've already got a conflict of interest going."

"Oh?"

I jerked a thumb at Binder. "This guy. I said the next time he operated in Chicago, we were going to have a problem."

"Christ," Binder said. He said it in Cockney. It came out "kroist." He looked at Nicodemus and said, "I told you this was an issue."

"Whatever problem you have with Mr. Tinwhistle is your personal problem, Dresden," Nicodemus said. "Until such time as the job is over, I expect you to treat him as a professional peer and an ally. If you fail to do so, I will regard it as a failure to repay Mab's debt to me and, regrettably, will be forced to make such an unfortunate fact public knowledge."

Translation: Mab's name would get dragged through the mud. I knew who she would take it out on, too.

I glanced back over my shoulder at Karrin, who had taken up a stance behind me and to one side, her expression distant, dispassionate, her eyes focused on nothing in particular. She gave a slight shrug of her shoulders.

"Okay," I said, turning back to Nicodemus. I eyed Binder. "I'm giving you a three-day pass, Binder. But bear in mind that I'm going to hold you responsible for what you do in my town at the end of it. I'd be cautious if I were you."

Binder swallowed.

At that, Ascher stood up. "Hi," she said, smiling

brightly. "You don't know me. I'm Hannah. Back off my partner before you get hurt."

"I know who you are, hot stuff," I drawled, not standing. I set my staff down across the table. "And I already backed off your partner. You can tell from how there aren't any splatter marks. Play nice, Ascher."

Her smile vanished at my response, and her dark eyes narrowed. She drummed her nails on the tabletop exactly once, slowly, as if contemplating a decision. A smirk touched her mouth. "So you're the infamous Dresden." Her eyes went past me, to Karrin. Ascher was a foot taller than she was. "And this is your bodyguard? Seriously? Aren't they supposed to be a little bigger?"

"She represents the Lollipop Guild," I replied. "She'll represent them right through the front and out the back of your skull if you don't show a little respect."

"I'd like to see her try," Ascher said.

"You won't see it," Karrin said softly.

The room got quiet and intent for a moment, though I never heard Karrin move. I knew she'd be standing there, not looking directly at anyone, watching everyone. That's a scary look, if you know what really dangerous people look like. Ascher did. I saw the tension start at her neck and shoulders, and make her clench her jaw.

"Easy, Hannah," Binder said, his tone soothing. He knew what Karrin could do on a fast draw. She'd dispatched some of his minions for him the last time he'd been in town. "Dresden's given a truce. We're all professionals here, right? Easy."

"Ladies and gentlemen," Nicodemus said in a patiently strained paternal tone. He went to the head of the table, of course, and seated himself. "Can we please settle down and get to work?"

"Fine with me," I said, not looking away from Ascher and Binder, until Ascher finally sniffed and returned to her seat.

"Would you care to sit, Miss Murphy?" Nicodemus asked.

"I'm fine," Karrin said.

"As you wish," he said easily. "Deirdre?"

Deirdre picked up an armful of folders and came around the table, passing them out to everyone seated. She rather pointedly skipped Karrin, who ignored her. I opened my rather thin folder, and found a cover page that read: DAY ONE.

"Everyone here knows the general objective," Nicodemus said, "though I'm going to be leaving specific details vague, for the time being. I trust that I need not emphasize the need for secrecy to anyone here. Our target has a great many ways of gathering information, and if he gets wind of our venture from any of them, it will certainly come to an abrupt and terminal conclusion for all of us."

"Keep your mouth shut," I said, loudly enough to be a little annoying. "Got it."

Nicodemus gave me that not-smile again. "In order to make clear to you all the potential gains to be had in this enterprise, you shall each be paid two million dollars upon our successful removal of my particular goal, guaranteed."

Karrin's breath stopped for a second. My stomach did an odd thing.

Man. Two million dollars.

I mean, I wasn't gonna take Nicodemus's money. I wasn't doing this for the money. Neither was Karrin. But neither of us had ever been exactly wealthy, and there were always bills to pay. I mean, stars and stones. Two million bucks would buy you a lot of ramen.

"In addition," Nicodemus continued, "you are welcome to whatever you can carry away from the target. There is an unfathomable amount of wealth there—more than we could take away with a locomotive, much less on foot."

"What kind of wealth?" Binder asked. "Cash, you mean?"

"For what that is worth," Nicodemus said, an edge of contempt in his voice. "But that is collected more as a curiosity than anything else, I suspect. The real trove contains gold. Jewels. Art. Priceless artifacts of history. Virtually every rare and valuable thing to have gone mysteriously missing over the past two thousand years has wound up there. I would suggest that perhaps filling a few packs with precious gemstones might be the most profitable and least traceable course of action for each of you, but if you simply must have something more distinctive, you are welcome to take it if you can carry it and if it does not slow down our egress. I think it easily possible for each of you to beat the cash payment by an order of magnitude."

So, not two million each.

Twenty-two million each.

That was so much money, it almost didn't have a real meaning . . . which was a real meaning all by itself.

"And what are you after?" Ascher asked, openly suspicious. "If you're willing to dish out two million to each of us, you certainly aren't hurting for money. You don't need a backpack of diamonds."

Her reasoning made me like her a little more. Her tone doubled it.

Nicodemus smiled. "I'll make that clear to you before we go in. For now, suffice it to say that it is a single, small article of relatively little monetary value."

Liar, I thought.

"As I said to Dresden before, he has known me only as an adversary. Much of my reputation has been made from those who have opposed me—those who survived the experience, that is." He smiled and took a sip of coffee. "There is another side to that coin. One does not operate for as many years as I have by betraying allies. It simply isn't practical. Certainly, one uses every weapon one has when dealing with foes—but when I work with associates, I do not turn aside or leave them behind. It is not from any sense of sentiment. It is because I do business with many people over the course of centuries, and treachery is a bad long-term investment. It simply isn't good business."

Liar, I thought. But maybe a little less emphatically than I had before. What he was saying made sense. In the supernatural world, there were plenty of people and things that counted their life spans in centuries. Wrong a wizard when he's young, for example, and you could wait three hundred years to find out he was never able to put it behind him— and has been working to gain the clout he needs to make it clear to you that your actions were unacceptable. Cross a vampire, and it could haunt you for millennia.

A certain degree of cutthroat pragmatism was what made any kind of alliance between various supernatural entities possible. I'd seen it between my grandfather and a professional assassin called the Hellhound. I'd seen it when squaring off against various bad guys, over the years, most of whom were willing to make a deal of some kind. Hell, I'd *done* it, with Mab, and she was doing it again with Nicodemus by sticking me here.

So it was entirely possible that he was on the up-and-up. Or at least that he was as sincere as I was about following through on the whole alliance thing. We had to get his McGuffin and get out again. Until then, I was betting, he might be good to his word.

And after that, everything would be up in the air.

On the other hand, Nicodemus had gone out of his way to remove as much memory of himself as possible from the human race, by destroying records of his deeds over the centuries. Guys who are on the up-and-up don't go to those lengths to hide what they've done.

Not that it mattered. Mab had given her word. I had to play nice until we had grabbed the loot from Hades, or until Nicodemus tried to stick a knife in my back.

Fun, fun, fun.

I flipped to the second page of the folder and found a photo of a woman I knew, and hadn't seen in . . . Hell's bells, had it been almost ten years? She hadn't changed much in that time, except for maybe looking leaner and harder. I wasn't sure she'd be at all happy to see me, and I knew for damned sure what she would think of Nicodemus.

And since when had I become the guy that things happened to ten years ago?

Nicodemus continued in his lecture voice. "Entry to the target in the Nevernever requires us to find a matching site here in the mortal world. That means breaking into a high-security facility in the real world before we can even get started in the Nevernever."

I raised my hand.

"Pursuant to that," Nicodemus said, and then paused. He sighed. "Yes, Mr. Dresden?"

"You've got to be kidding me," I said. "She's never going to work with you."

"Probably not," Nicodemus agreed. "She may, however, work with *you*. We need an expert in security systems with a working knowledge of the supernatural world. The pool of such individuals is rather small. I've arranged a meeting with her at a local event in approximately ninety minutes. You and Miss Ascher will make contact and convince her to join our cause."

"Suppose she won't?" I asked.

"Be more convincing," he said. "We need her in order to proceed."

I clenched my teeth, and then nodded once. Hell, if he needed her to make it happen, then by screwing this up, maybe I could make sure it didn't. "Fine. But it's me and Murphy."

"No," Ascher said. "It's me and Binder."

"I'm afraid the event is a formal one," Nicodemus said. "I've taken the liberty of securing appropriate attire and identities for Dresden and Miss Ascher, neither of which would be compatible with Miss Murphy or Binder. Perhaps Miss Murphy could serve as your driver. She has the shoes for it."

I couldn't actually hear Karrin grind her teeth, but I knew she had.

"Binder," Nicodemus said, "I have another errand for you. You'll need to pick up the fourth—pardon, Miss Murphy, the fifth—member of the team at the train station. He's stated that he'll only meet someone he knows."

Binder nodded once. "Who is it?"

"Goodman Grey."

Binder's face went pale. "Ah. Yes, I've worked with the gent."

"Who is he?" Ascher asked.

"He's . . . not a man to cross," Binder said. "But a pro. I'll pick him up. Smoother that way."

Ascher pressed her lips together, as if she didn't like it, but nodded. "Fine, then." She looked down the table at me and smiled. "Well, Dresden, it looks like it's time to put on our party dress."

"Gee," I said. "What fun."

And I closed the folder on the picture of Anna Valmont.

Chapter

Eight

Deirdre brought me a garment bag and pointed me to a small employees' kitchen and break room with another pair of work lights set up in it. I went in, closed the door, and opened the garment bag. There was a black tux inside with all the necessary accoutrements. I held it up enough to determine that it looked like a tolerable fit.

For a moment, I had a few paranoid misgivings. What if the entire point of the exercise had been to get me to take off the coat so that they could open fire with a machine gun and grease me through the wall? I already knew what it was like to be shot, and I was pretty well over the experience. Visions of Sonny Corleone danced in my head.

But I didn't think that was going to happen. Karrin was on guard outside. There was no way they'd move a gun into position without her at least making noise to warn me. Then, too, Nicodemus had plans in motion. I didn't think he'd want to jeopardize his "faithful associate" image until he could screw everyone over much more dramatically and permanently. And if he just murdered me outright, Mab would take it personally. I don't care how long you've been in business. If you cross Mab, you can skip your next five-year plan.

So I doffed the coat, stripped down, and started getting dressed in the tux.

I was at pretty much the damnedest point of the process when the door opened again, and Hannah Ascher prowled into the room, carrying a garment bag of her own.

She gave me a slow and blatant once-over, that small smirk still on her mouth.

I'm pretty sure the temperature of the room didn't literally go up, but I couldn't have sworn to it. Some women have a quality about them, something completely intangible and indefinable, which gets called a lot of different things, depending on which society you're in. I always think of it as heat, fire. It doesn't have to be about sex, but it often is—and it definitely was with Hannah Ascher.

I was extremely aware of her body, and her eyes. Her expression told me that she knew exactly what effect she was having on me, and that she didn't mind having it in the least. I'd say that my libido kicked into overdrive, except that didn't seem sufficient to cover the rush of purely physical hunger that suddenly hit me.

Hannah Ascher was a damned attractive woman. And I'd been on that island for a long, long time.

I turned my face away from her and tried to ignore her while I laid out my cummerbund. Mighty wizards do not get rattled because someone sees them standing around in their boxer briefs.

"Damn, Dresden," she said, taking a few steps to one side and looking me over again. A slow smile spread over her mouth. "Do you work out?"

"Uh," I said. "Parkour."

The answer seemed to amuse her. "Well. It's definitely working for you." She hung the garment bag up on a cabinet handle and unzipped it by feel, her eyes on me the whole time. "So many scars." She had long arms. Her fingers brushed my shoulder. "What's that one?"

The touch sent a zing of sensation down my spine and through my belly. There wasn't anything magically coercive about it. I'd been on alert for that kind of nonsense from the moment my feet had hit the shore. It was worse than that—chemistry, pure and simple. My body had the idea that Ascher was exactly what I needed, and it wasn't paying any attention to my brain.

I pulled my shoulder away from her, gave her a glare, and said, "Hey. Do you mind?"

She folded her arms, her smile widening. "Not at all. Where'd you get it?"

I glowered and turned back to my tux. "The FBI shot me, maybe twelve years ago."

"Seriously?" Hannah asked. "It faded out really well."

"It's like that with wizards," I said.

"Your left hand," she said. "That's from fire."

"Vampire's flunky," I said. "Homemade flame-thrower."

"Which Court?" she asked.

"Black."

"Interesting," she said, and stripped out of her sweater in one smooth motion.

Her body was exactly as pleasant to look at as the contours of the sweater had promised, possibly more so. My libido approved vigorously.

I hurriedly turned my back. "Hey."

"You're kidding, right?" she asked, something like laughter in her voice. "Turning your back, really? On this? What kind of big-time badass are you, anyway, Dresden?"

"The kind who doesn't know you, Miss Ascher," I said.

"That's a fixable problem, isn't it?" she asked, her voice teasing. "And it's 'Miss Ascher' all of a sudden, huh? I wonder why that is."

Her black satin bra hit the counter in my peripheral vision. It had little bits of frilly lace along the edges.

I hurriedly jumped into the pants before I embarrassed myself. "Look," I said. "We're working together. Can we just get the job done, please?"

"Not nearly so many scars on your back," she noted. "You don't run from much, do you?"

"I run all the time," I said, stuffing my arms into the shirt. "But if you let yourself get attacked from behind a lot, you don't get scars. You get a hole in the ground."

Her boots made some clunking sounds on the floor. Socks and jeans joined the bra on the counter. "This thief we're picking up," she said. "You two have some history, huh?"

"Sort of," I said. "She stole my car."

She let out a brief laugh. "And you let her?"

"She gave it back," I said. "I bailed her out of trouble once."

"Think you can get her to go with us?"

"If it was just me, it would be more likely," I said.

"Or maybe you'd try to throw a wrench into the works by making sure she didn't get on board," she said, her tone wry. "After all, you like Nicodemus so much."

Oops. The woman was sharp. "What?" I asked.

"Based on your response, I'm going to assume that you don't have much of a poker face, either," she said. Cloth made soft rustling sounds. "Don't feel bad. It's one of the things I'm good at. I've got a feel for people."

"Meaning what?"

"Meaning that I can tell that right now, you're wound up tighter than twenty clock springs," she said. "You're nervous and scared and angry, and you're about to explode with the need to have sex with something. I've met guys fresh out of prison who aren't bursting at the seams as hard as you."

I paused in the midst of fastening cuff links.

"Seriously, I can promise you that you are impaired right now. You should blow off a little steam. Be good for you."

"You're an expert, eh?" I asked. My voice sounded a little rough.

"On this?" she asked, her voice teasing again. "I'm not bad. Zip me?"

I turned to find her facing away from me. She was wearing the hell out of a little black dress accented with shining black sequins. Her legs were excellent. There wasn't much of a back to the dress, but there was a short zipper running a few inches up from the top of her hips. I was pretty sure she could have managed it alone. But I took a step over to her and did it up anyway.

She smelled like late-afternoon sunshine on wildflowers. Her long, curling hair touched the backs of my hands as they moved.

I felt the Winter in me stirring, taking notice of whatever had gotten to my sex drive, hungry for an outlet. That wasn't a good thing. Winter thought sex was almost as much fun as violence, and that they went even better mixed together. Like chocolate and peanut butter.

I started multiplying numbers in my head and stepped away again, focusing on getting dressed, and eight times eight, and putting on socks without sitting down or noticing the woman whose gaze remained on me.

"Man," she said finally. "You've been burned more than once."

I fastened the pretied tie onto the collar and straightened it by feel. "You have no idea."

"Fine," she said, her voice steady and calm. "You don't want to have fun at work, that's cool. I like you. I like your style. But this job is important to me, and to my partner. Get it right. You screw us over, and you and I are going to have a problem."

"You really think you can take on a Wizard of the White Council, Miss Ascher?" I asked.

"I have so far," she said, without a trace of threat or bravado.

I turned to face her and found her on something almost like eye level with me, thanks to a pair of heels that went with the dress. She was fastening a diamond tennis bracelet onto her left wrist.

I stepped up close to her and took the ends of the bracelet in my fingers. "You should hear my terms, too,"

I said, and as I did, I could hear the Winter in my voice, making it quiet and cold and hard. "This town is my home. You hurt any mortals in my town, I take you out with the rest of the trash. And you should remember the state of my back, if you start thinking about putting a knife in it. Try it, and I'll bury you." The clasp closed, and I looked up to see her keeping a straight face—but I could see considerable uncertainty behind it. She drew her arm back from me a shade too quickly, and kept her eyes on my center of balance, as if she was expecting me to take a swing at her.

I'd had to talk tough to monsters and dangerous people before. I just couldn't remember doing it while sharing a somewhat intimate domestic moment, like getting dressed together, or while helping them put on jewelry. There was something in that gesture that made Hannah Ascher a person first, a woman, and a dangerous warlock second. And I had effectively threatened her during that moment—which had probably just made me, to her, a dangerous Warden of the White Council slash paranormal criminal thug first, and a human being second.

Super. Harry Dresden, intimidator of women. Probably not the best foot to get off on with someone with whom I was about to face considerable intrigue and danger.

Maybe next time, I'd just stick a gun in her face.

"You look great," I said in a voice that sounded a lot gentler than it had a few seconds before. "Let's get to work."

Chapter
Nine

The Peninsula is one of the ritzier of the ritzy hotels in Chicago, and it has a grand ballroom measurable in hectares. The serious events of Chicago's nightlife rarely start before eight—you need time for people to get home from work and get all pretty before they show up looking fabulous—so when we arrived around seven thirty, Ascher and I were unfashionably early.

"I'm going to be right down here on the street," Karrin said from the front seat of the black town car Nicodemus had provided. She had checked it for explosives. I'd gone over it for less physical dangers.

"Not sure how long it will take," I said. "Cops going to let you loiter?"

"I still know a few guys on the force," she said. "But I'll circle the block if I have to. If you get in trouble, send up a flare." She offered me a plastic box with a boutonniere made from a sunset-colored rose in it. "Don't forget your advertising."

"Not like I need it," I said. "I'll recognize her."

"And she'll recognize you," Karrin said. "If she doesn't

know she's supposed to talk to you, she might avoid you. It's not exactly hard to see you coming."

"Fine." I took it, opened the box, and managed to stab myself in the finger with the pin while trying to put the damned thing on my lapel.

"Here," Ascher said. She took the flower, wiped the pin off on a tissue, and passed it to Karrin, along with whatever tiny bit of my blood had been on it. Then she fixed the flower neatly to the tux. She wasn't making any particular effort to vamp, but her dress was cut low, giving me several eyefuls during the process. I tried not to notice and was partially successful.

"Here we go," Karrin said, and got out of the car. She came around and opened the door for me. I got out, and helped Ascher out, and she flashed enough shapely leg to keep anyone on the hotel staff out front from noticing me except in passing. Karrin got back in the car and vanished with quiet efficiency, and I gave Ascher my arm and escorted her inside.

"Try not to look like that," Ascher said under her breath, after we were in the elevator.

"Like what?" I asked.

"Like you're expecting ninjas to leap out of the trash cans. This is a party."

"Everyone knows there's no such things as ninjas," I scoffed. "But it will be something. Count on it."

"Not if we do it smooth," Ascher said.

"You're going to have to trust me on this one," I replied. "There's always something. It doesn't matter how smooth you are, or how smart the plan is, or how plain the mission—something goes wrong. Nothing's ever simple. That's how it works."

Ascher eyed me. "You have a very negative attitude. Just relax and we'll get this done. Try not to look around so much. And for God's sake, smile."

I smiled.

"Maybe without clenching your jaw."

The doors opened and we walked down a hallway to the grand ballroom. There were a couple of security guys outside the door dressed in the hotel's colors, trying to look friendly and helpful. I breezed up and presented them with our engraved invitation and fake IDs. I'd say this for Nicodemus—he didn't do things halfway, and his production values were outrageous. The fake driver's license (in the name of Howard Delroy Oberheit, cute) looked more real than my actual Illinois driver's license ever had. They eyed me, and then my license, closely, but they couldn't spot it as a fake. Ascher (née Harmony Armitage) gave the guards a big smile and some friendly chatter, and they didn't look twice at her ID.

I couldn't really blame them. Ascher looked like exactly the kind of woman who would be showing up to a blue-chip evening event. In me, the hotel's thugs recognized another of their kind—and one who was taller and had better scars than they did. But with Hannah on my arm, they let me pass.

The interior of the ballroom had been decorated in a kind of Chinese motif. Lots of red fabric draped in swaths from the ceiling to create semi-curtained partitions, paper lanterns glowing cheerfully, stands of bamboo, a Zen garden with its sand groomed in impeccable curves. The hotel staff was mostly women in red silk tunics with mandarin collars. Caterers in white coats and black ties were just getting a buffet fully assembled. When we came in, I couldn't see them, but I could hear a live band running through a number—seven pieces of brass, drums, and a piano, playing a classic ballroom piece.

I scanned the room slowly as we entered, but I didn't see Anna Valmont standing around anywhere.

"So this thief we're meeting," Ascher said. "What's her story?"

"She used to belong to a gang called the Church-mice," I said. "Specialized in robbing churches in Europe. Nicodemus hired them to swipe the Shroud of Turin for him a few years back."

Ascher tilted her head. "What happened?"

"The three of them got it," I said. "I suspect they tried to raise their price. Nicodemus and Deirdre killed two of them, and he would have killed Anna if I hadn't intervened."

Her eyes widened slightly. "And now Nicodemus wants her to help him?"

I snorted softly through my nose. "Yeah."

Ascher studied me for a moment with her eyes narrowed. "Oh."

"What?" I asked her.

"Just . . . admiring the manipulation," she said. "I mean, I don't like it, but it's good."

"How so?" I asked.

"Don't you see?"

"I try not to think like that," I said. The caterers uncovered the silver trays holding the meat, and a moment later the smell of roasted chicken and beef wafted up to my nose. My stomach made an audible sound. I'd been cooking for myself over a fireplace for a long, long while. It had been sustenance, but given my culinary skills, it hadn't really been food, per se. The buffet smelled so good that for a minute I half expected to hear the pitter-patter of drool sliding out of my mouth.

"If you don't, someone else will," Ascher said. "If nothing else, you've got to defend yourself . . . Hey, are you as hungry as I am?"

"Uh-huh," I said. "And we've apparently got some time to kill."

"So it wouldn't be unprofessional to raid the buffet?"

"Even Pitt and Clooney had to eat," I said. "Come on."

We raided the buffet. I piled my little plate with what I hoped would be a restrained amount of food. Ascher didn't bother. She took a bit of almost everything, stacking food up hungrily. We made our way to one of many tables set up around the outskirts of the ballroom while the band went through another number. I picked one that gave us a view of the door, and watched for Anna Valmont to arrive.

She didn't appear over the next few moments, though a few of Chicago's luminaries did, and the numbers in the room began to slowly grow. The hotel staff began taking coats and drifting through the room with trays of food and drink, while the caterers began to briskly move back and forth through the service entrances, like a small army of worker ants, repairing the damage to the buffet almost the moment it was done. It seemed to mean so much to them that I was considering doing a little more damage myself, purely to give them a chance to repair it, you understand. I try to be nice to people.

I was just gathering my empty plate to show my compassionate, humanitarian side when one of the hotel staff touched my arm and said, "Pardon me, Mr. Oberheit? You have a telephone call, sir. There's a courtesy phone right over here."

I looked up at the woman, wiped my mouth with a napkin, and said, "All right. Show me." I nodded to Ascher. "Be right back."

I got up and followed the staffer over to a curtained alcove by one wall, where there was a phone. We were more or less out of the way of everyone else in the room there.

"Miss Valmont," I said to the staffer, once we were there. "Nice to see you again."

Anna Valmont turned to face me with a small and not terribly pleasant smile. The last time I'd seen her, she'd been a peroxide blonde. Now her hair was black, cut in a neat pageboy. She was leaner than I remembered, almost too much so, like a young, feral cat. She was still pretty, though her features had lost that sense of youthful exuberance, and her eyes were harder, warier.

"Dresden," she said. " 'Mr. Oberheit,' seriously?"

"Did you hear me criticizing your alias?" I asked.

That got a flash of a smile. "Who's the stripper?"

"No one you know, and no one to mess with," I said. "And there's nothing wrong with strippers. How've you been?"

She reached into her tunic and carefully produced a thickly packed business envelope. "Do you have my money or not?"

I arched an eyebrow at that. "Money?"

That got me another smile, though there was something serrated about it. "We have history, Dresden, but I don't do freebies and I'm not hanging around for chitchat. The people I had to cross for this aren't the forgiving type and have been on my heels all week. This envelope is made of flash paper. Cough up the dough or the data and I turn to smoke."

My mind was racing. Nicodemus had set up a job for Anna Valmont—it was the only way he could know that she would be here, and that she would be meeting the guy with the sunset-colored rose. So it stood to reason that whatever information he'd had her take, it might be valuable, too.

I checked around me quickly. I couldn't see the table from where I stood, but Ascher wasn't in sight. "Do it," I said, turning back to Valmont. "Destroy it, now, quick."

"You think I won't?" she asked. Then she paused, frowning. "Wait a minute . . . What's the con here?"

"No con," I said low. "Look, Anna, there's a lot going on and there's no time to explain it all. Blow the data and vanish. We'll both be better off."

She tilted her head, her expression suddenly skeptical, and she drew the envelope up close against her in an unconscious protective gesture. "You give me a hundred grand up front for this with another hundred on delivery, and then tell me to wreck the data? It's not like this is the only copy."

"I wasn't the one who hired you," I said intently. "Hell's bells, you stole my car once. You think I've got that kind of cash? I'm just the pickup guy, and you don't want to be involved with this crew. Get out while you can."

"I did the job, I get my money," she said. "You want to trash the data, fine. You pay for it. One hundred thousand."

"How about two million?" Ascher said. She eased into the alcove, holding a champagne flute with no lipstick marks on the rim.

Anna looked at her sharply. "What?"

"Two million guaranteed," Ascher said. "As much as twenty if we pull off the job."

I ground my teeth.

Valmont looked back and forth between us for a second, her expression closed. "This job was an audition."

"Bingo," Ascher said. "You've got the skills and the guts. This is a big job. Dresden here is doing what he always does, trying to protect you from the big bad world. But this is a chance at a score that will let you retire to your own island."

"A job?" Anna said. "For who?"

"Nicodemus Archleone," I said.

Anna Valmont's eyes went flat, hard. "You're working with him?"

"Long story," I said. "And not by choice." But I realized what Ascher had been talking about before. Nicodemus had picked Anna Valmont and sent me to get her because he'd been calculating her motivations. Anna owed me something, and she owed Nicodemus something more. Even if she didn't pitch in to help me, she might do it for revenge, for the chance to pull the rug out from under Nicodemus's feet at the worst possible moment. He'd given her double the reasons to get involved. The money was just the icing on the cake.

Valmont wasn't exactly a slow thinker herself. "Twenty million," she said.

"Best-case scenario," Ascher said. "Two guaranteed."

"Nicodemus Archleone," I said. "You remember what happened the last time you did a contract with him?"

"We tried to screw him and he screwed us back harder," Anna said. She eyed Ascher, as a couple more hotel staff flitted by the alcove. "What happens if I say no?"

"You miss the score of a lifetime," Ascher said. "Nicodemus has to abandon the job." She looked at me. "And Dresden is screwed."

Which was true, now that Ascher was here and had seen me trying to derail the job. Unless I killed her to shut her up, something I wasn't ready to do, she'd tell Nicodemus and he'd put the word out that Mab's word was no good anymore. Mab would crucify me for that, no metaphor involved. Worse, I was pretty sure that such a thing would be a severe blow to Mab's power in more than a political sense—and Mab had an important job to do.

All of which, I was certain, Nicodemus knew.

Jerk.

"Is that true?" Valmont asked.

I ground my teeth and didn't answer. A crew of four caterers carrying a large tray went by.

"It's true," Valmont said. "The job. Is it real?"

"It's dangerous as hell," I said.

"Binder is in," Ascher said. "Do you know who that is?"

"Mercenary," Valmont said, nodding. "Reputation for being a survivor."

"Damn skippy," Ascher replied. "He's my partner. I'm along to keep Dresden here from getting all noble on you."

"That true?" Valmont asked me.

"Son of a bitch," I said.

Valmont nodded several times. Then she said, to Ascher, "Excuse us for a moment, would you?"

Ascher smiled and nodded her head. She lifted her glass to me in a little toast, sipped, and drifted back out of the alcove.

Valmont leaned a little closer to me, lowering her voice. "You don't care about money, Dresden. And you aren't working for him by choice. You want to burn him."

"Yeah," I said.

Something hot flared in Valmont's eyes. "Can you?"

"The job is too big for him to do alone," I said.

"A lot of things could happen," she said.

"Or you walk," I said, "and it doesn't happen at all. He's out millions of bucks he's already paid, and there's no job."

"And he just crawls back into the woodwork," Valmont said. "And maybe he doesn't come out for another fifty years and I never have another chance to pay him back."

"Or maybe you get yourself killed trying," I said. "Revenge isn't smart, Anna."

"It is if you make a profit doing it," she said. She clacked her teeth together a couple of times, a nervous gesture. "How bad is it for you if I walk?"

"Pretty bad," I said, as a second crew of caterers went by with another huge tray. "But I think you should walk."

A hint of disgust entered her voice. "You *would*. Christ." She shook her head. "I'm not some little girl you need to protect, Dresden."

"You're not in the same weight class as these people either, Anna," I said. "That's not an insult. It's just true. Hell, I don't want to be there."

"It isn't about how big you are, Dresden," she said. "It's about how smart you are." She shook her head. "Maybe you need my help more than you know."

I wanted to tear out my hair. "Don't you get it?" I asked. "That's exactly what he *wants* you to think. He's a player who's been operating since before your family tree got started, and he's setting you up."

Naked hatred filled her voice. "He killed my *friends*."

"Dammit," I said. "You try to screw him over, he'll kill you just as fast."

"And yet you're doing it." She put the envelope carefully away in her tunic. "Last time around, I thought I had it all together. I didn't think I needed your help. But I did. This time, it's your turn. Get the stripper and tell her we'd better get moving."

"Why?"

She touched the envelope through the tunic. "Like I said. The former owners have been kind of persistent since I took this from their files."

"Who?"

"The Fomor."

"Balls—those guys?" I sighed, just as the horns blared and the band revved up into a swing number. "Okay, let's g—"

The caterers came by again, all eight of them this time, in their identical uniforms, moving industriously. They were carrying two big trays, and abruptly dumped them onto their sides. The shiny metal covers clanged and clattered onto the floor, the sound lost in the rumble of drums, and from beneath them came two squirming, slithering *things*.

For a second, I wasn't sure what I was looking at. It was just two mounds of writhing purple-grey flesh mottled with blotches of other colors. And then they just sort of *unspooled* into writhing, grasping appendages and a weird bulbous body, and suddenly two creatures that looked like the torso of a hairless, gorilla-like humanoid grafted to the limbs of an enormous octopus came scuttle-humping over the floor toward us, preceded by a wave of reeking, rotten-fish stench and followed by twin trails of yellowish mucus.

"Hell's bells," I swore. "I *told* her so. Nothing's ever simple."

Chapter Ten

So, what do you call abominations like that? I wondered in an oddly calm corner of my brain as adrenaline kicked it into high gear. Octogorillataurs? Gorilloctopi? How are you going to whale properly on a thing if you don't even have a name for it?

More to the point, nameless hideous monsters are freaking terrifying. You always fear what you don't know, what you don't understand, and the first step to having understanding of something is to know what to call it. It's a habit of mine to give names to anything I wind up interacting with if it doesn't have one readily available. Names have power—magically, sure, but far more important, they have psychological power. Something horrible with a name holds less power over you, less terror, than something horrible without one.

"Octokongs," I pronounced grimly. "Why did it have to be octokongs?"

"Are you *kidding* me?" breathed Anna Valmont. Her body tensed like a quivering power line, but she didn't panic. "Dresden?"

At the other end of the hall, the band hit the first chorus of the swing number, drums rumbling. The octokongs came a-glumping toward us, ten limbs threshing, octopus and gorilla both, nearly human eyes burning with furious hate, but they weren't what had me the most worried. The Fomor were a melting pot of a supernatural nation, the survivors of a dozen dark mythologies and pantheons that had apparently been biding their time for the past couple of thousand years, emerging from beneath the world's oceans in the wake of the destruction of the Red Court of Vampires. They'd spent the last couple of years giving everyone a hard time and making thousands of people vanish. Nobody knew why, yet, but the Fomor's covert servitors on land looked human, had gills, and acted like exemplary monsters—and they were what I was more worried about.

Behind the octokongs, the servitors in the caterer uniforms crouched down into ready positions, drawing out what looked chillingly like weighted saps, and every one of them was focused on Valmont. The beasties were just the attack dogs. The servitors were here to make Anna Valmont vanish—alive. One could only have nightmares about what people who get their kicks stitching gorillas to octopi might do to a captive thief.

I didn't have any of my magical gear on me. That limited my options in the increasingly crowded public venue. Worse, they'd gotten close to us before coming at us. There was nowhere to run and no time for anything subtle.

Lucky for me.

I'm not really a subtle guy.

I summoned forth my will, gathering it into a coherent mass, and crouched, reaching down and across my body with my right hand. Then I shouted, *"Forzare!"* as I rose, sweeping my arm out in a wide arc and unleashing a slew of invisible force as I did.

A wave of raw kinetic force lashed out from me in a crescent-shaped arc, catching both octokongs and all eight of the servitors, sending them tumbling backward.

The sudden, widely spread burst of magic also sent the heavy covered platters flying, and one of them hit edge-on and slashed right through one of the floor-to-ceiling windows of the ballroom. A genuine hotel staffer caught the edge of the spell and went sprawling as though clipped by an NFL linebacker. Hanging sheets of red fabric blew in a miniature hurricane, some of them tearing free of their fastenings and flying through the room. A couple of small tables and their chairs went spinning away—and almost every lightbulb in the place abruptly shattered in a shower of sparks.

People started screaming as flickering gloom descended, though as luck would have it, the band still had light enough to play by and, after a stutter, kept going. The octokongs, knocked back several yards before they could spread out their tentacles and grab onto the floor, let out enormous, feral roars of defiance, and at that terrifying sound, genuine panic began to spread through the ballroom. A few seconds later, someone must have pulled a fire alarm, because an ear-piercing mechanical whoop began to cycle through the air.

So, basically: Harry Dresden, one; peaceful gathering, zero.

I grabbed Valmont by the hand and darted to one

side, shoving scarlet cloth aside with my other hand and running blindly forward through it. The Fomor would be on our heels any second. Anything I could have unleashed that would have killed or disabled the Fomor crew would have caused even more collateral damage and might have gotten someone killed in the relatively limited confines of the ballroom. All I'd done was knock them back on their heels—but I wasn't trying to win a fight. I just wanted to get us out in one piece.

I didn't know where Ascher had gotten off to, but the Fomor were after Valmont. Ascher had survived being hunted by the White Council for years. I imagined she could get herself out of a hotel without my help.

"What are we doing?" Anna shouted.

"Leaving!"

"Obviously. Where?"

"Fire stairs!" I called back. "I'm not getting stuck in an elevator with one of those things!"

We plunged out of the obscuring curtains, and I tripped on a chair, stumbled, and banged my hip hard into the buffet table. I might have fallen if Valmont hadn't hauled on my arm.

I pointed toward the door the caterers had been using and got my feet moving again. "There! Fire stairs down the hall, to the right."

"I saw the signs too," she snapped.

We rushed through the doors, rounded the corner, and I found myself facing two more of the flat-eyed Fomor servitors, both of them bigger and heavier than average and wearing their more common uniform—black slacks with a tight black turtleneck.

And machine guns.

I don't mean assault rifles. I mean full-on automatic weapons, the kind that come with their ammunition in a freaking box. The two turtlenecks had obviously been placed to cover the stairs, and they weren't standing around being stupid. The second I came around the corner, one of them lifted his weapon and began letting loose chattering three- and four-round bursts of fire.

In movies, when someone shoots at the hero with a machine gun, they hit everything around him but they don't actually hit *him*. The thing is, actual machine guns don't really work like that. A skilled handler can fire them very accurately, and can lay down so many rounds that whatever he's shooting at gets hit. A lot. That's why they *make* machine guns in the first place. Someone opens up on you with one of those, and you have two choices—get to cover or get shot multiple times. I was less than fifty feet away, down a straight, empty hallway. He could barely have missed me if he'd been *trying*.

I threw back my right arm, hauling Anna Valmont behind me, and lifted my left arm, along with my will, snapping out, *"Defendarius!"*

Something tugged hard at my lower leg, and then my will congealed into a barrier of solid force between us and the shooter. Bullets struck it, sending up flashes of light as they did, revealing it as a half-dome shape with very ragged edges. The impact of each hit was visceral, felt all the way through my body, like the beat of a big drum in a too-loud nightclub. Heavy rounds like that were specifically designed to hit hard and penetrate cover. They could kill a soldier on the other side of a thick tree, chew apart a man in body armor, and reduce concrete walls to powder and rubble.

Without a magical focus to help concentrate my shield's energy, it took an enormous amount of juice to keep it dense enough to actually stop the rounds, while slowing them down enough to keep them from simply ricocheting everywhere. Rounds like that would penetrate the walls and ceiling of the Peninsula as if going through soft cheese. Innocent people five floors away could be killed if I didn't slow the bullets as they rebounded, and the metal-clad slugs bounced and clattered to the floor around me.

That didn't deter the turtleneck. He started walking slowly forward in the goofy-looking, rolling, heel-to-toe gait of a trained close-quarters gunman, the kind of step that kept his eyes and head and shoulders level the whole time he was moving. He kept firing steady, controlled bursts as he approached, filling the hallway with light and deafening thunder, and it was everything I could do just to keep the bullets off of us.

Holding the shield in place was a job of work, and within seconds I had to drop to one knee, reducing the size of the shield needed as I did. I had to hold on for a little longer. Once the turtleneck ran dry, he'd have to change weapons or reload his magazine, and then I'd have a chance to hit back.

Except that his buddy was advancing right next to him, *not* firing. Ready to take over the second the first turtleneck's weapon ran out. Gulp. I wasn't sure I had the juice to hang on *that* long.

I was missing my shield bracelet pretty hard at that

point—but it hadn't been with me when I woke up under the island of Demonreach, and I hadn't had the time or the resources to make another one since. My new staff would have done just fine, but it was just a little bit harder to sneak that thing into a formal gathering.

I needed a new plan.

Valmont shouted something at me. I was concentrating so hard, I barely heard her the first time. "Close your eyes!" she screamed. Then she tensed and moved and something flew over the faintly glowing top edge of my shield and clattered to the ground at the turtlenecks' feet.

The two shooters reacted instantly, diving away, and a second later there was a flash of utterly blinding white light and something slapped the air of the hallway like a giant's palm.

I hadn't gotten my eyes closed in time, and my vision was covered in red and purple spots, my ears ringing in a steady, high-pitched tone, but the shield had protected me from the force of the small explosion, and my head was clear enough that I could stagger to my feet and get out of the deadly hallway, Valmont pulling me along in her wake.

"Jesus Christ," she swore in a vicious tone as we ran. "It was just some goddamned *files*. Other stairway!"

Going back into the darkened ballroom after the stroboscopic hallway had left my eyes helplessly trying to adjust. "I can't see yet," I said, and felt her take my hand. "Okay, go!"

Valmont started running, and I lurched blindly along with her, holding her hand like an NBA-sized toddler and trying not to fall down. We crossed what had to have been most of the ballroom before Valmont suddenly stopped. My rented shoes were not exactly hell on wheels for traction, and I all but fell over her before I could stop, too.

"What?" I asked.

"Quiet," she hissed. "One of those things at the door."

"You have any more flash-bangs?" I said, lower.

"Most girls don't even carry the one, you know," she said rather primly. "I can't tell you how many jobs I've done without a hitch since the last time I saw you, Dresden. You walk through the door and everything goes to hell."

"That's embroidered on my towels, actually," I said. I blinked my eyes hard, several times, and could barely make out the shape of one of the octokongs waiting at the door. Well, technically, it was waiting *over* the door, its tentacles spread out along the ceiling, sticking to it like some enormous spider, apelike arms hanging down. Valmont had stopped us behind a column, deep in the shadows created by the emergency lights in the hallway beyond the octokong. "Wow, those things are ugly." I blinked some more. "Okay, stay close."

"Can you see?"

"Yeah, almost. We'll make a run for it. If it comes at us, I'll knock it away and we meep-meep right the hell out of here."

"Meep-meep." Valmont's voice was dry. "It's so nice to work with a mature professional."

"Fine. We extract, exfiltrate, whatever," I said. I changed hands, shifting hers to my left, making sure my right was free. "Here we go."

And we ran for the door.

The octokong started slorping down the wall, all tentacles and slime and harsh, ugly grunting sounds, but it didn't just drop, and though I was ready to unleash another blast of force at it, we scooted by a couple of inches ahead of the nearest tentacle tip, and into the hallway, free and clear, even more easily than I'd planned.

So naturally, alarm bells started going off in my head.

There was a doorway across the hall, and I didn't slow down. I lowered my shoulder and hit it with the weight of my entire body, and with the full power of the Winter Knight.

I don't wanna say I'm strong when I've got my Winter Knight on—but I've lifted cars. Maybe it isn't really comic-book-style superstrength, but I'm a big guy, I'm no lightweight, and that door splintered, its lock tearing free of its wooden frame as if it had already half rotted out. I went through it, my shoulder sending up a hot pulse of discomfort, dragging Valmont with me.

The *second* octokong had been waiting on the inside of the hallway, already plunging down at us, and if we'd paused for even a fraction of a second, it would have nabbed us both. Instead, I crashed into a rack of brooms and mops at the back of a large cleaning closet, snapping several handles and putting a huge dent in the drywall. I sort of bounced off of it, my eyes still blurry with spots, stunned.

"Dresden!" Valmont cried.

I spun to see her lurch and grab onto a heavy metal shelf of cleaning products. I'd lost hold of her at some point. No sooner had she grabbed on than one of her legs was jerked out from beneath her, and her hands were wrenched free of the shelf.

I snapped my arms out and caught her before she could be hauled out of the closet, becoming cognizant of a purple-grey tentacle wrapped around her ankle as I did. I went to the floor, lashing out with all the power of my legs, and sent the door swinging closed with vicious force, neatly severing the tip of the octokong's tentacle.

There was a furious bellow from outside the door.

"Get behind me, get behind me!" I shouted at Valmont, keeping the door pressed shut with my legs. She scrambled over me in the darkness inside the closet, her limbs lean and solid beneath her disguise. A second later, there was a click, and light from a tiny flashlight flooded the room as she used it to start scanning the shelves.

I expected the octokong to come shoving against the door, but instead there were several smaller impacts, and then suddenly the door let out a shriek as it was simply torn into pieces and ripped away from me. I caught a flash of multiple tentacles holding various shattered pieces of the door, and then the octokong was coming through the doorway, low, propelled by still more tentacles and its apelike arms.

I let out a scream and kicked it in the chest with both feet, tagging it hard enough to draw a coughing roar of surprise from it and send its heavy torso tumbling back into the hallway—but its tentacles caught the doorframe with clearly supernatural power, arresting its momentum and beginning to send it hurtling back into me.

I lifted my hand and screamed, *"Forzare!"* A second wave of kinetic energy lashed through the air and caught the octokong, pressing outward, and for half a dozen seconds the strength of my will contended with all of those tentacles and arms.

The shield in the hallway had taken too much out of me. I could feel my will beginning to buckle, the spell beginning to falter. The octokong pressed closer and closer to where I lay prostrate, my arm extended. Little stars gathered at the edges of my vision.

And then there was a shriek, a high-pitched howling sound that was absolutely industrial in its tone and intensity. There was a flash of light, blue-white and so bright that it made Valmont's stun grenade look like a camera's flashbulb by comparison, and the air itself was rent with a miniature thunderclap as a sphere of fire the size of my two fists appeared in the same space as the octokong's skull.

It was there for a fraction of a second, pop, like a short-lived soap bubble.

And when it was gone . . . all that was left was blackened bone and a cloud of fine, fine black powder.

The octokong convulsed, all ten limbs writhing, but it didn't last long. The headless corpse thrashed around for a moment, and the blackened remnants of the skull went rolling off of it, cracking and crumbling as it did.

Hannah Ascher appeared over the body, her party shoes held in one hand, her dark eyes blazing. "Dresden? You okay?"

I just stared at her for a second.

Hell's bells.

I mean, don't get me wrong. I'm a Wizard of the White Council. But what I'd just witnessed was a display of precision and power so awesome that I would barely have believed it from a senior Council member, much less a freaking warlock younger than me. Fire's a tricky, tricky magic to use. Call up enough power to do damage, and you have to fight to control it. The hotter you make it, the more it spreads out, consumes, destroys. This fire spell had been positively surgical.

I mean, I'm good with fire.

But Hannah Ascher was *good* with *fire*.

Ye gods, no wonder the Wardens hadn't brought her in yet.

"Thanks," I said, climbing to my feet. And then I reached out and shoved her away as the *first* octokong came swarming through the doorway behind her and pounced, tentacles flailing.

I had time to get my arms up and then the weight of the thing drove me flat to the floor. I tried to fight it, but there was nothing to fight—I was pinned beneath a fleshy web of tentacles that ripped and tore and bit at me through my clothes. I barely managed to wrench my head free of the slimy, stinking thing and get a breath, and because I did I was in time to see Anna Valmont step out of the cleaning closet and hurl a cup of some kind of powdered concentrate into the octokong's eyes.

The thing shrieked in agony, pure agony, and half of its tentacles lifted off of me instantly in a vain attempt to protect its face and head. The beast writhed in torment, and I managed to get a leg into place to shove it off me. I pushed myself to my feet.

"Go!" I shouted at Ascher and Valmont. "Go, go, go!"

They didn't need any more encouragement. We fled down the hallway, leaving the screaming octokong behind us, and all but flew down the stairs.

"There," I snapped at Ascher on the way down. "We got her out and she's helping. You happy?"

"Yeah, Dresden," she said, her tone cross. "I'm happy. I'm thrilled. I'm freaking joyous. Now shut up and run."

And I fled the hotel, blood oozing out to stain my shredded tux.

I didn't mind so much.

I'd like to see Nicodemus try to get his deposit back on that.

Chapter Eleven

On the way down the stairs, Anna Valmont ditched her tunic and pants, and proved to be wearing a little party dress beneath. Once she'd kicked off her shoes and socks, she blended in with every other society girl fleeing the building. A small bag belted around her waist and concealed beneath the tunic became a clutch. She pulled her hair off, ditched the wig, and shook out shoulder-length dark blond hair from beneath it, fashionably tousled. She put on sunglasses, and appropriated Hannah Ascher's heels. She hurried a little, caught up to the last group to head out in front of us, and blended in with them seamlessly. By the time we'd reached the ground floor, the shapeless, shorter, brunette hotel staffer had vanished, and a tall and lean blond woman in a black dress was tottering out of the building along with all the rest of them.

Valmont was no dummy. The Fomor servitors were waiting outside, in their caterer uniforms, scanning everyone leaving the building with their flat, somehow amphibian gazes.

"I'll run interference. You get her to the car," I muttered to Ascher as we exited the building.

Then I pointed a finger at the nearest servitor and thundered, "You!"

The man turned his eyes to me. I felt the rest of them do the same. Good. The more of them that were looking at me, the fewer eyes there were to notice Valmont making good her escape. I stalked over to the servitor like a man spoiling for a fight. "What do you people think you're doing? I mean, I've heard of getting your sushi fresh, but that's just plain ridiculous."

Fomor servitors were not known for their bantering skills. The man just stared at me and took an uneasy half step back.

"I've got half a mind to sue!" I shouted, waving an arm in a broad, drunken gesture. "Do you *see* the state of my tux? You've taken something from me tonight. My wardrobe's peace of mind!"

By now, I was getting the attention of all kinds of people—evacuated guests, hotel staff, passersby on the sidewalk. There are a limited number of blood-covered economy-sized males ranting at the top of their lungs in a shredded tuxedo, even in Chicago. Sirens were wailing too, coming closer. Emergency services were en route. Motorcycle cops and prowl cars were already beginning to arrive, lickety-split here in the heart of the city.

I saw the servitor take note of the same thing. His weight shifted uneasily from foot to foot.

"Yeah," I said in a lower, quieter voice. "I don't know which of the Fomor you serve. But tell your boss that Harry Dresden is back, and he says to stay the hell out of

Chicago. Otherwise, I'm going to knock his teeth out."
I paused. "Assuming, uh, he has teeth, I mean. But I'll
knock something out. Definitely. You tell him that."

"You dare to threaten him?" the servitor whispered.

"Just stating facts," I said. "You and your crew better
go. Before I start ripping off your collars and asking the
police and reporters what's wrong with your necks."

The servitor stared at me with empty eyes for a long
moment. Then he turned abruptly and started walking.
The other guys in caterer uniforms went with him.

"Subtle," came Karrin's voice.

I turned to find her standing maybe ten feet behind
me, her arms crossed, where her hand would be close to
her gun. Had the servitor or his buddies drawn a weapon,
she'd have been in a good position to draw and start
evening the odds.

"Murph," I said. "Did they get out?"

"They're waiting." Her eyes flickered with distress as
they swept over me. "Jesus, Harry. Are you all right?"

"Aches a bit. Stings a bit. I'm fine."

"You're bleeding," she said, hurrying closer. "Your
leg. Hold still." She knelt down and I suddenly realized
that she was right—my leg was bleeding, the leg of my
pants soaked, blood dripping from the hem of my pants
leg and onto my rented shoes. She rolled the bloodied
cloth up briskly.

"You've been shot," she said.

I blinked. "Uh, what? I don't feel shot. Are you sure?"

"There's a hole right through the outside of your
calf," she said. "Little on both sides. Christ, they must
have been close."

"M240," I said. "From maybe thirty feet."

"You got lucky—it missed the bone and didn't tumble." She pulled a handkerchief from her jacket pocket and said, "This is what Butters warned you about. Not being able to sense your own injuries. I've got to tie this off until we can get it taken care of. Brace."

Her shoulders twisted as she knotted the cloth around my calf and jerked it tight. That tingled and stung a little, but it didn't hurt any more than that. I suddenly realized that Winter was sighing through me like an icy wind, dulling the pain.

I also suddenly realized that Karrin was kneeling at my feet. The Winter in me thought that was all *kinds* of interesting. Something very like panic fluttered through my chest, something far more energetic and destabilizing than the fear I'd felt in the conflict a few minutes before.

"Uh, right," I said, forcing my eyes away. "What are we doing standing around here? Let's go."

Karrin rose and looked up at me, her expression torn between concern and something darker. Then she nodded and said, "Car's over here. Follow me."

Once in the car, I looked back over my shoulder at Ascher and Valmont while Karrin got us moving. We cruised out just as the majority of the emergency vehicles arrived. Valmont was staring out the window, her face unreadable behind her sunglasses. Ascher was looking over her shoulder, watching the scene behind.

When she finally turned around to see me looking at her, her face split into a wide smile, and her dark eyes glittered brightly. "Damn," she said, "that was intense."

"More for some than others," Karrin said. "Miss Ascher, I'm going to take you back to the slaughterhouse to meet up with your partner."

Ascher frowned. "What about you?"

"Dresden's shot."

Ascher blinked. "When?"

"Getting me out," Valmont said, still staring out the window. "He got shot pushing me behind him."

"I'm taking him to someone who can help," Karrin said. "Tell Nicodemus that Valmont is with us."

Ascher frowned at that, and eyed Valmont. "That what you want?"

"I'm not going to see that guy without Dresden around," Valmont said. "You were smart, you wouldn't, either."

"Let her be," I said quietly. "Ascher's a big girl. She can make her own choices."

"Sure," Valmont said.

Ascher frowned at me for a long minute before saying, "I hear a lot of stories about you."

"Yeah?" I asked.

"The warlock who became a Warden," she said. "And then refused to hunt warlocks for the Council."

I shrugged. "True."

"And they didn't kill you for it?" Ascher asked.

"Middle of a war," I said. "Needed every fighter."

"I hear other things. Wild things. That you help people. That you'll fight anyone."

I shrugged a shoulder. It hurt a little. "Sometimes."

"Is he always like this?" Ascher asked Karrin.

"Only when he's bleeding out," Karrin said. "Usually you can't get him to shut up."

"Hey," I said.

Karrin eyed me, a faint glimmer of humor somewhere in the look.

I shrugged a shoulder tiredly. "Yeah. Okay."

"So if you're such a tough guy," Ascher said, "how come I didn't see you kicking ass and taking names in there?"

I closed my eyes for a moment. I didn't feel like explaining to Ascher about how the Winter Knight was built to be a killing machine, one that moved and struck and never paused to think. I didn't feel like explaining what could have happened if I'd let that particular genie out of the bottle in the middle of one of Chicago's premier hotels. Karrin was right. I'd burned down buildings like they were going out of style in the past. A fire in the Peninsula could have killed hundreds. If I'd lost control of the instincts forced upon me by the Winter mantle, I might have killed even more.

What I did want to do, in the wake of the life-and-death struggle, was rip her party dress off and see what happened next. But that was the Winter in me talking. Mostly. And I wasn't going to let that out, either.

"We weren't there to kill Fomor," I said. "We went to get Valmont. We got her. That's all."

"If I hadn't been there," Ascher said, "that thing would have torn you apart."

"Good thing you were there then," I said. "You've got some game. I'll give you that. Fire magic is tricky to use that well. You've got a talent."

"Okay," Ascher said, seemingly mollified. "You've got no idea how many guys I've worked with that don't want to admit they got saved by a girl."

"Gosh," I said, glancing at Karrin. "It's such a new experience for me."

Karrin snorted, and pulled the car over. We'd made it back to the slaughterhouse.

"Tell Nicodemus we'll be back at sunrise," I said.

Valmont said nothing. But she took off the slightly too large shoes and passed them back to Ascher.

"Sure," Ascher said. "Don't bleed to death or anything. This is too interesting."

"Meh," I said.

She flashed me another smile, took her shoes, and slid out of the limo. Karrin didn't pause to watch her reenter the building, but pulled out again at once.

I looked back over my shoulder at Valmont. "You okay?"

She took off the sunglasses and gave me a very small smile. "Nicodemus. He's really back there?"

"Yeah," I said.

"And you're going to burn him?"

"If I can," I said.

"Then I'm good," she said. She turned her eyes back to the night outside. "I'm good."

Karrin stared at Valmont in the mirror for a moment, frowning. Then she set her jaw and turned her eyes back to the road.

"Where?" I asked her quietly.

"My place," she said. "I called Butters the minute the alarms started going off at the hotel. He'll be waiting for us."

"I don't want anyone else tangled up in this," I said.

"You want to take on the Knights of the Blackened

Denarius," Karrin said. "Do you really think you can do it alone?"

I grunted, tiredly, and closed my eyes.

"That's what I thought," she said.

The limo's tires whispered on the city streets, and I stopped paying attention to anything else.

Chapter

Twelve

Karrin's house is a modest place in Bucktown that looks like it should belong to a little old lady—mainly because it did, and Karrin never seemed to have the time or heart to change the exterior much from the way her grandmother had it painted, decorated, and landscaped. When we pulled up, there were already cars on the street outside. She slid the town car into the drive and around to the back of the house.

Before she had settled the car into park, I turned to Valmont and asked, "What's in the file?"

"A profile of a local businessman," Valmont replied at once.

"Anyone I know?"

She shrugged, reached into her purse, and passed me the file, which she had rolled up into a tube. I took it, unrolled it, and squinted at it until Karrin flicked on a reading light. It was on for about five seconds before it stuttered and went out.

"Nothing's ever easy around you, is it?" she said.

I stuck my tongue out at her, tugged my mother's silver

pentacle amulet out of my shirt, and sent a gentle current of my will down into it. The silver began to glow with blue-white wizard light, enough to let me scan over the file.

"Harvey Morrison," I read aloud. "Fifty-seven, he's an investment banker, financial adviser, and economic securities consultant." I blinked at Karrin. "What's that?"

"He handles rich people's money," she said.

I grunted and went back to reading. "He goes sailing in the summer, golfing when the weather is nice, and takes a long weekend in Vegas twice a year. No wife, no kids." There was a picture. I held it up. "Good-looking guy. Sort of like Clooney, but with a receding hairline. Lists his favorite movies, books, music. Got a biography of him—grew up in the area, went to some nice schools, parents died when he was in college."

"Why him?" Karrin asked me.

I looked back at Valmont.

She shrugged her shoulders. "He looked pretty unremarkable to me. No obvious graft or embezzling, which is a given for someone operating at his level."

"Honest men?" I asked, with minimal cynicism.

"Smart crooks, when they steal," she said. "He's a trusted functionary like hundreds of others in this town."

"Gambling problem?"

She shrugged. "Not an obvious one, from his records. The Fomor don't rate him as a particularly vulnerable target for manipulation."

"They have files on money guys?" I asked.

"They've been buying information left and right for the past couple of years," Valmont said. "Throwing a lot of money around. It's been a real seller's market."

"What do you mean?"

"Everyone's buying," Valmont said. "Fomor, White Court, Venatori, Svartalves, every paranormal crew who isn't trying to keep a low profile. That's why I ran this job—it's the third one this month. You want to make some fast money, Dresden, and know some juicy secrets, I can put you in touch with some serious buyers."

I blinked at that information. "Since when have you been all savvy on the supernatural scene?"

"Since monsters killed my two best friends." She shrugged a shoulder. "I made it my business to learn. I was sort of startled at how easy it was. No one really seems to spend all that much effort truly hiding from humanity."

"There's no need to," I said. "Most people don't want to know, wouldn't believe it if you showed them."

"So I've realized," Valmont said.

"Why him?" Karrin asked. "What's Nicodemus's interest?"

I pursed my lips and sucked in my breath through my teeth thoughtfully. "Access," I said. "Gotta be."

"What do you mean?"

I held up Harvey's picture. "This guy can get us something that no one else can. It's the only thing that makes sense."

"Whose money does he handle?" Karrin asked.

I scanned the file. "Um . . . there's a client list here. Individuals, businesses, estates, trusts. Most of it is just numbers, or has question marks. Several of them are listed as unknown."

"Pretty standard," Valmont said. "Guys like that operate at high levels of discretion. What has Nicodemus told you about this job?"

"The final objective, and you," I said. "None of the steps in between."

"Keeping you in the dark," she said. "Keeps the carrot in your mind, but makes it harder for you to betray him if you aren't sure what comes next."

"Jerk," I muttered. "So we don't know what Nicodemus has in mind yet, but I bet you anything that Harvey here is step two."

"Makes sense," Karrin said.

"All right," I said. "No details to any of the Chicago crew, okay? We're playing pretty serious hardball. If word of this leaks, it could reflect on Mab badly, and that could get a little crucifixiony for me."

Karrin grimaced. "So you also want to keep them in the dark and give them information on an as-needed, step-by-step basis?"

"Don't want to," I said. "Need to. The irony is not lost on me, but like I said, I'm playing this one kind of close to the chest."

I closed my eyes again and checked on my body. The same feelings of vague discomfort and weariness seemed to permeate my limbs, and a faint twinge of what might have been the beginnings of a muscle cramp tugged at my back. The silver stud in my ear continued to weigh a little too much, and to pulse with cold at the very edge of comfort.

A gut instinct told me that Mab's little painkiller wasn't actually helping me, *except* to hide the pain I would otherwise be feeling. I'd poured out a lot of energy into just a couple of spells back at the hotel, and doing it without my tools had been hard work. I'd been forced to draw upon the Winter mantle just to keep the pace I needed to stay alive. There wasn't any hard information on how the mantle would interact with my abilities, since to the best of my knowledge there had never been a Winter Knight with a wizard's skills before—but I was pretty sure that the more I leaned on that cold, dark power, the more comfortable I would get in doing so, and the more potential it would have to change who and what I was.

Whatever was in my head was close to killing me. I suddenly felt all but sure that Mab's gift had two edges. Yes, it made me feel well enough to run around getting in danger—but it also left me weak enough to need the Winter mantle now more than ever. It was probably her way of telling me I needed to employ it more.

But sooner or later, doing that would change me, the way it had changed everyone who had come before me.

If it hadn't changed me already.

I felt scared.

After a long moment of silence, Karrin said, "We'll do it your way for now. Let's go on in."

I forced myself to shake off the dark thoughts and the fear that went with them. "You got my stuff?" I asked.

"Trunk."

I got out and slogged over to the town car's trunk. I got my duffel bag and staff out of it, and slung the reassuring weight of my duster over my shoulder to don once I got patched up and into some comfortable clothing. Maybe I would sleep in it.

It had been that kind of day.

*   *   *

I stopped inside Karrin's kitchen, on the tile floor, so that I wouldn't get blood on the carpet, and found Waldo Butters waiting for me.

Butters was a scrawny little guy in his midforties, though from his build you could mistake him for someone a lot younger. He had a shock of black hair that never combed into anything like order, a slender beak of a nose, glasses, and long, elegant fingers.

"Harry," he said when I came in, offering me his hand. "We have got to stop meeting like this."

I traded grips with him and grinned tiredly. "Yeah, or I'll never be able to pay your bill."

He looked me up and down critically. "What the hell happened? You get in a fight with a street sweeper?"

"Octokongs," I said. "And a turtleneck with a machine gun."

"Right calf," Karrin said, bringing Valmont in out of the cold and locking the door behind her. "He's been shot."

"And you're letting him walk around on it?" Butters demanded.

Karrin gave him a look that would have curdled milk. "Next time I'll stick him in my purse."

He sighed and said, "Look, Harry, I know you don't feel the pain, but you are *not* invincible. Pain's there for a damned reason." He waved a hand at one of the kitchen chairs and said, "Sit, sit."

The kitchen was a tiny one. I sat. Butters was a medical doctor, though he spent most of his time cutting up corpses as an Illinois medical examiner, and since the hospitals tended to get a little twitchy when you walked in with gunshot wounds, he'd taken care of such injuries on the down low for me before.

Butters unwrapped my leg, muttered under his breath, and said, "Let's get him on the table. Help me extend it."

"Yeah," Karrin said.

They fussed about extending her kitchen table for a minute, and then she nudged me and said, "Come on, Harry, I'm not lifting you up there."

That said, she still got her shoulder beneath my arm and helped me up, and then helped me lift my legs onto the table. It seemed a lot harder than it should have been to get myself into place.

"Butters," I said, "you going to slash up my tux?"

"Just hold still," he said, picking up a pair of safety scissors out of his bag of medical tools.

"Awesome," I said, smiling. "I'm just going to close my eyes for a minute."

"Karrin, would you hang out with Andi, please. It's bad enough that I'm working on him like this. I don't need my elbows being crowded, too."

"Right," she said. "We'll be in the living room."

"Okay, Harry," Butters said. "Let me get to work."

"How you and Andi doing?" I asked him. "Still good?"

He didn't react to my mention of his girlfriend. "Try not to move."

I did that. The earring pulsed, waves of sleepy cold coming out a little faster than they had that morning. Butters prodded at the bullet wound with something, and I noted that it probably would have hurt like hell without the presence of Winter in my weary body. I opened my eyes long enough to see him swabbing out the injury with a plastic tool coated with what must have been some kind of antibiotic.

He was running it all the way through the hole in my leg.

I shuddered and closed my eyes again.

Day one of working with the Knights of the Blackened Denarius and I'd already been shot and ripped up by a pair of hideous abominations—and that had been doing something relatively simple and safe, by the standards of the rest of the operation.

I had this sinking feeling that day two was going to be worse.

Thirteen

*O*pen *your eyes, you fool. She's right in front of . . .*

I jerked my head up off the table, blinking. There had been a voice in my ear, as clear as day, speaking in a fearful, angry tone. "What?"

Time had gone by. Butters stood at the sink, cleaning his gear. He paused and looked over his shoulder at me, scowling, and said with perfect authority, "Lay. Down."

I did. The earring felt like a chip of ice, so cold that I was about to start shivering. "Did you say something?" I asked him.

"No," he said, frowning. "You were pretty out of it, man. I was letting you rest."

"Someone else in here?"

"No, Harry," he said.

"I could have sworn . . ."

He looked at me expectantly, raising one eyebrow. "Sworn what?"

I shook my head. "Beginning of a dream, maybe."

"Sure," Butters said.

"Am I going to make it, doc?"

He snorted. "Barring infection, you should be fine. No, wait—you *should* be in a hospital on an IV and then in a bed for a week. But knowing you, you're probably going to keep doing whatever stupidly dangerous thing you're doing. You probably won't bleed to death while you're doing it, now."

I lifted my head enough to examine myself. My clothes were gone, except for my pants, and they'd lost most of the right leg. Take that, Nicodemus's heist budget. I had several cuts bandaged. I had fresh stitches in two of the cuts, plus at both ends of the hole in my leg, maybe a dozen altogether, and . . .

"Is that *Super Glue* holding these cuts closed?"

"Super Glue and sutures, and if I could figure out a way to duct-tape them all shut, I'd do that, too."

"I'll take the roll with me, just in case," I said. "Can I get dressed, then?"

He sighed. "Try not to move too fast, okay? And be careful standing up. I don't think the blood loss was too serious, but you might be a little dizzy for a while."

I got up, slowly, and found my duffel bag. I pulled a set of fresh clothes out, ditched the rest of the tux, and tugged them on.

"So what *are* you doing?" Butters asked as I did. "Karrin's been more tight-lipped than usual."

"It's better if I don't say, for now," I said. "But before I do anything else, I need to pay off a debt."

He frowned at me. "What?"

I finished dressing, reached into the duffel bag, and withdrew a block of oak wood. It had taken me most of a month and several botched attempts to get the proportions correct, but in the end I had finally managed to carve a modestly accurate replica of a human skull. Once I'd gotten it carved, I'd boned it with tools I'd made from several curved and pointed sections of a deer's antler Alfred had found for me, and then I'd gone to work. Now, the wooden skull was covered in neat, if crowded, inscriptions of runes and sigils much like those on my staff.

"Four months it took me to make this," I said, and held it out to Butters. I didn't know exactly who else was in the house, or how much they might hear, so I didn't want to mention Bob the Skull out loud. The adviser-spirit was far too valuable and vulnerable a resource to advertise. "Give this to our mutual friend and tell him we're even. He'll be able to tell you what to do with it."

Butters blinked several times. "Is this . . . what I think it is?"

I stepped closer to him and lowered my voice to a near whisper. "A backup vessel for him," I confirmed. "Not as nice as the one he has, but it should protect him from sunrise and daylight if he needs it. I made a deal with him. I'm paying up."

"Harry," Butters said. He shook his head slowly. "I'm sure he'll be very pleased."

"No, he won't," I snorted. "He'll bitch and moan about how primitive it is. But he'll *have* it, and that's the important thing."

"Thank you," Butters said in a carefully polite tone, and slipped the wooden skull into his bag. "I'll get it to him."

I blinked a couple of times. "Uh, man? Are you okay?"

He looked at me for a moment before turning back to

the sink and continuing to wash things. "It's been a long year," he said. "And I haven't slept in a while. That's all."

That wasn't all. I mean, I'm not exactly a social genius, but I could see that he was clearly anxious about something.

"Butters?" I asked.

He shook his head and his voice came out harder and cooler than I would have expected. "You should probably stop asking, Harry."

"Yeah, I should probably eat more vegetables, too," I said, "but let's face it. That isn't going to happen. So what's up?"

He sighed. Then he said, "Harry . . . did you ever read *Pet Sematary*?"

I frowned. "Yeah, like, a long time ago . . ." My stomach twisted a little. "What are you saying exactly? You think I came back wrong?"

"You were *dead*, man," Butters said. "People were . . . Look, when you were here, you were the sheriff in town, in a lot of ways. You died and *things* started moving on Chicago. Not just the Fomor. Ghouls have been lurking around. Stuff came out of Undertown. The vampires started putting people in their pockets. Even the straights started to notice. Molly did what she could, but the price she was obviously paying to do it . . ."

I watched his face as he spoke. His eyes were focused out at a thousand yards, his hands moving more and more slowly. "And your ghost showed up, and that was . . . you know. Weird. But we all figured that, hey, you hadn't lived like the rest of us. It figured you wouldn't die the same way, either."

"Technically, it was more of a code-blue situation . . . ," I began.

"You didn't say that at the time," Butters said.

I opened my mouth and then closed it again. He was right. I hadn't. I mean, I hadn't known back then, but he'd had a considerable amount of time to get used to the idea of me being an ex-wizard.

"Then you show up again, when things are getting worse and worse," he said, smiling faintly. "I mean, bad-ass big brother Harry, back from the dead, man. I don't think you can know what that was like for us. You've had the kind of power you have for so long, I think maybe you've got very little clue what it feels like to walk around without it. You don't know what it was like to sit there helplessly as bad things happened to people while you couldn't do more than fumble around and maybe help someone once in a blue moon." He let out a bitter little laugh. "Oh, the skull could tell me all kinds of things. I'm not sure that made it any better, knowing all about what was happening, without having the strength to do anything but slink around and do little things when you could—just hardly ever when you wanted to."

"Butters," I said.

He didn't hear me. "And then to suddenly see that protector back, when you thought he was gone for good, when things were getting even worse." He shook his head, his eyes welling. "It was like an IV of pure hope, man. Superman had his cape again. The sheriff was back in town."

I bowed my head. I was pretty sure I knew what was next, and I didn't like it at all.

"Except . . . you weren't back in town, were you," he said. "You stayed out on Creepy Island. You didn't do anything. And then Molly was gone, too, so we didn't even have *that* going for us. Will and Georgia both got put in the hospital last year, you know. For a while we weren't sure they were going to make it. They have a little girl now. She almost wound up an orphan. Everyone's lost someone over the past couple of years, or knows someone who has. And you stayed on Creepy Island."

"I had to," I said.

Butter's jawline hardened. "Try to see this from my perspective, Harry," he said. "Ever since Chichén Itzá, you haven't been you. Do you even get that?"

"What do you mean?" I asked.

"You made a deal. With *Mab*," he said simply. "You apparently died. Your ghost showed up claiming you had died, and got us all to do things. Then you show up alive again, only you've got freaky Winter faerie powers. You were here for a *day* before Molly was gone, with freaky Winter faerie powers of her own. And you've been back for a year, living out on that island where hardly anyone can get to you, not talking, not helping, not *here*." He looked at me for the first time. "Not *you*. Not the you we all know. The guy who came to gaming every week. Who we went to drive-in movies with."

I stuffed my hands in my pockets.

"I know that things happen to people," he said. "And maybe you've got excellent and real reasons for doing what you've done. But . . . at the end of the day, there's just no replacement for being *here*. We're losing people. Kids. Old folks. Hell, there was this thing killing people's *pets* for a while." He turned back to his washing. "It's enough to make a guy a little bit cynical. And now you show up again, only you're not talking about what you're doing. People are worried that you're going to go bad like the other Winter Knights have." He spun back to me, his dark eyes hard and pained. "And when you sit up from being sewn up, what's the first thing you do? Hey, Butters? How you doing, Butters? Sorry about beating up your girlfriend? Didn't mean to wreck your computer room, man? No. The first thing you start talking about is *paying off a debt. Just like one of the Fae.*"

Which made a cold chill go through my stomach. Butters might not have all the facts, he might not have the full story, but . . .

He wasn't wrong.

He started slapping his stuff back into his bag, though his voice stayed gentle. "I'm afraid, man. I know what's going on out there now, and it's scary as hell. So you tell me, Harry. Should I be anxious about Superman hanging out with Luthor? When I find out more about what you're dragging Karrin into, is it going to make me less worried? Because I'm not sure I know you anymore."

It was maybe fifteen seconds before I could answer.

"It isn't going to make you any less worried," I said quietly. "And I still can't talk to you about it."

"Honesty," he said. He nodded a couple of times. "Well. At least we've got that much. There's orange juice in the fridge. Drink some. Get a lot of fluids in the next few days."

Then Butters took his bag and walked out of the kitchen.

He looked at least as tired as I felt. And I could see how afraid he was, and how the fear had worn him down. He had doubts. Which, in this world, was only smart. He had doubts about me. That hurt. But they were understandable. Maybe even smart. And he'd been up-front with me about it all. That had taken courage. If I truly had been turning into the monster he feared, by being honest with me about it, he would've just painted a huge target on his face. He'd done it anyway—which meant that he wasn't sure, and he was willing to risk it.

And most important, when I'd needed his help, he'd shown up and given it.

Butters was good people.

And he wasn't wrong.

I heard quiet talking going on in the living room, between Butters and Karrin and another female voice—Andi, presumably. A moment later, the door opened and closed again. The quiet of an emptier house settled over the place.

Karrin appeared in the doorway.

"You heard that, huh?" I asked.

"Yeah," she said. "I did." She crossed to the refrigerator, opened it, and took out a jug of orange juice. She got a plastic drinking glass out of the cupboard and poured it full. Then she passed the juice to me.

I grimaced and drank some, then stared down at the rest. "You agree with him?"

"I understand him," she said.

"But do you agree?"

"I trust you," she said.

Three words. Big ones. Especially coming from her. For a moment, they filled the room, and I felt something tight in my chest ease out of me.

I looked up at her and smiled with one side of my mouth. She answered it.

"Maybe you shouldn't," I said.

The smile deepened around her eyes. "Maybe I'm a big girl who can make up her own mind."

"Maybe you are," I allowed.

"It's been a hard year," she said. "They're tired, and scared. People lose faith sometimes. They'll come around. You'll see."

"Thanks," I said quietly.

She put her hand on my arm and squeezed, then let go of me. "I set Valmont up in the guest bedroom," she said. "You're in my room. I'm on the couch."

"I'll take the couch," I said.

"You don't fit on it, bonehead. You're the one who got shot, remember? And I need you in the best shape possible if we're going to do this."

I swirled the orange juice in the glass. She had a point.

Mister appeared in the doorway, then flung himself at my shins. I pulled the injured one back so that his shoulder hit my left shin alone. I leaned down to rub his notched ear. "Where have you been, fuzzball?"

"It's funny," Karrin said. "He vanishes whenever Andi shows up for some reason."

I remembered a scene of perfect havoc in the living

room of my old apartment, and it made me smile. "Maybe she's not a cat person," I said.

"Drink your juice," she said. I did. She filled up the glass and watched me drink it down again before she was satisfied.

"Okay," she said. "Valmont's already gone to bed. Go sleep. We're getting an early start tomorrow, and you need to be sharp."

This wasn't my first rodeo, and Karrin had a point. You don't survive situations like this by shorting yourself on vital rest for no reason. Besides, I'd already dealt with enough for one evening. Let the day's trouble be enough for the day.

I headed back toward Karrin's bedroom and paused as I entered the living room.

There were guns on the coffee table. Like, a lot of them, broken out on cloths, being cleaned, leaned against a nearby chair, where a large equipment bag waited to receive them. Karrin's favorite little Belgian carbine was there, along with what looked like a couple of space guns. "New toys?" I asked.

"I'm a girl, Harry," she said, rather smugly. "I accessorize."

"Is that a bazooka?"

"No," she said. "That is an AT4 rocket launcher. Way better than a bazooka."

"In case we have to hunt dinosaurs?" I asked.

"The right tool for the right job," she answered.

"Can I play with it?"

"No. Now go to bed."

She settled down on the couch and started reassembling one of her handguns. I hesitated for a moment. Did I have the right to drag her into the kind of conflict I was about to start?

I bottled that thought real quick, with a follow-up question: Did I have the capability to *stop* her from being involved, at this point?

Karrin looked up at me and smiled, putting the weapon together as swiftly and as automatically as other people tie their shoes. "See you in the morning, Harry."

I nodded. The best way to get her through this was to focus and get it done. She wouldn't leave my side, even if I wanted her to. *So stop dithering around, Harry, get your head in the game, and lay Nicodemus and company out so hard that they never have the chance to hurt her.*

"Yep," I said. "See you in the morning."

Chapter

Fourteen

Whatever it was about the mantle of Winter I held that sustained me during action, it didn't seem to have nearly as much interest in looking after me once I was safe somewhere.

I had too many stitches to hop into Karrin's shower, but I bathed myself as best I could with a washcloth and a sink full of warm water and a little soap, and then fell down in the bed. I'd been there for maybe ten seconds before the distant weariness became acute, and the low burn and dull ache of dozens of cuts and bruises swelled up to occupy my full attention.

I was too tired to care. I thought about getting up and getting some aspirin or something for maybe a minute and a half, and then sleep snuck up on me and sucker punched me unconscious.

I dreamed.

It was one of those fever dreams, noisy and bright and disjointed. I don't remember many of the details—just that I could never keep up with what was happening, and I felt as though as soon as my eyes would focus on something, everything would change, and as soon as I caught up to the action that was happening in the dream, it would roar off in a different direction, leaving me struggling to reorient myself, trying to keep up the pace with my feet dragging in the mud. The whole while, I was conscious of several other Harry Dresdens in the dream, all of them operating a little ways off from me, doing their own confusion dance in parallel to mine, and we occasionally paused to wave at one another and exchange polite complaints.

Toward the end of it, I found myself driving along some random section of road in my old multicolored Volkswagen Bug, the *Blue Beetle*, scowling ahead through heavy rain. My apprentice, Molly, sat next to me.

Molly was in her midtwenties and gorgeous, though she still looked a little too lean to my eyes. Her hair, which had seemed to be colored at random ever since she was a teenager, was now long and white-blond. She wore old designer jeans, a blue T-shirt with a faded recycling symbol on it, and sandals.

"I hate dreams like this," I said. "There's no plot—just random weird things happening. I get enough of that when I'm awake."

She looked at me as if startled and blinked several times. "Harry?"

"Obviously," I said. "It's my dream."

"No," she said, "it kind of *isn't*. How are you doing this?"

I took my hands off the steering wheel long enough to waggle my fingers and say, in a dramatic voice, "Wizard."

Molly burst out into a warm laugh. "Oh, good Lord,

it's an accident, isn't it? Are you finally off the island, then? How's your head?"

At that, I blinked. "Wait. Molly?"

"Me," she said, smiling, and leaned across the car. She snaked an arm around my neck for a second and leaned her head against my shoulder in a quick hug. There was a sense of warmth to the touch that went beyond the normal sense of a dream, a sense of another's presence that was too absolute to question. "Wow, it's good to hear from you, boss."

"Wow," I said. "How is this happening?"

"Good question," she said. "I've been attacked in my dreams, like, fifty times since the New Year. I thought I had my defenses locked up pretty tight."

"Attacked? By who?" I asked.

"Oh," she said in an offhand tone, "the Sidhe, mainly."

"Wait," I said. "Aren't you supposed to be their princess?"

"In the flesh, sure," Molly said, her eyes sparkling. "In dreams, though, they can come at me anonymously, so every punk thinks he's tough. It's like the Internet for faeries."

"What jerks," I said.

"No," she said, "not at all. Look, Harry, Maeve was a really, *really* awful Winter Lady. I have a job to do. The Sidhe just want to be sure I'm up for it. So they test me."

"By coming at you?" I asked.

"Quietly, where Mab can't see," Molly said. "It actually kind of reminds me of when Mom used to leave me in charge of all my little brothers and sisters at home. Only more felonious."

I blinked at that and let out a short bark of laughter.

"There, good, a smile," she said. "They step up. I swat them down. It's nothing personal," she continued. "Then I get back to business. Which, by the way, is why you haven't heard much from me. Sorry. I've had about a hundred and fifty years of Maeve's backlog to deal with. What's your excuse?"

"I've been sending messengers every day for the last six months," I said.

Molly's eyes widened, then narrowed. "Mab."

"Mab."

"Grrr," she said. "You need me?"

"The day before yesterday. There's this thing in my head that's going to kill me in the next couple of days. Demonreach says you can help. Apparently, Mab thinks so, too."

Molly's blue eyes went icy. "Or she wouldn't have intercepted your messengers. That bitch. If I'd known . . ." She chewed on her lower lip. "She's got me doing something that I can't get out of right away."

"What, it isn't convenient?" I asked.

"I'm under two miles of ice at the moment," she said. "It took me a day to get here—that's why I'm asleep now. What's the situation?"

I told her.

"Oh, God, Harry!" she said. "Nicodemus, really? Is Sanya there?"

"No," I said, then amended it. "At least, not yet."

"A Knight will be there," she said. "That's how it works. And I'm on the way." Her expression became distressed, and a moment later the dream world started flickering, and I was suddenly driving in a small herd of *Blue Beetles*, all of them filled with slightly different versions of Harry Dresden and Molly Carpenter. I had to slalom the VW through them.

". . . there as soon as I can . . ." came Molly's voice, distantly, and then I was driving alone.

The traffic got worse and worse and more confusing, and then there was a loud screech of tires and twisting metal, a bright light, and a sensation of tumbling and falling in exaggerated, graceful slow motion.

The radio blared with static and a woman's voice spoke in the tones of a news commentator. ". . . other news, Harry Dresden, Chicago wizard, blindly charges toward his own destruction because he refuses to recognize simple and obvious truths which are right there in front of him. Dresden ignored several excellently placed warnings, and as a result is expected to perish in the next forty-eight hours . . ."

I hauled myself out of the dream and sat up in bed, shaking and sweating, with my instincts keyed up for danger and certain that I was no longer alone in the room.

My instincts were half right.

Karrin shut the door behind her almost silently and padded over to the bed in the dim glow of a reflected streetlight outside. She was wearing a long, faded CPD T-shirt and her hair was back in a simple ponytail. She also had her favorite SIG in her hand, held down at her side.

"Hey," she half whispered. She stopped at the side of the bed. "I heard noises. Are you all right?"

I rubbed at my eyes with one hand. Had my dream of

Molly been just that? A dream? Or had it been something more? I knew that a lot of crazy stuff was possible when it came to dreaming, and I knew that it had *felt* incredibly real, but that didn't mean that it had *been* real. "Dreams," I muttered. "Sorry. Didn't mean to wake you."

"I wasn't really sleeping anyway. You were muttering, moving around a lot." I heard her set the SIG down on the bedside table. She was maybe a foot and a half away from me, and from that close, I could smell her. Clean laundry, some kind of vaguely floral deodorant, a hint of sunlight-warmed skin, a trace of cleaning solvent from tending to her guns. A second later, she laid her hand across my forehead.

"You're running a temperature," she said. "Fever dreams are the worst. Sit tight." She went into the bathroom and came out a minute later with a Dixie cup of water and four pills. "Ibuprofen," she said. "How's your stomach?"

"Fine," I muttered. "It's the cuts and bruises that are bothering me." She passed me the pills and the water and I swallowed both and put the cup down on the table. "Thanks."

She picked up the cup and turned to drop it in the trash can, and the light from the bathroom highlighted the strong, curved muscles in her legs as she did. I tried not to notice how much that appealed to me.

But Karrin did.

She paused that way, looking at me obliquely, noticing me noticing her. Then she turned and reached around the bathroom door to shut off the light. The motion showed me even more of her legs. Then the light shut off and we were in sudden darkness. She didn't move.

"Your eyes," she said quietly. "You've only looked at me like that a few times. It's . . . intense."

"Sorry," I said. My voice sounded rough to me.

"No," she said. Cloth rustled softly. Her weight pushed down on the edge of the bed. "I . . . I've been thinking about what we talked about last year."

My throat suddenly felt dry, and my heartbeat accelerated. "What do you mean?"

"This," she said. Her hand touched my chest and slid up to my jaw. Then her weight shifted the bed a little more in the darkness, and she found my mouth with hers.

It was a good kiss. Slow. Warm. Her lips were soft and gentle and explored mine in gentle surges. I could hear her breathing getting faster, too, and her fingers slid up into my hair, her short nails scratching over my scalp and then tracing down over my neck to my shoulder.

Desire flooded through me in a sudden surge of hot, hungry need, and the Winter in me rose up with a howl, demanding that I sate it. Every instinct in my body told me that Karrin was there, and warm, and real, and pressing more of her body against mine through one fragile layer of cloth—that she was mine for the taking.

I didn't move my hands. But I broke from the kiss with a gentle groan and said, "Karrin."

"I know," she said, breathing harder, not drawing away, her breath hot against my skin. "This thing you have with Mab. It pushes you. I know."

Then she took my hand and guided it to her hip. After a second, she moved it lower, below the hem of the shirt, and then slid it up. I felt the soft skin and tight muscle of her thigh, the curve of her hip as she moved my hand up to her waist.

She was naked beneath the shirt.

I absolutely froze in place. It was the only alternative to doing something sudden and primal.

"What?" she breathed.

Something in me that had nothing to do with Winter howled at me for stopping, urged me to start moving my fingers, to get the shirt out of the way, to explore further. I beat it down with a club.

She was too important. This wasn't something I could decide with my glands.

Unfortunately, my head wasn't getting thoughts through to my mouth. "You aren't . . . I'm not sure if I can . . . Karrin, I *want* this, but . . ."

"It's all right," she said quietly.

"I'm not sure," I said again. I wanted her. But I wanted it to be about more than desire. I could have that if I wanted—mindless, empty sex is not exactly in short supply among the Sidhe of Winter.

But that kind of thing can eat you hollow, if you let it. And Karrin was courage and loyalty and brains and heart and so much *more* than mere need and desire.

I tried to explain that. Words just sort of sputtered out. I wasn't even sure they were in the right order.

She slid her hand over my mouth after a few faltering moments. I could hear the smile in her voice as she spoke. "I've had a year to think about this, Harry. And I don't want to wake up one day and realize that I was too scared to take the next step." She leaned down and kissed one of my eyelids, her mouth gentle. "I know that you're a good man. And I've never had a friend like you." She leaned down and kissed the other eyelid. "And I know you've been alone for a long time. So have I. And I'm right here. And I want this. And you want this. So would you please shut up and *do* something about it."

My fingers flexed, all by themselves, savoring the warmth and texture, the soft, tight skin over the curve of her hip, and she shivered and let out a breathless little sigh.

That set something off. I slipped my other hand around her and all but lifted her on top of me. Karrin was made of muscle, but she was still small, and I was a hell of a lot stronger than I had been at any other point in my life. I pulled her atop me, her breasts pressing against my chest through the cotton shirt, and tightened my hands on her lower back, sliding them down, feeling softness, warmth, drawing another gasp out of her.

I groaned and said, "I don't know if I can control . . . I don't want to hurt you."

In answer, she found my mouth again with hers, and the kiss was pure, hungry fire. I pressed back into it, our tongues touching, dancing, and she started pushing and kicking the bedsheets down.

"I spar with Viking warriors, Harry," she snarled. "I'm not made of glass. You need this. *We* need this. Shut *up*, Dresden." Then her mouth was on mine again, and I stopped thinking about anything else.

The kiss got hotter, her hands bolder. I got lost in running my fingers up and down the length of her back, beneath the shirt, from the nape of her neck, down over the supple muscles beside her spine, down over the curves of her hips to her thighs and back, over and over, skin on skin. Her mouth traveled to my jaw, my ear, my neck, sending jolts of sensation coursing down my body, until it became almost more than I could bear.

I let out a snarl and rolled, pinning her beneath me, and heard her gasp. I caught her wrists and slammed them to the mattress, gripping tight, and slid down her body until my mouth found her sex. She tasted sweet, and she let out gasping, breathless sounds as I explored her with my lips and tongue, rising excitement in every shivering motion of her body, in the increasingly frantic roll of her hips and arch of her back. She twisted her wrists, using them as an anchor point so that she could move—and then her breathing abruptly stopped, her body arching up into a shivering bow.

She gasped a few seconds later, twisting and twitching in reaction, and I could see her again in the dim street-light, her face flushed with passion, her eyes closed. I was hard, so hard it hurt, and lunged up her body again, this time pinning her wrists down above her head.

"Yes," she hissed. "Now. Please."

My God, there are times when the sexiest thing a woman can give a man is permission.

I didn't hold back.

She was slippery and hot and I could only barely keep myself from simply taking, going. Some tiny bit of me managed to slow things down as I began to press into her—until she got her legs up and dug her heels into my hips, pulling me hard inside her.

After that, I didn't even try.

She twisted her wrists free of my grip and twined her arms around my neck. She pulled me down frantically, and

the difference in our heights made it awkward to get my
mouth down to hers without withdrawing from her, and
there was no way I was going to do that. I managed. Our
mouths were frantic on each other, breath mingling as our
bodies surged in rhythm. She writhed against me, her eyes
rolling back in her head as she climbed again, her back
arching into a sudden bow once more, a soft, soft moan
torn from her as she shuddered against me. I didn't stop as
she came down from the climax, and she only grew more
frantic, her body rolling to meet each thrust. "Now," she
breathed. "Don't hold back. Don't hold back."

And suddenly I couldn't, wouldn't, didn't want to. I
braced my hands on the bed, holding my weight off of
her, and could think of nothing but how good it felt,
about the pleasure building and building.

"Yes," Karrin hissed. "Come on."

I reached the shuddering edge—

—and felt something cold and hard press against my
temple.

I opened my eyes and saw her holding her SIG against
the side of my head. And as I watched, a second set of
eyes, glowing with a hellish violet light, opened above her
eyebrows, and a burning sigil of the same fire, in a shape
vaguely reminiscent of an hourglass, appeared on her
forehead.

Her voice changed, became lower, richer, more sensual.
"Hell hath no fury like a woman scorned," she purred.

And then she pulled the trigger.

I sat up in Karrin's bed choking down a short cry.

I blinked my eyes several times, struggling to order my

thoughts, fighting sleep out of my head. The silver earring in my left ear felt like a tiny lump of frozen lead, heavy and arctic. I was breathing hard and covered in a light sweat, and some of the cuts were burning with discomfort. My body hurt everywhere—and worse, was utterly keyed up with frustrated, not quite consummated sexual arousal.

I lay back in bed with a groan.

"Oh come on," I panted. "Not even in the *dream*? That's ri-goddamned-diculous!"

A moment later, the light in the hall clicked on, and the bedroom door opened.

Karrin was standing there in her CPD T-shirt and pair of big loose gym shorts, holding her SIG loosely at her side. "Harry?" she said. "Are you . . . ?" She paused, eyed me, and arched one dark gold eyebrow.

I grabbed a pillow, plopped it down over my hips, on top of the covers, and sighed.

She regarded me for a second, her expression difficult to read. "Save it for fight night, big guy," she said. She started to turn and then paused. "But once we're clear of this mess . . ."

She smiled, and looked back at the pillow. Her smile was an amazing thing, equal parts joy and wickedness.

"Once we're clear, we should talk."

I found myself blushing furiously.

She gave me that smile again, and said, "See you in the morning."

Then she shut the door and left me in bed alone.

Yet somehow, thinking of that smile, I didn't really mind.

Chapter
Fifteen

Karrin, Valmont, and I showed up at the slaughterhouse at dawn. As I came up the stairs and out
onto the catwalk, Jordan and one of the other squires
were hastily walking apart, with the mien of teenagers
who had been doing something they were supposed to
do. Jordan was tucking a small notebook into his pocket
as he did.

"Hi, Jordan," I said brightly. "Whatcha doin'?"

He glowered at me.

I walked up to him, smiled down, and said, "Let me
see the notebook, please."

Jordan continued glowering at me. He looked aside at
the other squire, who by now was standing forty feet
away at an intersection of two strips of catwalk, evidently
where he was supposed to be standing guard. The other
squire resolutely ignored Jordan.

I held my hand out and said, "Humor me. I'm going
to stand here until you cooperate or Nicodemus comes
looking."

Jordan's lips twisted into an unpleasant grimace. Then

he took the notebook from his pocket and slapped it into my hand.

"Thanks," I said, opening it to the page that had evidently been written on most recently, and read.

10 goats now.

The reply was written in a blocky, heavy hand—presumably the other squire's.

SO WHAT?

So one went missing last night, and another one in the last hour. Where did they go?

DID YOU TELL THE LORD ABOUT IT?

Yes, of course.

WHAT DID HE SAY?

Nothing.

THEN THAT'S WHAT YOU'RE SUPPOSED TO KNOW.

Something is in here with us. Dangerous. Can't you feel it?

SHUT UP AND DO YOUR JOB.

But what i—

And the script ended in a hasty scrawl.

I finished reading it and eyed Jordan. "You have to wonder about it when your boss doesn't want any questions, kid."

Karrin cleared her throat, pointedly.

"Oh, I want them," I drawled. "I'm just not answering them right away." I passed the notebook back over to Jordan. "That what Nick has the goats in here for, then, eh? He's feeding something."

Jordan's face went pale but he didn't respond in any way.

"Your boss, kid," I said. "He's hurt a lot of good people. Killed some of them."

For a second I flashed back on a memory of Shiro. The old Knight had given his life in exchange for mine. Nicodemus and company had killed him, horribly.

I still owed them for that.

Something of that must have shown in my face, because Jordan took a step back from me, swallowed, and one of his hands slipped toward the sling of his shotgun.

"If you were smart," I said, "you'd get away from this place. Comes time for the balloon to go up, Nicodemus is going to feed you into the meat grinder the second it becomes convenient for him. I don't know what he's promised you guys—maybe Coins of your own, someday. Your very own angel in a bottle. I've done that. It's not all it's cracked up to be."

Jordan, in addition to looking worried, also looked skeptical.

Not a lot of guys who pick up a Blackened Denarius manage to put it back down again, I guess.

"Take it from me," I said. "Whatever you've been told—the Fallen are bad news." I nodded to him and walked past him. Karrin and Valmont hurried to keep pace with me as I descended toward the factory floor.

"What was the point of that?" Karrin asked.

"Sowing seeds of discord," I replied.

"They're fanatics," she said. "Do you really think you're going to convince them of anything now?"

"He's a fanatic," I said. "He's also a kid. What, maybe twenty-three? Someone should tell him the truth."

"Even when you know he isn't going to listen?"

"That part isn't mine to choose," I said. "I can choose to tell him the truth, though. So I did. The rest is up to him."

She sighed. "If he gets the order, he'll gun you down without blinking."

"Maybe."

"There are only ten goats in the pen today," she noted.

"Yeah. The guards think something is in here with them, taking them."

"They think? But they haven't seen whatever it is?"

"Apparently not."

Karrin looked around the warehouse. At least eight or ten hard-looking men with weapons were standing with a clear view of the goat pen. "I find that somewhat disturbing."

"Yeah," I said. "Tell me about it. There're only so many ways to hide. I'll see if I can spot it."

"Do you think it was here with us yesterday?"

"Yeah. Probably."

She muttered something under her breath. "That's not too creepy or anything. Can't you just wizard-Sight it?"

"I could," I said. A wizard's Sight, the direct perception of magic with the mind, could cut through any kind of illusion or glamour or veil. But it had its drawbacks. "But the last time I did that, I got a look at something that had me curled into a ball gibbering for a couple of hours. I don't think we can afford that right now. I'll have to use something more subtle."

"Subtle," Valmont said. "You."

I sniffed and ignored that remark, as it deserved.

"Ah," Nicodemus said, as we reached the pool of light around the conference table. "Mr. Dresden. I'm glad to see you here on time. Will you have doughnuts?"

I looked past him to the snack table. It was indeed piled with doughnuts of a number of varieties. Some of them even had sprinkles. My mouth started a quick impression of a minor tributary.

But they were doughnuts of darkness. Evil, damned doughnuts, tainted by the spawn of darkness . . .

. . . which could obviously be redeemed only by passing through the fiery, cleansing inferno of a wizardly digestive tract.

I walked around the table to the doughnut tray, eyeing everyone seated there as I did.

Nicodemus and Deirdre were present, looking much as they had yesterday. Binder and Ascher sat there, too, a little way down the table, speaking quietly to each other. Binder, in his dark, sedate suit, was eating some kind of pastry that didn't look familiar to me.

Ascher had a plate covered in the remnants of doughnuts that she was apparently struggling to redeem from the hellfire even now. She had changed back into her jeans-and-sweater look, and bound up her hair. A few ringlets escaped here and there and bounced slightly as she spoke. She gave me a small nod as I went by, which I returned.

Seated at the table a little apart from everyone else was an unremarkable-looking man who hadn't been there yesterday. Late thirties, if I had to guess, medium height, solid-seeming, as if he had more muscle to him than was readily apparent beneath jeans and a loose-fitting designer athletic jacket. His features were clean-cut, pleasant without being particularly handsome. He had a slightly dark complexion, and the right bone structure to pass for a resident just about anywhere in the Western Hemisphere, and in chunks of the rest of the world. His dark hair had a few threads of grey in it.

One thing about him wasn't average—his eyes. They were kind of golden brown with flecks of bronze in them, but that wasn't the strange part. There was a sheen to them, almost like a trick of the light, a semi-metallic refraction from their surface, there for a second and then gone again. They weren't human eyes. They looked human in every specification, but something about them was just off.

Something else about him bothered me, too . . .

He was entirely relaxed.

Nobody in that damned building was relaxed. It was an inherently disturbing place, riddled with dark energy. It was filled with dangerous beings. I know I looked tense. Karrin was walled up behind her poker face, but you knew she was an instant away from violence. Binder looked like he was trying to watch everyone at once, the better to know when to beat a prudent retreat, and Ascher's gaze kept hunting for targets. Nicodemus and his daughter sat with a kind of studied air of disinterest, feigning confidence and relaxation, but they were the paranoid type by nature. When I looked at them, I knew they were ready to throw down at a moment's notice. Even Valmont looked like she was ready to dart suddenly in any direction necessary, like a rat daring a trip across open floor for something it wanted to eat.

Every one of us was exuding body language that

warned the others that we were potentially violent or at least hyperalert.

Not the new guy.

He sat slouched in his chair with his eyes half-closed as though he could barely keep them open. There was a half-empty Styrofoam cup of coffee in front of him. He'd drawn hash marks in it with his thumb and played a few rounds of tic-tac-toe with himself in a gesture of pure boredom. There was no sense of violence or alertness in him, no wariness, no caution. None at all.

Now, that made the hairs on my neck stand up.

Either this guy was stupid or insane, or he was dangerous enough that he genuinely was not bothered by this roomful of people—and Nicodemus did not seem the type to recruit the stupid or insane for a job like this one.

I secured a doughnut and coffee. I checked with Karrin and Valmont. Neither wanted to save the doughnuts from Nicodemus's corruptive influence. Not everyone can be a crusader like me.

"I was pleased to hear that you were successful last night," Nicodemus said. "Welcome to our enterprise, Miss Valmont."

"Thank you," Valmont said, her tone carefully neutral. "I cannot tell you how pleased I am to have this opportunity."

That brought a knife-edged smile to Nicodemus's face. "Are you?"

She smiled back, a pretty and empty expression. Then as I sat, she settled into the chair next to me, making it a statement to the room. Karrin took up her stance behind me, as before.

"You have the files, I trust?" Nicodemus asked.

I reached into my duster and paused with my hand there for a moment too long before beginning to draw the file out again, a shade too quickly.

Everyone jumped, or performed some vague equivalent of the gesture. Binder flinched. Nicodemus's fingers tightened slightly on the tabletop. Deirdre's hair twitched, as though thinking about becoming animate and edged. Ascher's shoulder rolled in a tiny back-and-forth motion, as though she'd stopped herself from lifting a hand in a defensive gesture.

The new guy remained lazily confident. He might have smiled, very slightly.

I put the file on the tabletop, tilted my head at the new guy, and asked, "Who's he?"

Nicodemus stared at me for a moment before answering. "Everyone, please meet Goodman Grey. Mr. Grey has kindly consented to assist us in our endeavor. I've already briefed him on each of you."

Grey looked up and swept those odd eyes up and down the table.

They stopped and locked on Karrin.

"Not everyone," he said. His voice was a resonant baritone, with a very gentle accent on it that might have been from somewhere deep in the American South. "I don't believe you mentioned this woman, Nicodemus."

"This is Karrin Murphy," Nicodemus replied. "Formerly of the Chicago Police Department."

Grey stared at her for a long time and then said, "The loup-garou videotape. You were in it with Dresden."

"Set the Wayback Machine for a damned long time ago," I said. "That tape went missing."

"Yes," Grey said, not quite amicably. "And I wasn't actually talking to you, wizard, was I now?"

That made everyone at the table notice. It got quiet and they got still, waiting to see what would happen next.

One thing you learn hanging out with people like Mab—you don't show weakness to predators. Especially not to the really confident ones.

"Not yet. I should ask you," I replied, "how thick do you think that wall behind you might be? When you go flying through it a few seconds from now, do you think you'll knock out a whole section, or just a little chunk the size of your head and shoulders?"

Grey blinked at that, and then turned a wide smile on me. "Seriously? You want to whip them out already? You've been here for about two minutes."

I took a bite of my doughnut, swallowed it (heavenly), and said, "You're not the toughest thing I've ever seen. You're not even close."

"Oh," Grey said. "You don't say."

Though he didn't rise or stir, the air got thick.

Karrin broke the silent tension by putting a small, restraining hand on my shoulder. "That was me in the video," she said.

Grey's eyes went back to her. "You took a shot right past this idiot's ear to take out that guy behind him. That takes some resolve. Good for you."

"I'm a better shot now," she said.

Grey lifted an eyebrow. "Damn, threats from both of you?" He turned his gaze on Valmont. "How about you, sister? Want to jump on this train?"

Valmont didn't meet his gaze. "I don't know you," she said.

Grey snorted. He considered me for a moment. Then he said, "Nicodemus?"

"Hmmm?"

"Do you need the wizard for the rest of the plan?"

"I'm afraid so."

"What about Murphy?"

"Not particularly."

Grey exhaled through his nose, his eyes glittering. "I see." Then he nodded and said, "Shall we put a pin in this, Dresden, until later?"

"Absolutely," I said. "Nicodemus?"

This time Nick's reply was warier. "Yes?"

"What is this jerk good for?"

"I'm the only person in the world who can get you where you want to go," Grey drawled.

"Yeah?" I asked. "Why? What do you do?"

Grey smiled. "Anything. This week, I'm opening doors."

"You've already opened the one that said AN ASS KICK-ING," I assured him. "We'll get to it eventually."

Grey regarded me levelly. Then he got up, moving lazily, and settled down in the chair next to Deirdre and Nicodemus, another statement. He took a slow sip of his coffee and studied Karrin the way a recently fed mountain lion might watch a baby mountain goat taking its first steps: with calm, patient interest.

"Thank you, gentlemen, for putting that aside for the nonce," Nicodemus said smoothly. He did not seem displeased either by Grey's choice of seats or by the focal point of his attention. "Dresden, may I assume you are ready to get to work?"

"When you assume," I said, "you make an ass out of you." I took another bite of doughnut and said, "Yeah, fine."

"The file, please."

I grunted and slid it down the table. Nicodemus promptly passed it over to Grey.

Grey opened the file and started reading it. Those odd eyes of his flicked over pages as if he could take in their entire contents with a glance, then moved to the next. He finished it in maybe six or seven seconds.

"Well?" Nicodemus asked.

"For the simple part, that's enough," Grey replied. "But to pull it off properly, I'll need a sample. A fresh one."

"We'll add that to today's list," Nicodemus said. He nodded to Deirdre, who got up and went around the table, passing out thin manila folders labeled DAY TWO. We each got one. I opened mine up to find a top page that simply read:

PHASE ONE PREPARATION:
WEAPONS
SPELLS
ENTRY

"We have considerable work in front of us today," Nicodemus said. "Binder, I've already had the weapons brought in for your associates to use, but we'll need to see to their maintenance and loading. Perhaps Miss Murphy will be willing to assist with that."

"Sure," she said. "Why not."

Nicodemus smiled. "Miss Valmont, you'll find a schematic for a vault door in your folder. You'll need to be able to open it without damaging it. Today will be the day you plan your approach and requisition whatever equipment you need. Just make a list and give it to one of the squires."

Valmont flipped to the next page, frowning, and studied a diagram. Then she said, "This is a Fernucci."

"Yes."

"I'm not going to say it's impossible," she said. "But what I will say is that I've never cracked one successfully before and I don't know anyone who has. Easier to blow it."

"But we will not be doing so," Nicodemus replied calmly. "Life is challenge. Rise to it."

"Great." She shook her head. "What, are we hitting Vegas or something? Who has a vault door like this around this town?"

"We'll discuss that at the evening meeting," Nicodemus said. "Miss Ascher, Mr. Dresden. Phase One will require us to breach a secure building. We may need to make entry through a wall, neatly, without an explosion, and we will certainly need a loud and obvious distraction to occupy the attention of local security forces while we enter. Those tasks will fall to you two."

I grunted and eyed Ascher. "You want walls or noise?"

"He said loud and obvious," Ascher replied, her voice light. "That screams Dresden to me."

"And we don't want the building collapsing on us," Karrin added in a murmur.

I sniffed and said, "Fine. I'll make the noise, then."

"Releasing enough energy to open a hole without an explosion? That's tricky," Ascher said. "I can adapt a spell I know, but I'll need some time to practice it."

"You have until sundown," Nicodemus said. "Deirdre, you will take Mr. Grey to the factor's address and assist him in obtaining a sample."

"No," I said. "These two stay. I'll go get the sample."

Nicodemus looked up at me sharply.

I showed him my teeth. "Grey's a shapeshifter, isn't he?" I asked. "You're going to use him to duplicate poor Harvey there."

"If we are?" Nicodemus asked. There was an edge of frost to his words. He didn't like that I'd figured out the next step of his plan.

"Harvey lives in my town," I said. "You turn these two psychos loose on Chicago, and Harvey winds up dead somewhere. So I'll do it. I'll get the sample your doppelgänger needs without killing anyone."

"Where's the fun in that?" Grey wondered aloud.

"The fun part is where you get to live," I replied. "Besides. If his death is discovered before we pull the job, don't you think someone's going to be able to put two and two together and figure out that the place is about to get hit? So we do it smart."

Grey sighed and looked at Nicodemus. "Honestly. Where do you find these people?"

Nicodemus never took his eyes off me. "Agreed," he said finally. "Finesse seems a wiser option." His dark eyes sparkled maliciously. "The three of you should have no problem accomplishing the task."

"What?" I asked.

"Grey, Deirdre, and Dresden will run this particular errand," he said, "while the rest of us busy ourselves here." He paused. "Unless, of course, Dresden, you wish to cease lending me your support."

I ground my teeth. I wanted to give him a solid punch in the nose—but that would not be upholding Mab's honor. "No," I said.

"Deirdre and Mr. Grey will bear witness to your sincerity."

My eyes tracked over to Deirdre, who was regarding me with a wide, intense smile that made her dark eyes too bulgy and conveyed a number of awful things. Her hair had begun to slither back and forth over her suit jacket's shoulders.

Grey just looked at me with that calm smile. He made a little motion of his hand, pantomiming sticking a pin into something. Or maybe pulling it out again.

"Oh, goodie," I muttered. "Field trip."

Sixteen

Harvey kept an office just off Logan Square, on the second floor of a brownstone he shared with a Chase bank. I drove us past the building and then around the square twice in Nicodemus's black town car, using the time to think. It was a sunny morning, promising a mild spring day.

"You are literally driving in circles," Grey noted, from the passenger seat.

"Harvey shares a building with a bank," I pointed out.

Grey made an unhappy sound.

"What difference does that make?" Deirdre asked from the backseat.

"They'll have at least one armed guard on-site," Grey said, "and probably more than one. Additionally, everyone there will have rapid access to alarms that will summon the local constabulary."

"Then we'll take him quickly and go," Deirdre said.

"A broad-daylight kidnapping," I said. "In view of all this foot traffic, bank customers and . . ." Even as I spoke, a white sedan with blue and white bubs and a sky blue horizontal stripe rolled through on the opposite side of the square's roundabout. "And Chicago PD patrol cars, which regularly prowl through here."

Grey sighed. "He's right. We're going to have to be patient."

"Can't keep circling the square," I said, pulling off. "We'll hit the next street over, try to find someplace we can park that gives us a view of the building."

Deirdre scowled at me in the rearview mirror. "The simplest way is to walk in, kill him silently, and take what we need. No one will be the wiser until the body is discovered."

"Point," Grey said.

"Simple, all right," I said. "I mean, we don't know his schedule today, who is coming to his office, where he is expected to be, who might raise a cry if he goes missing, or anything like that, but why let inconvenient little things like facts slow us down?"

Deirdre's scowl turned into a glower. Her hair whipped back and forth a few times, like an agitated cat thrashing its tail. I ignored her and drove slowly down the street on the other side of the bank building. It was early enough that I managed to find a parking space with a view of Harvey's office door, and I wedged the town car inexpertly into it.

"There's his car," Grey noted, as I did. "Our man comes in to work early."

"Maybe he loves his job."

"How tiresome," Grey said. He settled back in his seat with his odd eyes half-closed and unfocused.

"So?" Deirdre asked. "What are we going to do?"

"Await developments," Grey said.

"Harvey will leave eventually," I said, "to get lunch, if nothing else. We'll follow him until he's somewhere a little less likely to result in alarms and swarms of cops."

Deirdre didn't like that. "We are on a schedule."

"I guess Daddy should have thought of that before he decided to proceed without telling anyone his plans," I said. "We could have gotten started days ago."

"Patience, Miss Archleone," Grey advised, barely moving his lips as he spoke. He had the look of someone who was comfortable with the idea of spending a lot of time waiting. The man had worked stakeouts before. "We have a little time—and we can always do it the direct way should we need to change our minds."

And we waited.

"Why?" Grey asked me abruptly, a couple of silent hours later.

"Why what?" I asked. I needed a bathroom break, but I didn't want to wander off and take the chance that the two of them would roll up and kill Harvey the minute I wasn't looking.

"This man is no one to you," Grey said. "Why does it matter if he lives or dies?"

"Because killing people isn't right," I said.

Grey smiled slightly. "No," he said. "I'm being serious."

"So am I," I said.

"A random hardpoint of irrational morality?" he asked.

"I've heard your reputation, Dresden. You don't mind killing."

"If I've got to, I will," I said. "If I don't have to do it, I don't. Besides. It's smarter."

Grey opened his eyes all the way and turned his head toward me. "Smarter?"

"You kill someone, there's always someone close to them who is going to take it hard," I said. "Maybe a lot of someones. You remove one enemy, but you make three more."

"Do you honestly think Harvey has someone ready to avenge him should we take his life?" Grey asked.

"He's got whoever he works for," I pointed out. "And he's got the cops and the FBI. If we make a corpse of him, we risk warning our target and setting large forces in motion that could skew this whole deal."

"Kill them as well," Deirdre said sullenly.

"I thought we were on a schedule," I sniped back at her waspishly. I turned to Grey again. "The point is, killing someone is almost never the smart move, long term. Sometimes it's got to be done if you want to survive—but the more you do it, the more you risk creating more enemies and buying yourself even more trouble."

Grey seemed to consider that for a moment, and then shrugged. "The argument is not entirely without merit. Tell me, wizard, does it give you some sort of satisfaction to protect this man?"

"Yeah."

He lifted his eyebrows. "Hmm."

"Good, you want to keep him alive now," I said. It's

just possible that I might have sounded sarcastic. "That was easy."

Grey resumed his waiting posture, eyes slipping out of focus again. "It doesn't matter to me, either way. I've no objection to killing for professional reasons, and no need to do it when doing so would be stupid."

"I thought you said it would be fun."

That made Grey bare his teeth in a smile. "Always. But just because something is pleasurable doesn't mean it is appropriate."

"Look," Deirdre said, her voice suddenly intent.

I did. Three people in overcoats were walking up to Harvey's building. They skipped the entrance in front and headed for the staircase in back. Two of them were men, fairly bulky. The third was a petite woman.

All three moved with a clarity and intensity of purpose that marked them as predators.

"Poachers," Grey noted. There was a low, growling tone to his voice.

I peered at the woman a little more closely, and shot Deirdre a look over my shoulder. "Is that—?"

Her eyes were wide. She nodded tightly. "My mother."

Fantastic.

Polonius Lartessa was another Knight of the Blackened Denarius, the bearer of Imariel. She was also Nicodemus's estranged wife, a sorceress, and an all-around piece of bad news.

"What's she doing here?" I demanded.

Deirdre stared intently at the woman. "I'm not sure. She's supposed to be in Iran. She wasn't supposed to know that—" Deirdre cut herself off abruptly.

So. The wife was cutting in on Nicodemus's action—assuming Deirdre was telling the truth, which I couldn't.

"We can't let her take the factor from us," Grey said calmly. He unbuckled his seat belt and got out of the car. "Come on."

Deirdre bit her lip. But then she got out, following Grey, and I went with them.

Chapter
Seventeen

"**G**rey," I said, hurrying to catch up.

"Hmm?"

"How is walking up and starting a fight with Tessa any better than doing it with Harvey?"

"It isn't," he said. "But the alternative may be losing him. Unacceptable."

"Then we don't lose him," I said. "How good is your Nicodemus impersonation?"

Grey narrowed his metallic eyes. "What did you have in mind?"

"You two go up and distract them," I said. "One big happy family. I go in the front door and get Harvey the hell out of there. Quietly."

Grey considered it for a moment and then nodded once. "I doubt I'll be able to fool his wife for more than a moment. But then, you only need a moment."

Deirdre grimaced. "Just press your lips together as hard as you can and keep quiet. He gets like that when he's angry. I'll talk."

Grey's mouth turned up into a grin. Then he winked at me and just *melted*.

One second, the plain man in jeans and an athletic jacket was there. The next, it was Nicodemus, head to toe, black suit and all—and not just in appearance. Grey's posture changed, along with his walk, the way he held his head, right down to the smug, wary eyes. "Why, thank you, Deirdre," he said in a perfect imitation of Nicodemus's gravelly voice. "Such a dear child."

Deirdre stared at Grey for a second in something between fascination and disgust. Then she said to me, "Hurry. Imariel will realize Anduriel isn't there before long."

I nodded and took off at a jog. I vaulted a large cast-iron fence behind the building (Parkour!) and hustled down an alley no wider than my shoulders between the bank building and its neighbor, keeping the bank between me and the approach of Tessa and her goons, the way a squirrel will circle and hide behind the trunk of a tree. I stopped at the corner to check and be sure that they'd gone out of sight, found the coast clear, then ran down the length of the front side of the bank and went up the stairs to Harvey's office three steps at a time.

The front door had a simple logo on it that read: MOR-RISON FIDUCIARY SERVICES. I went on in and found myself in an office decorated with tastefully spartan sensibilities. There was a receptionist's desk, though no one was at it, and an open door leading into what was obviously a working office.

"Just a moment," called a man from the other room. "I'll be right with you."

I didn't give him a moment. The way the office was laid out, the rear entrance had to open directly into Harvey's office, and Tessa and company might appear there anytime.

Harvey's office was as elegant as his entry, but more crowded with the tools of his trade—computers and office equipment and bookshelves and files. The man himself sat behind the desk with his shirtsleeves rolled up, hunched over a computer keyboard, fingers flying as he watched figures and diagrams of some kind rolling by on his screen.

No sooner did I set foot in the office than the computer started making an odd buzzing noise and the scent of scorched insulation filled the air. An instant later, Harvey's screen turned blue, covered in white text.

"What?" he said, baffled. Then he slapped the side of the monitor and repeated, "What? You have *got* to be *kidding* me . . ." He turned his gaze toward me, annoyance all over his face, and suddenly froze as he saw my expression and my quarterstaff. "Uh," he said. "Who the hell are you?"

"Come with me if you want to live," I said.

"Excuse me?"

"No time," I said. "It isn't your fault, but you're into some bad business, Harvey. There's a woman with two hired goons about to come up your back steps, and they aren't here to sell you a magazine subscription."

"What?" he said. "Do you have an appointment?"

"Are you freaking kidding me?" I growled, and stalked over to his desk. "Get up and come with me."

"Now see here, young man," Harvey stammered. "I

will not be ordered about in my own place of business. If you do not leave immediately, I will summon the authorities."

There just wasn't time for this dance. So I stepped around the desk, grabbed his upper arm in my left hand, and hauled him to his feet.

"Take your hands off of me at once!" he shouted.

"I'm trying to help you," I told him, dragging him back out into the front room by main force. "You are going to thank me for this later—"

The front door opened, and two *more* goons stepped into the office, different men from the ones Tessa had with her. Dammit. I hadn't been keeping an eye out for them on the way in. Of course, if we'd thought to cover both exits, Tessa and her people would have done the same.

The two men saw us and immediately plunged their hands into their jackets, going for their shoulder holsters.

I was quicker. I thrust Harvey behind me with my left hand and pointed my staff at the two men with my right, summoning up a burst of will and snarling, *"Forzare!"*

The runes carved into the staff flared into a pale green-white light, and a wave of force caught both men. One of them was slapped against the wall hard enough to dent the drywall, while the other went reeling back out the door and was thrown down the steps.

The thug who hit the drywall was tough. He bounced off it, completed drawing his silenced pistol, dropped to a knee, and aimed at Harvey.

No time to pull together a shield, not without the advantage of a specialized magical tool to make it happen. So I spun, putting my back between the shooter and

Harvey, bowed my head forward as far as I could, and hunched my shoulders.

The gun coughed, *clack, clack, clack*. Slugs smashed against my back, only to be defeated by the painstaking protective energies I had spell-wrought into the leather duster I wore. I counted eight hits, all of which felt like taking a Little League fastball to the back—painful but not debilitating. Then the gun fell silent and I heard the metallic click of a magazine being released.

I whirled and slashed the end of my staff at the gunman. The heavy oak smashed against the wrist of his gun hand and knocked away the fresh magazine he'd been about to load. I followed up with a backswing and hit him on the jaw right below his ear and sent him sprawling to the floor, the gun tumbling free.

I kicked the gun away from him, and hauled Harvey to his feet. He was staring at the downed gunman, aghast.

"That . . . that man just tried to kill you."

"No," I said. "He just tried to kill *you*. Seriously, dude, what part of *come with me if you want to live* did you not understand?"

I hauled Harvey along with me again, and this time he wasn't resisting me. We headed for the door just as the sound of breaking glass cut in from the office.

"What was that?" he panted.

"Trouble," I said. "Hurry."

I led the way, staff in hand, a shield spell ready to leap into reality if the second gunman proved to be waiting for us, but there was no sign of him.

"You're in pretty good shape, Harvey," I said as I led him down the stairs. "You a jogger by any chance?"

"Uh," he said. "I swim. And do yoga."

"No, Harvey," I said. "You run. You run marathons every morning before breakfast. Make me believe it. Move." I broke into a run down the sidewalk, dodging a little bit of foot traffic now and then. Harvey hurried to keep up, breathing harder than was strictly warranted by the exercise. We'd gotten past the bank and to the next strip of brownstone buildings before I heard a shout behind me. Tessa had appeared in the doorway to Harvey's office. She focused on me, and even from that distance I could feel the malice in her gaze. She pointed a finger at me and two goons took up the chase.

I ducked down the next alley between buildings, circling back toward where I hoped Grey and Deirdre would be waiting to give me some backup, but they were not to be found. As I looked, I saw Tessa emerge from the back door of Harvey's office and begin hurrying after us. There wasn't much foot traffic on this block, and I saw Tessa shuck out of her overcoat on the run. In another moment, she'd take her demonic form and close in on us.

If she was truly out to disrupt her husband's plans, Tessa wasn't worried about causing a scene. If she could stir up the city's police forces, so much the better. She'd happily become that hideous bug thing she turned into and rip Harvey's skull apart.

"Dammit," I said, fleeing down the street, away from Harvey's office and my compatriots. I didn't have much choice. Tessa had me outnumbered. I might have been able to take my chances in a fight with her and some armed thugs, but I couldn't fight them and protect Harvey at the same time. If I stood my ground, they'd take him. So I ran, to buy myself some time to think.

As I did, I realized that I didn't have to beat them in a fight. All I had to do was stall them, or hold them off long enough for Deirdre and Grey to catch up with me. While I didn't trust either of my companions to give a damn about me, they needed Harvey to carry out the plan, and the farther I ran, the more likely it was that I might accidentally lose my own backup.

We reached a building that had been abandoned; its windows were boarded up and covered with graffiti. It would have to do. I whirled toward it, unleashed another blast of energy from my staff, and blew a hole the size of a garbage can in the plywood and the glass beyond.

"Come on," I said. "Stay close."

"What are you doing?"

"We're playing hide-and-seek," I said, and lunged into the building. Harvey stared slack-jawed at me for a second, but then glanced back toward Tessa.

His face went pale, and his eyes widened. He made a few strangled noises, and then thrust himself through the hole, almost sprawling into the broken glass. I caught him and set him on his feet.

The building had been a retail store of some kind, and most of it was one large room. There were still clothing racks scattered around the place, along with the detritus of long-term abandonment. The only light came in around the edges of its boarded-up windows, and through the hole I'd blasted. Shadows crawled everywhere.

I headed deeper into the building, stumbling blindly over things on the floor while my eyes struggled to shift from the light of the spring morning to the gloom of the store's interior. I almost ran into a wall before I saw it, but once I had, I was able to make out just enough shapes to realize that the shop had a doorway leading back to some restrooms and what were probably managerial offices of some kind.

I pushed Harvey into the hallway, then stepped into the doorway between him and the rest of the shop, raising my staff to the horizontal and preparing a shield spell. It wasn't anything like ideal, but it was a better defensive position than I could get on the street outside. They'd all have to come at me from the same direction. "Stay low," I advised him. "Don't go anywhere."

"We should be running," he panted. "Shouldn't we? Calling the police?"

"Cops got better things to do than get killed," I said.

He blinked. "What?"

"Seriously, you don't recognize that reference either? Hell's bells, Harvey, do you even go to the movies?"

Shadows moved in the shaft of light provided by my impromptu portal, and figures entered the abandoned store. Three gunmen, then four—and then something that might have been a praying mantis, only hundreds of times too large, complete with googly, faceted bug eyes and a second set of glowing green eyes open above them.

It took Tessa only a second to spot me. Then she darted toward me over the floor, moving with terrible, insectlike speed, and I triggered the shield spell. The runes on my staff flared green-white again, and a fine curtain of blue-green light washed out from the oak, covering the doorway.

Tessa stopped in front of it, maybe ten feet away. Then she pointed at the door with one long leg and said, in a perfectly normal human voice, "Open fire."

The gunmen didn't hesitate. Their silenced weapons went *clickity-clack*, and sparks and flashes of light bounced up from my shield where the bullets struck. Foiling them wasn't a terrible strain. Subsonic ammunition is slow-moving by its very nature, and each individual round carried considerably less force when it struck than it would have at full speed.

"Hold," the mantis-thing said.

The gunmen stopped firing.

The giant bug stared at me for a long moment. Then its jaws opened, and opened, and opened some more, and Tessa's face and head emerged from its mouth, flaccid chitin peeling back like a hood. Her skin and hair were covered in some kind of glistening slime. She was an odd one to look at. She didn't look like she could be out of her teens when she didn't have wardrobe to lend her its gravitas, and her apparent youth was magnified by the fact that she was a tiny woman, under five feet tall. She was pretty, the high school girl next door.

Of course, she'd been walking the earth for more than a millennium before there *were* any high schools.

"Hello, Dresden," Tessa said.

"Hi, Tessa," I replied.

"The upright hero Harry Dresden," she said, "working for Nicodemus Archleone. Did Lasciel finally talk you into taking up her Coin?"

"Pretty sure you know that she didn't," I said.

She shrugged one shoulder. The motion was absolutely eerie on her insectoid body. "True. But I cannot imagine what else might compel a man like you to work for the likes of my husband."

"Long story," I said. "Now go away."

She shook her head. "I can't do that, I'm afraid. You have something I want. I want you to give it to me."

"It would never work out for us," I said sadly. "I'd be too worried about you biting my head off afterward to live in the moment."

"Don't flatter yourself," she said. "Give the mortal to me. Make me take him from you and you will share his fate."

"Who are you?" Harvey asked in a shaking, bewildered voice. "What on earth have I done to you?"

Tessa clicked her tongue. "Don't trouble yourself with such questions, little man. You won't have them for very much longer."

"Oh, God," Harvey said.

"I'll make you a deal," I said. "Walk away and I won't call the Orkin man."

In reply she lifted an insect leg and hissed a word. A shaft of rotten-looking greenish light streaked toward my shield. I gritted my teeth and held it steady, turning back the attack, feeling the strain of holding the shield beginning to build.

"This isn't a negotiation," she said. "You've already lost. You're trapped, and you can't keep that shield up forever. Give him to me and I will grant you safe passage."

She was right, of course. I couldn't hold the shield forever, or even for long. The moment it dropped, she and her boys would cut loose with everything they had and that would be that. She might or might not be sincere about the offer of free passage, but if she was . . .

If she was, then this was my chance to derail Nicodemus's heist. If Tessa, one of Nicodemus's own circle, interfered and overpowered me, that wouldn't be my fault. I could end this mess and get out while still preserving Mab's reputation. Mab would applaud this solution.

And all I had to do was let Tessa kill Harvey.

No. I wasn't ready to hand over anyone to one of the monsters if I could help it. I might have made some bad choices along the way, but I wasn't that far gone. Besides, I couldn't trust her word anyway. She was just as likely to kill me for the fun of it as to let me walk away in one piece.

"Why don't you go back to the roach motel you crawled out of?" I replied.

She shook her head and sighed. "Such a waste of potential." Then she turned her head to one of her minions and nodded. "Take them both."

The gunmen did something I hadn't expected, at that point—they dropped their weapons and started shucking out of their coats and jackets. As they did, they began to jerk and contort. Joints popped and flesh rippled. Their shirts distended as their shoulders hunched to inhuman proportions, and their faces stretched out into almost canine muzzles, teeth extending into fangs and tusks. Their hands thickened and lengthened, with long claws extending from their tips.

"OhmyGodOhmyGodOhmyGod," Harvey whispered, his breath coming in panicked gasps. "What is that?"

"Ghouls," I said grimly. "Strong, fast, hard to kill."

"What are they going to do?"

"Rip through the walls, come at us from all sides, kill us, and eat us," I said.

And, in professional silence, the ghouls started ripping at the drywall on both sides of my defensive position in the doorway, to do exactly that.

Chapter

Eighteen

Tearing through drywall is a surprisingly noisy process. It breaks with loud crunching, snapping noises. Ghouls have been known to claw their way through inches of stone mausoleum wall to get to a nice rotten corpse to eat, and they had very little trouble with drywall and wood, their claws and hunched shoulders ripping through it at a steady pace.

We had maybe sixty seconds, at most, before they would be romping through the wall and into the building on either side of us.

"They're coming," Harvey gasped. "They're going to get us. What do we do?"

My own heart was beating a lot faster than it had been a moment ago. Ghouls were no joke. And a close, confined space like this was the worst possible situation in which a wizard could take them on. My spell-armored duster wouldn't be of much help when one of them was chewing on my head. It doesn't matter how many times you've faced danger. When your life is under threat and you know it, you're scared, end of story.

Fear—real, silvery, adrenaline-charged fear—rocketed through me.

"Um," I said, not panicking. "We . . ."

I was going to say "back up." I really was. But Tessa was staring at me with a smug, gloating expression on her face, and I was suddenly infuriated. Tessa was special. The last time I'd seen her, she'd put a good man in the hospital for months and left him permanently maimed. It was a miracle, literally, that he'd lived at all.

She hurt my friend.

The Winter surged up inside me in time with my rage, and I suddenly put a much higher priority on the fact that I still *owed* her for that.

"Get behind me and stay close," I growled instead.

"What?" Harvey blurted.

I had the satisfaction of seeing Tessa's gloating expression falter for a fraction of a second, tipped off by something in my face, maybe, before I dropped my shield, extended my staff in my right hand, called upon Winter, and snarled, *"Infriga!"*

A howl of arctic air billowed out onto the display floor, blanketing every object in it—the floor, the ceiling, and the walls—in an instant layer of flash-frost. The sudden shift in temperature condensed the air into frozen mist, a fog thick enough to cut visibility to five or six feet—a situation that would be much more to the advantage of the team with fewer members, making it harder for the enemy to coordinate their superior numbers.

I strode forward through the fog, closing the distance on Tessa so that I could get her in sight again before she recovered and started maneuvering on me. In a perfect world, I would have found her frozen into a block of bitterly cold Winter ice—but she was a sorceress, and not a dime-store amateur, either. As she came in sight through the fog, I saw her stumbling back, her foremost insect-arms crossed in a defensive gesture, her image blurry on the other side of a C-shaped wall of ice that had not quite managed to engulf her entirely.

I gestured with the staff and snarled, *"Forzare!"*

The frozen wall exploded into chunks and shards of knife-edged, crystalline ice, as deadly as a cloud of shrapnel. She tried to fling herself to one side, but stunned by the intensity of the attack, she didn't account for the ice-coated tile floor beneath her legs—floor that provided me with footing as sure and solid as a basketball court. Insect legs skittered wildly, and the ice tore into her chitin-covered body, sending splatters of dark green ichor everywhere, even as the mantis-head half slithered up over her human face, swallowing it down again. Hotly glowing green eyes opened above the insectoid mantis-eyes of Tessa's demonform, blazing with immortal rage, and as the swirling mists closed around them, the eyes of Tessa's patron Fallen angel were all that I could see of her.

"Hey, Imariel!" I snarled. "I got some for you, too! *Fuego!"*

As I spoke the words, I hurled the fusion of my will and elemental flame through my staff, imbuing the spell that ran through it with the silver-white fire of Creation itself. A basketball-sized comet of blazing soulfire soared through the air like a chord of triumphant choir music and detonated upon those glowing eyes in thunder and fury, in steam and even more mist. The eyes vanished in time with a teakettle scream of hellish fury and a thunderous crash of shattering brick from the far end of the building.

That bought me a little time, at least. I whirled and dragged Harvey behind me just as the quickest or luckiest of the ghouls loomed out of the mist and flung itself bodily at my head.

No time for a spell. No *need* for one. With the full power of Winter still singing through my limbs, I whirled my heavy oaken quarterstaff and met the leaping ghoul with a strike that used the full power of my arms, shoulders, hips, and legs. I struck it across one shoulder, and there was a wet, sickening crack of breaking bone and limbs being torn out of joint. I hammered the ghoul to the floor with the same blow, as if it had been an overeager kitten jumping at me, and drew a yowling shriek of surprised anguish from it as it landed.

My mind flashed to a pair of young wizards, brother and sister, tormented to death by ghouls on my watch, a few years back—and I remembered that I owed *them* a debt, collectively, as well. I kicked the downed ghoul hard enough to send it sliding away over the icy floor, and though it was already taxing my reserves to call up that kind of power, I again unleashed Winter, snarling, *"Infriga!"*

The ghoul had no defenses against that kind of magic. An instant later, there was a white, vaguely ghoul-shaped block of ice where the creature had been. The block kept sliding, grinding over the icy floor . . .

. . . and fetched up against the clawed feet of the other three ghouls.

The three stared at the block of ice for a startled quarter-second, and then, as one, fixed me with hate-filled eyes and let out snarls of utter fury.

Yikes.

Time slowed down as they crouched to spring toward me.

Entombing one ghoul in ice was one thing. Doing it to three of them was something else entirely. If I took the time to take out one of them, the other two would be upon me almost before the words had left my lips, and four ghouls minus two ghouls is two ghouls too many. When you're outnumbered as badly as I was, inflicting two-to-one casualties is just another way to say that you lost and got eaten.

I had to change the footing of this fight.

The ghoul on my left was a shade faster than his two fellows, and I sprang to my left, drawing him with me, creating a little more space between him and his companions. As his clawed feet left the ground, I gestured with my staff, calling upon Winter again and shouting, *"Glacivallare!"*

With a shriek, a sheet of ice a foot and a half thick rose from floor to ceiling in a ruler-straight line cutting diagonally across the sales floor. The ice clipped the lead ghoul's heels as it shot upward, slamming into the ceiling in front of the other two with an ear-tearing grinding noise.

My timing had been solid. It was a one-on-one fight again. I felt a surge of triumph.

That lasted for maybe a quarter of a second, and then the leaping ghoul hit me like a professional linebacker. Who was also a hungry cannibal.

He slammed into me hard enough to break ribs, and I had to hope that the crackling sound I heard was shifting ice. We went down hard, with me on bottom, my duster now sliding over the hard surface, dispersing some of the energy of the hit.

The ghoul knew exactly what it was doing. I'd tangled with them a few times before, and in a fight, ghouls are mostly all unfocused ferocity and brute strength, ripping and tearing at whatever they can reach. This one didn't do that. He got both hands on my staff, wrenching it aside with that hunched, fantastic strength, and ducked his head in close, going for my throat, for the immediate kill. I knew enough about hand-to-hand fighting to recognize technique and discipline when I saw it. It was the difference in fighting a furious drunken amateur and taking on a trained soldier or a champion mixed martial artist.

Over the years, I'd picked up some technique of my own, from Karrin and the others. I provided an instant's resistance against the ghoul's wrenching of my quarterstaff, then released it as I doubled up my body, pushing the ghoul up as hard as I could with my legs, trying to shove him to one side.

I didn't fling him off me or anything, but simultaneously taking his balance and giving him a solid impetus in a new direction let me dump him to the ice just as his jaws began to snap closed on my throat. I felt a flash of sensation there as his weight vanished, and I rolled frantically in the opposite direction, using the momentum of the push to get me going.

I came to my feet, a hair faster than the ghoul warrior,

already reaching for a fire spell in my mind—but without the aid of my staff to focus the energy of the spell more efficiently and effectively, I was a shade too slow getting it together. The ghoul came back to his feet, his claws digging at the ice, and promptly came at me with my own damned staff, whirling it like he knew how to use it.

I let out a yelp and started dodging. If we'd been standing on the street, he'd have tenderized me into a pulpy mess that he'd barely need to chew. But we weren't standing on the street. We fought in the frozen arctic air of the little store coated in Winter ice. The ice betrayed him at every movement, forcing him to constantly keep his balance in check, while to the Winter Knight it was as smooth and safe as a dance studio's floor. I ducked around empty clothes racks, dumping a couple of them at the ghoul as he came at me, hoping to knock him down, and changed direction constantly, hoping to open the gap between us or force him to lose his balance. All I needed was a portion of a second to bring another spell into play and end the fight.

Problem was, the ghoul knew it. He came at me smart and fast and balanced, and as long as he could keep doing it, he had me in a stalemate. All he had to do was hold me until his friends either ripped through the wall or loped around it, and I was done.

Stars and stones, I was missing my force rings right about then. And my blasting rod, and shield bracelet, and every other little magical craft tool I'd ever designed. But when my lab and its accompanying gear had been destroyed, it had severely cut down my options on what I could manufacture—and being stuck out on the island the whole winter with harshly limited resources, limited by what my brother could round up and bring on a boat, I'd not yet had a chance to set up anything as elaborate and as extensively personalized as a new lab. I'd managed the staff and the wooden skull, working at a laboriously glacial pace, but practically all I'd had to work with was a small set of knives and some sandpaper left over from the construction of the Whatsup Dock.

Preparation! Dammit, Harry. The key to survival as a wizard is preparation!

I could hear sledgehammer blows being delivered to my ice wall, and though I couldn't see it in the fog, I could *hear* the change of pitch in each impact, as the ice began to crack and shatter.

"Oh God!" Harvey shouted in a panic. I couldn't see him either, and I'd forgotten about him for a second. He was probably right where I'd left him, within a few feet of the wall, and able to see exactly what was happening.

The other two ghouls were coming through.

Something inside me started screaming along with poor Harvey.

It was time for a desperate risk.

I abruptly shifted direction and charged the warrior ghoul.

My staff flickered at my head. I raised my left arm to block, trying to take the blow on the meaty muscle of my forearm. Though I didn't feel any pain, the impact sent a flash of white light across my vision. My duster's sleeve caught some of the blow, but not much. Its defensive spells were really meant to slow and disperse fast-moving objects like bullets, or to stop the penetration of sharp things. A big blunt instrument had no subtlety, but it was merry hell to defend against.

I found myself inside the quarterstaff's reach, and promptly slammed my head against the end of the ghoul's muzzle. He let out a yowl of surprise and anger, his forward momentum abruptly stalled, and I followed up with a one-armed push using every bit of muscle the Winter mantle could muster.

The ghoul staggered back several steps and then *his feet went out from under him*!

Hope sparked and kindled will. As the ghoul fell, I let out a triumphant howl of *"Infriga!"*

Winter howled into the little store for the fifth time in maybe sixty seconds, blanketing the fallen ghoul warrior in absolute cold and boiling fog. I panted frantically for a couple of seconds, until the fog boiled away enough to let me see the warrior ghoul in its frozen sarcophagus.

"Harvey!" I croaked. "Harvey, sound off!"

"Oh *God*!" Harvey sobbed. "Oh *God*!"

"Yeah, or that," I muttered, and hurried toward the sound.

I reached him just as the other two ghouls pounded their way through the wall. Harvey let out a shockingly high-pitched squealing sound and scrambled in helpless panic on the slippery ice.

I raised my frost-coated right hand, gathered my will for another spell—

—and found a patch of white blankness in front of my eyes. I blinked and suddenly I was sitting on the ice next to Harvey, wondering how I'd gotten down there.

Winter, I realized. I called up too much power, too

fast, with too little chance to rest. I'd burned up my reserves of magical energy, to the point where it threatened
to rob me of consciousness. But even now, I didn't *feel*
magically exhausted.

*Of course you don't feel it, dummy. You're the Winter
Knight.*

I blinked a couple of times, and then looked down at
my left arm, which was sending me some sort of odd,
pulsing sensation.

My duster's sleeve was being distended from the inside
by something pointy. It took me an effort of conscious
observation and logical processing to realize that it was
my own broken arm.

A seven-foot section of the ice wall suddenly shattered
and fell to the floor with a groan.

I shoved myself to my feet with my good arm as the
other two warrior ghouls came through the opening.

No magic.

No weapons.

No options.

I set my teeth in a defiant, futile snarl and the ghouls
pounced.

Chapter
Nineteen

Both ghouls came at me, as the most dangerous target in sight, ignoring the sobbing Harvey. I didn't blame them. I'd have made the same call.

All three of us were wrong.

The warrior ghouls came at me from different angles, so that I could have nailed only one of them, even if I'd had the energy to call up another blast of Winter. It meant that one ghoul had to bound to one side and then rush me. The other one just leapt over Harvey's screaming figure.

Goodman Grey killed that one first.

As the ghoul passed over him, Harvey's eyes went cold and calm, and one arm swept out. I didn't see it actually change, as much as I had an impression that the arm was, for a second, in an entirely different shape—a hard, inward-curving sickle, moving with fantastic speed. There was a shearing sound combined with a *thunk*, like a schoolroom paper cutter, but wetter and meatier, and suddenly the ghoul's top and bottom halves were spinning off on separate arcs.

Then the second ghoul was on top of me, and even with the extra strength of the Winter mantle, it was everything I could do to keep its teeth off my throat. If it hadn't been for my duster, its claws would have shredded my torso in the second it took Grey to reach me.

There was a sense of motion more than anything I could actually see, and something vaguely gorilla-like seized the ghoul in enormous hands, and threw him away from me with such power that I heard joints dislocating from the force of the throw. The ghoul hit a still-standing portion of the wall of ice and went right through it, splattering fluids in the process. Before it had gone all the way through the wall, a blur that reminded me of some kind of big hunting cat hit it in midair and bore it to the ground, out of sight behind the fog and the rubble of the wall.

The ghoul let out a single, weak, gurgling scream.

Then it went quiet.

Something moved on the other side of the wall. A few seconds later, there was a long exhalation and Goodman Grey appeared, stepping calmly over what was left of the wall. Something was twitching in death on the floor beyond him, though I couldn't make out any details—and didn't want to. Ghouls don't die easy, and they don't go out any way but messy. The one he'd bisected was making scrabbling noises from two different directions in the fog.

He looked around for a moment, pursed his lips and nodded, and said, "Good move, splitting them up like that, and in the fog, too. Smart. Don't see that much in people your age."

"There's always more of them than me," I said, and got to my feet. I had a feeling that I didn't want to be sitting on the ground bleeding, with a broken arm, around Goodman Grey. You don't give predators like that ideas—and at that moment, the casually dressed, unremarkable-looking little guy was scaring me more than had the ghouls and Tessa together.

I kept any tremor out of my voice and asked, "Where's Harvey?"

"Over here," Grey said. He looked exactly as relaxed as he had before, as if he had just paused to throw away an empty paper cup, rather than tearing two ghouls to shreds. His eyes lingered on my wounded arm. "I only had a few seconds to make the switch and he wouldn't quiet down. I had to knock him out."

I gave Grey a hard look. Then I took a couple of steps to the frozen ghoul who had taken my staff from me and reached down to wrench it free of the Winter ice. It crumbled for me obligingly, yielding the tool back into my hand. A couple of the ghoul's clawed fingers broke off and came with it. I shook them off of it with a grimace, turned to Grey, and said, "Show me."

He lifted his eyebrows at me for a moment. He might have smiled a bit, but nodded and waved for me to follow him. He didn't seem in the least worried about turning his back on me.

Hell's bells. For all I knew, the shapeshifter had eyes in the back of his head.

Grey led me to the side of the sales floor, where old metal-frame shelves had once held magazines. He grabbed one and hauled it easily aside.

Harvey Morrison's corpse lay on the other side.

His throat had been cut, neatly, by something sharp. There was an unholy mess on the floor around him. His eyes were open and staring sightlessly up at the ceiling. The blood was still pulsing out, though he was white enough that I knew that it was too late. He was dead. His body was still figuring it out.

I lifted my eyes slowly to Grey.

The shapeshifter stared down at Harvey with a very faint frown on his face. He looked up at me and said, "Huh. Awkward."

"You think this is funny?" I asked him. I knew my voice sounded hot.

"I think it stinks," Grey said, and looked back at Harvey. "I only choked him out."

"You would say that, though, if you were trying to screw me over."

"No, I wouldn't," Grey said. "I'd tell you I cut his cowardly throat because it was simpler."

"You would?"

"It's not as if you frighten me, Dresden. Lying well takes a lot of effort, and it gets old after a few centuries. Mostly I don't bother." He nudged Harvey's shoulder with the toe of his shoe. "But someone went to a lot of effort to get this done. Did it fast. Got out just as fast."

"Where's Deirdre?" I asked.

"She was supposed to be chasing her mother away after you bloodied her nose for her." He knelt down on the floor beside Harvey and then leaned closer, inhaling through his nose like a hound. "Nngh." He considered for a moment. "Too much fresh blood and damned ghoul stench. Can't get anything through it." He looked up at me. "What about you?"

"If I had twenty-four hours to collect gear and another five or six to go over the place, maybe I could turn up something," I said.

We looked at each other. I think we were both thinking that the other one wasn't telling us something he knew. Except that I was actually ignorant, whereas I was pretty sure Grey had scented more than he let on. But he struck me as the suspicious sort.

Evidently, Grey had me figured the same way. He let out an impatient sigh. "Wizard. You know I'm telling you the truth, right?"

"Right," I said. "Sure you are. We're a trustworthy bunch of Boy Scouts."

That got what almost looked like a genuine wry smile out of him. He leaned down and closed Harvey's eyes with one hand, the motion almost respectful. In the same gesture, he ran his fingers through the thickening puddle of blood.

"What are you doing?" I asked.

"Getting what we came for," he said. "Got to have the blood sample for what's coming up. You'll have to tell Nicodemus where I am."

"And where's that?"

"Morrison Fiduciary Services, for the rest of the day," he said. "The point of not killing Harvey was to avoid the possibility that he'd be noticed if he went missing. So he's about to not go missing."

"You're going to fake being a confidential and knowledgeable financial expert to people you've never met before for the rest of the day?" I asked him, my voice heavy with sarcasm.

"Yes," Grey said calmly.

I felt my eyebrows going up. "You're that good?"

"I'm better," he said. His eyes glinted weirdly and it made me shudder.

"What about Harvey's body?"

"He didn't have any family. And you've got two ghouls on ice," he said. "Leave them where they are. They'll take care of him for us when they thaw out."

That made me grind my teeth. "Maybe I should take them out now. Those guys were different than the usual ghoul. I don't feel like giving them a second shot at me."

"Whatever," Grey said. "I need to get moving."

Grey started lapping the fresh blood out of his cupped hand. He grimaced, and then shuddered, and a second later, he looked exactly like the corpse at his feet, clothes and all. He leaned over and took Harvey's glasses out of his shirt pocket. He wiped the blood off them on a corner of Harvey's shirt, and then put them on. "Better get someone to look at that arm, eh?"

I eyed my broken arm distractedly and then said, "Grey."

"Yeah?"

"I'm not leaving Harvey's body to be eaten by ghouls. And if you've got a problem with that, then we can discuss it right now."

Grey looked at me with Harvey's face and then nodded once. "Your call. You do it."

And he padded off through the rapidly thinning fog toward the opening I'd blasted in the store's window, and vanished onto the street.

I looked down at Harvey's corpse. Then I said, "I'm sorry." It seemed inadequate. I was going to promise him that I would punish his murderer—but Harvey was beyond that now.

The dead don't need justice. That's for those of us who are left looking down at the remains.

I pushed the heavy shelves back in front of Harvey's body. The authorities would probably find him in a couple of days. It wasn't dignified, but there wasn't a lot more that I could do—and I really didn't feel like making a run on Hades' vault only to find a batch of mythological badasses waiting to kill us all the moment we came in. So I did what I could.

I didn't have much left in the way of a magical punch. But I did have the strength of my good arm and a big heavy stick. I used them to shatter the frozen ghouls into chunks, and then I left the store too, and shambled back out to the rental car, feeling tired and sick and useless.

Chapter Twenty

I wasn't sure where I was driving. The important thing was to drive.

Some part of me was noting, with more than a little alarm, that I was not behaving in any kind of rational fashion. The numbers weren't adding up. I had a badly broken arm. We were on the clock. I had left Karrin by herself among that crew, though I felt fairly sure that Ascher and Binder wouldn't kill her out of hand, and that Nicodemus had no good reason to do so. Yet. But I had only Grey's word that he had gone where he said he meant to go. For all I knew, he'd doubled back to the warehouse to indulge his interest in Karrin. Unlikely, maybe, but I still didn't like the idea of leaving her there.

On the other hand, I couldn't go back either. Not with my arm hurt like that. Showing weakness to that crew was not an option.

I checked to be sure that my arm wasn't bleeding. It wasn't, but I nearly crashed into a car that had come to a stop in front of me while I was looking. Whatever the mantle of the Winter Knight did for me, the damage was catching up to me now. Maybe I couldn't feel the pain, but the mantle had to draw its energy from something, and the most logical source was me. The pain didn't hurt, but it was still being caused by a very real injury, and covering that pain was costing me in exhaustion and focus.

I needed help.

Right. Help. I should drive to Butters, get him to set the arm and splint it.

But instead I found myself parking the car in front of a pretty, simple, Colonial home in Bucktown. It was a lovely house, unpretentious and carefully maintained. There was a large oak tree out front, a couple more in the back, and a freshly painted white picket fence surrounded the front yard. A new mailbox, handmade and hand-carved, rested on a post beside the fence's gate. Metallic gold lettering on the mailbox's side read: THE CARPENTERS.

I put the car in park and eyed the house nervously.

I hadn't been there since my last trip to Chicago, the year before. I'd stopped by when I'd been pretty sure no one was home, like a big old coward, to collect my dog, Mouse, for a secret mission.

Doing so had permitted me to craftily dodge my first meeting with my daughter since I'd carried her from the blood-soaked temple in Chichén Itzá, from the deaths of thousands of vampires of the Red Court—and from her mother's body, dead by my hand.

Her name was Maggie. She had dark hair and eyes, just like Susan, her mother.

Beautiful Susan, who I'd failed, just like I'd failed Harvey.

And after that, I'd taken Molly Carpenter out and gotten her involved with some of the most dangerous beings I knew. Because she'd been helping me, Molly had fallen prey to the power games of the Sidhe—and now, for all I knew, she wasn't even truly human anymore.

Molly, who I'd failed, just like I'd failed Harvey.

What the hell was I doing here?

I left the car and shambled up to the gate. After a brief pause, I opened it, and continued to the front door.

I knocked, wondering who might be home. It was the middle of the day. The kids would all be in school. For a second, I debated fleeing, driving away. What was I hoping to accomplish here? What could I possibly do here that would make victory in my treach-off with Nicodemus any more likely?

It was wholly against reason.

I stood on the front porch of Michael Carpenter's house, and only then did I realize that I was crying, and had been for a while. Again, I considered simple, childish flight. But my feet didn't move.

A moment later, a good man opened the door.

Michael Carpenter was well over six feet tall, and if he didn't have quite the same musculature he'd carried when he'd been an active Knight of the Cross, he still looked like he could take most men apart without breaking a sweat. His brown hair was more deeply threaded with silver than it had been before, and his beard was even more markedly grizzled. There were a few more lines on his face, especially around the eyes and mouth— smile lines, I thought. He wore jeans and a blue flannel work shirt, and he walked with the aid of a cane.

He'd gotten the injury fighting beside me because I hadn't acted fast enough to prevent it. I'd failed Michael, too.

My view of him went watery and vague and fuzzed out completely.

"I think I need help," I heard myself whisper, voice little more than a rasp. "I think I'm lost."

There was not an instant's hesitation in his answer or in his deep, gentle voice.

"Come in," my friend said.

I felt something break in my chest, and let out a single sob that came out sounding like a harsh, strangled groan.

I sat down at Michael's kitchen table.

Michael's house had a big kitchen that looked neater and a lot less cluttered than the last time I'd seen it. There were two big pantries, necessary for the provisioning of his platoon-sized family. The table could seat a dozen without putting the leaves in.

I squinted around. The whole place looked neater and better organized, though it had always been kept scrupulously clean.

Michael took note of my gaze and smiled quietly. "Fewer people occupying the same space," he said. There was both pride and regret in his voice. "It's true, you know. They grow up fast."

He went to the fridge, pulled out a couple of beers in plain brown bottles, and brought them back to the table. He used a bottle opener shaped like Thor's war hammer, Mjolnir, to open them.

I picked up the bottle opener and read the inscription

on it. " 'Whosoever holds this hammer, if he be worthy, shall wield the power of Thor.' Or at least to crack open a beer."

Michael grinned. We clinked bottles and drank a pull, and I put my arm up on the table.

He took one look at my sleeve and exhaled slowly. Then he said, "Let me help."

I eased out of my duster, with his aid, my arm and wrist flickering with silvery twinges of sensation as the sleeve came off. Then I eyed my arm.

The bone hadn't actually come out of the skin, but it looked like it would only take a little push to make it happen. My forearm was swollen up like a sausage. The area around the upraised bone was purple and blotchy, and something that looked like blisters had come up on my skin. Michael took my arm and laid it out straight on the table. He began to prod it gently with his fingertips.

"Radial fracture," he said quietly.

"You're a doctor now?"

"I was a medical corpsman when I served," he replied. "Saw plenty of breaks." He looked up and said, "You don't want to go to the hospital, I take it?"

I shook my head.

"Of course not," he said. He prodded some more. "I think it's a clean break."

"Can you set it?"

"Maybe," he said. "But without imaging equipment, I'll have to do it by feel. It could heal crookedly if I'm not good enough."

"I'd kill most of that equipment just by walking into the room with it," I said.

He nodded. "We'll have to immobilize the wrist right away once it's done."

"Don't know if I can afford that."

"You can't *not* afford it," he replied bluntly. "Assuming I get it set, one twist of your hand will shift the bone at the break. You've got to immobilize and protect it or the ends will just grind together instead of healing."

I winced. "Can you do a cast?"

"There's too much swelling," he said. "We'll have to splint it and wait for the swelling to go down before it can take a proper cast. I could call Dr. Butters."

I flinched at the suggestion. "He's . . . sort of wary of me right now. And you know how much he doesn't like working on living people."

Michael frowned at me for a moment, studying my face carefully. Then he said, "I see." He nodded and said, "Wait here."

Then he got up and went out his back door, toward his workshop. He came back a few moments later with a tool-bag of items and set them out on the table. He washed his hands, and then took some antibacterial towelettes to my arm. Then he took my wrist and forearm in square, powerful hands.

"This will hurt," he advised me.

"Meh," I said.

"Lean back against the pull." Then he began pulling with one hand, and putting gentle pressure on the upraised bone with the other.

It turned out that even the Winter Knight's mantle has limits. Either that, or the batteries were low. A dull, bone-deep throb roared up my arm, the same pain you feel just before your limbs go numb while submerged in freezing water, only magnified. I was too tired to scream.

Besides.

I had it coming.

After a minute of pure, awful sensation, Michael exhaled and said, "I think it's back in place. Don't move it."

I sat there panting, unable to respond.

Michael wrapped the arm in a few layers of gauze, his hands moving slowly at first, and then with increasing confidence—old reflexes, resurfacing. Then he took the rectangular piece of sheet aluminum he'd brought in from his workshop, gave my arm a cursory glance, and used a pair of pliers and his capable hands to bend it into a U-shape. He slid it over my hand at the knuckles, leaving my thumb and fingers free. The brace framed my arm most of the way to my elbow. He slid it back off and adjusted the angle of the bend slightly before putting it back on. Then he took a heavier bandage and secured the brace to my arm.

"How's that?" he asked, when he was finished.

I tested it very, very gingerly. "I can't twist my wrist. Of course, there's a problem with that."

"Oh?"

I spoke as lightly as I could. "Yeah, I can't twist my wrist. What if there's some incredibly deadly situation that can only be resolved by me twisting my left wrist? It could happen. In fact, I'm not quite sure how it could *not* happen, now."

He sat back, his eyes steady on my face.

I dropped the joking tone. "Thank you, Michael," I said. I took a deep breath. There was no point in saying anything else, here. It must have been the broken arm talking, telling me it was a good idea to open up to someone. "I should go."

I started pushing myself up.

Michael took his cane, hooked the handle around my ankle and calmly jerked my leg out from beneath me. I flopped back into the chair.

"Harry," he said thoughtfully. "How many times have I saved your life?"

"Bunch."

He nodded.

"What have I asked you for in return?"

"Nothing," I said. "Ever."

He nodded again. "That's right."

We sat in silence for a long time.

Finally, I said, very quietly, "I don't know if I'm one of the good guys anymore."

I swallowed.

He listened.

"How can I be," I asked, "after what I've done?"

"What have you done?" he asked.

It took me another minute to answer. "You know about Mab. What I am now. The deal I made."

"I also know that you did so intending to use that power to save your daughter's life."

"You don't know about Susan," I said. I met his eyes. "I killed her, Michael."

I don't know what I looked like—but tears suddenly stood out in his eyes. "Oh, Harry." He looked down. "She turned, didn't she? What happened?"

"That son of a bitch, Martin," I said. "He . . . he set

her up. Sold out the family that had Maggie. I think he did it to set me on a collision course with the Red King, maybe hoping to focus the White Council on the war effort a little harder. But he had inside knowledge of the Reds, too. He'd worked for them. Was some kind of double agent, or triple agent—I don't know. I don't think he was running a grand scheme to get to one specific moment . . . but he saw his chance. The Red King was getting set to kill Maggie as part of a ritual bloodline curse. The curse was meant to kill me and . . . other people, up my family tree."

Michael raised his eyebrows.

"But the ritual was all loaded up and Martin saw a chance to wipe out the whole Red Court. All of them. He popped Susan in the face with the knowledge of his treachery and she just *snapped* . . ." I shuddered, remembering it. "I saw it coming. Saw what he was doing. Maybe I could have stopped it—I don't know—but . . . I didn't. And she killed him. Tore his throat out. And . . . she started to change and . . ."

"And you finished the ritual," he said quietly. "You killed her. You killed them all."

"The youngest vampire in the whole world," I said. "Brand-new. And they all originated from a single point— the Red King, I guess. Their own curse got every one of them. The whole family."

"Every Red Court vampire," Michael said gently, "was a killer. Every one of them, at one point, chose to take someone's life to slake their thirst. That's what turned them. That choice."

"I'm not shedding tears over the Red Court," I

said, contempt in my voice. "The fallout from taking them all out at once . . . I don't know. Maybe I wish I could have done it differently. With more planning."

"One doesn't destroy an empire built on pain and terror neatly," Michael said, "if history is to be any indicator."

I smiled bleakly. "It was a little hectic at the time," I said. "I just wanted to save Maggie."

"May I ask you a question?"

"Sure."

"After she started to turn . . . how did you subdue Susan?"

I sat for a time, trying to remember the moment less clearly.

"You didn't," he said gently, "did you?"

"She . . . she was turning. But she understood what was happening."

"She sacrificed herself," Michael said.

"She allowed *me* to sacrifice her," I snarled, with sudden, boiling fury. "There's a difference."

"Yes," Michael said quietly. "There's a cost for you in that. A burden to be carried."

"I kissed her," I said. "And then I cut her throat."

The silence after I said that was profound.

Michael got up and put a hand on my shoulder.

"Harry," he said quietly, "I'm so sorry. I'm so sorry you were faced with those awful choices."

"I never meant . . ." I swallowed. "I never meant for all those things to happen. For Susan to get hurt. For Mab's deal to stick. I never meant to keep it."

Real pain touched his eyes. "Ah," he said quietly. "I'd . . . wondered. About the after."

"That was me," I said. "I arranged it. I thought . . . if I was gone before Mab had a chance to change me, it would be all right."

"You thought . . ." Michael took a slow breath and sat down again. "You thought that if you died, it would be all right?"

"Compared to me becoming Mab's psychotic monster?" I asked. "Compared to letting the Reds kill my daughter and my grandfather? Yeah. I regarded that as a win."

Michael put his face in his hands for a moment. He shook his head. Then he lifted his face and looked up at his ceiling, his expression a mixture of sadness and frustration and pain.

"And now I've got this thing inside me," I said. "And it pushes me, Michael. It pushes and pushes and pushes me to . . . do things."

He eyed me.

"And right now . . . Hell's bells, right now, Mab has me working with Nicodemus Archleone. If I don't, there's this thing in my head that's going to come popping out of it, kill me, and then go after Maggie."

"*What?*"

"Exactly," I said. "Nicodemus. He's robbing a vault somewhere and Mab expects me to pay off a debt she owes him. He's formed his own Evil League of Evil to get it done—and I'm a member. And to make it worse, I dragged Murphy into it with me, and I'm not even telling her everything. Because I *can't*."

Michael shook his head slowly.

"I look around me, man . . . I'm trying to do what

I've always done, to protect people, to keep them safe from the monsters—only I'm pretty sure I'm *one of them*. I can't figure out where I could have . . . what else I might have done . . ." I swallowed. "I'm lost. I know every step I took to get here, and I'm still *lost*."

"Harry . . ."

"And my friends," I said. "Even Thomas . . . I was stuck out on that island of the damned for a year. A *year*, Michael, and they only showed up a handful of times. Just Murphy and Thomas, maybe half a dozen times in more than a year. It's just a goddamned boat ride away, forty minutes. People drive farther than that to go to the *movies*. They know what I'm turning into. They don't want to watch it happening to me."

"Harry," Michael said in a low, soft voice. "You . . . you are . . ."

"A fool," I said quietly. "A monster. Damned."

". . . so *arrogant*," Michael breathed.

I blinked.

"I mean, I was accustomed to a certain degree of hubris from you, but . . . this is stunning. Even on your scale."

"What?" I said.

"Arrogant," he repeated, enunciating. "To a degree I can scarcely believe."

I just stared at him for a moment.

"I'm sorry," he said. "I know you were expecting me to share words of wisdom with you, maybe say something to you about God and your soul and forgiveness and redemption. And all those things are good things that need to be said in the right time, but . . . honestly, Harry. I wouldn't be your friend if I didn't point out to you that you are behaving like an amazingly pigheaded idiot."

"I am?" I asked, a little blankly.

He stared at me for a second, anger and pain on his face—and then they vanished, and he smiled, his eyes flickering as merrily as a Christmas Eve fire. I suddenly realized where Molly got her smile. Something very like laughter bubbled just under the surface of his words. "Yes, Harry. You idiot. You are."

"I don't understand," I said.

He eyed our beers, which were empty. That tends to happen with Mac's microbrews. He went to the fridge and opened another pair of bottles with the power of Thor, and put one of them in front of me. We clinked and drank.

"Harry," he said, after a meditative moment, "are you perfect?"

"No," I said.

He nodded. "Omniscient?"

I snorted. "No."

"Can you go into the past, change things that have already happened?"

"Theoretically?" I asked.

He gave me a level stare.

"I hear that sometimes, some things can be done. But apparently it's tricky as hell. And I've got no idea how," I said.

"So can you?"

"No," I said.

"In other words," he said, "despite all the things you know, and all the incredible things you can do . . . you're only human."

I frowned at him and swigged beer.

"Then why," Michael asked, "are you expecting perfection out of yourself? Do you really think you're that much better than the rest of us? That your powers make you a higher quality of human being? That your knowledge places you on a higher plane than everyone else on this world?"

I eyed the beer and felt . . . embarrassed.

"That's arrogance, Harry," he said gently. "On a level so deep you don't even realize it exists. And do you know why it's there?"

"No?" I asked.

He smiled again. "Because you have set a higher standard for yourself. You think that because you have more power than others, you have to do more with it."

"To whom much is given, much is required," I said, without looking up.

He barked out a short laugh. "For someone who repeatedly tells me he has no faith, you have a surprising capacity to quote scripture. And that's just my point."

I eyed him. "What?"

"You wouldn't be twisting yourself into knots like this, Harry, if you didn't care."

"So?"

"Monsters don't care," Michael said. "The damned don't *care*, Harry. The only way to go beyond redemption is to choose to take yourself there. The only way to do it is to stop caring."

My view of the kitchen blurred out. "You think?"

"I'll tell you what I think," Michael said. "I think that you aren't perfect. And that means that sometimes you make bad choices. But . . . honestly, I don't know if I would have done any differently, if it had been one of my children at risk."

"Not you," I said quietly. "You wouldn't have done what I did."

"I *couldn't* have done what you did," Michael said simply. "And I haven't had to be standing in your shoes to make those same choices." He tilted his beer slightly toward the ceiling. "Thank you, God. So if you've come here for judgment, Harry, you won't find any from me. I've made mistakes. I've failed. I'm human."

"But these mistakes," I said, "could change me. I could wind up like these people around Nicodemus."

Michael snorted. "No, you won't."

"Why not?"

"Because I know you, Harry Dresden," Michael said. "You are pathologically incapable of knowing when to quit. You don't surrender. And I don't believe for a *second* that you actually intend to help Nicodemus do whatever it is he's doing."

I felt a smile tug at one corner of my mouth.

"Hah," Michael said, sitting back in his chair. He swallowed some more beer. "I thought so."

"It's tricky," I said. "I've got to help him get whatever he's after. Technically."

Michael wrinkled his nose. "Faeries. I never understood why they're such lawyers about everything."

"I'm the Winter Knight," I said, "and I don't get it either."

"I find that oddly reassuring," Michael said.

I barked out a short laugh. "Yeah. Maybe so."

His face grew more serious. "Nicodemus knows treachery like fish know water," he said. "He surely knows the direction of your intent. He's smart, Harry. He's got centuries of survival behind him."

"True," I said. "On the other hand, I'm not exactly a useless cream puff."

His eyes glinted. "Also true," he said.

"And Murphy's there," I said.

"Good," Michael said, rapping the bottle on the table for emphasis. "That woman's got brains and heart."

I chewed on my lip and looked up at him. "But . . . Michael, she wasn't . . . for the past year . . ."

He sighed and shook his head. "Harry . . . do you know what that island is like, for the rest of us?"

I shook my head.

"The last time I was there, I was shot twice," he said. "I was in intensive care for a month. I was in bed for four months. I didn't walk again for nearly a year. There was permanent damage to my hip and lower back, and physically, it was the single most extended, horribly painful, grindingly humiliating experience of my life."

"Yeah," I said.

"And," he said, "when I have nightmares of it, you know what I dream about?"

"What?"

"The island," Michael said. "The . . . presence of it. The malevolence there." He shuddered.

Michael, Knight of the Cross, who had faced deadly spirits and demons and monsters without flinching, shivered in fear.

"That place is horrible," he said quietly. "The effect it

has . . . It's obvious that it doesn't even touch you. But I don't know if I could go back there again, by choice."

I blinked.

"But I know Molly went back there. And you tell me Karrin did, too. And Thomas. Many times." He shook his head. "That's . . . astounding to me, Harry."

"They . . . they never said anything," I said. "I mean, they never spent the night, either, but . . ."

"Of course they didn't," he said. "You already beat yourself up for enough things that aren't your fault. People who care don't want to add to that." He paused, and then added gently, "But you assumed it was about you."

I finished the beer and sighed. "Arrogance," I said. "I feel stupid."

"Good," Michael said. "It's good for everyone to feel that way sometimes. It helps remind you how much you still have to learn."

What he said about the island tracked. I remembered my first moments there, how unsettling it was. I had talent and training in defending myself against psychic assault, and I'd shielded against it on pure reflex, shedding the worst that it could have done to me. Wizard. And not long after that, I'd taken on Demonreach in a ritual challenge that had left me the Warden of the place, and exempt from its malice.

Thomas hadn't had the kind of training, the kind of defenses I did. Molly, who was more sensitive than me to that kind of energy, must have found it agonizing. And Karrin, who had been assaulted psychically before . . . damn.

They'd all picked up more scars for me, on my behalf,

without a word of complaint—and I'd been upset because they hadn't been willing to take more.

Michael was right.

I'd gotten completely focused on myself.

"It occurs to me," I said, "if I wasn't being the Winter
Knight . . . Mab would have picked another thug." Mab
had even told me who she would have gone after—my
brother, Thomas. I shuddered to think what might have
happened, if the temptations of Winter had been added
to those he already bore. "Someone else would be bearing this burden. Maybe someone it would have destroyed
by now."

"It occurred to you just now?" Michael asked. "I
thought of it about five seconds after I heard about it."

I laughed and it felt really good to do it.

"There," Michael said, nodding.

"Thank you."

I meant it for a lot of things. Michael got it. He inclined his head to me. "There is, of course, an elephant
in the room, of which we have not spoken."

Of course there was.

Maggie.

"I don't want to make her into a target again," I said.

Michael sighed patiently. "Harry," he said, as if speaking to a rather slow child, "I'm not sure if you noticed
this. But things did not turn out well for the last monster
who raised his hand against your child. Or any of his
friends. Or associates. Or anyone who worked for him.
Or for most of the people he knew."

I blinked.

"Whether or not that was your intention," Michael

said, "you did establish a rather effective precedental message to the various predators, should they ever learn of her relationship to you."

"Do you think Nicodemus would hesitate?" I asked. "Even for a second?"

"To take her from this house?" Michael asked. He smiled. "I'd love to see him try it."

I lifted my eyebrows.

"A dozen angels protect this house, still," Michael said. "Part of my retirement package."

"She's not always in the house," I said.

"And when she isn't, Mouse is with her," he said. "We got him attached to her as a medical assist dog. He prevents her from having panic attacks."

I made a choking sound, imagining Mouse in a grade school. "By making everyone else around her panic instead?"

"He's a perfect gentleman," Michael said, amused. "The children love him. The teachers let the best students play with him on recess."

I imagined my enormous moose of a dog on a playground, trotting around after Maggie and other kids, with that dopey doggy grin on his face, cheerfully going along with whatever the kids seemed to have planned, moving with tremendous care around them, and shamelessly cadging tummy rubs whenever possible.

"That's kind of awesome," I said.

"Children frequently are," Michael said.

I chewed on my lip some more. "What if . . . Michael, she was there. She was in the temple when . . ." I looked up. "What if she remembers what I did?"

"She doesn't remember any of it," Michael said.

"Now," I said. "Stuff like that . . . it has a way of popping up again."

"If it does," he said, "don't you think she deserves to know the truth? All of it? When she's ready?"

I looked away. "The things I do . . . I don't want any of it to splash on her."

"I didn't want it to touch my children, either," Michael said. "Mostly, it didn't. And I don't regret my choices. I did everything in my power to protect them. I'm content with that."

"My boss has a few differences in policy compared to yours."

"Heh. True, that."

"I need to get moving," I said. "Seriously. I'm on the clock."

"We aren't done talking about Maggie," he replied firmly. "But we'll take it up soon."

"Why?" I asked. "She's safe here. Is she . . . She's happy?"

"Mostly," he said amiably. "She's your daughter, Harry. She needs you. But not, I think, nearly as much as you need her."

"I don't know how you can say that to me," I said, "after Molly."

He tilted his head. "What about Molly?"

"You . . . you know about Molly, right?" I asked.

He blinked at me. "She's been doing great lately. I saw her last weekend. Did she lose her apartment or something?"

I looked back at him in dismay, realizing.

He didn't know.

Michael didn't know that his daughter had become the Winter Lady. She hadn't told him.

"Harry," he said, worried, "is she all right?"

Oh, Hell's freaking bells. She hadn't *told* her parents?

That was so Molly. Unimpressed by a legion of wicked faeries—terrified to tell her parents about her new career.

But it was her choice. And I didn't have the right to unmake it for her.

"She's fine," I blurted. "She's fine. I mean, I meant, uh . . ."

"Oh," Michael said, a look of understanding coming over his face. "Oh, right. Well, that's . . . that's fine. Behind us now, and it all worked out."

I wasn't sure what he was talking about, but it was getting me out of making a major problem for Molly. I rolled with it. "Right," I said. "Anyway. Thank you, again. For too much."

"If it's ever too much," he said, "I'll thump you politely on the head."

"You'll have to, for it to get through," I said.

"I know." He rose, and offered me his hand.

I shook it.

"Michael," I asked, "do you ever . . . miss it?"

His smile lines deepened. "The fight?" He shrugged. "I'm very, very happy to have the time to spend with my wife and children."

I narrowed my eyes. "That . . . wasn't exactly an answer."

He winked at me. Then he walked me to the door, leaning on his cane.

By the time I got to the car, the icy ache in my arm

had dulled down to a buzzing sensation. I was recovering. I'd get some anti-inflammatories into me before I got back, to help with the swelling. No, I couldn't feel the pain, but that didn't mean that it wouldn't be smart to do whatever I could to take the pressure off the mantle, to save my strength for when it counted. I needed to pick up some other things too, thinking along the same lines.

Whatever Nicodemus had planned, it would go down in the next twenty-four hours, and I was going to be ready for it.

Chapter
Twenty-one

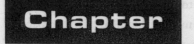

I rolled back up to the slaughterhouse just before the rented town car's transmission gave out on me altogether.

It sort of cheered me up, actually. I hadn't wrecked a car with my wizardliness in a long time. And it just couldn't have happened to a nicer guy's rental vehicle. For a moment, I felt a sudden, sharp pining for my old Volkswagen, which made about as much sense as anything else I'd been doing that day. The *Blue Beetle* had been uncomfortable and cramped and it had smelled a bit odd, not to mention that it was put together from the cannibalized scraps of a bunch of other late-sixties VWs—and I must have looked absolutely ridiculous crouched behind its wheel. But it had been *my* car, and while it hadn't run like a race car, it *did* run, most of the time.

Suck it, rental town car. The built-in talking GPS computer hadn't lasted two blocks.

"Jordan!" I boomed as I came in. I tossed a paper bag with a couple of cheeseburgers in it at the Denarian squire. "Chow down, buddy. They're hot, so don't let the cheese burn your ton— Oh, right. Sorry."

Jordan scowled at me and fumbled with the bag and his shotgun until he managed to balance the two. I clapped him on the shoulder in a genial fashion and rolled on by. I pointed at the guard at the next post and said, "You don't get cheeseburgers. You didn't say nice things to me like Jordan did."

The guard glowered at me in silence, of course. It was an act. No one could resist my bluff and manly charisma. In his heart of hearts, he wanted to be friends with me. I just knew it.

As I descended to the floor of the slaughterhouse, Karrin looked up from a long worktable absolutely covered in guns. She tracked my entrance, her expression touched with both wariness and . . . a certain amount of incredulity.

"Harry?" she asked, as I came down the last few steps.

"Who else would I be?" I asked. "Except that jerk Grey, but he's too busy being Harvey to be me." I took another paper bag from Burger King and plopped it down in front of Karrin, then dumped the loaded duffel I'd picked up from a military surplus store off where it hung over my shoulder. "Figured you might be hungry."

She eyed the fast-food bag. "I'm not sure I'm *that* hungry."

"Whoa, whoa, hold on there, Annie Oakley. You did *not* just say that," I said. "Not right to my face."

A slow smile spread over her mouth and reached her eyes. "Harry."

"I . . ." I exhaled. The talk with Michael had made me

feel about twenty tons lighter, at least on the inside. "Yeah. I guess maybe it is." I felt my own smile fade. "Harvey's dead."

Her face sobered and her eyes raked over me, stopping on my arm. "What happened?"

"Polonius Lartessa showed up with a squad of soldier-ghouls and whacked him," I said. "Unless maybe it was Deirdre who did it. Or Grey. I had ghouls all over my face when it happened."

"Who took care of your arm for you?"

"A good man," I said.

She stared at me for a moment and then her eyebrows lifted. "Oh," she said. Her eyes glittered. "*Oh*. That explains some things, then."

"Yeah," I said, bouncing my weight lightly on my toes. "The point being, someone's trying to screw with the job before we even get going."

"What a crime," Karrin said.

I grunted. "If Tessa's trying to stop Nicodemus, I've got to wonder why."

"She's married to him?" she suggested drily.

"That's vengeance-worthy, all right," I said. "But . . . I don't know. I hate working in the dark."

"So what's the move?"

I chewed my lip and said, "Nothing's changed for us. Except . . ."

"Except what?" she asked.

"Except someone's going down for Harvey before this is done," I said.

"Yeah," she said. "I can get behind that."

I took a long look at the table. "Uzis," I noted.

"They're a classic," Karrin said. "Simple, reliable, durable, and *not* assault rifles."

That was good for the innocent bystanders of Chicago. Pistol ammunition wasn't nearly as good at flying through an extraneous wall or ten and killing some poor sap sitting in his apartment two blocks away. Which wasn't to say that they weren't insanely dangerous—just less so than a bunch of AK-47s would have been. Nicodemus wasn't doing that to be thoughtful. Either he'd bought what was available, or else he had a reason to cause only limited collateral damage.

"Can Binder's goons handle them?" she asked.

"I assume so," I said. "They seemed to take to guns pretty easily the last time. Check with Binder on it."

"Check with Binder on what?" asked Binder, appearing from farther down the factory floor. He was carrying a sandwich in one hand, a cup of what might have been tea in the other.

"Speak of the devil and he appears," I said.

Binder sketched me a courtly little bow, rolling his sandwich as he did.

"Your . . . people," Karrin said. "Do they know how to handle an Uzi or do they need some kind of orientation?"

"They'll be fine," he said, his tone confident, even cocky. "Don't ask them to fieldstrip and repair one, or for witty banter before they shoot, but for trigger work or reloading they're golden." His sharp, beady little eyes landed on my arm in its splint. "Does someone not know how to play well with others?"

His eyes went from me to start flicking around the

slaughterhouse. I could all but see the calculation going on in his head. One Harry, no Deirdre, no Grey.

"They're fine," I said. "We ran into some opposition around the accountant."

"Bookmark," Binder said, holding up two fingers. He turned and retreated, wolfing down his sandwich, and returned a moment later with Hannah Ascher in tow. Ascher had ditched her sweater in favor of a tank top, and she looked as if she'd just come off a treadmill. She was breathing lightly and her skin was sheened with sweat. There were bits of ash stuck in the fine hairs of her forearms and smudging one cheek. Like every other look I'd seen on her, it was an awfully intriguing one—easily translated to let a fellow imagine what she might look like during . . .

"Right, then," Binder said. "Resume."

"We staked out the accountant," I said. "Nicodemus's wife showed up with a crew of ghouls and went after him. The accountant was killed."

"The wife did it?" Ascher asked.

"Women," Binder said scornfully.

Karrin and Ascher both eyed him.

He folded his arms. "I'm a century older than any of you sprats," he said. "I'll stand by that."

"I'm pretty sure I didn't kill Harvey," I said. "My gut says it wasn't Grey. Other than that, your guess is as good as mine."

"Eh?" Binder said, nodding toward me conspiratorially. "Women."

Karrin gave me a very level look.

I coughed. "The female of the species is deadlier than the male?"

She snorted, and picked up the next Uzi in the row.

"I don't understand. Why would Nicodemus's wife be trying to sabotage him?" Ascher asked.

"Maybe she wants to cop the job," Binder said wistfully. "Lot of money."

"Nah," I said. "Money isn't her thing."

" 'Fraid you'd say that," he said. "Personal?"

"Let's just say that 'dysfunctional' doesn't even come close to that family."

"Bloody hell," Binder said. "Why does everyone have to get bloody personal? No bloody professional pride anymore." He glowered at me. "Present bloody company included."

"Language," Ascher said, wincing.

"Sod off," he said. "Where're Deirdre and Grey?"

"Grey's doubling the accountant," I said. "No clue about Deirdre."

Binder made a growling sound.

"Hey," Ascher said. "Has anyone else been keeping track of how many goats are in the pen?"

"Eight," said Karrin and Binder together.

I did a rough calculation. "It's eating one goat at every meal."

That got me a round of looks.

I shrugged. "Something's here. It stands to reason."

Ascher and Binder both looked around the factory floor. Ascher folded her arms as if she'd suddenly become cold.

"Big," Karrin noted calmly. "If it eats that much."

"Yeah," I said.

"And quiet."

"Yeah."

"And really, really fast."

Binder shook his head. "Bloody hell."

"What is it?" Ascher said.

"Could be a lot of things," Binder said. "None of them good." He squinted at me. "Muscle, you think?"

"Maybe where we're going, we need something with that kind of physical power," I said.

Ascher scowled. "Or maybe it's there to clean us up after the job."

"We wouldn't have been given a chance to become aware of it if that was the case," Karrin said.

"Unless that's what Nicodemus wants us to think," Binder said.

Us. I liked the sound of that. The more people I could incline against pitching in on Nicodemus's side when it all hit the fan, the better. "Let's not go down that rabbit hole," I said. "We've got problems enough without adding in paranoia."

"Too right," Binder said. "Job worth twenty million each, with an invisible monster nipping about the place and a psychotic ex trying to bugger us out of tweaking the nose of a bloody Greek god. What have we got to be paranoid about?"

"Look," I said, "at the best, it means Nicodemus isn't telling us everything."

"We knew that already," Ascher said.

I shrugged a shoulder in acknowledgment of that. "At worst, it means someone on the inside is giving information to some kind of opposition."

Ascher narrowed her eyes. "That's rich, coming from the opposition."

I waved a hand. "At this point, I'm playing the game. I'll get in and out again, because if I don't, Mab is going to have my head." Well, technically, she'd have the splattered pieces, but they didn't need the details. "I'm not looking to derail the train before then."

Ascher looked skeptical. Binder looked pensive. Karrin finished her inspection of the next Uzi and picked up another one.

"Ash-my-girl," Binder said, and jerked his head toward the other end of the factory floor.

She nodded, and the two of them moved off, walking close and speaking quietly.

Karrin watched them go, and then asked me, "What do you think they're talking about?"

"Same as us," I said. "Wondering when someone's going to pull the rug out from underneath them, and how they're going to get out of it in one piece."

"Or maybe thinking about doing a little pulling themselves," she said.

"Or maybe that," I said. "But . . . they won't do it until after they've got their packs loaded with jewels."

"How do you figure?"

"Binder," I said. "He's a mercenary, plain and simple."

"Unless that's what he wants us to think," Karrin said.

"Unless that," I said. I exhaled slowly. "This whole thing," I said, "is going to come down to guessing who isn't what they look like."

"Who *is*?" Karrin asked, her hands moving surely over the weapon. "Ever."

"Point," I said. "But it's going to be about guessing

motivations. Whoever's done a better job of figuring out what the other wants wins."

Her mouth quivered at the corners. "Then we might be in trouble. Because your motivations have . . . never exactly been mysterious, Harry."

"Not to you," I said. "To someone like Nicodemus, I must seem like an utter lunatic."

Karrin let out a short laugh. "You know what? I think you're probably right." She manually cycled the action of the Uzi, caught the round as it was ejected, then put the weapon down and nodded. "That's it. Forty of them."

I grunted. "Didn't some biblical guy have forty soldiers to take on an army or something?"

"Gideon. He had three hundred."

"I thought that was the Spartans."

"It was also the Spartans," Karrin said. "Except that they had about four thousand other Greeks there with them in addition to their three hundred."

"Three hundred makes a better movie. Who had forty guys, then?"

"You're thinking of how many days and nights it rained on Noah's ark."

"Oh," I said. "I was sure somebody had forty guys."

"Ali Baba?"

"He didn't *have* forty guys," I said. "He ripped off forty guys."

"Maybe you're remembering cartoons again," Karrin said.

"Probably," I said. I stared down at the guns. "Forty of those demon suit guys. With Uzis."

She grimaced. "Yeah. Gonna take me maybe three hours just to load all the clips."

"What kind of target is tough enough that it needs forty demon soldiers with submachine guns to assault?"

Karrin shook her head. "Military installation?"

I grunted.

"You don't plan for this many guns if you don't intend to use them," Karrin said. "If it comes down to Binder's goons shooting people . . ."

"We sure as hell don't stand around and watch it happen," I assured her.

She nodded. "Good." She twisted her mouth in distaste. "Won't that upset Mab, if you bail out?"

"Her Royal FreezePop-iness can get upset—but if she claims to be surprised, I'll laugh in her face."

"But it could mean she kills you," she said quietly.

"Could mean she tries," I said, aiming for cocky and confident.

Karrin looked away, the motion a little too sharp. She didn't go so far as to need to blink tears from her eyes or anything, but for a moment she looked about ten years older. She nodded. It looked like she wanted to say something.

"Karrin?" I asked.

She shook her head once and said, "I've got to get these clips loaded."

"Want help?"

"Sure."

We set to the task of loading a hundred and twenty thirty-two-round magazines with 9mm rounds. Thirty-eight hundred bullets or so. Even with speed-loading tools, it took a while, and we worked in companionable silence, broken occasionally by the passing guard or an increasingly gentle, intermittent series of whumping sounds that came from the far end of the factory floor—Ascher, presumably, practicing her breaching spell.

Just as we were finishing up, bootsteps came from the opposite direction and I looked up to see Nicodemus marching toward us, a pair of his squires tromping along behind him. Deirdre walked beside him, in her human form, her expression unfriendly and otherwise unreadable.

"Weapons ready?" he asked Karrin, without stopping.

"All set."

"Excellent. Conference table, please."

"Why?" I asked. My left hand hadn't been good for much beyond holding the magazine as I loaded rounds, and the fingertips of my right hand felt raw.

Nicodemus went on by and glanced over his shoulder at me, his eyes lingering on my splint. "Grey is back. It's time to talk about our target."

Chapter
Twenty-two

We gathered at the conference table again, and Anna Valmont slid into the seat beside me.

"Hey," I said. "How goes the grease job?"

She eyed me and smiled faintly. "I am, in this crew, what is known as a grease man. A grease man is the person who can get you into someplace you otherwise couldn't get into by yourself." Her voice turned wry. "A grease job is something else."

"Right," I said, narrowing my eyes, nodding. "Got it. So how goes the man greasing?"

Valmont let out a shallow chuckle. "Got to admit, I wouldn't mind being the first to take on one of those Fernucci monsters and win."

"Can you?"

She nodded slowly. "I think it's possible."

Grey sauntered in, looking exactly as he had that morning, and sat down at the table.

"Order, please," Nicodemus said, as Grey sat down next to Deirdre. "We'll make this quick and then break for a meal, if that's all right with everyone."

"All right with me," Ascher drawled. She looked sweat-ier and more smudged than she had a few hours before, but her expression was unmistakably smug. "I'm raven-ous."

"I know just what you mean," Nicodemus said. "Deir-dre?"

Once more, Deirdre circled the table with folders that were labeled simply GOAL.

"I've been meaning to ask," I said. "Does this master plan of yours come with health coverage?"

"Dresden," Nicodemus said.

"Because that kind of thing is getting to be more and more important. I mean, I know the government proba-bly means well and all, but those people, honestly."

Nicodemus eyed me.

"Life insurance seems like something that would be worthwhile, too." I looked up at Ascher and winked. "Maybe we should strike until we get a whole-life policy."

Ascher flashed me a quick grin and said, "I've always thought that insurance was more or less betting against myself."

"Nah," Binder said. "In my experience, you're just playing the odds."

"Children," Nicodemus said with a sigh, "shall we fo-cus on the matter at hand?"

"But I haven't even had the chance to dip Deirdre's pigtails in my inkwell," I said.

Deirdre glowered at me, her eyes glinting.

"Fine," I said, and subsided.

"Each of you," Nicodemus said, "brings something to the table that we need in order to reach our final destination. The manor of the Lord of the Underworld, Vault Seven."

"You mean Ha—"

"Shall we *not* speak his name for the next twenty-four hours or so, please, Mr. Dresden?" Nicodemus said in a pained tone. "Unless you prefer him to be ready and waiting for all of us, including yourself? Granted, the likelihood of him taking notice of any one of us, in particular, is vanishing small, but it seems prudent to take a few simple steps."

"Whatever," I said. I thought he was being pretty fussy. What with books and movies using him as a character, and mythology courses being taught all over the world, I figured Hades got to hear his name spoken in one form or another tens if not hundreds of thousands of times every day.

Each utterance of a powerful supernatural being's name is . . . kind of like sending him a page, a ping for his attention. If I could have a phone that survived longer than an hour, and it tried to get my attention ten thousand times a day, I'd throw the damned thing into a hole. The big supernatural beings, especially the very human-like Greek gods, probably reacted in much the same way. Odds were good that I could sit chatting for an hour or two and mention his name several times, yet he wouldn't even notice my relative handful of pings among all the others. It took a deliberate and rhythmic repetition, usually at least three times, to really get a signal through the noise.

But on the other hand . . . there was always the chance that Hades just *might* feel my utterance of his name and randomly decide to take a moment to pay attention. That probably wouldn't be good. So despite giving Nicodemus lip, I shut up.

"Once we gain entry to the Underworld vault . . . ," Nicodemus began.

I held up my hand and said, "Question?"

Nicodemus's left eye began to twitch.

I didn't wait for him to respond. "You're planning on just jumping straight to the vault? Hell, not even Hercules could do that. It was kind of a journey to get in. There was a bit with a dog and everything. Do you really think we're going to just hop right past all of the defenses around the realm of the king of the Underworld?"

That got everyone's attention, even Grey's. They all looked at Nicodemus, interested in the answer.

"Yes," Nicodemus said in a flat tone.

"Oh," I said. "Just like that, eh?"

"Once we're inside the vault," Nicodemus said, as if my question was not interesting enough to waste more time on, "there will be three gates between us and our goal. The Gate of Fire, the Gate of Ice, and the Gate of Blood."

"Fun," I said.

"Obviously," Nicodemus said, "Ascher was chosen for her capability with fire. As the Winter Knight, you, Dresden, will obviously handle the Gate of Ice."

"Right," I said. "Obviously. What about the Gate of Blood?"

Nicodemus smiled pleasantly.

Of course. Old Nick had probably spilled more blood than the rest of us in the room together, if you didn't count Deirdre. "Exactly what does each of these gates entail?"

"If I knew that," Nicodemus said, "I'd not have bothered recruiting experts. Each of us will take point on our specific gate, with the rest of the team backing whatever play they decide is important. Once we're through, we'll be in the vault. It's quite large. You'll have a few minutes to gather whatever it is you feel you need to take with you. After that time, I'm leaving. Anyone who lags behind is on his or her own."

I held up my hand again, and didn't bother waiting for a response. "What are you after?"

"Excuse me?" Nicodemus asked.

"You," I said. "Vault Seven is awfully specific. And you don't care much about money. So I have to wonder what's in there that you are so interested in."

"That's hardly your concern," Nicodemus said.

I snorted. "The hell it isn't. We're all sticking our necks out—and if things don't go well, we might have an angry *god* on our tails. I want to know what's worth that, other than the twenty million. After all, a lot of things could go wrong. Maybe you wind up dead, purely by someone else's hand on the way in—maybe I want to grab that whatsit for myself."

There was a mutter of agreement from Binder, and nods from Karrin and Valmont. Even Ascher looked curious. Grey pursed his lips thoughtfully.

"Should I fall, the rest of you will already be dead," Nicodemus said calmly.

"Indulge me," I said. "This deal is already starting to

stink. A reasonable person might walk based purely on what happened today."

That brought a low round of mutters, and Valmont asked, "What happened today?"

I told her about Tessa and her ghouls and Deirdre and Harvey. That made Valmont's lips compress into a line. She knew better than most what was left when a Denarian tore into a mortal, and two out of three possible suspects were Knights of the Coin.

"That has no bearing on our mission," Nicodemus said.

"The hell it doesn't," I said. "I don't know about the rest of you, but the last thing we need is his crazy ex jumping into things on some kind of vengeance kick."

"It's not about that," Nicodemus said.

"Then what is it about?" I asked. "I dealt with the White Council my whole life, so I'm used to being treated like a mushroom—"

"Eh?" Ascher asked.

"Kept in the dark and fed bullshit," Binder reported calmly.

"Ah."

"—but this is going beyond the pale, even for me. You ask us to trust you about the plan to get into what should be an impenetrable vault. You ask us to trust you that our share will be waiting next to whatever it is you want. You ask us to trust you and believe that Tessa isn't on some kind of jihad that will get us all killed, but won't tell us what it is about." I looked around the table at my criminal confederates. "Trust is kind of a two-way street, Nicodemus. It's time to give something."

"Or you'll do what, precisely?"

"Or maybe we'll all walk away from a bunch of empty promises without a sliver of proof to back them up," I said.

Nicodemus narrowed his eyes. "Dresden and his woman are obviously in accord," he said.

Karrin scowled.

Nicodemus ignored her. "What about the rest of you?"

"What he said," Valmont said quietly.

Ascher folded her arms, frowning.

Binder sighed. "Twenty. Million. Quid. Think, girl."

"We can't spend it if we're dead from sticking our heads into a hole and getting them whacked off," Ascher said firmly.

Nicodemus nodded. "Grey?"

Grey tented his fingertips in front of his lips for a moment and then said, "The personal aspect of this interference troubles me. A job of this sort requires pure professionalism. Detachment."

Binder made a nonverbal sound of agreement with Grey's statements.

"I will not walk away from a job once I've agreed to it—you know how I operate, Nicodemus," Grey continued. "But I would sympathize if another professional of less ability and less rigid standards did so."

Nicodemus regarded Grey thoughtfully for a moment. "Your professional recommendation?"

"The wizard has a point," Grey said. "He is an annoying, headstrong ass, but he isn't stupid. It would not be foolish for you to invest some measure of trust to balance what you ask for."

Nicodemus mused over that for a moment and then nodded his head. "One ought not hire an expert and then ignore his opinion," he said. Then he turned to the rest of us. "Vault Seven contains, in addition to a standard division of gold and jewels, a number of Western religious icons. It is my intention to retrieve a cup from the vault."

"A wha'?" Binder asked.

"A cup," Nicodemus replied.

"All this," Binder said, "for a cup."

Nicodemus nodded. "A simple ceramic cup, something like a teacup, but lacking any handle. Quite old."

My mouth fell open and I made a choking sound at approximately the same time.

Grey pursed his lips and let out a slow whistle.

"Wait," Ascher said. "Are you talking about what I *think* you're talking about?"

"Jesus, Mary, and Joseph," Karrin said quietly.

Nicodemus made a face in her direction. "Miss Murphy, please."

She gave Nicodemus a small, unpleasant smile.

Binder clued in a second later. "The bloody Holy Grail? Is he bloody kidding?"

Valmont turned to me, frowning. "That's real?"

"It's real," I said. "But it was lost more than a thousand years ago."

"Not lost," Nicodemus corrected me calmly. "It was collected."

"The cup that caught the blood of Christ," Grey mused. He eyed Nicodemus. "Now, what possible use could you have for that old thing?"

"Sentimental value," Nicodemus said with a guileless smile, and straightened the skinny strands of his grey tie. "I'm something of a collector of such artifacts myself."

The tie wasn't a tie, unless you meant it in a very literal sense. It was a length of simple old rope, tied into the Noose—the one that Judas used to hang himself after betraying Christ, if I understood it correctly. It made Nicodemus all but unkillable. I didn't know if anyone else in the world knew what I knew: that the Noose didn't protect him from itself. I'd nearly strangled him with it the last time we'd crossed trails—hence his roughened voice.

Grey didn't look like he believed Nicodemus's answer, but that hadn't stopped him from being satisfied with it. He looked around the room and said, "There. You know more than you did. Is it enough?"

"Tessa," I said. "What's her beef with you going after the Grail?"

"She wants it for herself, of course," Nicodemus said. "I'll deal with Tessa before we launch. It won't become an issue for the job. You have my personal guarantee."

Grey spread his hands. "There," he said. "That's good enough for me. Binder?"

The stocky little guy screwed up his eyes in thought and nodded slowly. "Ash?"

"All right," Ascher said. "Sure. That's enough for me, for now."

"But . . . ," I began.

Ascher rolled her eyes. "Oh, don't be such a whiny little . . ." She turned to Binder. "Git?"

"Git," he confirmed.

"Don't be such a whiny little git, Dresden," Ascher said. "I'm hungry."

The more I could force Nicodemus to bend, the more of his authority would drain away from him. The more someone else defended him, the more he would stock-pile. Time to try another angle. "And you aren't the only thing in here that is," I said to Ascher, and pointed at the goat pen. "Before I go anywhere else, I want to know what's been picking off the livestock."

"Ah," Nicodemus said. "That."

"Yeah, that."

"Does it matter?"

I glowered at him. "It kind of does," I said. Then, thoughtfully, I raised my voice to carry a little farther. "Whatever big, ugly, stinking, stupid thing you've got hanging around in here with us probably doesn't deserve to be in this company. Given our goal, I don't see the point in taking along a mindless mound of muscle."

Grey winced.

I felt it almost at once. The hairs on the back of my neck suddenly started trying to crawl up onto my scalp. Part of me kicked into a genuine watery-bellied fear reaction, something purely instinctive, a message from my primitive hindbrain: A large predator was staring at me with intent.

"Yeah, got your attention now," I muttered under my breath. I raised my voice to address Nicodemus. "Point is, Grey's right. It's time to share some details. So who is the last guy on the crew?"

"I certainly never meant to frighten anyone," Nicode-mus said. "But I suppose I don't have the same point of view as you children. I can understand your apprehension."

Bull. He'd known exactly what he was doing, setting out the goats and letting us get the idea in our heads. From the start, he wanted us to know that he had something big and bad and dangerous hiding in reserve.

"If you don't mind," Nicodemus said to the room at large, "I think introductions are in order."

The nape of my neck was trying to slither away and find a good place to hide when the smell hit me first. It was thick and pungent, bestial—the smell of a large animal in the immediate proximity. A few seconds later, the goats started panicking in their pen, running back and forth and bleating to one another in terror.

"What the hell," Valmont breathed, looking around uneasily.

I didn't join her in rubbernecking. I was extending my awareness, my wizard's senses, searching for the subtle vibration of magical energies at work in the air. I'd never been able to throw up a magical veil so good that it could mask odor, but just because I couldn't do it didn't mean that it was impossible. The one huge weakness of veiling magic was that it was still *magic*. If your senses were sharp, and you were reasonably sure a veil was present, you could find that source of magical energy if you looked hard enough.

I found it after a moment's intense concentration— about ten feet directly behind me.

I turned kind of casually in my chair, folded my arms, fixed my gaze on the empty space where I'd felt the energy coming from, and waited, trying to look bored.

It faded into sight, slowly, an utterly motionless figure. It was human in general shape, but only generally. Muscle covered it in ropy layers and in densities that were too oddly proportioned to be human—so much muscle that you could see its outlines through a thick layer of greyish, straggly hair that covered its body. It was well over nine feet tall. Massive shoulders sloped up to a tree-trunk-sized neck, and its head was shaped strangely as well, sloping up more sharply than a human skull, with a wide forehead and a brow ridge like a mountain crag. Eyes glittered way back in the shadows beneath that brow, glinting like an assassin's knives from a cave's mouth. Its features were heavy and brutish, its hands and feet absolutely enormous—and I had met the creature's like before.

"Stars and stones," I breathed.

That massive brow gathered, lowered. For a second, I thought there had been distant thunder outside, and then I realized that the nearly subsonic rumbling sound was coming from the thing's chest.

It was growling.

At me.

I swallowed.

"This," Nicodemus said into the startled silence, "is the Genoskwa. He, of course, knows you all, having been the first to arrive."

"Big one, isn't he," Binder said, in a very mild voice. "What's his job?"

"I share Dresden's concerns about the availability of our target's vault," Nicodemus said. "There have, in the past, been rather epic guardians protecting the ways in and out of this particular domain. The Genoskwa has consented to join us in order to serve as a counterweight, should any such protection arise."

"An ogre?" Ascher asked.

"Not an ogre," I replied immediately. "He's one of the Forest People."

The Genoskwa's growl might have gotten a little louder. It was so deep that I had a hard time knowing for sure.

"What's the difference?" Ascher asked.

"I once saw one of the Forest People take on about twenty ghouls in a fair fight," I said. "It wasn't even close. If he'd been playing for keeps, none of them would have survived."

The Genoskwa snorted a breath out through his nose. The sound was . . . simply *vile* with rage, with broiled, congealed hate.

I held out both of my hands palms up. I'd rarely seen the kind of power that River Shoulders, the Forest Person I'd met several times before, had displayed, physically and otherwise, and it seemed like a really fantastic idea to mend some fences if possible. "Sorry about what I said earlier. I figured Nicodemus had a troll stashed around here or something. Didn't realize it was one of the Forest People. I've done a little business with River Shoulders in the past. Maybe you've heard of—"

I don't even know what happened. I assume the Genoskwa closed the distance and hit me. One minute I was trying to establish some kind of rapport, and the next I was about a dozen feet in the air, flying across the factory floor, tumbling. I saw the conference table, the windows, the ceiling—and Jordan's incredulous face staring down at me from a catwalk, and then I hit the brick wall and light briefly filled my skull. I mean, I didn't even notice when I fell and hit the floor—or maybe I just can't remember that part.

I do remember that I came up fighting. The Genoskwa walked over the conference table—he just *stepped over it*—and covered the distance to me in catlike silence, in three great strides, moving as lightly as a dancer despite the fact that he had to weigh in at well over eight hundred pounds.

I threw a blast of Winter at him, only to see him make a contemptuous gesture and spit a slavering, snarling word. The ice that should have entombed him just . . . drained away into the floor beneath him, grounding out my magic as effectively as a lightning rod diverts the power of a thunderbolt.

I had about half of a second to realize that my best shot had bounced off him with somewhat less effect than I would have had if I'd slugged him with a foam rubber pillow, and then he hit me again.

Aerial cartwheels. Another flash of impact against a wall. Before I could fall, he had closed the distance again—and his enormous hands drove a rusty old nail into my left pectoral muscle.

Once the steel nail had broken the surface of my skin, my contact with the mantle of the Winter Knight shattered, and I was just plain old vanilla me again.

And that meant pain.

A whole lot of pain.

The mantle had suppressed the pain of my broken

arm, among other things, but once it was taken out of the circuit, all of that agony came rushing into my brain at the same time, an overload of torturous sensation. I screamed and thrashed, grabbing the Genoskwa's wrist with both hands, trying to force his arm and the nail he still held away from me. I might as well have been trying to push over a building. I couldn't so much as make him acknowledge my effort with a wobble, much less move him.

He leaned down, huge and grey and horrible-smelling, and pushed his ugly mug right up into mine, breathing hard through his mouth. His breath smelled like blood and rotten meat. His voice came out in a surprisingly smooth, mellow basso.

"Consider this a friendly warning," he said, his accent harsh, somehow bitter. "I am not one of the whimpering Forest People. Speak of me and that flower-chewing groundhog lover River Shoulders in the same breath again, and I will devour your offal while you watch."

"Frmph," I said. The room was spinning like some kind of wacky animated drunk scene. "Glkngh."

The nail evidently robbed some of the power from Mab's earring, too. Someone drove a railroad spike into each temple, and I suddenly couldn't breathe.

The Genoskwa stepped back from me abruptly, as though I was something unworthy of his attention. He faced the rest of the room, while I clawed desperately at the nail sticking out of my chest.

"You," he said to the people seated at the table. "Do what Nicodemus says, when he says. Or I will twist off your head." He flexed his huge hands, and I suddenly noticed that they were tipped in ugly-looking, dirty claws. "Been here most of two days, and none of you ever saw me. Followed some of you all over this town last night. None of you saw me. You don't do your job now, no place you run will keep you from me."

Those at the table stared at him, stunned and silent, and I realized that my plan for stealing Nicodemus's thunder and destabilizing his authority over the crew had just gone down in flames.

The Genoskwa was apparently satisfied with his entrance. He strode to the pen and, as if it had been an appetizer at a sports bar and not a nimble animal trying desperately to avoid its fate, he plucked up a goat, broke its neck using only one hand, and vanished again, gone more suddenly than he had appeared.

Karrin was at my side a second later, grabbing the nail with her small, strong hands—but the pain was just too damned much. I was fading.

"Well," I dimly heard Nicodemus say, "that's dinner."

Going, going.

Gone.

Chapter

Twenty-three

I hadn't been to this place in a very long time.

It was a flat, empty floor in some vast, open, and unlit space that nonetheless somehow didn't echo with its emptiness, as if there were no walls from which sounds could reflect. I stood in a circle of light, though I couldn't quite make out the source of illumination above me.

It was the first time, though, that I'd ever been standing there alone.

"Hey!" I called out into the empty space. "It's not like my own subconscious can up and disappear, you know! If you've got something you want to say, hurry it up! I'm busy!"

"Yeah, yeah," called a voice from the darkness. "I'm coming. Keep your pants on."

There were shuffling footsteps, and then . . . I appeared.

Well, it wasn't me, exactly. It was my double, though, a mental image of myself that had appeared a few times in the past, and that I would probably avoid mentioning to any mental health professionals who had signed mandatory reporting clauses. Call him my subconscious, my id, the voice of my inner jerkface, whatever. He was a part of me that didn't surface much.

He was dressed in black. A tailored black shirt, black pants, expensive black shoes. He had a goatee, too.

Look, I never said my inner self was hideously complex.

In addition to his usual outfit, he also wore a pin on his left breast—a snowflake, wrought from silver with such complexity and detail that one could see the crystalline shapes of its surface. Whoa. I wasn't sure exactly what the hell *that* meant, but given how my day was going, I was reasonably sure it was nothing good.

There was someone with him.

It was a smallish figure, covered in what looked like a black blanket of soft wool. It moved slowly, hunched, as if in terrible pain, leaning hard against my double's supporting arms.

"Uh," I said. "What?"

My double sneered at me. "Why is it that you've never got the least goddamned clue what's happening inside your own head. Have you ever noticed this trend? Doesn't it bug you sometimes?"

"I try not to overthink it," I said.

He snorted. "Hell's bells, *that's* true. We have to talk."

"Why can't you just send dreams like everyone else's subconscious?"

"I've been trying," he said, and shifted into a voice that sounded suspiciously like Bullwinkle the cartoon moose. "But somebody's been busy not overthinking it."

I arched an eyebrow. "Oh, wait. That . . . that dream with Murphy? That was you?"

"All the dreams are me, blockhead," my double said. "And I swear, dude, you have got to be the most repressed human being on the face of the planet."

"What? Maybe you didn't notice, but I'm not exactly bending over backwards for anybody."

"Not oppressed, moron. *Re*pressed. As in sexually. What is *wrong* with you?"

I blinked, offended. "What?"

"You were doing okay with Susan," he said. "And Anastasia . . . Wow, there's really something to be said for experience."

I felt myself blushing and reminded myself that I was talking to me. "So?"

"And what about all the things you missed, dummy?" he asked. "You had the shadow of a freaking angel who could have shown you any sensual experience you could possibly have *imagined*, but did you take her up on it? No. Mab's been *throwing* girls at you. You could literally make one phone call and have half a dozen supernaturally hot Sidhe girls playing rodeo with you anytime you wanted, and instead you're playing hopscotch over the cages of has-been demons. Hell, Hannah Ascher would have gotten busy with you if you wanted."

"It's Parkour," I said defensively. "And just because I don't go to bed with everything with a vagina doesn't mean I'm repressed. I don't want it to be just sex."

"Why *not*?" my double said, exasperated. "Go forth and freaking multiply! Drink from the cup of life! Carpe femme! For the love of God, get *laid*."

I sighed. Right. Id me didn't have to be concerned with long-term consequences. He was my instinctive, primitive self, driven by my most primal impulses. I wondered, briefly, if *id* and *idiot* came from the same root.

"You wouldn't get it," I said. "It's got to be more than just physical attraction. There's got to be respect and affection."

"Sure," he said, his tone absolutely acidic. "Then how come you haven't banged Murphy yet?"

"Because," I said, growing flustered, "we aren't . . . We haven't gotten to . . . There's been a lot of . . . Look, fuck off."

"Hah," my double said. "You're obviously terrified of getting close to someone. Afraid you'll get hurt and rejected. Again."

"No, I'm not," I said.

"Oh, please," he said. "I've got a direct line to your hindbrain. I've got your fears on Blu-Ray." He rolled his eyes. "Like *she* isn't feeling exactly the same thing?"

"Murphy isn't afraid of anything," I said.

"Two ex-husbands, and the last one married her little sister. He might as well have sent her a card that said, 'I'd like you, only you're too successful. And old.' And you're a freaking wizard who is going to live for centuries. Of course she's freaking out about the idea of getting involved with you."

I frowned at that. "I . . . You really think so?"

"No, dolt. *You* really think so."

I snorted. "Okay, guy, if you're so smart. What do I do?"

"If having something real is so important to you, man up and go *get* her," my id said. "You could both be dead tomorrow. You're heading for the realm of freaking *death*, for crying out loud. What the hell are you waiting for?"

"Uh," I said.

"Let me answer that for you," he said. "Molly."

I blinked. "Uh, no. Molly's a freaking kid."

"She *was* a freaking kid," my double said. "She's heading for her late twenties, in case you forgot how to count. She's not all that much younger than you, and the proportional distance is only shrinking. And you like her, and you trust her, and the two of you have a ton in common. Go get laid *there*."

"Dude, no," I said. "That is not going to happen."

"Why not?"

"It would be a serious violation of trust."

"Because she's your apprentice?" he asked. "No, she isn't. Not anymore. Hell's bells, man, she's practically your boss when you get right down to it. At the very least, she got promoted past you."

"I am not having this conversation," I said.

"Repression *and* denial," my double said acerbically. "Get thee to a therapist."

The figure next to him made a soft sound.

"Right," the double said. "We don't have much time. Murphy's pulling the nail out."

"Time for *what*?" I asked. "And who *is* that?"

"Seriously?" he asked. "You aren't going to use your intuition even a little, huh?"

I scowled at him and at the other figure and then my eyes widened. "Wait . . . Is that . . . is that the *parasite*?"

The shrouded figure shuddered and let out a pained groan.

"No," my double said. "It's the being that Mab and that stupid Alfred have been *calling* a parasite."

I blinked several times. "What?"

"Look, man," my double said. "You've got to work this out. Think, okay. I can't just *talk* to you. This near-dream stuff is my best, but you've got to meet me halfway."

I narrowed my eyes. "Wait. You're saying that the parasite isn't actually a parasite. But that means . . ."

"The wheel is turning," my double said, in the tone of a reporter covering a sports event. "The fat, lazy old hamster looks like he's almost forgotten how to make it go, but he's sort of moving it now. Bits of rust are falling off. The cobwebs are slowly parting."

"Screw you," I said, annoyed. "It's not like you've showed up with a ton to say ever since . . ." I trailed off and fell entirely silent for a long moment.

"Ah," he said, and pointed a finger at me, bouncing up onto his toes. "Ah hah! Ah hah, hah, hah, the light begins to dawn!"

"Ever since I touched Lasciel's Coin," I breathed quietly.

"Follow that," my double urged me. "What happened next?"

"Touching the Coin put an imprint of Lasciel in my head," I said. "Like a footprint in clay, the same shape as the original. She tried to tempt me into accepting the true Lasciel into my head along with her, but I turned her down."

My double rolled his wrist in a "keep it moving" gesture. "And then?"

"And then the imprint started to change," I said. "Lasciel was immutable, but the imprint was made of me. A shape in the clay. As the clay changed, so did the imprint."

"And?"

"And I gave her a name," I said. "I called her Lash. She became an independent psychic entity in her own right. And we kind of got along until . . ." I swallowed. "Until there was a psychic attack. A bad one. She threw herself in the way of it. It destroyed her."

"Yeah," my double said quietly. "But . . . look, what she did was an act of love. And you were about as intimate with her as it gets, sharing the same mental space. I mean, it's funny, you get twitchy when you start considering *living* with a woman, but having one literally inside your head was not an issue."

"What do you mean?"

"Christ, you're supposed to be the intellect here," my double said. *"Think."* He stared at me for a long moment, visibly willing me to understand.

My stomach fell into some unimaginable abyss at the same time my jaw dropped open. "No," I said. "That isn't . . . that's not possible."

"When a mommy and a daddy love each other *very much*," my double said, as if speaking to a small child, "and they live together and hug and kiss and get intimate with each other . . ."

"I'm . . ." I felt a little ill. "You're saying . . . I'm *pregnant*?"

My double threw up his arms. *"Finally*, he gets it."

In years and years and years of experience as a wizard, I'd dealt with concepts, formulae, and mental models that ranged from bizarre to downright insanity-inducing.

None of them had, in any way whatsoever, ever prepared my head to wrap around this. At all. Ever. "How is that . . . That isn't even . . . What the *hell*, man?" I demanded.

"A spiritual entity," my double said calmly. "Born of you and Lash. When she sacrificed herself for you, it was an act of selfless love—and love is fundamentally a force of creation. It stands to reason, then, that an act of love is fundamentally an act of creation. You remember it, right? After she died? When you could still play the music she'd given to you, even though she was gone? You could hear the echoes of her voice?"

"Yeah," I said, feeling dazed.

"That was because a part of her remained," my double said. "Made of her—and made of you."

And very gently, he drew back the black blanket.

She looked like a child maybe twelve years old, in the last few weeks of true childhood before the sudden surge of hormones brought on the chain of rapid changes that lead into adolescence. Her hair was dark, like mine, but her eyes were a crystalline blue-green, the way Lash's had often appeared. Her features were faintly familiar, and I realized in a surge of instinct that her face had been constructed from those of people in my life. She had the square, balanced chin of Karrin Murphy, the rounded cheeks of Ivy the Archive, and Susan Rodriguez's jawline. Her nose had come from my first love, Elaine Mallory, her hair from my first apprentice, Kim Delaney. I knew because they were *my* memories, right there in front of me.

Her eyes were fluttering uncertainly, and she was shivering so hard that she could barely stand. There was frost forming on her eyelashes, and even as I watched it started spreading over her cheeks.

"She's a spiritual entity," I breathed. "Oh, my God. She's a spirit of *intellect*."

"What happens when mortals get it on with spirits," my double confirmed, though now without heat.

"But Mab said she was a parasite," I said.

"Lot of people make jokes, refer to fetuses like that," he said.

"Mab called her a monster. Said she would hurt those closest to me."

"She's a spirit of intellect, just like Bob," my double said. "Born of the spirit of a fallen freaking angel and the mind of one of the most potent wizards on the White Council. She's going to be born with knowledge, and with power, and be absolutely innocent of what to do with them. A lot of people would call that monstrous."

"Argh," I said, and clutched at my head. I got it now. Mab hadn't been lying. Not precisely. Hell, she'd as much as told me that the parasite was made of my essence. My soul. My . . . me-ness. Spirits of intellect had to grow, and my head was a limited space. This one had been filling it up for years, slowly expanding, putting more psychic and psychological pressure on me—reflected in the growing intensity of my migraines over that time.

If I'd realized what was happening, I could have done something sooner, and probably a lot more simply. Now . . . I was overdue and it was looking like this was going to be a very, very rough delivery. And if I didn't have help, I'd be in much the same shape as a woman giving birth alone and encountering complications. Odds were good that my head wouldn't be able to stand the pressure of such a being abruptly parting ways with me, fighting its way out of a space that had become too small, in sheer instinct for its own survival. It could drive me insane, or kill me outright.

If that happened, it would leave the newly born spirit of intellect alone and bewildered in a world it didn't understand, but about which it had lots and lots of data. Spirits like Bob liked to pretend they were all about rationality, but they had emotions, attachments. The new spirit would want to connect. And it would try to do so with the people who mattered most to me.

I shuddered, imagining little Maggie suddenly gaining a very, very seriously dangerous imaginary friend.

"See?" I demanded of my double. "You *see*? *This* is why you don't go around having sex with everyone all the time!"

"You're the brain," he said. "Figure it *out*." The lights flickered and he looked up and around. "Ugh," he said. "Nail's coming out."

He was right. I could feel a faint pang in my chest, and a fading echo of the agony in my head. Frost continued covering the little girl, and she sighed, her knees buckling.

My double and I both stooped down and caught her before she could fall.

I picked her up. She didn't weigh anything. She didn't look dangerous. She just looked like a little girl.

Her eyes fluttered open. "I'm sorry," she stammered. "Sorry. But it *hurts* and I c-c-couldn't talk to you."

I traded a look with my double and then looked down

at her. "It's okay," I said. "It's okay. I'm going to take care of it. It'll be all right."

She sighed slightly and her eyes closed. Frost covered her in fine layers upon layers, as the spell on Mab's earring wrapped her in sleep and silence, stilling her—for now—and turning her into a beautiful white statue.

I hadn't even known she was there—and she was entirely my responsibility.

And if I didn't handle it, she would kill me being born.

I passed her carefully to my double. "Okay," I said. "I've got it."

He took her, very gently, and gave me a nod. "I know she's weird. But she's still your offspring." His dark eyes flashed. "Protect the offspring."

Primal drives indeed.

I'd torn apart a nation protecting my physical child. I was looking at part of the reason why. That drive was a part of me, too.

I took a deep breath and nodded to him. "I'm on it," I said.

He wrapped the girl in a blanket and turned to carry her back into the darkness. He took the light with him, and darkness swallowed me again.

"Hey," my double called abruptly, from the distance.

"What?"

"Don't forget the dream!" he said. "Don't forget how it ended!"

"What is that supposed to mean?" I asked.

"You flipping *idiot*!" my double snarled.

And then he was gone along with everything else.

Chapter

Twenty-four

I opened my eyes and saw the ceiling of Karrin's bedroom. It was dark. I was lying down. Light from the hallway came creeping under the bedroom door, and was almost too bright for my eyes.

"That's what I'm trying to tell you," Butters's voice was saying. "I don't *know*. There's no AMA-approved baseline for a freaking wizard Knight of Winter. He could be in shock. He could be bleeding from the brain. He could be really, really *sleepy*. Dammit, Karrin, this is what *hospitals* and practicing physicians are for!"

I heard Karrin blow out a breath. "Okay," she said, without any kind of heat. "What *can* you tell me?"

"His arm's broken," Butters said. "From the swelling and bruising, badly. Whatever put that dent in the aluminum brace on it—did he get it taken care of in a tool shop?—rebroke it. I set it again, I *think*, and wrapped it up in the brace again, but I can't be sure I did it right without imaging equipment, which would probably explode if he walked into the room with it. If it hasn't been set right, that arm might be permanently damaged." He blew out a breath. "The hole in his chest wasn't traumatic, by his usual standards. It didn't go through the muscle. But the damned nail was rusty, so I hope he's had his tetanus shots. I gave the hole another stitch and I washed the blood off the nail."

"Thank you," Karrin said.

Butters's voice was weary. "Yeah," he sighed. "Sure. Karrin . . . can I tell you something?"

"What?"

"This thing he's got going with Mab," Butters said. "I know that everyone thinks it's turned him into some kind of superhero. But I don't think that's right."

"I've seen him move," she said. "I've seen how strong he is."

"So have I," Butters said. "Look . . . the human body is a pretty amazing machine. It really is. It can do really amazing things—much more so than most people think, because it's also built to protect itself."

"What do you mean?" she asked.

"Inhibitors," Butters said. "Every person walking around is about three times stronger than they think they are. I mean, your average housewife is actually about as strong as a fairly serious weight lifter, when it comes to pure mechanics. Adrenaline can amp that even more."

I could hear the frown in Karrin's voice. "You're talking about when mothers lift cars off their kids, that kind of thing."

"Exactly that kind of thing," Butters said. "But the body can't function that way all the time, or it will tear itself apart. That's what inhibitors are built for—to keep you from injuring yourself."

"What does that have to do with Dresden?"

"I think that what this Winter Knight gig has done for him is nothing more than switching off those inhibitors," Butters said. "He hasn't added all that much muscle mass. It's the only thing that makes sense. The body is capable of those moments of startling strength, but they're meant to be something that you pull out of the hat once or twice in a lifetime—and with no inhibitors and no ability to feel pain, Dresden's running around doing them *all the time*. And there's no real way he can know it."

Karrin was silent for several seconds, digesting that. Then she said, "Bottom line?"

"The more he leans on this 'gift,'" Butters said, and I could picture him making air quotes, "the more he tears himself to shreds. His body heals remarkably, but he's still human. He's got limits, somewhere, and if he keeps this up, he's going to find them."

"What do you think will happen?"

Butters made a thoughtful sound. "Think about . . . a football player or boxer who has it hard and breaks down in his early thirties, because he's just taken too damned much punishment. That's Dresden, if he keeps this up."

"I'm sure that once we explain that to him, he'll retire to a job as a librarian," Karrin said.

Butters snorted. "It's possible that other things in his system are being affected the same way," he said. "Testosterone production, for example, any number of other hormones, which might be influencing his perception and judgment. I'm not sure he's actually got any more real power at *all*. I think it just *feels* that way to him."

"This is fact or theory?"

"An informed theory," he said. "Bob helped me develop it."

Son of a bitch. I kept quiet and thought about that one for a minute.

Could that be true? Or at least, more true than it wasn't?

It would be consistent with the other deal I'd worked out with a faerie—my godmother, Lea, had made a bargain to give me the power to defeat my old mentor, Justin DuMorne. Then she'd tortured me for a while, assuring me that it would give me strength. It did, though mostly, in retrospect, because I had believed it had.

Had I been magic-feathered by a faerie *again*?

And yet . . . at the end of the day, I *could* lift a freaking car.

Sure you can, Harry. But at what price?

No wonder the Winter Knights stayed in the job until they died. If Butters was right, they would have been plunged into the crippling agony of their battered bodies the moment the mantle was taken from them.

Sort of the same way I had just been rendered into agonized Jell-O when the Genoskwa had shoved a nail into me.

"I worry," Butters said quietly, "that he's changing. That he doesn't know it."

"Look who's talking," Karrin said. "Batman."

"That was one time," Butters said.

Karrin didn't say anything.

"All right." Butters relented. "A few times. But it wasn't enough to keep those kids from being carried off."

"You pulled some of them out, Waldo," Karrin said. "Believe me, that's a win. Most of the time, you can't even do that much. But you're missing my point."

"What point?"

"Ever since you've had the skull, you've been changing, too," Karrin said. "You work hand in hand with a supernatural being that can scare the crap out of me. You can do things you couldn't do before. You know things you didn't know before. Your personality has changed."

There was a pause. "It has?"

"You're more serious," she said. "More . . . intense, I suppose."

"Yeah. Now that I know more about what's really happening out there. It's not something influencing me."

"Unless it is and you just don't know it," Karrin said. "I've got the same evidence on you that you have on Dresden."

Butters sighed. "I see what you did there."

"I don't think you do," she said. "It's . . . about choices, Waldo. About faith. You have an array of facts in front of you that can fit any of several truths. You have to choose what you're going to allow to drive your decisions about how to deal with those facts."

"What do you mean?"

"You could let fear be what motivates you," Karrin said. "Maybe you're right. Maybe Dresden is being turned into a monster against his knowledge and will. Maybe one day he'll be something that kills us all. You're not wrong. That kind of thing can happen. It scares me, too."

"Then why are you arguing with me?"

Karrin paused for a time before answering. "Because . . .

fear is a terrible, insidious thing, Waldo. It taints and stains everything it touches. If you let fear start driving some of your decisions, sooner or later, it will drive them *all*. I decided that I'm not going to be the kind of person who lives her life in fear of her friends' turning into monsters."

"What? Just like that?"

"It took me a long, long time to get there," she said. "But at the end of the day, I would rather have faith in the people I care about than allow my fears to change them—in my own eyes, if nowhere else. I guess maybe you don't see what's happening with Harry, here."

"What?" Butters asked.

"This is what it looks like when someone's fighting for his soul," she said. "He needs his friends to believe in him. The fastest way for us to help make him into a monster is to look at him like he is one."

Butters was quiet for a long time.

"I'm going to say this once, Waldo," she said. "I want you to listen."

"Okay."

"You need to decide which side of the road you're going to walk on," she said gently. "Turn aside from your fears—or grab onto them and run with them. But you need to make the call. You keep trying to walk down the middle, you're going to get yourself torn apart."

Butters's voice turned bitter. "Them or us, choose a side?"

"It's not about taking sides," Karrin said. "It's about knowing yourself. About understanding *why* you make the choices you do. Once you know that, you know where to walk, too."

The floorboards creaked. Maybe she'd stepped closer to him. I could picture her, putting her hand on his arm.

"You're a good man, Waldo. I like you. I respect you. I think you'll figure it out."

A long silence followed.

"Andi's waiting on me to eat," he said. "I'd better get going."

"Okay," Karrin said. "Thank you again."

"I . . . Yeah, sure."

Footsteps. The front door opened and closed. A car started up and then drove away.

I sat up in bed, and fumbled until I found Karrin's bed-side lamp with my right hand. The light hurt my eyes. My head felt funny—probably the result of being bounced off of walls. I'd lost my shirt, again. Butters had added some more bandages and the sharp scent of more antibiotics to my collection of medical trophies. My arm had been ban-daged again, inside its aluminum brace, and the brace was held in a sling tied around my neck.

I got out of bed and wobbled for a minute and then shambled across the floor to the bedroom door. Karrin opened it just as I got there, and stood looking up at me, her expression worried.

"God, you are turning into a monster," she said. "A mummy. One bit at a time."

"I'm fine," I said. "Ish."

She pursed her lips and shook her head. "How much of that did you hear?"

"Everything after his usual 'I'm not really a physician' disclaimer."

Her mouth twitched. "He's just . . . He's worried, that's all."

"I get it," I said. "I think you handled it right."

That drew a sparkle from her eyes. "I know I did."

"Batman?" I asked.

"He's been . . ." She folded her arms. "You-ing, I suppose. With you gone from the city and Molly gone, the streets haven't been getting any safer. Marcone's crowd have taken up the fight against the Fomor, whenever their territory is threatened, but their protection costs. Not everyone can afford it."

I grimaced. "Dammit," I muttered. "Damn Mab. I could have been back here months and months ago."

"Waldo does what he can. And because he has the skull, that's more than most."

"Bob was never meant to be used in the field," I said. "He's a valuable resource—until he attracts attention to himself. Once he's been identified, he can be countered or stolen, and then the bad guys get that much stronger. It's why I tried not to take him out of the lab."

"The Fomor started taking children last Halloween," Karrin said simply. "Six-year-olds. Right off the streets."

I grimaced and looked down from her steady gaze.

"We'll sort something out," Karrin said. "You hungry?"

"Starving," I said.

"Come on."

I followed her to the kitchen. She took a pair of Pizza 'Spress pizzas from the oven, where she'd had them staying warm. They had almost settled onto the table before

I started eating, ravenous. The pizza was my favorite. Not good, but my favorite, because it had been the only pizza I could afford for a long, long time, and I was used to it. Heavy on the sauce, light on the cheese, and the meat was just hinted at, but the crust was thick and hot and flaky and filled with delicious things that murdered you slowly.

"Present for you," Karrin said.

"Mmmmnghf?" I asked.

She plopped a file folder down on the table beside me and said, "From Paranoid Gary the Paranetizen."

I swallowed a mouthful and delayed getting another long enough to ask, "The one who found the deal with the boats last year? Crazy-but-not-wrong guy?"

"That's him," she said.

"Huh," I said, chewing. I opened the folder and started flipping through printed pages of fuzzy images.

"Those are from Iran," Karrin said. "Gary says that they show a functioning nuclear power plant."

The images were obviously of some sort of installation, but I couldn't tell anything beyond that. "Thought they had big old towers."

"He says they're buried in that hill behind the building," Karrin said. "Check out the last few images."

On the last pages of the folder, things in the installation had changed. Columns of black, greasy smoke rolled out from multiple buildings. In another image, the bodies of soldiers lay on the ground. And in the last image, up on the hillside, which was wreathed in white mist, or maybe steam . . .

Three figures faced one another. One was a large man

dressed in a long overcoat and wielding a slightly curved sword in one hand, an old cavalry saber. He carried what might have been a sawed-off shotgun in the other. His skin was dark, and though his head hadn't been shaved like that the last time I'd seen him, it could really have been only one person.

"Sanya," I said.

The world's only Knight of the Cross was standing across from two blurry figures. Both were in motion, as if charging toward him. One was approximately the same size and shape as a large gorilla. The other was covered in a thick layer of feathers that gave an otherwise humanoid shape an odd, shaggy appearance.

"Magog and Shaggy Feathers," I muttered. "Hell's bells, those Coins are slippery. When were these taken?"

"Less than six hours ago," Karrin said, "according to Paranoid Gary. The Denarians are up to something."

"Yeah," I said. "Deirdre said that Tessa was supposed to be in Iran. That makes sense."

"In what way does that make sense?"

"Nicodemus wants to pull a job over here," I said. "He knows there's only one Knight running around. So he sends Tessa and her crew to the other side of the world to stir up major-league trouble. Let's say Gary's right, and Iran has a nuclear reactor running. And something goes horribly wrong with it. You've got an instant regional and international crisis. Of course a Knight gets sent to deal with it—where he can't get to Chicago, or at least not in time to do any good."

Karrin took that in silently, and I went back to eating. "So you're saying, we're on our own."

"And the bad guys keep stacking up higher and higher," I said.

"The Genoskwa, you mean," Karrin said.

"Yeah."

She shuddered. "That thing . . . seriously, a Bigfoot?"

"Some kind of mutant serial killer Bigfoot, maybe," I said. "Not like one of the regular Forest People at all."

"I can't believe it," Karrin said.

"It's no weirder than any number of—"

"Not that," she said. "I can't believe you met a Bigfoot and you never told me about it. I mean, they're famous."

"They're kind of a private bunch," I said. "Did a few jobs for one, a few years back, named River Shoulders. Liked him. Kept my mouth shut."

She nodded in understanding. Then she got up and left the kitchen, and came back a moment later with her rocket launcher and an oversized pistol case. She set the rocket launcher down and said, "This will take out something Bigfoot-sized, no problem."

I opened my mouth and then closed it again. "Yeah," I admitted. "Okay."

She gave me a nod that did not, quite, include the phrase "I told you so." "I like to be sure I've got enough firepower to cover any given situation." She put the case on the table and slid it over to me. "And this is for you."

I took the case and opened it a little awkwardly, using mostly one hand. In it was a stubby-looking pistol that had been built with a whole hell of a lot of metal, to the point where it somehow reminded me of a steroid-using weight lifter's gargoylish build. The damned thing could have been mounted on a small armored vehicle turret. There were a number of rounds stored with it, each the size of my thumb.

"What the hell is this?" I asked, beaming.

"Smith and Wesson five hundred," she said. "Short barrel, but that round is made for taking on big game. Big, Grey, and Ugly comes at you to make another friendly point, I want you to give him a four-hundred-grain bullet-point reply."

I whistled, hefting the gun and admiring the sheer mass of it. "I've got one broken wrist already, and you give me this?"

"Ride the recoil, Nancy," she said. "You can handle it." She reached out and put her hand on the fingers of my left hand, protruding from the sling. "We'll handle it. We'll get this thing with Nicodemus done, and get that parasite out of your head. You'll see."

"Yeah," I said. "We've got a problem there."

"What's that?"

"We can't kill the parasite," I said. "We have to save it."

Karrin gave me a flat look and, after a brief pause, said, "What?"

"We, uh . . . Look, it's not what I thought it was. My condition isn't what we thought it was, either."

She eyed me carefully. "No? Then what is your condition, exactly?"

I told her.

"Come on," I said. "Get up."

She sat on the floor, rocking back and forth helplessly

with laughter. Her plate with its slice of pizza had landed beside her when she'd fallen out of her chair a few minutes before, and hadn't moved.

"Stop it," she gasped. "Stop making me laugh."

I was getting a little annoyed now, as well as embarrassed. My face felt as though it had a mild sunburn. "Dammit, Karrin, we're supposed to be back at the slaughterhouse in twenty minutes. Come *on*, it's just not that funny."

"The look"—she panted, giggling helplessly—"on your . . . face . . ."

I sighed and muttered under my breath and waited for her to recover.

It took her only a couple more minutes, though she drifted back into titters several times before she finally picked herself up off the floor.

"Are you quite finished?" I asked her, trying for a little dignity.

She dissolved into hiccoughing giggles again instantly.

It was highly unprofessional.

Chapter
Twenty-five

By the time we got back to the slaughterhouse, the sun had gone down, and the night had come on cold and murky. Rain had begun to fall in a fine mist, and the temperature had dropped enough that I could see it starting to coat the city in a fine sheet of ice.

"Ice storm," Karrin noted as she parked the car. "Perfect."

"At least it'll keep people in," I said.

"Depending on how this goes, that might cut down on innocent bystanders," she said. "Is Mab messing with the weather again?"

I squinted out at the weather. "No," I said, immediately and instinctively certain of the answer. "This is just winter in Chicago being winter in Chicago. Mab doesn't care about innocent bystanders."

"But she might care about giving you an advantage."

I snorted and said, "Mab helps those who help themselves."

Karrin gave me a thin smile. "That thing you did, with the Genoskwa. You threw magic at it."

"Yep."

"It didn't work, I guess."

"Nope," I said. "I hit him with my best shot, something Mab gave me. Just drained off him, grounded out."

"Grounded," she said. "Like with a lightning rod?"

"Exactly like that," I said. "The Forest People know magic, and they're ridiculously powerful, but they understand it differently than humans do. The one I knew used water magic like nothing I'd ever seen or heard of before. This Genoskwa . . . I think he's using earth magic the same way. On a level I don't know a damned thing about."

"Pretend I don't know a damned thing about earth magic either," Karrin said, "and bottom-line it for me."

"I threw the most potent battle magic I know at him, and he shut it down with zero trouble. I'm pretty sure he'll be able to do it as much as he wants."

"He's immune to magic?" Karrin asked.

I shrugged. "If he senses it coming and can take action, pretty much," I said. "Which makes me think that he's not all that bright."

"Hell of a secret to give away when his goal wasn't to actually kill you."

"No kidding," I said. "Maybe he gave me too much credit and assumed I already knew. Either way, I know now."

"Right," Karrin said. "Which gives you an advantage. You won't bother trying to blast him with magic the next time."

I shuddered, thinking of the creature's sheer speed and power, and of exactly how little he feared me. I touched the handle of my new revolver, now loaded and in my duster pocket. "With any luck, there won't be a next time."

Karrin turned to me abruptly, her expression earnest. "Harry," she said quietly, "that thing means to kill you. I know what it looks like. Don't kid yourself."

I grimaced and looked away.

Satisfied that she'd made her point, she nodded and got out of the car. She'd slung one of her space guns (she'd called it a Kriss) on a harness under her coat, and you almost couldn't see it when she moved. She rolled around to the trunk, looked up and down the street once, and then took out the rocket launcher and slung it over her shoulder. In the dark, in the rain, it looked like it might have been one of those protective tubes that artists use, maybe three and a half feet long.

"Really think you can hit him with that thing?" I asked.

"It's weapon enough to handle him," she said. "If I have to."

I squinted up at the drizzling mist and said, "I'm getting tired of this job."

"Let's get it done, then," Karrin said.

This time, when we rolled in, Jordan wasn't on duty. Maybe he'd been given a shift off to get some sleep. Or maybe Nicodemus was so sure I was about to break through his conditioning and suborn him that he'd moved the kid to a less vulnerable post. Yeah. That was probably it.

When we came in, most of the crew was already downstairs, gathered around the conference table. Even the Genoskwa was standing around in plain sight, albeit in a deep patch of shadow that reduced his visible presence to an enormous, furry shadow. Only Nicodemus and Deirdre were absent—and I spotted Deirdre standing silently on one of the catwalks, looking down at the table, where Binder was telling some sort of animated anecdote or joke.

She looked . . . disturbed. Don't get me wrong—a girl who goes around biting the tongues out of men's mouths is disturbed one way or another, but the Denarian killer looked genuinely troubled, or distressed, or something.

Karrin caught me looking at her and sighed. "We can't afford another damsel, Dresden."

"I wasn't thinking that," I said.

"Sure you weren't."

"Actually," I said, "I was thinking she looked vulnerable. Might be a good time to confront her about how Harvey died."

Karrin clucked her tongue thoughtfully. "I'll be at the table."

"Yeah."

She descended the stairs, and I ambled out along the catwalk to stand beside Deirdre.

She looked up at me as I approached, her eyes flat. But then her gaze shifted back to the room below.

"And then I said"—Binder snickered, evidently coming to the punch line—"why did you wear it, then?"

Hannah Ascher burst out in a short, hearty belly laugh, and was joined, more quietly, by Anna Valmont. Even Grey smiled, at least a little. The expression looked somehow alien on his oddly unremarkable features.

Deirdre stared down at them all, her expression dispassionate, like a scientist observing bacteria. Her eyes flickered toward me for a second as I approached, her body tensing slightly.

Being a genius interrogator, I asked her, "So. Why'd you kill Harvey?"

She looked at me for a few seconds, then turned her eyes back to the room below, to watch Karrin come to the table. There was a moment of silence from everyone as they took in her armament. Then Grey rose, suddenly dapper, and offered to help her with the rocket launcher like it was a coat. Karrin let him, giving him an edged smile that she directed past him, to the shadows where the Genoskwa lurked.

"I didn't kill the accountant," she said quietly. "Nicodemus said not to."

That surprised me a little. If she wanted to hide herself from me, she didn't need to go to the effort of lying. All she had to do was stay silent.

"He said that to all of us," I said. "Maybe he said something else to you privately."

"He didn't," she said. "My mother killed him with a spell she calls the Sanguine Scalpel."

"The cuts looked a lot like the ones you would inflict," I said.

"A cut throat is a cut throat, wizard."

Tough to argue with that one. "And you chased her."

"I went to say . . . to talk to her, yes."

"What did she have to say?"

"Personal things," Deirdre replied.

I narrowed my eyes.

Something wasn't jiving here. Deirdre was demonstrating absolutely no emotion about her mother, which in my experience is the next best thing to impossible for almost anyone. Hell, even *Maeve* had carried enormous mother issues around with her. If Tessa was really trying to beat Nicodemus and Deirdre to the Holy Grail, there should have been something there. Frustration, irritation, fear, anger, resignation, *something*.

Not this distant, cool clarity.

Tessa wasn't after any Grail.

But what else could motivate her?

Deirdre looked up from below and studied me calmly. "He knows that you mean to betray him, you know."

"Makes us even," I said.

"No, it doesn't," she said, in that same distant voice. "Not even close. I've seen him disassemble men and women more formidable than you, dozens of times. You don't have a chance of tricking him, out-planning him, or beating him." She stated it as a simple fact. "Mab knows it, too."

"Then why would she send me?"

"She's disposing of you without angering your allies at *her*. Surely you can't be so deluded that you don't see that."

A slow chill went through me at the words.

That . . . could make a great deal of sense, actually. If Mab had decided not to use me after all, then my presence was no longer needed—but enough people thought well of me that they could prove extremely trying for her, should they set out to seek revenge.

Of course, that wasn't how Mab played the game.

When she set something up, she did it so that no matter what happened, she would run the table in the end. Mab probably intended me to do exactly what she'd told me she sent me to do. But what she *hadn't* said was that she'd set it up so that it wouldn't hurt her too badly if I failed. If I was too incompetent to work her will, she would regard me as a liability, to be dispensed with—preferably without angering my allies. Nicodemus would get the vengeance-level blame for my death if I failed, and Mab would be free and clear to choose a new Knight.

I felt my jaw tightening and loosening. Well. I couldn't really have expected anything else. Mab struck me as the kind of mother who taught her children to swim by throwing them into the lake. My entire career with her would be shaped the same way—sink or swim.

"We'll see," I said.

She smiled, very slightly, and turned back to regard the table below. Grey was sitting with Karrin, speaking quietly, a smile on his face. She had her narrow-eyed expression on hers, but a smile also lurked somewhere inside it. He was being amusing.

Jerk.

"Is there anything else you'd like to ask me?" Deirdre asked.

"Yeah," I said quietly. "Why?"

"Why what?"

I gestured around. "Why this? Why do you do what you do? Why bite out the tongues and murder hirelings and whatnot? What makes a person *do* something like this?"

She fell silent. The weight of it became oppressive.

"Tell me, child," she said. "What is the longest-lasting relationship in your life?"

"Uh," I said. "Like, in terms of when it started? Or how long it continued?"

"Whichever."

"My mentor in the White Council, maybe," I said. "I've known him since I was sixteen."

"You see him daily? You speak to him, work with him?"

"Well, no."

"Ah," she said. "Someone that close to you. Who shares your life with you."

"Uh," I said. "A girlfriend or two. My cat."

A small smirk touched her mouth. "Temporary mates and a cat. One cat."

"He's an awesome cat."

"What you are telling me," she said, "is that you have never shared your life with another over the long term. The closest you have come to it is providing a home and affection for a being which is entirely your subject and in your control."

"Well, not at bath time . . ."

The joke did not register on her. "You have had nothing but firefly relationships, there and then gone. I have watched empires rise and fall and rise again beside Nicodemus. You call him my father, but there are no words for what we are. How can there be? Mortal words cannot possibly encompass something which mortals can never embrace and know. Centuries of faith, of cooperation, of trust, working and living and fighting side by side." Her mouth twisted into a sneer. "You know nothing of commitment, wizard child. And so I cannot possibly explain to you why I do what I do."

"And what is it that you think you're doing with him, exactly?" I asked her.

"We," she said, with perfect serenity, "are fighting to save the world."

Which, if true, was about the creepiest thing I'd run into that day.

"From what?" I asked.

She smiled, very faintly, and finally fell silent.

I didn't press. I didn't want to hear anything else from her anyway.

I withdrew and went down to the table with the others.

". . . dinner," Grey was saying. "Assuming we're all alive and filthy rich afterward, I mean."

"I certainly can say no," Karrin replied, her tone light with banter. "You're a little creepy, Grey."

"Goodman," Grey said. "Say it with me. 'Goodman.'"

"I was a cop for twenty years, Grey," Karrin said. "I can recognize a fake name when I hear it."

I settled down next to Karrin and pulled the new revolver out of my pocket, put it on the conference table right where I could reach it and said to Grey, "Hi."

Grey eyed me and then the gun. Then he said to Karrin, "Does he make these kinds of calls for you?"

"You'll have to try a little harder with something a little less obvious than that," Karrin said. "Honestly, I'm sort of hoping he shoots you a little. I've never seen a round from that beast hit somebody."

Grey settled back in his seat, eyeing me sourly. "Bro," he said, "you're totally cockblocking me."

In answer, I picked up the monster revolver. "No," I said, and then I freaking cocked it, drawing the hammer back with my thumb. Rather than a mere click, it made a sinister ratcheting sound. "*Now* I'm cockblocking you."

The table got completely quiet and still. Anna Valmont's eyes were huge.

"Touché," Grey said, nodding slightly. "Well, there was no harm in my asking the lady, was there?"

"None to her," I agreed amiably. "Murphy, should I shoot him anyway?"

Karrin put a finger to her lips and tapped thoughtfully. "I've got to admit, I'm curious as hell. But it seems a little unprofessional, as long as he backs off."

"Hear that?" I asked Grey.

"You people are savages," Grey said. He shook his head, muttered something beneath his breath, and rose to stalk away from the table and settle down not far from the Genoskwa—who did not object. The two exchanged a very slight nod, and began to speak in low voices in a language I did not recognize.

I lowered the hammer carefully and put the revolver down. The table was silent for another long moment, before Binder said in a jovial tone, as if he had never stopped speaking, "So there I was in Belize with thirty monkeys, a panda, and a pygmy elephant . . ."

He had begun to tell a story that everyone around the table thought was completely fabricated, while he insisted that every detail was absolutely true, when Nicodemus entered the factory through emergency doors on the floor level, letting in a blast of freezing mist and winter air. He had added a long coat to his ensemble, and he dropped it behind him as he strode forward across the floor. His shadow slid over the floor beside him, too large and never quite in sync with the rest of him.

"Good evening," he said, as he took his seat at the head of the table. "Ladies and gentlemen, please give me your attention. Wizard Dresden, if you would, please give us a brief primer on the nature of Ways and how they open."

I blinked as every eye on the table turned to me. "Uh," I said. "Ways are basically passages between the mortal world and some portion of the Nevernever—the spirit world. Any point in the mortal world will open a Way to somewhere, if you know how to do it. The Way opens to a place that shares something in common with the point of origin in the mortal world. Uh, for example, if you wanted to open a Way to Hell, you'd have to find a hellish place in the mortal world and start from there. If you want to go to a peaceful place in the Nevernever, you start with a peaceful place here. Like that. Chicago is a great place for Ways—it's a crossroads, a big one. You can get just about anywhere from here."

"Thank you," Nicodemus said. "Our goal is to open a Way into the secured facility containing our objective." He accepted a large sheet of rolled paper from a squire who had hurried up to hand it to him. "Bearing all those factors in mind, I'm sure you'll understand why we will begin the job here."

With a flick of his wrist, he unrolled the large sheet of paper.

It proved to be blueprints, a floor plan. I frowned and stared at it, but it didn't look familiar.

Karrin made a choking sound.

"Murph?" I asked.

"Ah," Nicodemus said, smiling. "You know it."

"It's a vault," Karrin said, looking up at me. "A vault that belongs to a lord of the underworld."

I felt myself clench up in a place that didn't bear much more clenching. "Oh," I said weakly. "Oh, Hell's bells."

Binder jerked a thumb at me. "What is he on about?" he asked Karrin.

Karrin put a forefinger on the plans. "This is the Capristi Building," she said. "It's the second most secure facility in the city." She took a deep breath. "It's a mob bank. And it belongs to Gentleman John Marcone, Accorded Baron of Chicago."

Chapter
Twenty-six

I'd been afraid it would come to something like this, though I'd held out hope that Nicodemus would come up with a better way of getting to where we needed to go. Like maybe burning down a building around our ears and hoping to open a Way at the last second. That would have been merely dicey.

Marcone was *dangerous*.

"Gentleman" Johnnie Marcone had clawed his way to the top of Chicago's outfit back when I had first set up business in town, and he had ruled the city's crime with an iron fist ever since, with an eye toward making organized crime safer, more efficient, and more businesslike. It worked. A lot of cops thought he had more power than the government. Those cops kept their mouths shut about it, for the most part, though, because he commanded more cops than the government, too.

Then, a few years back, he'd sought and gained the title of freeholding lord under the Unseelie Accords, the legal document that was the backbone of civilized relations between supernatural nations. He was the first vanilla human being on record as having done so, and he had claimed, fought for, and held Chicago against all comers thus far, as its Baron.

Though, to be fair, I'd been out of town for a lot of that time.

Still, I didn't think it would be smart to cross him if I wasn't prepared to go right to the mat, for keeps. Marcone commanded an army of thugs and hired killers, some of whom were truly excellent at their jobs. He kept a small squad of Einherjaren, dead-but-not-gone Viking warriors, on retainer, and I had seen them efficiently take on some of the toughest nasties I've ever encountered. He had at least one freaking Valkyrie on the payroll—and the man himself was ruthless, intelligent, and absolutely without fear.

I thought getting into it with Marcone was going to be about two steps shy of getting into it with Hades himself. But all I said out loud was, "Hoo boy."

"Problem, Dresden?" Nicodemus asked.

"Marcone is not someone to cross lightly," I said. "Not only that, but he's a member of the Accords."

"I'm not," Nicodemus said. "Not any longer."

"I am," I said. "Twice. As a Wizard of the White Council and as the Winter Knight."

"I'm sure the White Council will be stunned and disappointed should you not conform to their policy," Nicodemus said. "And as for Mab—you are, in effect, simply my tool during this operation. As far as she is concerned, any obligation you incur with regard to the Accords can be laid at my feet, not hers."

He was right, twice, which made me scowl. "My point

is," I said, "Marcone is not a man to be taken lightly. If you hit him, he hits you back. Harder."

"Indeed," Nicodemus said. "He has an excellent reputation. He would have made a fine monarch only a few centuries ago."

Good King John Marcone? I shuddered at the thought. "Let's say we hammer our way into his building," I said. "Fine. It's probably doable. Getting back out again is going to be the hard part—and even if we do *that*, it isn't over. He isn't going to forget, or let it go."

"Dresden's right," Karrin said. "Marcone doesn't suffer intrusions on his territory. Period."

"We will do what we have come to do," Nicodemus said calmly. "If necessary, reparations to the Baron can be considered once our mission is accomplished. I believe I can make the point to him that accepting such restitution will be more cost-effective than pursuing more personal collection efforts."

I traded a look with Karrin, and could see that she was thinking the same thing I was.

Nicodemus had abducted Marcone himself, not so many years back, as part of one of his schemes. Mab had, in fact, sent me to bail Marcone out, back when I'd just owed her a couple of favors. I still remembered Marcone as a helpless prisoner. The image had kind of stuck in my memory.

He would never forget that. There are some things money can't buy: One of them is redemption from the vengeance of Gentleman Johnnie Marcone.

And if Karrin and I went along with this plan, it would mean as much as declaring war on the Baron of Chicago.

"What do you think?" I asked her.

Karrin could do the math. She knew exactly what I was talking about. "Had to happen sometime."

"Heh," I said. "Right."

"I don't get it," Binder said. "Look, if he's a man of business, why don't we just make him a proposition and cut him in for a piece of the action?"

"A valid notion," Nicodemus said. "But it is not possible."

"Why not?"

"In the first place," Nicodemus said, "the vault houses materials belonging to more persons than our principal target alone. Marcone has become something of a notoriously neutral party in the affairs of the modern supernatural world. Svartalfheim, the White Court, Drakul, and a number of other individuals of similar weight have entrusted a portion of their wealth to his keeping, and he has given his word to protect it to the best of his ability."

"That's it, then," I said to Binder. "He won't bargain. Guy's a murderous asshole, but he's good to his word."

Binder settled back, frowning. "What's the other reason, then?"

"If he *let* us in, it would change the nature of the place," I said before Nicodemus could answer. "We're trying to open a Way into a jealously guarded vault. We probably won't be able to do it from a vault that's been opened to the public."

"Exactly," Nicodemus said. "Barring a few security systems requiring specific countermeasures, I have complete confidence that we can seize the building. Holding it until the job is done and escaping it with our hides is another matter, and that, Mr. Binder, is where you and your associates will play a critical role."

Binder grunted and leaned forward to study the map. "How long will I need to hold it?"

"An hour, at most," Nicodemus said.

"Barring anyone manipulating time on us between here and there," I put in.

Nicodemus gave me a sour frown and said, "We shall be finished in one hour—one way or the other." He pointed to a portion of the floor plans. "Here is the master vault door. That, Miss Valmont, is your responsibility—"

"Hang on," Binder said. "If you leave me playing doorman, how am I supposed to collect my backpack of jewels, eh? I can't go off to the Nevernever and leave my lads here behind me. That'll cut the connection between us. I'm not doing this job on salary."

"I suggest your partner carry and fill two packs," Nicodemus said. "I will undertake to carry your pack out myself and give it to you upon my return. As I am, with the possible exception of Grey, the one most likely to survive to escape, this arrangement would give you a greater chance of successfully receiving your payment than anyone else here."

Binder squinted at Nicodemus and sat back in his seat, obviously thinking it over. "What do you think, Ash?"

Hannah Ascher shrugged, which any red-blooded hetero male would have found utterly fascinating. It wasn't just me. "If you'll trust me to pick your share, I'm willing."

Binder grunted and then nodded slowly. "I like the red ones."

"I'll remember," Ascher promised.

I idly scratched at an itch on the back of my neck. "So what's the big deal with Valmont cracking the door? And why drag poor Harvey into this?"

"Poor Harvey," Nicodemus said, with all the sympathy of a bullet in flight, "was our principal's factor in Chicago. He had exclusive access to the vault in question, which is kept shut by the best vault door money can buy in combination with what is known as a retina scan. A retina scan—"

"We know what a retina scan is," Ascher said impatiently. "But why do you need it? Why not just blow the vault instead of going to all the trouble of getting Grey to duplicate the guy?"

"Same deal as before," I said. "We're trying to get into a secure vault, not one that's been blown the hell open already. If we alter the place in the real world too much, we screw up the Way to the one in the Nevernever." I glanced at Nicodemus and thumped a finger on the blueprint. "Our target has a private vault here?"

"Precisely. An inner security room inside the main vault. This location is one of several in which he acquires additional items for his collection by proxy," Nicodemus said.

I had to give Nick this much: He'd thought this business through, lining up like to like, the way you needed to do to make magic work. "So first we have to get to the main vault?"

"Through two security doors, which Miss Ascher will see to with her newly practiced spell," Nicodemus said, "the better not to activate the seismic sensors in the vault that will lock down the building more thoroughly and force us to take much more destructive measures to gain access."

I nodded. "Then Valmont does the door on the main vault, and Grey does the private security room with the retina scan." I blinked and eyed Grey. "Right down to his retinas, seriously?"

Grey looked up from where he sat in the shadows and gave me a modest smile.

I shuddered visibly. "You are an extremely creepy man," I said. I looked back at Nicodemus. "I can see a possible problem."

"Yes?"

"Marcone is not a dummy," I said. "He's gone up against supernatural powers more than once. He knows that sooner or later, he and I are going to get into it. He doesn't make mistakes often, and he never fails to learn from them. He'll have supernatural precautions as well as physical ones."

"Such as?" Nicodemus asked.

"If I was him," I said, "I'd have something rigged to shut down all the electronic gizmos and close off the vault as soon as the building's power got disrupted— which just might happen when Ascher and I start throwing magic around. In fact, I'd set it up to happen as soon as any amount of magic started flying."

"It would be smart," Binder said in agreement. "Don't think it'd be too hard to fix, either. Have circuits set up around the place, something delicate that would go out without too much trouble."

"Like the ones in cell phones or something," I added.

"Those things go to pieces if a wizard looks at them funny."

"Yeah," Binder said, nodding. "I can use one, but only just. Had to start keeping it powered off when I took up with Ash, here."

"Assuming such a . . . wizard alarm, I suppose, exists," Nicodemus said, "how shall we defeat it?"

"Not a problem for me," Binder said. "It wouldn't even blink. These two, though, we'd have to . . ."

I eyed Binder sourly and rubbed at the itch on my neck again.

"Sorry, mate," he said. He sounded genuine about it. "Thorn manacles," he said to Nicodemus. "You know the ones?"

"I have some in stock," Nicodemus said. "Though mine are svartalf make, not faerie. Steel. I suppose they'll keep the talent of you and Miss Ascher suppressed as much as possible. Simpler than keeping running water flowing over you both, in any case."

He gave me a small smirk when he said it. He'd once had me chained up under a freezing-cold stream to prevent me from using my talents to escape or make mischief. If another good man hadn't given himself in exchange for me, I might have died there. Thorn manacles were uncommon but by no means unattainable magical bindings that accomplished the same thing, dampening a wizard's powers to the point of uselessness.

And they hurt like a son of a bitch. In fact, if he had some that worked the same way but were made of steel, they were going to hurt *me* to an outstanding degree, given how they functioned.

I returned Nicodemus's smirk with a wintry smile.

Binder continued, either ignoring or not noticing the look between Nicodemus and me. "Once the two of them are inside, get them into a circle before the manacles come off," Binder said. "That will contain the excess energy when they work their mojo. It should help."

"Mmm," Nicodemus mused. "We'll have to change the entry plan. Dresden won't be able to provide a distraction. We'll have to use more"—he glanced toward the Genoskwa—"overt means."

In the darkness, a faint gleam of yellow appeared beneath the Genoskwa's eyes.

Hell's bells, the thing was smiling.

Karrin shot me a look. She was thinking the same thing I was: The Genoskwa wasn't going to distract anything, except by ripping its head off. Depending on when we went in, God only knew how many people might be in that bank—people with absolutely no knowledge of its provenance. Even the building's security forces wouldn't necessarily know they worked for the outfit. And hell, when you got right down to it, I wasn't willing to feed even a mobster to something like the Genoskwa at Nicodemus's behest.

I rubbed at my neck again and said, "Nah, I got it still."

"Excuse me?" Nicodemus said.

"Noisy distraction? I'll handle it. No sense showing our secret weapon early if we don't have to do it, right?"

Nicodemus smiled faintly. "What, wizard? Without your talents?"

"I hadn't planned on using them anyway," I said. "Could be someone was going to get hurt during this.

The White Council takes a pretty dim view of magic used for that kind of thing—and I have to think about my future. You want loud and obvious? Not a problem."

The Genoskwa's voice came rumbling from the shadows. "He's soft."

"He's smart," I said in harsh rejoinder. "The harder you hit things on the way in, the harder Marcone's going to be ready to hit back on the way out. Hell, if you make a big enough stink, you'll have the cops there, too. There are only about thirteen thousand of those guys running around Chicago, but I'm sure the eight of us can handle them. Right?"

The Genoskwa let out a low growl. "I am not afraid of them."

"Sure you aren't," I said. "That's why you cruised all over the place invisible the past two days, because you didn't care if you were spotted."

"Gentlemen," Nicodemus said, his voice raised and slightly tense. And then he paused, frowning, his head cocked partly to one side, as if trying to identify a distant sound.

Ascher suddenly looked up, frozen in the act of scratching her arm again, and said, "Dresden? Do you feel that?"

The itching on the back of my neck resolved itself into a full-on creepy sensation, the awareness of someone watching me. I closed my eyes and extended my other senses, reaching out with my talent to feel for magic in the air around me—and found the eavesdropping spell almost at once.

Ascher had already given us away with her comment, so there was no point in being cute about it. "Someone's listening in on us," I breathed, coming to my feet.

"Where?" Nicodemus spat.

Ascher pointed to the far end of the slaughterhouse. "There, not far. Just outside, I think."

The sensation abruptly vanished as the spell winked out of existence—but not before I'd found the spell's focus—the thaumaturgic version of the bug that had been planted so that the eavesdropper could hear us.

"Binder," Nicodemus said at once.

Binder had already produced a hoop of wire from his suit coat's pocket. He moved to a clear space of floor, gave it a toss with a flick of his wrist, and the wire unreeled and unfolded into a circle almost three feet across. It landed on the floor even as Binder spoke a few words, and filled with amber light.

Binder was a chump sorcerer, but he had one trick that he could do really, really well—summoning a small army of creatures from the Nevernever that he had somehow bound to his will. It took him less than two seconds to whistle up the first of his suits—humanoid figures dressed in something that resembled a badly fitted suit, their proportions and features looking almost normal, until one looked at them a little more closely. The demonic servitor flung itself up out of the circle like an acrobat emerging from a trapdoor in the stage, and Binder tapped his foot down onto the circle of wire in perfect time, releasing the suit from the circle's confinement as it tumbled clear. Then he lifted his foot and dropped it down again in metronomic time as a second suit emerged from the Nevernever, and a third, and a fourth, and so on.

"Spell's gone," Ascher reported. "He heard us. He's running."

"He's heard too much," Nicodemus said, and turned to Binder. "Can your associates track him?"

"Like bloodhounds," Binder confirmed.

Nicodemus nodded. "Kill him."

Binder let out a short whistle and cocked a finger in the direction Ascher had indicated. The suits needed no more indication than that. They bounded off in that direction with greater than human agility.

I jerked my head at Karrin and stalked away from the table.

"What?" she hissed.

In answer, I dug into the bandages over my arm until I found the object, hidden from me until I had finally focused my attention on it—a rounded, black Pente stone that had been worked into the bandages when they had been reapplied. There were a number of familiar runes painted over its dark surface in metallic gold. I'd used the exact same spell design myself more than once, back in the day, when I'd been learning how it worked.

"What's that?" Karrin asked.

"The bug," I hissed quietly. "The one the listener was using to hear us. It got put in the bandages over my arm when it was reset."

Her eyes widened. "But . . ."

"Yeah," I said, and watched as more of the suited servitors poured forth from the Nevernever to streak into the night in pursuit. "It's Butters. They're going to kill him."

Chapter

Twenty-seven

"**G**o," Karrin said. "I'll catch up."

"How are you going to find me?"

She gave me a quick roll of her eyes. "Harry, please."

Right. Karrin had been a Chicago cop for twenty years. She'd find me whether I wanted her to or not. I touched her shoulder, called upon Winter, and took off at a sprint, staff clenched in my right hand.

As I ran, I could feel the power of the Winter mantle infusing my body, my senses, and my thoughts. Binder's suits were hounding after the prey in a pack, moving in instinctive coordination, their leaders slowing the pace slightly until a few of the ones with a later start could catch up, the better to bring down the prey together.

I caught up to the rearmost suits and passed them before I'd even exited the slaughterhouse, which sent a rush of elation through me. Slowpokes. But they were necessary. I couldn't hunt Butters down by mys—

I faltered for a few steps, and forced multiplication tables to start running through my head. I wasn't hunting down Butters. I was keeping *them* from hunting him down. And I had to figure out a way to do it without overtly turning on Nicodemus and company and shaming Mab.

That particular line of reason seemed to interfere mightily with the flow of energy from the Winter mantle, as if it simply didn't understand why it was going to all this trouble for so incomprehensible a goal.

Butters is one of mine, I snarled at it, *and we're not letting these chumps kill him unless that's what I decide should happen.*

Territory and power—those were things that Winter could sink its teeth into. I regained my stride as we exploded from the exit of the slaughterhouse and into the near-silent mix of sleet, rain, and frozen, slippery cold that was a Midwest ice storm.

The ground outside the slaughterhouse was already freezing over; not in a uniform sheet, but in treacherous patches of various consistencies of nearly transparent slush, invisible ice, and wet concrete, with very few visible cues to differentiate between them. The streetlights gleamed off of all of them with benevolent cheer, and the suits started slipping at random, further slowing them. I adjusted my pace only enough to be sure of putting my feet on the least slippery option available at every stride, trusting the instincts of the mantle to guide me.

Butters was sprinting across the small gravel parking lot, maybe seventy yards ahead of his pursuers. I could recognize his build and his shock of dark hair from where I was, though he was wearing a long, billowing overcoat and a rather bulgy-looking backpack and moving more slowly than he should have been. In the lowering skies, the mixed rain and lumpy snow, the sounds seemed muffled and close, as if everything was happening indoors. I could hear Butters's quick, clean breaths, his pants of effort as he slowed, nearing the street.

I hoped he was about to throw himself into a getaway car. Instead, he fumbled at his backpack and spun in a comical circle trying to pull something off of it. As he whirled beneath the yellow cone of illumination cast by a streetlight, I saw him take a wide-looking skateboard off where it had been fastened to the pack and slam it to the concrete.

"You've got to be kidding me," I muttered. "A freaking skateboard?"

The suits saw it and surged ahead. I'd seen them move before, and they could pounce like mountain lions. They'd be within a long leap of him in seconds.

Butters threw a glance over his shoulder, his face pale, his eyes huge behind his glasses, and stepped hard onto the skateboard, setting it into motion. He fumbled at a short strap on the front of the board, crouching and taking hold of it with the same intensity as a water-skier about to be launched into motion.

"Go, go, go!" he screamed.

And then a small inferno of orange sparks erupted from the wheels of the skateboard, and the damned thing took off down the empty street at the speed of a motorcycle.

I felt my jaw drop open for a second—and then a bubbling chuckle rolled up out of my chest. Butters, it seemed, had been using more of my old artifice spells, doubtless learned from Bob the Skull. That particular one looked an awful lot like the one I'd put together in my one ill-advised attempt to create a wizardly classic: a flying broomstick. The experiment had damned near killed me, and scared me enough that I abandoned its use until I had a better understanding of the aerodynamics involved, but I'd never even considered applying it to something that wouldn't necessarily flip me upside down while in motion and carry me into buildings at suicidal speeds. Why had I never applied the same magic to a freaking bicycle?

Or to a skateboard?

Butters didn't have the kind of power it took to be even a serious sorcerer—but the little guy had knocked together a number of useful magical tools over the past couple of years, also with Bob's help, and it looked like those exercises had developed into a real gift for creating magical artifices. But how the hell was he powering the damned things? Wizardly tools like that were like toys that needed batteries to work, but Butters didn't have the strength to power any but the simplest toys. So what was he using as a battery?

Oh. Oh, *no*.

The suits let out howls of excitement and began lengthening their strides. They weren't done, not by a long shot, and they started curling the path of their pursuit, bounding over the fence surrounding the property, leaping over the landscaping of nearby buildings. I went with them, leaping the same fences. One of the suits slipped and hit the chain link at better than thirty miles an hour, with moderately gruesome results.

Another suit might have accidentally caught the end of my quarterstaff in the teeth as we both leapt a six-foot hedge, and wound up slamming into the side of an office building at the same pace, but it was pretty dark, what with the rain and sleet and snow and all, and I just wasn't entirely sure what happened. Heh.

By the time we hit the next cross street, I saw Butters fling out an arm. There was another glitter of orange sparks, this time in a long line, and I saw some kind of dark fiber whip out from his hand and wrap around a streetlight's pole. He leaned into it with a high-pitched, half-panicked whoop of excitement, and used the line to carry the racing skateboard through a tight ninety-degree turn without slowing down. There was another sparkle of orange campfire sparks along the length of the line, and the thing evidently let go of the pole, as he kept sailing down the street, heading north.

Suits were letting out hunting cries at regular intervals by now, and running unimpeded on streets that were still warm enough from the day's light to resist the ice. I knew that Binder could probably have forty or fifty of the damned things on the street by now, and that they were smart enough to communicate and work cooperatively. I had to hope that Butters would have the good sense to continue heading in one direction—every turn in the chase would give his more numerous pursuers a chance to maneuver, closing in around him, like hounds around a panicked rabbit.

He kept fleeing down the street, but the smooth surface that let him use his—and I can't believe I'm going to use this phrase—enchanted skateboard also gave an advantage to his pursuers. The street was still warm enough from the sunlight of the day, and the passage of early-evening traffic meant that the falling precipitation had been given less time to settle, and consequently ice had not yet begun to clog it. The suits and I began to close the distance, and I couldn't act to discourage them in the excellent lighting without risking observation.

Then came what I had feared might happen. A pair of suits, maybe a little leaner and faster than their companions, vectored in on the chase from a side street, using the cries of their companions to coordinate their attack. They bounded forward in a rush, and it was only because Butters had his left leg forward, and so was facing them as they came, that he saw them close on him.

I'll give the little guy credit. He didn't panic. Instead, he dropped his free hand into his coat, seized something, and smashed it to the street in his wake, shouting a word as he did. There was a flash of light on some kind of glass globe, and then it shattered on the concrete, expanding into a cloud of thick grey mist, just in front of his pursuers.

The two suits hit the mist, unable to avoid it in their surge of closing speed, and plunged into it and out the other side—where their steps abruptly slowed, and the pair of them stumbled to a halt, looking around them blearily as Butters and his orange-sparking skateboard whooshed on down the street.

As the rest of the pack passed the spot, the suits dodged around the cloud of grey mist, and the two who had stopped gave their packmates a startled, confused look and then took off in belated pursuit again, obviously straining to catch up. That was when I realized what I'd just seen, and I went by the cloud of mist cackling madly.

Mind fog. Better than ten years ago, a foe had used the

enchanted mist to blanket an entire Wal-Mart store, rendering the memory of everyone inside it temporarily nonfunctional and effectively blurring the previous hour or so of experience beyond recall. Bob and I had worked out the specifics of how the spell must have operated in the aftermath of the case. Obviously, Butters and Bob had, between them, figured out how to can the stuff.

Butters rocketed on down the street, dodging around a couple of slow-moving cars, used his lightpole-lariat again twice in quick succession, and careened onto Michigan Avenue, heading into the heart of downtown, where the towers and lights of Chicago burned brightest in the freezing haze.

That gave even the demonic suits pause. Cities aren't just streets and buildings—they are collectives of sheer will, of the determination of every person who helped build them and every soul whose work and life maintains them. To something from the Nevernever, a place like downtown Chicago is an alien citadel, a source of power and terror. Mordor, basically. (One does not simply walk into Mordor—except that was *exactly* what everyone in the story did anyway.)

Similarly, Binder's goons were not sufficiently impressed with the Loop to let it stop them from pursuing Butters. They put on a surge of speed and gained on him, and for a moment, it looked like they might nab him again—but he hurled a second glass globe of forget-me mist to the street and disrupted the pursuit at exactly the right moment. Butters let out a shriek of terrified defiance and shook his fist at his pursuers as several staggered in confusion, stumbling into their packmates.

Then the Genoskwa appeared out of nowhere on the sidewalk in front of a café and kicked a stone planter the size of a hot tub directly into Butters's path.

Butters had maybe a whole second to react and nowhere near enough time to steer around the planter. The Genoskwa had acted with calm, precise timing. Butters did the only thing he could do: He let go of the skateboard strap and leapt into the air.

He wasn't wearing padding and he didn't have a helmet. That dopey little skateboard had been moving at thirty miles an hour, and all that waited to receive him was cold asphalt. If he'd been in a car with an airbag, I'm sure he'd have been fine—but he wasn't.

I ground my teeth and prepared a spherical shield to catch him with—but while that would protect him from the fall, it would also mean that he could be briefly held inside it until his momentum was spent. Without the skateboard, the suits or the Genoskwa would catch him in a few heartbeats, and I would be forced to fight to defend him, bringing my mission to an unfortunate conclusion.

So be it. You don't leave friends, even friends twisted up with mistrust, to the monsters.

But instead of falling onto the street and splattering, or into my shield and getting us both subsequently killed, Butters's too-billowy overcoat flared with orange sparks and spread out into a giant, cupped wing shape. He windmilled his arms and legs with a high-pitched, creaking shout, and then tucked himself into a ball while the orange light seemed to gather the coat into a resilient sphere around him—one that bounced once when it hit the street, and then rolled several times, dumping him onto the street more or less on his feet.

The little guy darted straight away from the Genoskwa, for which I did not blame him, up the steps of the nearest building—as it happened, the Art Institute of Chicago. The nearest of the suits leapt at his unprotected back.

I flung my staff forward with a howl of *"Forzare!"* and smashed the suit with invisible power in midair, flinging him just over Butters's shoulder as he leapt. "Dammit!" I howled, with as much sincerity as I could muster— which wasn't much. "Clear my line of fire!"

Butters shot an aghast look over his shoulder at me, and stumbled away, fetching up against the northernmost of the two lion statues outside the Art Institute. He darted a look at the statue, licked his lips, and hissed something beneath his breath.

Orange light flooded out of the inner folds of his coat and promptly seeped into the bronze of the statue, con- firming how he was managing all of these tricks.

Bob.

Bob the Skull was running around loose, like some kind of bloody superhero sidekick.

Bob had been the one powering the skateboard. Bob had guided the ropes that had flown from Butters's wrist. Bob had manipulated Butters's coat to bring him in to a safe landing.

Damn. Bob was kind of awesome.

It only stood to reason. Though Bob was a spirit, he had always been able to manipulate physical objects—and if he had mostly only done so with fairly small, fairly light things in the past, like romance novels or his own skull, there was no reason that I knew that he might not have tried something larger. I'd always assumed he simply lacked the motivation.

But I'd rarely removed Bob from my lab for a *reason*. To be exercising that kind of control over the spirit, Butters had to be in possession of Bob's skull, like, *right now*. He was actually *carrying* the skull around, probably in that backpack, and that meant that Bob's allegiance was as fragile as Butters's ability to remain in physical possession of the skull itself. If someone like Nicodemus got hold of the skull, with Bob's centuries of experience and knowledge, I shuddered to think what my old friend might be used to accomplish.

Of course, that concern abruptly dwindled to a secondary issue as I realized what Butters had commanded the spirit to do.

Orange firelight-sparks suddenly erupted from the eyes of the enormous bronze lion. Then, moving exactly as if it had been a living beast, the thing turned its head toward me, crouched, and let out an enormous and authentically leonine roar.

"Oh, crap," I said.

"Hold them off!" Butters shouted.

The lion roared again.

"Dammit, Butters," I snarled under my breath, "I'm helping!"

And then several tons of living bronze predator, guided by the intelligence and will of the most powerful spirit of intellect I had ever encountered, flung itself directly at my head.

Chapter

Twenty-eight

It had been a good long while since I'd had a freaking lion coming at me, and at the time it had been one of the genuine flesh-and-blood variety, from the zoo. I'd never had something made entirely of metal try to kill me before, unless you counted the instruments of the occasional would-be vehicular homicide that came my way, and never both at the same time—so actually that made this a first.

And that's important in a job. Fresh challenges. What would I do without them?

Without the Winter mantle on my side, I think Bob might have taken my head off of my shoulders. But instead, I ducked, fast enough and low enough to avoid the enormous paw that flashed toward me in anticipation of the move, and Bob flew over me, crashing into a pair of Binder's suits with juggernaut enthusiasm. They went flying like ninepins, and the bronze lion whirled toward me, far too fast for something so massive, and crouched to leap at me again.

And one of the lion's golden orange glowing eyes, the

one away from the street, shivered down in the barest little wink imaginable.

Bob *got it.*

My former lab assistant thundered, "Die, traitor!" and then roared again.

"Watch out, he's loose!" I screamed to a nearby suit, reeling back toward him and fighting to keep the sudden grin off my face. "He'll tear us all apart!"

"Rargh!" Bob screamed and came rushing at me again.

I flung myself to one side at the last second, when the suit wouldn't see Bob coming until it was too late. The bronze lion smashed into the suit, sending it tumbling in a whirl of broken limbs, to smash into the side of the Art Institute. It exploded into gelatinous clear goo, its physical vessel simply too mangled to enable the spirit Binder had summoned to continue animating it, and the lion let out a roar of triumph, and turned toward the next nearest suits.

"I'll get him!" I shouted. I pointed my staff at Bob and snarled, *"Fuego!"* A blast of pure fire erupted from the staff, missed the rampaging lion statue by inches, and took a pair of suits full-on, setting them ablaze and causing them to issue weird howls of frustration and rage as it began to consume their physical forms.

Furious, the burning suits flung themselves at Bob, and the hunting-pack mentality of the demons prompted the others to leap at the rampaging statue as well. Bob roared, his eyelights blazing merrily, and started batting them around like Mister playing with multiple catnip lures on a string.

I hopped back from the immediate vicinity of the

havoc and looked around wildly for Butters. I checked his last direction but saw nothing—except an empty plastic sports-drink bottle rolling slowly down the sidewalk, pushed by the mild wind coming in from the north, exactly like the kind I used to store a potion in when I made one.

Butters was in the wind. Hell, maybe literally. It had been a long time since I'd brewed that escape potion that had saved me from a toad demon, but if I'd had a twenty, I'd have bet it against a piece of bubble gum that Butters had duplicated my old formula and used it to pull a quick vanishing act in the confusion.

Because confusion there was: The explosions and roaring and noise had done exactly what I had hoped they would, and attracted attention. Though the muffling effect of the weather had dulled the sounds, and though it was well after business hours, that didn't mean that the area around us was wholly empty of life. Lights had begun to flick on. Faces had begun to appear at windows in nearby buildings.

One of the cardinal points of common sense, in the supernatural world, is that you don't get yourself involved with mortal authorities. The average individual mortal (or twenty) might not be a match for a real supernatural predator. I'm pretty sure the serious bad guys, like the hulking, hairy one standing in the shadows across the street from the Art Institute, could take on a riot's worth of mortals without hesitation, and expect victory. But in a city like Chicago, starting a rumble with humanity wouldn't mean fighting a score of mortals, or a couple of hundred. It would mean thousands, and more important, it would mean tangling with those who had the training and equipment to be a genuine threat.

People had actually begun to appear on the street, from inside the café and a nearby sandwich shop. Cell phones were coming out. And Chicago PD had maybe half a dozen stations within a mile of where I stood.

"What are you waiting for?" I shouted toward the Genoskwa, and pointed at the animated statue. "Lend a hand, big guy!"

The Genoskwa glowered at me for a second, and then at the rampaging Bob. There was a flash of ugly yellow tusks, a glitter of malicious and angry eyes, and then the creature faded from sight, turning as it vanished, and starting up the street in the direction Butters had last been going.

Worse, there was a sound of rushing wind overhead, and something dark and swift passed between me and some of the higher lights in the area, sending a multitude of wavering, flickering shadows across the street. I squinted up into the rain and mist, and saw nothing but a large, winged form, moving fast, in the same direction.

Well, crap.

Nicodemus and Anduriel had taken to the air. I had no doubt that the Genoskwa could track Butters as well as any hound, and that escape potion, if that's what he'd used, would only transport him a relatively short distance, maybe a couple of blocks. It would be only a matter of time before Nicodemus spotted Butters or the Genoskwa picked up his trail—and he no longer had Bob to propel his skateboard or cover his back.

I ground my teeth, and Bob sent another one of Binder's suits flying past me. I ducked absently. My instincts told me to get moving again, as quickly as possible. I told them to shut the hell up. I could go sprinting off in some direction, but that was unlikely to result in accomplishing anything. I took a moment to lever the Winter mantle away from my thoughts, and found them clearer. The Winter Knight was not needed here.

I ran down the street to the discarded sports bottle and snagged it. Just as I did, one of those mini-SUVs sliced through the slush in the middle of the avenue, sliding only slightly to one side as it braked, and Karrin stuck her head out the window. "Get in!"

I ran for the vehicle as Karrin stared in fascination at the sight of more than a dozen suits swarming over the lion, struggling to overturn it, and the huge thing twisting and spinning like a dervish trying to keep them off, orange eyelights blazing.

"Huh," Karrin said. "That's new."

I slammed the door shut and said, "It's Bob. Butters let him off the chain."

"Is that good?" she asked.

I stuffed my staff mostly into the back and fumbled with the bottle. "It's exciting, anyway. Butters gave them the slip, but Nicodemus and the Genoskwa are on his trail."

"Is our cover blown?"

"Not yet," I said. "We're still bad guys. At least, enough to satisfy Mab. You know how confusing fights can be."

"Hah," Karrin said. "What's the plan?"

"Find Butters. Get me to somewhere I can step out of

the rain and give me a second to get a tracking spell running."

"No need," she said and started driving. "I know where he's going."

I blinked. "Where?"

"You're Butters. You know basically everything that's been going on in Chicago for the past dozen years. You've got a bunch of demons and supernatural bad guys including the Knights of the Blackened Denarius after you," she said. "Where would you go?"

I frowned, thinking. She was right about that. If Butters had been working that closely with Bob, he'd know pretty much anything the skull did, and he'd recognize Deirdre and Nicodemus by name—hell, he must have, which probably explained his mistrust. I'd declined to tell him anything about what I'd gotten Karrin into, and he'd listened in on me spending a day with a bunch of supercriminals and sitting down at a table with Nicodemus Archleone.

And where in this city would be the best place to go if one wanted protection from Fallen angels?

"Hell's bells," I breathed. "He's going to Michael's."

"Yeah," Karrin said, real anger in her voice. "Dammit, he knows better."

I blinked several times and then felt my jaw drop as a flash of intuition hit me. "The Swords are there, aren't they? And Butters knows it."

Her jaw tensed. She eyed me and gave me a single short nod. "I wanted one other person to know, in case something happened to me. My place isn't secure enough, even with what the Paranetters can do. And I'm sure as hell not going to trust those things to Marcone's people. Anything bad that tries to get into Michael's place has got a world of hurt coming down. It was the best I could think of."

"If they catch Butters before he gets there," I said, "he's dead. If you're wrong about where he's going, he's dead."

"And if we stop for a couple of minutes for you to get your mojo together, we might get there too late to do anything," she said, and bit her lip. She was coaxing as much speed from the little truck as she could, in this weather, its all-wheel drive churning steadily. "What do you think we should do?"

This was my fault. If I'd brought Butters in, at least far enough to understand what was going on, he wouldn't have gone poking around himself. But dammit, how could I have done it without . . .

Augh.

I hated this cards-close-to-the-chest thing.

I suck at cards. I'm more a Monopoly sort of guy.

"I hadn't talked to Michael in years," I said. "The first day I do, I set off a chain of events that has some heavy-weight monsterage heading right for his house."

"Yeah," Karrin said, "I noticed that."

"Maybe it isn't a coincidence," I said.

She arched one pale brow. "Faith, Harry? You?"

"Oh, blow me," I said, scowling. "Drive."

She bared her teeth in a fierce smile and said, "Buckle up."

I did, as the fine, freezing rain began to turn to heavy sleet.

Chapter
Twenty-nine

We were two blocks from Michael's place, back in the residential neighborhoods, when a cab all but teleported out of the sleet, moving too fast. It rolled through a stop sign and forced Karrin to slam on the brakes and swerve to avoid a collision.

The little SUV did its best, but it slid on the sleet-slickened street, bounced over the curb, through a wooden privacy fence, and wound up with its front wheels in someone's emptied pool.

Karrin slapped the vehicle into reverse and tried to pull out, but the rear tires spun uselessly on the ice. "Dammit!" she snarled. "Go. I'm right behind you!"

I grabbed my staff and leapt out into the sleet without hesitating, wrapping myself in Winter as I went running through the storm and into the hazy pseudo-darkness. I went straight for Michael's place, sprinting down a sidewalk briefly, and then cutting through yards, bounding over fences and parked cars (Parkour!) as I went.

I got to the Carpenters' home just as the cab that had caused our wreck slid to a gradual stop a few houses past

Michael's. Butters popped out of the back and threw several wadded bills at the driver, then put his head down and sprinted toward Michael's house. He looked pale and shaky. I sympathized. That potion had left me feeling like I'd just ridden a couple of dozen roller coasters, all at once, with a bad hangover. He hadn't run five steps before one of his feet went out from under him on the frozen, slippery sidewalk, and he went down hard. I heard his head rap the concrete, and then felt a sympathetic pang at the explosion of air from his lungs as the fall knocked the wind out of him.

I didn't slow down until I was close to Butters, sweeping my gaze around the neighborhood, and finding it quiet and still.

"Jesus!" Butters blurted out as I got close. He flinched away from me, raising one hand as if to ward off a blow, reaching for something inside his coat with the other.

"Hell's bells, Butters," I said on a note of complaint. "If I was going to hurt you, I'd have blasted you from way the hell over there."

"You *tried* . . . ," he wheezed, hand still poised inside his coat. "Stay . . . back. I . . . mean it."

"Hell's bells, you are smarter than this." I sighed and offered him my hand. "Come on. They're bound to be right behind you. You can't stay out here. Let me help you up."

He stared up at me for a second, clearly a little dazed from the fall, and just as obviously terrified.

I made an impatient clucking sound and stepped forward.

Butters fumbled what looked like a glass Christmas

ornament from his coat's inner pocket and flicked it at me weakly.

Winter was still upon me. I bent my knees a little and caught it on the fly, careful not to break it. "Whoa," I said. "Easy there, killer. I'd rather not have us both forget why we're standing out here in the sleet."

He stared up at me, struggling to draw a steady breath. "Harry . . ."

"Easy," I said. "Here." I passed the ornament back to him.

He blinked at me.

"Come on," I said. I bent down, got a hand under his arm, and more or less hauled the little guy to his feet. He slipped again at once, and would have fallen if I hadn't held him up. I steadied him, guiding his steps off the treacherous concrete and onto the grass in front of one of the houses. "There, easy. Come on, let's get you out of the cold at least."

He groaned and said, "Oh, God, Harry. You're not . . . You haven't . . ." We stumbled a few more steps and then he said, "I'm an idiot. I'm sorry."

"Don't be sorry," I said, looking around us warily. "Be inside."

"How bad have I screwed things up?" he asked.

"We move fast enough, nothing that can't be fixed," I said. Impatient, I ducked down enough to get a shoulder beneath his arm and more or less lifted him up, dragging him along with his feet barely touching the ground toward the Carpenters' yard.

Twenty yards.

Ten.

Five.

The wind rushed. Something shaped like black sails billowed in the sleet, and then swirling shadow receded, and Nicodemus Archleone stood between us and safety, a slender-bladed sword held in his right hand, blade parallel with his leg. He faced me with a small smile.

Behind him, his shadow stretched out for twenty yards in every direction, writhing in slow waves.

I drew up short. Butters's legs swung back and forth.

I took a step back and looked over my shoulder.

The Genoskwa blurred into vision through the thick sleet, maybe twenty feet back, staying in the shadows of a large pine tree, his enormous shaggy form blending into its darkness. I could see the gleam of his eyes, though.

"Ah, Dresden," Nicodemus purred. "You caught him. And in the nick of time."

I set Butters down warily, and kept him close to my side. The little guy didn't move or speak, though I could feel him shuddering with sudden intelligent terror.

"The little doctor," Nicodemus said. "Quite a resourceful rabbit, is he not?"

"He's quick," I said. "And not much of a threat. There's no reason not to let him go."

"Don't be absurd," Nicodemus said. "He's heard entirely too much—and my files on him say that he's been associated with Marcone's Chicago Alliance. Only an idiot wouldn't recognize a potentially lethal security leak." He tilted his head to one side. "He dies."

The Genoskwa let out a hungry, rumbling growl.

Butters stiffened. He did not look behind him. I didn't blame him. I didn't want to look back there either.

Nicodemus was enjoying this. "It seems, Dresden," he said, "that it is time for you to make a choice. Shall I make it easier for you?"

"What'd you have in mind?" I asked.

"Practicality," Nicodemus said. "Give him to me. I will take him from here. It will be quick and merciful." His eyes shifted to Butters. "It's nothing personal, young man. You became involved in something larger than you. That is the price you pay. But I've no grudge with you. You will simply stop."

Butters made a quiet, terrified sound.

"Or," Nicodemus said, "you can breach Mab's given word, wizard." He smiled. "In which case, well, I have no need of you."

"Without me," I said, "you'll never get through the second gate."

"Once I kill you," Nicodemus said, "I'm quite certain Mab will loan me her next Knight or another servant as readily as she did you, if it means a chance to make good on her word. Choose."

"I'm thinking about it," I said.

Nicodemus opened one hand, a gracious gesture, inviting me to take my time.

Giving him Butters wasn't on the table. Period. But fighting him did not seem like a good idea either. With Nicodemus on one side and the Genoskwa on the other, I did not like my chances at all. Even with the Winter Knight's mantle, I didn't know if I could have beaten either of these guys, let alone both of them at once.

If I gave him Butters, I might live. If I didn't, both of

us were going to die, right here next door to Michael's house.

I was out of options.

"You take the guy behind us," I muttered to Butters.

The little guy swallowed, and jerked his head in a tiny nod, gripping his Christmas ornament carefully.

Nicodemus nodded, his dark eyes glittering. The point of the slender sword swept up, lithe as a snake's flickering tongue, and his shadow began to dance and waver in sudden agitation. The Genoskwa let out another rumbling growl and stepped forward. I gripped my staff, and Butters's tremors abruptly stilled into an electrified tension.

And then Karrin stepped out of the sleet with her rocket launcher prepped and resting on her shoulder, aimed directly at Nicodemus.

"Hi," she said. "I really don't like you very much, Denarian."

"Hah," I said to Nicodemus. "Heh, heh."

His eyes slid from me to Karrin and back. His smile widened. "Ms. Murphy," he said. "You won't shoot."

"Why not?" Karrin asked brightly.

"Because it is obvious to me that you love him," Nicodemus said. "That weapon will kill the wizard, as well as your friend the doctor, if you fire it. At that range, I'm not at all certain that you would survive the blast, either."

Karrin seemed to regard that offering thoughtfully. Then she said, "You're right," and took several steps closer. "There. That should just about do it, don't you think?"

Nicodemus narrowed his eyes. "You wouldn't."

Karrin spoke in a very low, very calm voice. "People do crazy things for love. I'd rather kill us all and take you with us than let you harm him." Her voice became a bit sharper, and she took another pair of quick strides nearer Nicodemus. "Take one step closer, Tall, Dark, and Furry, and I blow us all to hell right now."

I checked over my shoulder, to see the Genoskwa pause in the act of slipping a little closer. Its cavern-eyes glittered in silent rage.

Karrin took a couple of slow steps toward Nicodemus, her eyes strangely bright. "Crazy, crazy things. Don't push me."

Nicodemus's smile turned into a smirk. "You proceed from a false assumption," he said. "You assume that your toy can actually threaten me or my companion."

Guy had a point, even if I didn't want to admit it. With that Noose around his neck, I was pretty sure Nicodemus would smirk just as hard at a flamethrower, or a giant meat grinder, for that matter.

"Actually, you're the one proceeding from a false assumption," Karrin countered in that same deathly calm voice, a decidedly odd light in her eyes, still approaching. "You think I'm holding a rocket launcher."

And with that she knocked some kind of concealed cap off the back of the rocket launcher's tube, and from its length withdrew a sword.

Check that. She withdrew a Sword.

It was a Japanese-style katana blade, set into a wooden cane sheath, in the same style as that of the apocryphal Zatoichi. Even as the false rocket launcher casing fell to the ground, the Sword's blade sprang free of its sheath, and as it did, *Fidelacchius*, the Sword of Faith, blazed with furious white light.

But more important, the *presence* of the Sword suddenly filled the night, a nearly subaudible thrumming like the after-vibration of a bass guitar string. It wasn't something that could be heard, precisely, or seen, or felt on the skin—but its presence was absolute, unquestionable, filling the sleet-streaked air. It was power, bone-deep, earth solid, and terrible in its resolution.

I think it was that power that wiped the smirk from Nicodemus's face.

His eyes widened in dismay. Even his shadow abruptly went statue-still.

Karrin's bid to narrow the distance between them as she had been speaking meant that she was only a few strides away. She closed in, her feet sure, barely seeming to touch the icy ground, and he barely lifted his blade to a defensive counter in time. The swords met in a clash of steel and a blaze of furious light, and she carried her momentum into him with a full-body check against his center of gravity.

"Watch the big guy," I hissed to Butters, and took a step toward Nicodemus and Karrin—then froze in place.

Nicodemus slipped on the treacherous ground as Karrin slammed into him, but he swept a leg back, dropped one knee to the ground, and prevented himself from falling. She pressed her advantage, their swords locked, each blade exerting lethal pressure against the other.

I didn't dare intervene. The least slip or mistake in balance from either of them would mean that the two razor-sharp blades would slice like scalpels into unprotected flesh.

I watched them strain silently against each other, strength against strength. Karrin wasn't relying on upperbody strength to get it done. Her arms were locked in tight against her body, her weight and her legs pressing forward against Nicodemus, and her two-handed grip on *Fidelacchius* gave her a significant leverage advantage against his one-handed grip. The edge of her sword pressed closer to his face with each straining heartbeat, until a thin, bright ribbon of scarlet appeared on Nicodemus's cheek.

He showed her his teeth, and the strain on his arm quivered through his entire body as he pushed the Sword back a precious half inch from his skin. "So," he hissed, "the burnout thinks she has found her new calling."

She didn't say anything back. Karrin's never been a big one for backtalking the bad guys without a damned good reason. It's not her fault. She's a practical soul. She took a slow, contained breath, and kept up the pressure, veering the blades, altering the direction slightly, so that the locked swords began a slow descent toward Nicodemus's throat.

"And you think you deserve to join the ranks of real Knights of the Sword," Nicodemus said, his voice smooth and confident. "You battered, scarred, broken thing. In my centuries I've learned exactly what is needed in a real Knight. You haven't got what it takes. And you know that. Or you'd have taken up the Sword before now."

Her eyes blazed, bright blue in her pale, frightened face, and she leaned forward, pressing the Sword closer to his neck, and the beating artery there. I'd seen how sharp the katana's blade was. It would take a feather's pressure and the movement of a blade of grass to open Nicodemus's neck once that steel reached his skin.

"You've never done this before," he said. "Been this close, this tense, this still—not in earnest. Do you know how many times I've talked to novices exactly like you, in situations almost exactly like this? I've forgotten more about real sword fighting than this pale modern world knows."

Karrin ignored him. She shifted her hips the barest fraction, seeking a slightly different angle of pressure. The blazing Sword dipped another fraction of an inch closer.

"Dresden," Nicodemus said, "I'm giving you ample chance to call off your dog before I put her down." His eyes flicked to me. "End the little doctor and come back to headquarters. There's no reason I should have to kill all three of you."

I ground my teeth. Getting myself killed defending Butters was one thing. Taking Karrin with me was something else. But I knew her. I knew what choice she would make, without needing to talk to her about it.

Karrin didn't let the monsters take her people, either.

But there just wasn't a good option open to me. The Genoskwa wasn't far from us, and the damned thing was fast. Even if Butters ran for the safety of Michael's place right now, he'd never get there before it caught him—and I couldn't slow the huge thing down with magic, either.

I only had one choice.

"All right," I croaked. "Dammit, all right."

I grabbed Butters and threw him out in front of me, pointing my staff at him and calling forth my will. The runes blazed up with the pale green-white light of the crystals beneath Demonreach, from whence the wood for the staff had come.

"Sorry about this, Butters," I said. "Nothing personal."

Nicodemus's eyes widened. Karrin's gaze flicked toward me for an instant, disbelieving and then resolute.

"Harry?" Butters asked.

"Forzare!" I thundered, and unleashed a blast of unseen force from the staff.

It took Butters full in the chest, hitting him like a charging bull and hurling him through the sleet—and over the little white picket fence into the nearest corner of the Carpenters' yard.

Everything happened in the same instant.

Nicodemus's left arm blurred and produced a short-barreled pistol from somewhere on his body. He jammed it into Karrin's belly and pulled the trigger half a dozen times.

I let out a scream of defiance and drew that monster revolver from my duster even as the Genoskwa came charging toward me. The Winter mantle made me faster than I could ever have been on my own, but even so there was no time for anything but a hip shot. The Genoskwa was maybe three feet away when the gun went off, thundering like a high-powered rifle. Then the huge creature hit me like a freight train, picking me up in its onslaught like a piece of litter being towed along by the breeze, and carried me across the street and into the side of the neighbor's minivan.

Metal crashed and crunched. Glass broke. Silver lightning ran through my body without causing me any real
pain. The carnivore stench of the Genoskwa filled my
nose. My arms slammed against the vehicle, but I hung
on to the pistol, shoved it against the creature's torso, yet
before I could shoot, it got hold of my wrist, its huge
hands wrapping my forearm as if I'd been a toddler, and
slammed it against the minivan, pinning the pistol there.
Its other hand landed on my head, claws pressing into my
skin as the thick fingers tightened on my skull like a nut-
cracker.

"Hold!" I heard Nicodemus shout, his voice sharp.

The Genoskwa let out a low growl. It had to turn its
shoulders and twist at the waist to look back at him, a
simian gesture—there was just too much muscle on that
huge neck to allow it the full range of motion. As a result,
I was able to see past it.

Karrin, apparently unhurt, still stood, and she had *Fidelacchius* pressed against Nicodemus's throat.

I blinked, and felt a sudden surge of ferocious pride.

She'd *beaten* him.

"I may be no true Knight," Karrin snarled into the
sudden silence, her voice tight with pain. "But I'm the
only one here. Tell the gorilla to let Dresden go or I take
your head off and give the Noose back to the Church
along with your Coin."

Nicodemus stared at her for a moment. Then he
opened his hands, slowly, and the sword and pistol both
tumbled to the frozen ground. The sleet rattled down in
silence.

"I surrender," he said quietly, his voice mocking. He

tilted his head slightly toward Butters. "And I relinquish my claim on the blood of the innocent. Have mercy on me, O Knight."

"Tell the Genoskwa to let him go," Karrin said.

Nicodemus held out his hand. The swarming shadows around him abruptly surged, condensed, flooded toward him. They gathered in his palm, and an instant later, a small silver coin gleamed there, marked with a black smudge in the shape of some kind of sigil. Without looking away from Karrin, he dropped the Coin, and it fell to the icy sidewalk without bouncing, as if it had been made from something far heavier than lead.

"Let Dresden go," Karrin said.

Nicodemus smiled, still, his eyes and hands steady. He reached up and undid the Noose tied about his throat, and let it fall to the ground beside the Coin.

Karrin bared her teeth. "Let him go. I'm not going to ask again."

Nicodemus smiled and smiled, and said, "Crush his skull. Make it hurt."

The Genoskwa turned back toward me, his eyes blazing from back beneath his cavernous brow, and his fingers tightened on my skull. I dropped my staff and tried to reach up to pry his hand off my head, but quickly realized that I was hilariously outclassed in the physical strength department. If I strained with my entire body, I might have a chance against one of the Genoskwa's fingers. I tried that. The vise tightened. My breathing turned harsh as red cracks began to spread through the silvery sensation.

"But I've surrendered," Nicodemus assured Karrin.

"It's very clear, what you must do." His smile had returned, and his voice dripped contempt. "Save me, O Knight."

"You son of a bitch," Karrin snarled. Her breath had begun to come in gulps. "You son of a bitch."

Pain finally began to hammer through the mantle of Winter. I heard myself make an animal sound as the Genoskwa's grip tightened. His breathing was getting faster and harsher, too. He was enjoying this.

My groan shook Karrin, visibly, her body reacting to the sound.

I saw it coming, what Nicodemus was doing. I tried to warn her, but as I began to speak, the Genoskwa rapped my head back against the minivan and nothing came out.

"Save me," Nicodemus said again, "and watch him die."

"Damn you!" Karrin snarled.

Her hips and shoulders twisted, to deliver the lethal slash.

The light of the blade died away as abruptly as that of an unplugged lamp. The thrum of power that resonated through the very air vanished.

Nicodemus rolled, moving like a snake, anticipating her perfectly and flowing away from the Sword with a sinuous motion of spine and shoulder. Karrin was thrown slightly off-balance by the lack of resistance, and his hands swept up and seized her wrists.

The pair of them struggled for a second, and then *Fidelacchius* swept up high, over Karrin's head. Her expression whitened in horror as she saw the Sword, now gleaming with nothing more than ordinary light.

Then, guided by Nicodemus's hands, the ancient Sword came smashing down onto the concrete of the sidewalk, the flat of the blade striking the frozen stone.

It shattered with a rising shriek of protesting metal, shards flickering in the streetlights. Pieces of the blade went spinning in every direction, sparkling reflected light through the darkness. Karrin stared at it with unbelieving eyes.

"Ah," Nicodemus said. The wordless sigh was a slow, deep expression of utter satisfaction.

Awful silence fell.

The Sword of Faith was no more.

Chapter
Thirty

Sleet rattled down.

A dog howled, somewhere a few blocks away, a lost and lonely sound.

Karrin's breath exploded from her in a sob, her blue eyes wide and fixed on the shattered pieces of the blade.

"Judge not, lest ye be judged, Miss Murphy," Nicodemus purred. And then he slammed his head into hers.

She reeled back from the blow, and was brought up short by Nicodemus's grip on her arm.

"It is not the place of a Knight to decide whether or not to take the life given to another," Nicodemus continued. Before she could recover, he struck her savagely, the heel of his hand cracking into her jaw with an audible crunching sound. "Not your place to condemn or consign."

Karrin seemed to gather herself together. She flicked a quick blow at Nicodemus's face, forcing him to duck, and then their hands engaged in a complex and swift-moving series of motions that ended with Karrin's left arm held out straight, while she was forced down to her knees on the freezing sidewalk.

I'd never seen her lose when it came to grappling for a lock. Never.

"I'm not sure what would have happened if you'd simply struck, without that condemnation," Nicodemus continued, "but it would seem that in the moment of truth, your intent was not pure." He twisted his shoulders in a sudden, sharp motion.

Karrin screamed, briefly, breathlessly.

I struggled against the Genoskwa's crushing grip. I might as well have been a puppy, for all the effect my best efforts had on the thing. I gathered my will and flung a half-formed working of power against him, but again, the energy grounded itself harmlessly into the earth as it struck him.

I could do nothing.

Nicodemus twisted Karrin, tilted his head to one side, and then drove his heel against her knee with crushing strength.

I heard bones and tendons parting at the blow.

Karrin choked out another sound of pain, and crumpled to the ground, broken.

"I was afraid, for a time, that you actually *would* leave the Sword out of it," Nicodemus said. He bent and recovered the Noose calmly, fastening it around his neck as casually as a businessman putting on his tie. "Survivors of Chichén Itzá—and there were more than a few, in part thanks to your efforts—describe your contribution to that conflict as impressive. You were obviously ready and in the right, that night. But you were never meant for more. Most Knights of the Cross serve for less than three days. Did you know that? They aren't always killed—they simply fulfill their purpose and go their way." He leaned down closer to her and said, "You should have had the grace to do the same. What drove you to take up the Sword, when you knew you weren't worthy to bear it? Was it pride?"

Karrin shot him a fierce glare through eyes hazed with pain and tears, and then looked over at me.

He straightened, arching an eyebrow. "Ah, of course," he said, his tone dry—yet somehow filled with venomous undertones. "Love." Nicodemus shook his head and picked up his sword with one hand, and the Coin with the other. "Love will be the downfall of God Himself."

Karrin snarled weakly, and flung the broken hilt of *Fidelacchius* at Nicodemus's head. He snapped his sword up, flicking it contemptuously away from him. The wooden handle landed in the Carpenters' yard.

Nicodemus stepped closer to Karrin, dropping the point of his sword again, aiming it at her. As he did, blackness slithered down his body again, onto the ground, his shadow spreading out around him like a stain of oil over pure water.

Karrin fumbled backward, away from him, but she could barely move with only one arm and one leg functioning. The wet sleet plastered her hair to her head, made her ears stick out, made her look smaller and younger.

I kicked at the Genoskwa through the red haze over my vision. With Winter upon me, I can kick cinder blocks to gravel without thinking twice. It was useless. He was all mass and muscle and rock-hard hide.

"Face it, Miss Murphy," Nicodemus said, keeping pace

with her. His shadow swarmed all over the ground around her, surrounding her. "Your heart"—the tip of his sword dipped toward it by way of illustration— "simply wasn't in the right place."

He paused there, long enough to give her time to see the sword thrust coming.

She faced him, her eyes fierce and frightened, her face pale with pain.

And the front door of the Carpenters' house opened.

Nicodemus's dark eyes flickered up at once, and stayed focused on the front porch.

Michael stood in the doorway to the house for a brief moment, leaning on his cane, surveying the scene. Then he limped down the steps and out onto the walk leading from the front porch to the mailbox. He moved carefully and steadily in the sleet, right up to the gate in the white picket fence.

He stopped there, maybe three feet from Nicodemus, regarding him steadily.

Sleet struck and melted into rain on his flannel shirt.

"Let them go," Michael said quietly.

Nicodemus's mouth turned up at one corner. His dark eyes shone with a dangerous light. "You have no power here, Carpenter. Not any longer."

"I know," Michael said. "But you're going to let them go."

"And why should I do that?"

"Because if you do," Michael said, "I'll walk out this gate."

Even where I was, I could almost see the blaze of hatred that flared out of Nicodemus's eyes. His shadow went insane, flickering from side to side, surging up the white picket fence like an incoming tide chewing at a stone cliff.

"Freely?" Nicodemus demanded. "Of your own choice and will?"

A critical point. If Michael willingly divested himself of angelic protection, there would be nothing his bodyguards could do. Angels have terrible power—but not over free will. Michael would be helpless.

Just like Shiro had been helpless.

"Michael," I grated. I was under some pressure. I sprayed a lot more spittle than I thought I would. "Don't do it."

Michael gave me a small smile and said chidingly, "Harry."

"There's no point," Karrin gasped, her voice thin and breathless, "in you dying too. He'll just come after us again, later."

"You'd both do the same for me," Michael said, and looked up at Nicodemus with that same quiet smile.

And then the sleet just . . . stopped.

I don't mean it stopped sleeting. I mean that the sleet stopped *moving*. The half-frozen droplets hung in the air, suspended like millions of tiny jewels. The slight wind vanished. The howling dog's voice cut off as abruptly as if someone had flipped a switch.

At the same time, a man appeared, outside the little gate. He was tall and lean with youth, broad-shouldered like a professional swimmer. His features were porcelain-fine. His hair was glossy black and curling, his skin a rich, dark caramel color, and his eyes glittered silver-green.

There was no fanfare about his appearance. One moment nothing was there, and the next moment he was.

His presence was as absolute as it was abrupt, as if the light of the street somehow picked him out more clearly, more sharply, than anyone else there. Even if the abrupt cessation of movement in the physical world hadn't been enough to tip me off, I could feel the power in him, radiating from him like light from a star.

He'd appeared to me in many different forms, but there was no possibility of mistaking his presence, his identity.

Mister Sunshine. The archangel Uriel.

His gaze was focused exclusively on Michael, and his expression was anguished.

"You need not do this," he said, his voice low, urgent. "You have given enough and more than enough already."

"Uriel," Michael said, nodding his head deeply. "I know."

The angel held up his hand. "If you do this, I can take no action to protect you," he said. "And this creature will be free to inflict upon you such pain as even you could not imagine."

A sudden, sunny smile lit Michael's face. "My friend . . ."

Uriel blinked, and rocked slightly, as if the words had struck him with physical force.

". . . thank you," Michael continued. "But I'm not the Carpenter who set the standard."

Nicodemus tapped Uriel on the shoulder. "Excuse me."

The angel turned to him, slowly. His face was resolute, his eyes flat.

"You are standing in the way of mortal business, angel," Nicodemus said. "Stand aside."

Uriel's eyes flickered, and frozen lightning exploded through the clouds overhead, thunder making the stand-still sleet-drops quiver.

"You make threats?" Nicodemus asked, contempt dripping from his voice like blood from a wound. "Perhaps you should cut your losses. You are without power in this matter, angel, and we both know it. You can do nothing to me."

And then Nicodemus lifted his left hand and, deliberately, calmly, tensed his forefinger beneath his thumb and flicked it out to tap the end of the angel's nose.

Uriel's eyes widened, and terrible light gathered around his head and shoulders. Looking at it hurt, burned the eyes, seared my mind with sudden memories of every shameful act I'd ever chosen to do, scorched me with the obvious truth of how easy it might have been to make a different choice. The light of Uriel's halo banished shadows and averted everyone's gaze.

Everyone's but Nicodemus's.

"Go on, angel," Nicodemus taunted, his shadow swelling and curling in slow, restless motion. "Smite me. Visit your wrath upon me. Judge me."

Uriel stared at him. Then the angel's gaze went to the shards of *Fidelacchius*. He closed his eyes for a moment, and turned his face away from the Denarian. The light of his halo flickered and died away. A tear slid down his cheek.

And he stepped aside and began walking away.

"Dude!" I said in protest. It was getting hard to see

through all the red. "What the hell kind of angelic protector are you? *Do something.*"

Uriel did not look back.

"Now, then," Nicodemus said to Michael. His sword had never ceased pointing at Karrin's heart. "If I release this pair, you will step through that gate?"

Michael nodded once. "I will. You have my word."

Nicodemus's eyes glittered. He looked up at the Genoskwa and nodded, and suddenly I was on the ground, untouched, with the giant thing looming over me. The shaggy, hulking creature stared at Uriel with hateful eyes, but then that feral gaze flickered up to the house, and around the yard, skipping from point to point, and looking at something that I couldn't see. The blood rushed back and forth through my head, pounding hard, and though Winter held the pain at bay, my vision pulsed darker and lighter with every heartbeat.

"Go on, Dresden," Nicodemus said. "Take her inside."

It took me a couple of tries to get to my feet, but I did it, stuffed my revolver back into my duster's pocket, and shambled over to Karrin.

She was in bad shape, obviously in severe pain. When I picked her up, she would have screamed if she'd had the breath. Michael opened the gate for me, and I carried her through it, into the yard, then put her down as carefully as I could on the grass.

Uriel, meanwhile, had gone to Butters's side. He crouched down and shook him. Butters started awake and sat up, rubbing at his head.

Uriel spoke to him in a low, intent voice, nodding toward the house. Butters swallowed, his eyes the size of teacups, and nodded. Then he got up and half ran around the house, into the backyard.

Uriel gave me an intent look.

Time, said a voice in my head. *Get me a little time.*

"I've kept my word," Nicodemus said to Michael. "Now it's your tur—"

"The hell you have," I spat. "You just ordered your goon to kill me. You've broken your contract with Mab."

Nicodemus shifted his gaze to me and looked amused. "That?" he said. "Goodness, Dresden, can you not recognize a ploy when you see one?"

"What ploy?" I demanded.

"I needed to put a little pressure on Miss Murphy," he said. "But you were never in any actual danger. Do you honestly think it would take the Genoskwa more than a few seconds to crack even a skull so thick as yours?" He smiled widely, clearly enjoying himself. "Why, it was no more an attempt to kill you than was your participation in the chase of the little doctor a betrayal of Mab's word that you would aid me."

Dammit. Nothing like a little pro forma quid pro quo action. By Mab's reckoning, I was pretty sure, Nicodemus and I had played this one out evenly. My actions in protecting Butters could be explained as bad luck and sincere incompetence. Nicodemus's attempt to kill me could be explained as a ploy to destroy the Sword.

His eyes narrowed. "And I fully expect you to continue to fulfill your half of the bargain, Dresden, regardless of what happens over the next few hours."

I ground my teeth and said, "You attacked Murphy."

"I warned you that I could not guarantee her safety,"

he said in a reasonable tone. "And in any case, she initiated the attack, if you recall. And she's not dead just yet." He showed me white teeth. "I'd say that I'm being more than reasonable. And so would your liege."

Again, he was right—by Mab's reckoning, he was indeed a reasonable man.

Uriel, meanwhile, had paced over to stand at Michael's right hand. I took up station on my friend's left.

"The bargain was made," Nicodemus purred, to Uriel, "his word freely given. You cannot stop him from fulfilling it."

"Correct," Uriel said, "but I can *help* him do so."

Nicodemus's smile slipped.

Calmly, Uriel turned to Michael. He put a hand on Michael's shoulder and gently took his cane away.

Michael blinked at Uriel, his arms going out for balance, his body tightening as if he expected to pitch over without the cane's support. And then he abruptly relaxed. He put some of his weight on his bad leg, and then a little more. And then he let out a little laugh and hopped on it a few times.

Just then, Butters came running back around from behind the house. There was a twig with a soggy brown oak leaf still attached to it in his hair, his knees were scuffed and marked with sap, and he was carrying a slender package wrapped in canvas and duct tape, almost as long as he was tall. Butters was tearing at the package as he ran over and then offered it to Michael.

Michael's eyes widened and went to Nicodemus as he stretched out his right hand, without looking, without *needing* to look, and withdrew from the canvas package a

Sword, a shining length of straight steel with a cruciform hilt. As Michael's fingers closed on it, *Amoracchius* exploded into white light, and for the second time in an evening, the quiet, ominous power of one of the Swords filled the air.

Nicodemus's eyes widened. "You cheat!" he snarled.

"I said I would come out to you," Michael said.

Then he lifted a work-booted foot and kicked the white picket gate off its hinges. It struck Nicodemus across the torso, driving him back into the street, and Michael Carpenter, Knight of the Cross, strode out of the open gate onto the icy sidewalk while the archangel looked on, silver-green eyes blazing in answer to the light of the Sword in Michael's hands.

"I'm out," Michael said. "*In nomine Dei*, Nicodemus, I have come to face you."

In the street, Nicodemus bared his teeth.

I was terrified for Michael.

And my heart soared.

"Hah-hah," I said, like the bully on *The Simpsons*, pointing at him. Then I walked out of the gate to stand beside my friend. I pointed my finger at my quarterstaff, fallen on the ground where the Genoskwa had held me, exerted my will, and called, *"Ventas servitas."*

A burst of wind rose and flung the staff into the air. I caught it, and called power into it, summoning green-white light and silvery soulfire into the channels of power that ran through its runes.

Uriel smiled tightly, his eyes hard, and the sleet began to fall once more. It burst into little drops of steam when it hit the runes on my staff.

"Two of you," I said to Nicodemus. "Two of us. What do you think, Nick?"

Michael faced him squarely, both hands on the hilt of *Amoracchius*. The Sword's light filled the air—and Nicodemus's shadow quailed before it.

Nicodemus finally stood back. He lowered his blade and said, "Dresden. I expect you back at our headquarters by four a.m." He turned to go.

"Not so fast, smart guy," I said.

Nicodemus paused.

"If I have to play by these stupid rules, so do you. I still get someone to watch my back during this job."

"Miss Murphy is more than welcome to do so."

"You put her out of commission," I said. "You didn't have to do that. You'd already beaten her."

"Then choose another," Nicodemus snapped.

I put a hand on Michael's shoulder and said, "I already have. And you're going to put up with it, or I'll consider it a release of obligation—and so will Mab."

Nicodemus simply stood, soaked by the sleet and unmoved by the cold. He stared at me in chilly silence for several seconds. Then he said, "So be it."

Shadows gathered around him, and vanished up into the stormy night, taking him with them. I looked left and right, and realized that the Genoskwa was already gone.

Michael was looking at me very oddly as he lowered the Sword.

"What?" I asked him.

"Charity," he predicted, "is not going to be pleased."

Chapter
Thirty-one

Once Nick and Big Shaggy were gone, I hurried to Karrin. She was on her back, shuddering, her eyes focused on nothing.

I turned to Uriel, pointed a finger at Karrin, and said, "Fix her."

Uriel grimaced. "I cannot." After a moment, he added, "I'm sorry."

"I am badly disappointed in you, Mr. Sunshine," I said. "Butters."

"Yeah, yeah," Butters said, already on his way to Karrin. "Jesus," he said after a moment. "Come on, we have to get her out of the cold and wet. Like, right now. She could be going into shock."

"I've got a fire going," Michael said. "We'll pull the couch up next to it."

I stripped out of my coat and put it on the ground next to her. We lifted her onto it. "Hey, Mr. Sunshine," I said, maybe a little more harshly than I could have. "Some cosmic limitation that keeps you from picking up your corner of the coat?"

Uriel blinked, but then hurried over to us and took one side of the coat willingly. We all picked up the coat with Karrin on it, trying to support her evenly. She made an incoherent sound of pain as we did. We carried her into the house together, with Butters opening doors for us.

Michael watched my face closely as we carried her.

"What?" I asked.

"You aren't angry," he said. "That she's hurt."

"Like hell I'm not," I said. "It's coming. After we take care of her. When it's time."

Michael grunted. "You aren't *more* angry than you would be if it was me. Or Butters, here."

I grunted. "She's not a delicate princess," I said. "She's a warrior. Warriors have enemies. Sometimes warriors get hurt." I felt my jaws clench. "And then their friends even things up."

"Damned right they do," Butters said.

Michael's eyes were steady. "Harry."

We had gotten Karrin into Michael's living room by then, and settled her slowly onto the couch. Good to his word, there was a fire burning in a neat stone fireplace inside. Once she was on the couch, I picked up one end, Uriel picked up the other, and we set the whole thing down in front of the fireplace where the heat of it would surround her.

"Towels," Butters said. "Blankets. Hurry."

"I'll get them," Uriel volunteered. He turned, paused, and then asked Michael, "Where are they?"

Michael directed him to the linen closet. He hurried off and returned a moment later, arms loaded with cloth.

"Good," Butters said, and seized them. He started

taking them to Karrin, drying her off. The heat and the chafing of the towels seemed to rouse her slightly, and she blinked her eyes several times.

"Michael," she said. "Michael?"

"I'm here," Michael said.

Karrin looked up, her face drawn, her eyes full of tears. "I'm sorry. I'm so sorry. I lost the Sword."

"Easy," Michael said gently. "We'll deal with it. You don't have to worry about it right now."

"We've got to get the wet clothes off," Butters said. "Do you have safety scissors?"

"In my kit," Michael said. "In the kitchen."

Uriel said, "I'll get it." He walked out and in, and passed the same red plastic toolbox Michael had used on me earlier to Butters.

"Sorry, Karrin," Butters said. "About your jacket." He went to work with the safety scissors, cutting Karrin out of her coat while trying not to move her arm and shoulder. She grunted with pain anyway.

"I didn't know what to do," Karrin said. "If I'd turned from him, he'd have come at my b-back. If I didn't go to Harry, he was g-going to die." Her eyes widened. "Harry, is he . . . ?"

"Here," I said. I found her right hand with mine. Her eyes rolled to me, and her fingers suddenly squeezed down tight on mine. Her hand was icy cold, and she was shivering harder.

"Harry," she said. "Thank God."

"Holy crap," Butters said. "There are bullet holes in her shirt."

"I blew it, Harry," she said. "Dammit, I blew it." She

was weeping openly now. "They're always too strong. There's always more of them, and they're always too strong."

"Karrin," I said. I took her face in my hands and made her look at me as Butters cut away at her shirt. "Shut up. You screwed up excellently. Okay? We all made it out. We're all going to be fine. Right, Butters?"

Butters gave me a tight look.

"But the Sword," Karrin said.

Michael leaned down and said, "Have faith, Ms. Murphy," he said, his voice serious. "Things are not always as bad as they seem. Sometimes, the darkness only makes it easier to see the light."

I looked up at Uriel, who compressed his lips into a grim line.

"Oh, thank God," Butters breathed. "She was wearing a vest."

"Of course I was wearing a vest," Karrin said, her voice for a second perfectly clear and slightly annoyed. She was shivering harder now. "Oh, God, cold."

Butters plucked at several small, bright bits of metal, passing them to Michael. "Four, five. How many shots did she take?"

"Five," Uriel supplied instantly.

"Twenty-twos," Michael said. "Maybe twenty-fives."

"No blood," Butters reported. "I think the vest stopped them all." He kept cutting her shirt away until he could see her injured shoulder. It was already swelling. "We've got to get the vest off of her."

"Why?" I asked.

"Because Kevlar doesn't stretch and she's going to

keep swelling, and because this needs a hospital. I'd rather she didn't have to answer any questions about a damaged bulletproof vest once we get there."

"It might not be safe," I said. "Why can't you take care of her here?"

"Because I don't have the tools I need to help her here, and I don't have the expertise to use them even if I did," Butters said, his voice hard. "Look, Harry, not everyone has got your ability to handle injury. Her shoulder is dislocated and there's probably additional damage. I haven't seen her knee yet, but from the shape of it I think he took her ACL. This isn't something she can just walk off, and if she doesn't get proper care, fast, it could cripple her for life. So as soon as I'm sure she isn't going into hypothermia, we're going to the hospital." He looked up at me, his eyes steady, his expression resolute. "And if you argue with me, I'm going to call her friends on the force and tell them that she needs help."

Rage made my vision pulse, and I snarled and clenched my hand into a fist, but Butters didn't back down.

"Harry," Michael said. He stepped in between us, and put a hand on my chest. "She can't stay here. She's in agony."

I blinked several times, and did math, pushing the Winter aggression further from my thoughts. The rage receded, leaving weariness behind, and my head started to hurt. "Right," I said. "Right . . . Sorry, Butters. Hey, Mr. Sunshine. You can put a protective detail on her, can't you?"

"I cannot," Uriel said.

"So useless," I muttered. The throbbing got worse, despite Mab's earring. "God, my head."

Michael's restraining hand became a steadying one, his voice sharpening with concern. "Harry? Are you all right?"

"Will be. Just . . . need a minute to rest."

"Uriel," Michael said, his voice softly urgent.

The room tilted to one side unexpectedly, and I flailed my arms to try to catch my balance. Michael caught my right arm. Uriel's nose caught my left, right in the aluminum brace, but the archangel managed to support me. Between the three of us, I found a chair and sat there in it for a minute while my head spun, briefly.

Uriel had a shocked, even startled look on his face.

And his nose was bleeding.

I was pretty sure that wasn't possible.

Uriel touched his fingers to his face and drew them away, bright with scarlet blood. He blinked at them, the expression almost childlike in its confusion. Tears welled in his eyes, and he blinked them several times, as if he wasn't sure what was happening.

Michael caught the direction of my stare, and his clear grey eyes widened. He straightened, staring at Uriel in shock.

"What have you done?" he asked.

"It was not within our power to heal what was done to you," Uriel said. "I'm sorry. It was not chance that brought you to harm, but choice."

Michael looked from the angel down to his leg and back. "What have you done?" he repeated.

Uriel looked from his shaking, bloodied fingers to Michael and said, "I have loaned you my Grace."

Michael's eyes became completely round.

"Wow," I said. "Uh . . . Isn't that . . . that kind of important?"

"It is what makes me an angel," Uriel said.

"Merciful Mother of God," Michael said, his voice awed.

"Uh," I said. "Isn't that . . . kind of overkill? I mean . . . Uriel, you've got the power to unmake solar systems."

"Galaxies," Uriel said absently.

"Harry," Michael said, "what are you saying?"

"Why?" I asked Uriel.

"I had to do something," he said. "I couldn't just . . . stand there. But my options are limited."

"Oh," I said. "I get it. I think."

"Harry," Michael said. "What are you talking about?"

"Um," I said, and rubbed at my aching head. "Uriel wanted to help you, but he couldn't exert his will over the situation to change it. Right?"

"Correct," Uriel said.

"But he could act in accordance with your will, Michael. Which was to go out and meet Nicodemus."

"Yes," Michael said.

"So he couldn't change you," I said. "And he couldn't change the world around you, at least not of his own will. But he could change himself. So he gave you his power in order to make your body function the way it used to. That way it isn't his will that's using the power. It's yours." The throbbing had begun to recede, slowly, and I looked up. "It's way more than you needed, but it's the only unit he had to work with. It's as if . . . he loaned you his giant passenger jet because you needed a reading light." I eyed the angel. "Right?"

Uriel nodded and said, "Close enough."

Michael opened his mouth in understanding. "Loaned," he said. "It won't last."

Uriel shook his head. "But this task is an important one. You need it. Use it."

Michael titled his head. "But . . . Uriel, if I were to misuse it . . ."

"I would Fall," Uriel said quietly.

I choked on the air.

Holy crap.

The last time an archangel Fell, I'm pretty sure there were extended consequences.

Uriel smiled faintly at Michael. "I'm confident that you won't." His smile turned a little green. "I would, however, appreciate it if you . . . did not push any buttons or pull any of the levers in my giant passenger jet."

"How could you do this?" Michael breathed.

"You need the reading light," Uriel said. "You have more than earned whatever help I can give. And you are a friend, Michael."

"What happens to you, while I . . . borrow your jet?" Michael asked.

"Transubstantiation," Uriel said. He gestured with his bloodied fingers.

Butters finally chimed in. "Holy. Crap. He's mortal?"

"And he can die," I said quietly.

Chapter
Thirty-two

The fire crackled.

"Because, obviously," I said, "there wasn't enough on the line already."

Uriel smiled. It was a tight, pained expression.

"Take it back," Michael said. "You've got to take it back, right now."

"I can do that," Uriel said. "If that is your choice, I will respect it."

Something in his voice triggered my instincts, and I said, "Michael, wait. Think about this."

"What's to think about?" Michael asked. "An archangel of the Lord is vulnerable."

"Right," I said, and spread my hands. "Almost as if he thinks this is important or something. Or maybe you figure Uriel for the kind of guy who hands out this kind of power all willy-nilly, every time the wind blows." I looked at Uriel. "Right?"

Uriel helped Butters get another blanket around the shuddering Karrin, watched us, and said nothing.

"Yeah," I said. "You can tell when you're on the right

track, because he shuts up and doesn't tell you a damned thing. It's about the Grail, isn't it? About what Nicodemus wants to do with it."

Uriel gave me a knowing look.

I flushed and said, "I'm playing my cards close to the chest, okay? I know it's about more than that."

He put his hand on Karrin's head and smiled at her encouragingly.

Michael shook his head and walked over to where he'd set *Amoracchius* after he'd drawn it from his belt once we had Karrin inside. He picked it up absently, and started cleaning the water from it carefully with one of the used towels. "You're asking me to make a very large choice."

"Yes," Uriel said.

"With potentially horrible consequences."

Uriel looked at him with sympathetic eyes and nodded.

"Can you tell me what is at stake, that I should risk this?"

Uriel frowned, considering the question for a moment. Then he said, "A soul."

Michael raised his eyebrows. "Oh," he said. "You should have said that from the beginning." He extended the Sword and looked down the length of its blade. "I'm not retired at the moment," he said. "What about my family?"

"The guards remain," Uriel said. "I have taken your place."

Michael exhaled and some of the tension eased out of him. "Right. Though this is going to draw attention here again."

"It might."

"And your protection doesn't extend to the merely mortal," Michael said.

"No."

"So mortals could enter, and kill you. Kill them."

"Potentially," he said.

"Guys," Butters said, "we need to get her to a hospital."

"Right," I said. "Here's the plan. Butters drives Murphy to the hospital and tells the guys at SI she needs looking after."

"Those guys can't stop someone like Nicodemus," Butters said.

"No," I said, "but they can force him to get noisy if he wants to get to her, and Nick won't want that until after the job. He might send some of his squires to do it, but SI can go up against them just fine. Michael, will you loan Butters a car?"

"Of course," Michael said.

"Good. They'll help you unload her at the emergency room, Butters."

"Right," Butters said. "Great."

"I'm going to go clean up out front," I said. "What's left of the Sword, shell casings, what have you. Those shots were muffled by the sleet, but we don't need to leave things lying around in case some busybody called the cops."

"Leaving me to talk to Charity alone," Michael said drily.

"Yeah, funny how that worked out," I said. "Where is she, anyway?"

"In the panic room with Mouse and the kids," Michael said. "Little Harry was all but bouncing off the walls, he was so excited. I didn't want him seeing . . ." He nodded toward Karrin. "I'll sound the all clear as soon as she and Butters leave."

"Good call," I said.

"What should I do?" Uriel asked.

"Sit," I said. "Stay inside. Don't put pennies in the outlets or play with matches or run with scissors."

"I don't understand," Uriel said.

"Take no chances," I clarified.

"Oh, yes." He frowned and said, "But I want to help."

"So sit," I said. "Sitting quietly is very helpful."

He sat down on the arm of the couch, frowning.

"I think this will hurt the least if one person carries her," Butters said.

"Right," I said, rising, and wobbled as the blood rushed to my head.

"Harry," Michael said, and pushed gently in front of me. He went over to Karrin and adjusted the couch to give him room to stand in front of her. He passed Butters a set of car keys.

"It's her left arm and leg that are hurt," Butters said. "Carry her right side against you and try to support her left knee."

"I'll be careful," Michael said, and lifted her gently, keeping her wrapped in the blankets. He didn't seem to have any trouble doing it. I mean, he didn't look like he'd gained muscle or anything, but his strength was certainly that of the Knight I remembered, and not of the lame contractor and Little League softball coach he'd been lately.

Karrin let out a soft sound of pain, and closed her eyes, breathing with steady, disciplined rhythm through her nose.

"Right, right," Butters said. He'd discarded his pack before, but he recovered it now, as we went outside and loaded Karrin into Michael's white pickup truck.

We got her in and buckled up, though she was obviously fighting the pain. Michael hurried back inside, out of the sleet. She opened her eyes once and gave me a little smile.

"Sorry," she said, "that I won't be there to watch your back."

"You did fine," I said. "We'll make sure you've got cover."

"Worry about yourselves," she said. "I can make some calls. Michael's a good man, but he doesn't always see things coming."

I bit my lip for a second, trying to decide if I should say anything. I decided not to. If she didn't know what was coming up, she couldn't possibly tip off anyone that I already knew part of what Nicodemus was up to.

I need to work on my poker face. She looked at my expression and smiled with one side of her mouth. "Need-to-know. I get it, Harry." She struggled to free her right hand from the blankets, so that she could put it on mine and squeeze. "Make the sucker punch count."

I winked at her. "I'll come see you soon."

"You'd better," she said.

Butters slammed the driver's-side door and brought the truck to life with a smooth rumble of V8 engine. He turned the heaters all the way up, first thing, and double-checked Karrin's seat belt. Then he adjusted the mirrors, muttered something about the truck being the size of a house, and said to me, "Close it up. I'll get you word as soon as I know anything."

I nodded and said, "Thanks, Butters."

He grimaced and said, "Thank me when I save your life."

"You've done that already," I said. "Back in the museum."

"So we're even?"

"Once you've made that swap, you don't keep counting, man," I said. "Drive safe."

I closed the door carefully, and watched Butters back the truck out onto the icy street. He put it into the lowest gear, and the tires crunched slowly down the street as he drove away.

He'd been out of the driveway for maybe twenty seconds when a flickering stream of campfire sparks came soaring down out of a nearby tree and through the windshield of the truck—Bob, returning to the skull still in Butters's backpack.

I watched until they were gone. Then I hurriedly cleaned up the scene, fake rocket launcher, Sword-shards, sheath, hilt, and shell casings all, and hurried back inside.

I shut the door behind me and leaned against it. For a second, I was alone.

I missed Karrin already. Logically, I knew that she probably wasn't in any immediate danger from Nicodemus and company, but some irrational part of me wanted to be the one who drove her to the hospital, terrified the doctors into perfection, and watched over her when she could finally sleep.

She'd looked so small like that, with her wet hair plastered down, swaddled in blankets.

And she wouldn't have been that way if I hadn't invited her along for the ride.

I mean, yeah, logically, I hadn't been the one to hurt her. Nicodemus had done that. But there was a great, seething tide of anger somewhere behind the walls of my mind, absolute fury that she had come to harm, and since it had no handy targets to crash upon, some stupid part of my brain had decided that I would do.

And now I was going to drag Michael into my mess as well. And if he got put in a compromising position the way Karrin had, the consequences might be significantly more severe.

And all because I'd been weak, and cut a deal with Mab.

I gritted my teeth and forced myself to stand on my own two feet again.

What was done was done. There was no point in tearing myself to shreds over it—especially since indulging in that kind of self-flagellation would not help me protect Michael or stop Nicodemus from obtaining one of the most powerful holy relics in the world.

There would be plenty of time to beat myself up later—assuming I lived long enough to do it.

Focus on the task at hand, Harry. Sort the rest out when you have time.

Yeah, sure. But isn't that the kind of thinking that got me into this mess in the first place?

I was trying to learn to play the game a few more moves ahead than I had in the past. Part of that had been keeping Karrin in the dark about what I had in mind for Nicodemus and company. But, man, that game was hard to play.

Bleak thoughts. I was roused from them by feet on the stairs. I looked up.

At the top of the stairs stood two figures—an enormous dog and a little girl.

The dog was grey, shaggy, and the size of a bantha. A bulky ruff of fur about his head and shoulders gave him a leonine look, and his dark eyes were bright, his slightly curled tail wagging so furiously that it looked like it might pull him over sideways. When Mouse saw me, he made a happy little chuffing sound, and his front paws bounced off the floor, but then he glanced to the girl beside him and held himself carefully still.

The little girl stood with her hands buried in the thick fur of Mouse's mane, as though she had refused to admit that she couldn't just circle her arms around his neck and tote him about like a teddy bear. She was wearing an old T-shirt of Molly's that read SPLATTERCON!!! across the front. The shirt hung past her knees and its sleeves went halfway to her wrists. She had big brown eyes the size of softballs, it looked like, and her dark brown hair hung straight down to her little shoulders.

Her features were a little long. I could see myself in the shape of her eyes, in the set of her chin. But she had her mother's full mouth and elegant nose.

Maggie.

My daughter.

My heart all but stopped beating—and then it lurched into high gear in pure terror.

What should I do? What should I say? I mean, I had known I was a father and whatnot, but . . . now she was *looking* at me. And she was a *person*.

She regarded me soberly from the top of the stairs for several long seconds before she said, "Are you Harry Dresden?"

She was missing a tooth from up front and off to one side. It was kind of adorable.

"Uh," I said. "Yeah. That's me."

"You're really big," she said.

"You think so?"

She nodded seriously. "Bigger than Mr. Carpenter."

"Um," I said. "How did you know it was me?"

"Because Molly showed me your picture," Maggie said. She moved her shoulders, as though attempting to hold Mouse up the way she might a favorite doll. "This is my dog, Mouse."

Mouse wagged his tail furiously and managed not to knock Maggie down while he did it.

"I know," I said. "I'm the one who gave him to you."

Maggie nodded. "That's what Molly said. She said you gave him to me 'cause you loved me."

"Yes," I said, recognizing the truth as I spoke it. "That's true."

She wrinkled up her nose, as if she had smelled something unpleasant. "Are you mad at me?"

I blinked several times. "What? No, no, of course not. Why would I be mad at you?"

She shrugged and looked down at Mouse's mane. "Because you aren't ever here. Never, ever."

Ow.

The Winter Mantle is pretty amazing, but there are some kinds of pain it can't do jack about.

"Well," I said after a moment, "I have a very tough job. Do you know what I do?"

"You fight monsters," Maggie said. "Molly told me so. Like Draculas and stuff."

Had Molly been filling in for me a little, while I was away? That . . . sounded a lot like the kind of thing Mab had done or ordered done when I was unavailable—taking up some of the duties of her vassal in his stead.

Maybe Molly was following in the same footsteps. Or maybe she was just being Molly, and being as kind as she could to the child. Or maybe it wasn't as simple as either-or.

"Yeah," I said. "Like Draculas and stuff. It's very dangerous and I do it a lot."

"Mr. Carpenter works harder than two men. That's what Missus Carpenter says."

"That's probably true," I said.

"But he comes home every night. And you haven't ever . . ." A thought seemed to strike her and she pressed a little closer to Mouse. "Are you going to take me away?"

"Um," I said, blinking. This was proceeding really quickly. "I, uh. Would you like that?"

She shrugged, almost hiding her eyes in Mouse's mane. "I don't know. My toys are all here. And my roller skates."

"That's very true," I said. "Um. Not tonight, any-way."

"Oh," she said. "Okay. Molly says you're really nice."

"I try to be."

"Is he nice, Mouse?"

Mouse continued wagging his tail furiously, and gave a quiet bark.

"Mouse is smart," she said, nodding. "Really super dog smart. We're reading *James and the Giant Peach*."

I blinked. Did she mean that she was reading the book to the dog or that *Mouse* was reading the book, too? I mean, I already knew that he was as smart as most people, but I'd never really considered whether or not he could learn to do abstract things like reading. It seemed like a very strange notion.

On the other hand, he *was* going to school. Hell, I only had a GED. If he stayed close enough to Maggie for long enough, the dog might wind up with more educa-tion than me. Then there'd be no talking to him.

"Don't tell people about Mouse, though, okay?" Maggie said, suddenly worried. "It's a top secret."

"I won't," I said.

"Okay. Do you wanna see my room?"

"I'd like that."

I came up the stairs, and Maggie let go of the dog's mane with one hand, to grab my right forefinger with it, and to lead me down the hall.

Maggie's room had, long ago, been Charity's sewing room. They'd cleaned it out and redecorated the little chamber, in purple and pink and bright green. There was a tiny kid-sized desk with a chair, and several toy boxes.

The toys had all been put neatly away. There were a couple of schoolbooks on the desk. A closet stood slightly open, and proved to have its floor covered in dirty clothes that hadn't made it into a small laundry hamper. There was a raised bed against one wall, the kind that usually came with a second one beneath it. There wasn't a lower bunk. Instead, there was a big futon mattress on the floor beneath the bed. Posters of brightly colored cartoon ponies adorned the walls, and the ceiling above the bed.

Once we were in the room, Mouse finally let out a few little whines and came over to me, grinning a big doggy grin. I spent a few minutes rubbing his ears and scratching him beneath the chin and telling him what a good dog he was and how much I'd missed him and what a good job he was doing. Mouse wriggled all over and gave my hands a few slobbery kisses and in general behaved exactly like a happy dog and not at all like a mystic, superpowered guardian creature from Tibet.

Maggie climbed a little ladder to her bunk, to watch the exchange closely. After a minute, Mouse leaned against me so hard that he nearly bowled me over, and then he happily settled down on the futon mattress beneath the little girl's bed.

"I have a monster under my bed, and it's *Mouse*," she said proudly. "There was another one there but me and Mouse slayerized it."

I lifted an eyebrow. I mean, any other kid, I might have thought she was reporting a recent game of pretend. But on the other hand . . . I mean, she *was* a Dresden and all. Maybe she was giving me the facts and nothing but the facts.

"He's the most awesome dog ever," I said.

That pleased her immensely. "I know!" She chewed on her lip thoughtfully, a gesture that reminded me so much of Susan that a tangible pang went through my chest. "Um," she said. "Would you like to . . . tuck me in?"

"Sure," I said.

She nodded and flopped down onto her pillow. I stepped up to the bed and took a few seconds to sort out the sheets and the blanket and to get them pulled over her. Once that was done, she said, "Would you like to read me a story?"

Mouse's tail thumped enthusiastically against the wall.

"Sure," I said. And we read *Where the Wild Things Are*. When I finished, she said, "You didn't do the voices right."

"Hmmm," I said. "Maybe I'll do better next time."

"I don't know," she said dubiously. "I guess you can try." She looked at my face searchingly for a moment and then said, in a tiny voice, "Do you want to be my dad?"

I went blind for a few seconds, until I blinked the tears away.

"Sure," I said. It came out in a tight croak, but when I said it she smiled at me.

By the time I'd finished the second run-through of Sendak's opus, she was asleep.

I made sure the blankets had her all covered up, and kissed her hair, and then crouched down beside Mouse and put my arms around him.

"Thank you, boy," I said. "Thank you for taking care of her."

He leaned against me, tail wagging, and snuggled his huge head into my ribs. I petted him some more. "I have to go soon. But I need you to keep her safe. The Carpenters, too. Okay?"

He chuffed and snuggled a little closer.

"Missed you too, boy," I said, rubbing his ears. "I just need a little time to figure this out. To figure out what comes next."

Had I decided that I was going to be a dad to Maggie now? I examined myself and realized that indeed I had. When did *that* happen? And why hadn't anyone kept me in the loop?

It had happened, I thought, the moment I had seen her, talked to her.

Oh my God.

That was terrifying.

And . . . exciting?

All things considered, I wasn't sure I could put a lot of trust in my emotions at the moment. But one thing was certain.

If I wanted to keep my word to my daughter, I'd have to come back. That meant staying alive tomorrow.

I got up, gave Mouse a final round of petting and scratching, and padded quietly from the room into the upstairs hallway. The lights in the other rooms were out—except for the one in Michael and Charity's room. A light burned there. The door was slightly open.

And I could see Charity, sitting on the edge of the bed in flannel pajamas, a tall blond woman with an excellent physique, whose hair was threading through with silver in style as she aged. Her tearstained face was miserable, as she spoke, presumably, to her husband, seated on the bed beside her. I couldn't see him from there.

Obviously Michael had intended that talk to take place in private.

I turned away from it and went back down the stairs. I sat down on the bottom steps and tried to clear my head.

A few minutes later, Charity came down the stairs and sat down next to me. I made room.

"Where's Michael?" I asked.

"Praying over the children," she answered. "He always does that before he leaves. In case . . ."

"Yeah," I said.

"You know," Charity said, "I had intended to punch you in the nose, twice, the moment I saw you again. Once to make it bleed, once to break it."

"Oh?"

"Mmm-hmm. The first time for trying to kill yourself. The second for using my daughter to do it."

"You, uh. You know about that? How?"

"I watch. I listen. Her reaction to reports of your death was . . . too much. It took time, but I eventually worked out why she was so furious at herself."

"You can hit me right now, if you think it would help," I said.

"No," she said tiredly. "I just wanted to tell you something."

"Yeah?"

She nodded. "Kids need their father to come home safe, Harry. Make sure it happens."

"I'll bring him back to you or die trying. I promise."

Charity glanced at me and then shook her head with a weary smile. "I wasn't talking about Michael, Harry. I meant you." She glanced back up the stairs, toward Maggie's room. "That child has lost everyone she's ever loved. Did you notice how close she stays to Mouse? Without him, I wonder if she'd be functioning at all. If anything should happen to you . . ."

"Ah," I said quietly.

"Maggie doesn't need to feel that pain again. Don't let her down."

I chewed on my lip and nodded with my watery eyes closed. "Right."

"And . . . please remember that Michael has children who need him, too. Please."

"I'll bring him back or die trying," I repeated.

Charity exhaled a shaky breath, and then touched my shoulder gently. "Thank you. God be with you and bring you home safe, Harry. Both of you."

Chapter
Thirty-three

At three thirty a.m., we rolled up to the evil lair in a soccer mom's minivan with a MY KID IS AN HONOR STUDENT AT . . . bumper sticker on the back. It is worth noting that by the standards of my life, this was not a terribly incongruous entrance.

Michael regarded the slaughterhouse for a moment after he had killed the ignition and said, "This is a bad place."

"Yeah," I said. I rubbed at the small of my back. I'd gotten a few hours' worth of sleep before we'd left, on the futon mattress on the floor beneath Maggie's bed. Mouse had been happy to snuggle up to me. The lummox likes to pretend he's still a tiny puppy that will fit on my lap if he tries hard enough, and I'd been too tired to argue with him. As a result, I'd had to practice defensive sleeping, and it had left my back a little twitchy.

On the upside, even the modest amount of sleep I'd gotten had done wonders to restore me, or at least the power of the Winter mantle. I felt practically normal, broken arm, gunshot wound, and all.

Michael was dressed in his old mail, which he had kept

clean and scoured free of rust despite his retirement. He wore body armor beneath it. He'd put his big white cloak with its bright red cross on the left breast over it.

"You sure you couldn't just put something black on?" I asked him. "You're going to clash with all the bad-guy robbery wear."

"That's the idea," Michael said.

"You don't get it, man," I said. "This building we're going to hit belongs to John Marcone. We're supposed to go in without taking down their electronic systems. That means there will be cameras and pictures. The blindest security tech in the world could identify you— and your guardian angels won't protect you from Marcone's people."

Michael shook his head. "It won't come to that."

"You say that," I said, "but you don't know what Marcone is like."

"Perhaps," he said. "But I *do* know what the Almighty is like, Harry. And He wouldn't give me the strength to do this only to have it result in harm to my family."

I grimaced. "Seems to me it would be polite of you to take a couple of prudent steps—like wearing dark clothes and a mask—so that the Almighty wouldn't need to go out of His way to arrange things for you."

He barked out a quick laugh and gave me a rueful smile. "So you *have* been listening to me, all this time." He shook his head. "Nicodemus and his ilk operate in the shadows, in secret. The Swords aren't meant for that. I have nothing to hide."

"Hey," I said, letting my voice be annoyed, "as shadowy ilk myself, I think I resent that statement."

Michael snorted. "You destroy buildings, fight monsters openly in the streets of the city, work with the police, show up in newspapers, advertise in the phone book, and ride zombie dinosaurs down Michigan Avenue, and think that you work in the shadows? Be reasonable."

"I will if you will," I said. "At least wear a ski mask."

"No," Michael said calmly. "The Lord is my helper, and I will not fear what man shall do unto me. Trust Him, Harry."

"Probably not in the cards," I said.

His smile widened. "Then trust me."

I threw up my hands. "Fine. Whatever. Are you sure your people can find someplace safe to keep the Grail if we get it back? Because apparently they go out and use the Coins to get snacks out of the vending machine, the things go back into circulation so fast."

"Part of the nature of the Coins is to *be* in circulation, as you put it," Michael said. "They can only be contained for so long. The Grail is a different proposition entirely. They'll keep it safe."

"And you know the rules I have to play by, right?" I asked.

"You have to help Nicodemus recover the Grail," he said. "After that, you can go weapons free."

"Right. And you'll respect that?"

"I will do what is right," Michael said.

I licked my lips. "Yeah, but . . . could you maybe put off doing what is right until we get clear of Mab's restrictions?"

"All things considered," Michael said, "no. I'm not taking chances."

Translation: He wasn't going to do anything—or *not* do anything—that might screw up Uriel's grace, no matter what.

Thank you, Mab, for this wonderful, wonderful game. Maybe next time we can play pin the tail on the wizard.

"I'm pretty sure Nicodemus is going to play it straight, at least until right before we get back to Chicago," I said.

"Why would he?"

"Because I'm going to say please."

Michael arched an eyebrow at me.

"I'm going to say it in his native tongue," I said.

"Power?"

"Bingo."

Nicodemus hadn't warned his squires what to expect, and when Michael strode in at my side, Jordan and his brothers-in-arms produced a truly impressive number of weapons in what appeared to be a state of pure panic.

Michael just stood there with his thumbs hooked into his belt, *Amoracchius* hanging quietly at his side in its scabbard. "Son," he said to Jordan, "don't you have anything better to do than point that thing at me?"

"Lower your weapons," I snarled in a voice loud enough to carry throughout the slaughterhouse. "Before I start downsizing your organization."

They didn't put their guns down, but my threat did make a lot of the squires eye me nervously. Go me.

"Hey, Nick," I shouted. "Your boys are all jittery. You want to calm them down or should I do it?"

"Gentlemen," Nicodemus called, a moment later, "I know who is with Dresden. Let them through."

Jordan and the others lowered their weapons with manifest reluctance, but kept their hands on them, ready to bring them to bear again at any time. Michael didn't move or take a threatening posture, but he swept his gaze from squire to squire, one by one.

They all dropped their eyes from his. Every one of them.

We started down to the conference table, and Michael said, "I feel sorry for these men."

"The tongue thing?" I asked.

"Removing their tongues is one way to keep their loyalty," Michael said.

"Yeah. I love people who mutilate my body parts."

He frowned. "It's designed to keep them isolated. Think what it does to them. They can't talk—so how much more difficult is it for them to connect with other people? To form the kinds of bonds that might let them free themselves of this cult? They can't taste their food, which precludes eating for pleasure—and eating together is one of the primary means of forming real relationships between human beings. Think how much more difficult it makes even the simplest of interactions with outsiders. And how the shared experience of that hardship means that one's fellow squires will always be the only ones who truly understand his pain." He shook his head. "It's the last step of their indoctrination for a reason. Once it's done, they no longer have a voice of their own."

"It's not the same as not having a *choice*," I said. "These guys have made their call."

"Indeed. After being manipulated by Nicodemus and Anduriel as unwise young men." He shook his head. "Some men fall from grace. Some are pushed."

"Once their fingers pull the trigger, does it matter?"

"Of course it matters," Michael said, "but it doesn't change what has to be done. I just wish they could find another way to fill the empty place inside them."

We'd reached the conference table by that time, where the crew was making final preparations. Anna Valmont, Hannah Ascher, and Binder were all there, dressed in close-fit, dark clothing, and each of them was wearing a shoulder holster. Valmont had a roll-up leather tool pouch laid out on the table and was going through various bits of equipment in it one by one. Ascher was sipping coffee, her bagel untouched on the plate in front of her. Binder was going over his gang's Uzis one more time.

The loading doors at one end of the slaughterhouse rolled open, and a pair of large stepside vans rumbled into the place a moment later. Several squires set about getting them lined up and then rolling their rear doors open.

"Morning, Dresden," Hannah Ascher said. "What happened to your girlfriend?"

"She's not my girlfriend," I said. "And she had a misunderstanding with Nicodemus."

Anna Valmont's eyes flicked up to me, hard.

"She's alive," I told her. "But she wasn't in any shape to go to work today."

"So you brought Captain Crusader instead?" Ascher asked. "He looks like a Renaissance fair."

Binder abruptly stood up, his eyes widening. "Bloody hell, girl. That's a Knight of the Sword."

Ascher frowned. "I thought there were only, like, three of those guys in the whole world."

"Two," Michael said, "at the moment."

Binder stared at Michael, and narrowed his eyes in calculation. "Aw, dammit. Dresden, this is what you do because Nicodemus gets in a tiff with your girlfriend?"

"She's *not* my g—" I rubbed at the bridge of my nose. "Look, I want someone I know and trust watching my back. Murphy couldn't do it, so he's doing it instead."

"What a load of tripe," Binder said. "You think I don't know what the Coins and the Swords are like with each other? You didn't bring him to watch your back. You brought him to fight."

"Let's just say I don't mind having a deterrent around," I said. "If Nicodemus plays it straight and keeps his word, I will too and we'll all get rich."

Binder scowled and eyed Michael. "Is that right, Knight?"

"Harry's generally a very honest man," Michael said. "I really don't care about the money, though."

Binder and Ascher both tilted their heads to one side, like dogs that have just heard a new noise.

Anna Valmont smiled and shook her head slightly, going back to checking her tools.

"So what happened last night?" Ascher asked me. "Binder's goons drew him a picture of a lion. The ones who came back, I mean."

"Yeah, it got a little crazy," I said.

"Did you get the guy?" Binder asked.

"Nah, he skated," I said. "Nobody's fault, really. Tricky, slippery little bastard."

Binder eyed me. "Yeah. Right. You give me a big speech about how you'll come down on my neck if I hurt anyone in your town. Then you two tear out of here to take up the chase, and Murphy winds up too busted up to continue after a 'misunderstanding' with Nicodemus."

I gave him a beatific smile. "Binder, relax. The op isn't in any danger. I made sure he's not going to go to anyone. That was the point of chasing him down in the first place, right?"

Binder frowned. "I thought the White Council didn't let you use mind magic."

Which I hadn't meant, at all, and which I really couldn't do, considering my utter lack of talent in that area, but Binder didn't know that. "I did what needed to be done," I said. "And think of it like this—I don't have to stomp on your neck now."

Binder looked skeptical, but he didn't push it—which was smart. Binder had a really formidable skill, but he was a one-trick pony. He wasn't up to facing a Wizard of the White Council directly, and he knew it.

Michael rounded himself up a cup of coffee and looked at me. I nodded, and he brought me back one. "That's a very large pen for just four goats," he noted.

Which meant that the Genoskwa had come back here last night, and gotten a couple more meals in. Damn, but that thing ate a lot. It ate more than something that size should have been able to consume—but a lot of supernatural creatures had supernatural metabolisms that helped fuel their exceptional speed and strength. Ghouls could put down forty or fifty pounds of meat in a meal, and need more the next day. Maybe Big Shaggy had a similar high-consumption engine fueling its physical power.

I sipped coffee and waited. At a quarter to four, Goodman Grey came ambling in. The unassuming-looking man stopped ten feet short of the table and stared hard at Michael. The Knight returned the shifter's look, and dropped the heel of his hand casually to the hilt of *Amoracchius*, resting it there with his fingers relaxed.

"What's wrong?" I asked him.

"I don't like that man very much," Michael said. "He's done terrible things."

"Obviously," Goodman Grey said, his tone wary. "I'm a monster for hire. But I've got no quarrel with you today, sir Knight."

"Maybe," Michael said. "Maybe not."

Grey's eyes flicked to me. "Do you really expect me to work with someone like this, wizard, on our side?"

"Yes," I said. "You've been hired, haven't you? Show a little professionalism."

Grey grunted and seemed to relax a little. "Well. I won't give him any cause to take issue with me. But if he does, don't think I won't take him apart."

"Pretty sure you can't," I told him. "But it might be fun to watch you try it."

Grey gave me a sour look and went over to the coffee-pot.

At five minutes to four, Nicodemus and Deirdre arrived together. Deirdre was in her demonic battle form, all purple scales and metallic ribbons of hair. Both sets of her eyes were focused on Michael warily. Nicodemus looked like he always did, but more smug. "Good morning, everyone," he said. "Table, please."

In the shadows back behind Nicodemus, I could see the hulking outline of the Genoskwa, lurking in silence.

We all gathered around the table, where Nicodemus had laid out a large piece of paper with a map of the bank drawn cleanly upon it. "This will be a simple entry," he said. He pointed at the front doors of the bank. "We'll go in through these doors. There will be between three and six security personnel, and I will expect Binder and Dresden to keep their attention and eventually neutralize them. The rest of us will head straight back to the vaults. There are two large security doors in the way, but we aren't going to bother opening them. Miss Ascher will go through the walls beside them here and here." He marked the appropriate places with a red pen. "After that, Miss Valmont and Mr. Grey will move forward into the main vault. Miss Valmont will open the vault's door, and Mr. Grey will open the target's private storage room. Once those systems have been circumvented and the doors opened, it will be safe to bring our wizards into the vault." He smiled widely. "And then the real fun can begin. Are there any questions?"

"What happens when we get where we're going?" I asked. "You got a map for that?"

"Unfortunately, no," Nicodemus said. "Though our path should be an obvious one. Our target uses active defenses to protect his vaults, not obfuscation."

"No map," I said. "Just some vague references to gates."

"One does not attain great reward without daring similarly great risk," Nicodemus said. "We will simply have to adapt to what we find as we enter."

I did not, for a minute, believe that Nicodemus had no further information about Hades' vault. But there wouldn't be much point in saying it.

"If that is all," Nicodemus said, "we shall load up. Dresden and his escort, Grey, and Valmont will be in the leftmost van. The rest of us will take the one on the right. I took the liberty of stocking them with heavy-duty back-packs for each of you, in order to allow you to gather up your shares. Mr. Binder, twenty of your associates in each van, if you please."

"Got it," Binder said. He produced his circle of wire and began calling up suits, issuing them an Uzi and a couple of spare clips as they arrived. They rushed to the waiting vans, leaping up into them with a will.

Michael watched and shook his head.

"Oh, cheer up, Mr. Carpenter," Nicodemus said. "By the time the sun rises this morning, you may be twenty million dollars richer."

"I have a family. I am already rich beyond measure," Michael said. "But I really wouldn't expect you to under-stand that."

Nicodemus's face went blank, his eyes cold.

I took note of *that*. It was far more reaction than I'd seen from him this whole time. Something about what Michael had said struck home.

"The time for talking and planning is over," Nicode-mus said. "Now is the time for action. Everyone get in the vans."

Chapter

Thirty-four

The inside of the van was crowded, with twenty of Binder's goons crammed in with the four of us, and a couple of squires driving.

"All right, Dresden," Grey said. "Let's have your wrists."

"What?" I said. "Oh, right. The manacles."

"What is he talking about?" Michael asked.

"Thorn manacles," I said. "They inhibit magical ability. They should greatly reduce the odds that I'll blow out any of the building's security systems by walking past—and we need them to stay up and functioning until we get all the doors open."

"His wrist is broken," Michael said to Grey. "Will they fit on his ankles?"

Grey held up a set of manacles on a heavy steel chain. They looked just like the ones I'd seen before, only they had the heavy gleam of steel to them, instead of that weird silvery metal the Sidhe used. The inner surfaces of the cuffs were lined with small, sharp thorns of steel. They would bite into the flesh when they were locked on—and with that steel breaking my skin, the Winter mantle would go to pieces.

That wasn't going to feel good.

"Doesn't matter," I said, eyeing them. "If either of the cuffs is on, I can't use the magic. Just have them both on one wrist and wrap the chain around to keep it out of my way. Gimme."

"Sure you don't want me to do it?" Grey asked.

"Nah, I dislike you enough already. I'll put them on." I took the manacles from Grey and gave Michael a look to let him know that I wanted him to pay attention. He frowned and did.

I elbowed myself enough room to wrap the chain around my wrist. Then I closed my eyes for a moment and took slow, deep breaths, concentrating. Blocking out pain was a lesson I'd learned a long time ago, and I could do it pretty well if I had time to prepare for it. Mostly, the bad guys aren't that courteous before they start hurting me, but fortunately this time the bad guy was me, and I was willing to cut myself a break. It took me a couple of minutes to erect the mental barriers, and then I opened my eyes, pulled up the sleeve of my duster, and fastened both manacles onto my right wrist, locking them on with their key.

Steel bit into my skin with a hundred tiny teeth, and the Winter mantle vanished. As suddenly as light comes on when you flip the switch, my body started reporting injuries.

My arm was pretty horrid, but my back had apparently turned into a single large contusion when the Genoskwa slammed me into that parked car. My calf burned steadily where I'd been shot. My feet were killing me, too, which—what the hell? Had I gotten a pair of shoes the wrong size or something? I was aching in the knees, and somehow I'd collected a cut on my tongue and on one of my gums—I hadn't really noticed them before, though I sure as hell felt them now.

And my head . . . oh, my aching head. Mab's little silver earring was as cold as an ice cream truck in Antarctica, but with its numbing influence reduced by the steel, my head felt like it was going to crack open and spill out streams of molten lead.

I realigned my mental shields for a moment, once I knew exactly what I was supposed to be blocking out, and then straightened up slowly.

"Harry," Michael said. "You just went pale."

"Hurts," I said shortly. "I'll be fine." I put the key to the manacles in my pocket, then picked up my oversized duffel bag and started rooting around in it. I'd tied a leather thong onto my wizard's staff, and now wore it over one shoulder like a rifle. "Grey, I'm going to be making all kinds of light and noise once we're inside. If you feel like doing something about the guards, try to make it nonfatal."

"Or what?" Grey asked.

"The manacles come off and I get upset with you," I said.

"Maybe I'll just let them shoot you," he said.

I gave him a pleasant smile. "If you do, who is going to open your Way to the vault, eh? Took me years of formal instruction to learn enough to make that happen. I guarantee you that Ascher can't pull that one off." I squinted at Grey. "Ask you something?"

"Sure."

"Why take money for something like this?" I asked. "Someone with your talents can get it any way he wants."

Grey shrugged. "No mystery. Everyone's got to pay the Rent," he said, and something in his voice put a capital letter on the last word.

"I don't get it," I said.

"I know," Grey replied placidly. "Not my problem."

"If you don't mind, gentlemen," Valmont said, speaking for the first time since we got in the van. "You may think your bits of the job are simple, but mine is the next best thing to impossible. I would appreciate some quiet, please."

I eyed Valmont, grunted, and fell silent, working to rearrange the contents of my duffel to my satisfaction.

It didn't take us long to get where we were going. The van came to a stop, and a moment later Jordan rolled up its rear door.

The Capristi Building is one of the last skyscrapers to be had on the north end of the city of Chicago proper, right across the street from Lincoln Park. It's made of white concrete and glass, a mediocre bit of soulless modern architecture that's all monotonous squares and right angles stretching up and up into the still-sleeting skies.

Between the weather and the time, the streets were almost completely empty and still—which actually bothered me a little bit. That stillness would have made our vans pretty obvious to anyone who saw them moving. I stepped out of the van, slipped on the ice, and would have fallen if I hadn't grabbed onto the truck. Right. No Winter mantle to help with the ice.

By now, there was half an inch of transparent ice lying over every surface in sight. Power lines were bowed down with the weight of it. In the park behind me, the trees were bent almost double, and here and there, branches had cracked and fallen beneath its weight. The streets had been a mess, and only careful driving and the weight of the heavily loaded vans had kept them from slithering all over the place.

A sign on the first floor of the Capristi Building read: VERITY TRUST BANK OF CHICAGO. Which was a fine name for a mob bank. The first floor was the bank's lobby, with the secure floors being on the levels below. At least half the outside of the building was glass, and I could see a security guard inside staring at the vans.

"Michael," I said, striding toward the guard, drawing my gear out of my duffel and preparing it. "Doors."

Michael stepped in front of me and said, as if reminding himself, "The building belongs to a criminal overlord and functions to assist him in his evil enterprise." Then he drew *Amoracchius*, made two sweeping slashes, and the glass fell entirely out of the door immediately in front of me.

I deployed the material I'd picked up the day before: specifically, a self-lighting butane torch and a bundle of two dozen large roman candles I had duct-taped together. I held the roundish bundle of fireworks under my left arm and was already lighting their fuses en masse with the butane torch as Michael leapt aside. By the time the guard had begun to rise from his chair, twenty-four twenty-shot roman candles were sending out screaming projectiles that detonated with deafening cracks of thunder.

It was a constant stream of fire and sound and light and smoke, and the poor guard had no idea how to react. He'd been fumbling for his gun when the first projectile went off not a foot from his nose, and before he could recover from that, two dozen more were going off all around him.

I hated to admit it, but . . . it was pretty gratifying. I mean, it was like holding my own personal pyrotechnic minigun, so many rounds were spewing out of the various roman candles. They filled the air with the scorched scent of sulfur and thick smoke that I hoped would confuse the surveillance cameras.

The guard was hit by twenty or thirty of the sizzling munitions in a couple of seconds, and flung himself down behind his desk, while I peppered the wall behind him with more of the raucous projectiles. While I did that, Grey bounded into the place, danced between the last few rounds from my bundle, and slugged the guard across the jaw with bone-cracking force.

The guard went down in a moaning heap.

Grey looked at something behind the desk and said, "He got to the silent alarm."

"Right," I said. I dropped the first bundle of roman candles and pulled the second one out of the duffel bag. I started walking toward the stairs down to the vault below as I lit the second bundle, and began hosing down the top of the stairway with more fireworks just as two more men in the same uniform came pelting up the stairs.

These two weren't as slow as the first one—and they had shotguns. That said, there's a really limited amount of damage you can do when you can't see or hear and loud things are going bang half an inch from your face, or giving you first-degree burns as they sizzle into your arm. They got a few aimless rounds off before Deirdre, in her demonform, swarmed past them, walking on her ribbons of hair as if they were the manifold legs of some kind of sea crustacean. A couple of them lashed out, slashing the shotguns in half, and the guards began to beat a hasty retreat back down the stairs.

Grey flung himself down the stairwell after them, not touching the stairs with his feet on the way, and there came the sounds of efficient and brutal violence from below, beneath the howling and banging of the fireworks.

"Clear!" Grey shouted.

I went to the top of the stairs and looked down. Grey had both guards lying back to back at the bottom of the stairs, in front of the first security door. He was busy using their handcuffs to cross-bind their wrists to one another.

I spattered him with the last few rounds from the roman candles. He rolled his eyes and gave me a disgusted look.

"Oops," I said, and discarded the exhausted bundle of fireworks.

Nicodemus appeared on the stairs beside me, looking down at Grey. He arched an eyebrow. "All three, still alive. Going soft, Grey?"

"They set off the silent alarm," Grey said. "Means the authorities are coming. It will be easier for Binder to convince them to sit and talk rather than simply assaulting the place if we have prisoners instead of corpses."

"I suppose that's true," Nicodemus said. He turned

and called, "Mr. Binder, bring your associates in, if you would, and prepare to defend the building. Miss Ascher, we are ready for you now."

I put the butane torch out, put it back in my duffel, and then slung my staff down off my shoulder. Nicodemus was eyeing me as I did.

"Fireworks," he said.

"You think you're the only guy in the world who can get things done without his supernatural gadgets?" I asked him.

He waved a hand at the smoke in his face and said mildly, "Let us hope that their firefighting systems do not include—"

An alarm began to blare, and sprinkler heads all around the first floor started up, spraying chilly, slightly stale-smelling water everywhere.

"—sprinklers," Nicodemus finished on a sigh.

Hannah Ascher came in, moving quickly, and eyed me with disgust. "Fireworks? Seriously?"

"Loud and distracting, remember?" I called after her, as she descended the stairs. "I am the king of loud and distracting."

"Not only do I have to burn through a wall," she muttered. "I've got to do it in a downpour, too."

"Get tough. It should help muffle the excess magical energy," I said, maybe a bit grumpily.

Ascher shot a look back up at me, and gestured at the sprinklers. "You did this on purpose?"

"Yeah, well. Sometimes, when I get bored, I stop and think."

She held up a small spray can. "How am I supposed to

lay out a circle on the floor when there's a layer of water over it? Did you think about that?"

"Deirdre," Nicodemus said.

Deirdre promptly swarmed halfway down the stairs, and then there were several sharp sounds of impact, as her metallic hair shot out, surrounding Ascher, and slammed onto the floor around her. The flat ribbonlike hairs spread out, edge down, scraping along the marble tile like a squeegee, sweeping the standing water away.

Ascher looked like she nearly had a heart attack when Deirdre did that, and cast a glare up at the Denarian. But then she took the can and sprayed a layer of what looked like some kind of aerosolized plastic or rubber onto the floor. She laid it out in a large circle around her, overlapping the circle onto the wall and continuing it up to a few inches above her head. It was lopsided, but technically a circle didn't have to be a perfect one to contain the magic. It was just a lot more efficient—not to mention professional—that way.

Ascher, who was looking damned appealing in her wet clothes (and dammit, how could I blame my reaction on the Winter mantle when it was being held at bay by iron?), went over the circle again, making sure the plastic spray was especially thick at the joints of the floor and wall. Then she nodded once, bent, and twisted her wrist so that a couple of drops of her blood fell from the manacles onto the circle. It snapped up into place at once, a screen of invisible energy, and she promptly unlocked her manacles and dropped them onto the floor at her feet. Then she narrowed her eyes, touched her finger to the wall inside the circle, and murmured a quiet word.

Light sprang out from her fingertip, sudden and fierce, and steam began to hiss up where droplets of water fell onto her hand or the wall. She began to move her fingertip slowly, and I watched as marble and the drywall and the concrete and metal beneath it began to crack and blacken and part. Glowing motes and sparks flew back from her, falling thickly on her hand and her arm, then blackening and dropping to the floor, burning holes in her sleeve but leaving her flesh, as far as I could see, untouched.

I lifted my eyebrows at that. I mean, I guess I could turn my finger into an arc welder, sure, but that wouldn't mean that my entire hand wouldn't burn to a crisp as I did it. That kind of inurement to the elements required an entirely different order and magnitude of talent— talent very few wizards, in my experience, possessed.

Man. When Ascher said she mostly worked with fire, she wasn't kidding.

Binder and his troops came into the bank while she was working, and Binder immediately scouted out the place and started assigning groups to various defensive positions. As he did that, Anna Valmont slid silently across the floor until she stood near me. She looked at the thorn manacles on my wrist.

"I can't stand to look at those things," she said. "It must hurt."

I bit down on a sharp reply. She wasn't looking for that by standing near me. "Yeah, pretty much."

She fiddled with her gear and licked her lips. "How long, do you think, before you can take them off?"

"No idea," I said. "Depends on Ascher, I guess."

There was a loud snapping sound and a squeal of parting metal from below, and Ascher half snarled, "That's right, bitch," and began putting her manacles back on in a businesslike fashion.

It had taken her less than three minutes to slice an opening large enough to admit a big guy into the reinforced wall.

She smeared the circle with her foot, and the excess energy of the spell dispersed into the air to be immediately smothered by the falling water. Then she put her hand on the cut section and began to push.

Grey slid in front of her and said, "Best let me go first, Miss Ascher." He set his shoulders and almost casually shoved the cut section of wall down, and it fell through to the hallway beyond with a satisfying boom—and was instantly echoed by the hollow, coughing blast of a shotgun from the hallway beyond.

Grey was flung off of his feet to the ground, where he promptly became the origin point of a growing puddle of blood.

Ascher let out a choked sound and flattened herself desperately to the side of the opening, into the shelter of the unexposed side of the stairwell.

The shotgun boomed twice more, and then Deirdre was through the opening. The shotgun went off again, and then a man screamed.

Then silence.

I snarled wordlessly. I rushed down the stairs to check on Ascher, and then peered through the hole in the wall. Deirdre crouched beyond it, on all fours like a wary cat, her hair spread out around her and moving slowly, like strands of kelp in a gentle current. A fourth guard lay unmistakably dead on the floor in front of her, his shotgun still gripped loosely in his hand.

"Grey," Nicodemus said, his voice tight.

Of course he was worried about Grey. Grey hadn't done his job with the retina scanner yet.

Ascher was shaken but untouched. I gave her shoulder a quick squeeze and turned to Grey, trying to remember what I knew about first aid and tourniquets.

I needn't have bothered. Grey had already begun sitting up even before I turned around, and his hair was mussed. Other than that, and the bloodied clothing, he looked entirely healthy. His expression was annoyed. "Damn, that hurts."

"Whiner," I said. "One little load of buckshot to the chest." I offered him my hand.

Grey stared blankly at my hand for a second, as if it had taken him a moment to remember what the gesture meant. Then he took it and I pulled him up to his feet. He wobbled once, and then shook his head and steadied.

"You okay?" I asked.

He gestured at all the blood on the floor. "Hit my heart. I'll be fine in a minute."

"Man," I said, impressed. "Takes a licking and keeps on ticking."

Grey showed me his teeth, then turned, poised and contained once more, and stalked through the doorway after Deirdre.

Hannah Ascher got slowly to her feet and stood staring down at the smeared puddle of blood on the floor. She swallowed and started back up the stairs.

I put out a hand and stopped her. "It'll take the cops time to get here, but you probably don't want to be standing around on the first floor when they do," I said.

"Too right," said Binder, coming up behind Valmont, still at the stairway's top and nudging her down like a bulldog herding a hesitant child. "Bullets are no respecters of persons. Go on, girl. And Ash, love, don't forget to fill my pack."

Ascher had a couple of empty black backpacks slung over her shoulder. "I know, I know. The red ones."

Nicodemus came to the top of the stairs, dragging the unconscious guard, and came down the steps, taking the guard along none too gently. Once he had the man to the bottom, he interlaced his handcuffs with those of the men already on the floor and cuffed him there.

"Well-done, Miss Ascher," Nicodemus said. "We'll secure the hallway and you can repeat your excellent performance on the second door. Miss Valmont, if you would accompany us, please—I'll want you working on the main vault door the moment we have access to it."

Anna Valmont tensed beside me, her fingers fretting over the surface of her tool roll, constantly wiping droplets of water away.

"Michael," I said, "why don't you go on in and make sure Valmont has everything she needs?"

Michael arched an eyebrow at me, but nodded, and came down the stairs to Anna Valmont's side. He gave her an encouraging smile, which she returned hesitantly, and the two of them went on through in the wake of the others.

"Dresden," Nicodemus said, his tone amused. "Surely

you don't think I'd do anything to the woman simply because her purpose had been served?"

"Not if you want that Way opened, you won't," I said.

Nicodemus smiled at me. He had buckled on a sword belt bearing the long blade he'd used earlier and a curved Bedouin dagger. "There, you see. You can learn to play the game after all." He vanished through the security door. A moment later, a huge shadow moved through the narrow stairway. I never saw the Genoskwa go by, but I felt the brush of patchy fur against the skin of my right hand, smelled a faint reek of its odor in the air, and bits of ash and the scent of burned hair came from the edges of the torched opening as the huge beast squeezed through it.

"This stinks," Binder said a moment later, his voice pitched low. "This stinks all to hell."

"Hah," I said. "Maybe it's just the furball."

He snorted, and we waited in silence for another three or four minutes, until Ascher reappeared, newly muddy with ashes and soot from burning through the second wall, wearing the manacles again. "That big thing creeps me out," she said.

"Too right," Binder said. "Gotta wonder what something like that wants with jewels, eh?"

He wasn't wrong about that.

"You're right," I said. "It smells."

Ascher traded a long look with Binder. "Should we leave?"

Binder grimaced. "And leave Old Nick unable to get through his fiery gate? He'd take that personally, I think. What is Uncle Binder's Rule Number Two?"

"Keep your eyes on the money," Ascher said.

"That's right," Binder said. "Don't take things personally, don't get emotional. We're professionals, love. Do the job, get paid, get gone."

"There could be more than money at stake here," I said quietly.

"Nick and his cup?" Binder asked. "Been a lot of bad men and a lot of powerful artifacts since this ball started spinning. It'll spin on."

"Maybe," I said. "Maybe not. Nicodemus is connected like few others. What if I could make you an offer?"

"Cash?" Binder asked.

I grimaced. "Well. Not as such."

He made a tsking sound and glanced at Ascher. "What's Uncle Binder's Rule Number One?"

"Money or nothing," she said. "Anything else costs too much."

He nodded. "So don't offer me favors, wizard, or lenience from the White Council, or power from a Faerie Queen. Those things aren't payment. They're pretty, pretty things with strings attached, and sooner or later you're all wrapped up like a bug in a web. Money or nothing."

"What about freedom?" I asked him. "The cops are going to have this place surrounded by the time we get back. Do you think you're going to fight your way out past an army of CPD?"

Binder let out a low belly laugh. "Look at you, Dresden. Damn, but you're a Boy Scout. This is a mob bank, belongs to your local robber baron. Eight minutes since the silent alarm went off, and where are the sirens? Where are the uniforms?"

I grimaced. I'd noticed that, too.

"You really think the alarms call the gendarmes?" He shook his head. "Twenty to one, it'll go to his people first. Then they can decide if they want to call in the coppers or handle the matter themselves."

Yeah. Marcone's people.

Gulp.

Binder busied himself making sure the groaning, stirring guards had been thoroughly disarmed and relieved of their handcuff keys. "Now, if you'll excuse me, odds are good if this Marcone of yours is so savvy, someone will start playing circle games with me. I'll need to be ready to counter them." He pointed a finger at Ascher.

"For the hundredth time, the red ones," Ascher said, quirking a slight smile.

"I'll buy us a nice tropical island with a nice beach, and get you a new swimsuit," he said, winking.

"You should be so lucky," Ascher said back.

"I'll hold the door for you lot. Don't be too long." Binder went up the stairs, his beady eyes sparkling, fairly bristling with energy.

"Huh," I said.

"What?" Ascher asked.

"You and Binder . . . not a thing?"

Ascher's mouth turned up bitterly at the corners. "Not for lack of trying."

"Well," I said, "kinda hard to blame him. You're damned attractive."

"Not *him*, trying," she said. "Me. He's turned me

down." She looked up the stairs for a moment and sighed. "Rule Number One. He's not into entanglements."

"Oh," I said, trying to imagine Ascher coming on to Binder and getting turned down. Granted, I'd turned her down too. Which . . . now that I thought about it, just couldn't have been awesome for her self-image.

Doesn't matter how pretty you are. What's important is how pretty you feel. No one feels pretty when they hear "no" often enough.

"Don't take this the wrong way," I said, "but you would not believe how many times I've had pretty girls who would have eaten me alive, like, literally, make a pass at me. Makes a guy a little tense about it."

Ascher scratched at her nose with one finger, making the manacles jingle. She grimaced as the thorns dug at her wrists. "Wait a minute. You're saying I'm *too* pretty to be attractive."

"To a guy in my business, maybe," I said. "Someone as alluring as you, there's a high twitch factor. Binder strikes me as the type to have the same kind of wariness."

Her voice turned thoughtful. "So if I'd been a little older and a little dumpier, maybe I'd have had some luck with you—like Murphy."

I scowled. "Murphy's made of muscle. You just can't see it under the suit and the body armor," I said. "And she hasn't gotten lucky with me either."

Ascher stared at me for a second and blinked slowly. "You're . . . serious, aren't you?"

"We're complicated," I said.

"Because you're twitchy?"

"And she's had a couple of divorces. And her ex-boyfriend kind of shot me."

"What?"

"I asked him to," I said hurriedly.

"What?"

My mouth just kept running. "Plus there was this whole initiation rite with Mab, except I think that only happened in my brain or something. Traumatic—like getting it on with a hurricane. I think it's kind of put me off sex in general."

Ascher stared at me for a second more, then shook her head and turned away. "Man," she said. "Don't take this the wrong way, Dresden, but thanks for turning me down. Kinda dodged a bullet on that one."

"Hey," I protested.

"Seriously," she said. "Way too much drama there for anyone sane."

"We're not dramatic," I said. "Just—"

"Complicated?" she asked. She shook her head. "It isn't complicated. You just open up and let someone in. And whatever comes after that, you face it together."

"It isn't that simple."

"The hell it isn't. You had a chance for that and you turned it down? You're a fucking idiot. I'm not making the same mistake."

Footsteps came from the hallway beyond the security door and Michael appeared, *Amoracchius* in hand. The Sword was glowing with a faint, angry light.

"Harry," he said. "Trouble."

"What's happening?"

"Nicodemus is about to kill Anna Valmont."

"And you're here?"

"Four of them and one of me," he said.

I got out the key to my manacles and made sure it was handy.

"Dresden," Ascher said, her voice tense, "if you blow out the electronics, you'll blow the whole job!"

"I love it when a posh bird talks dirty!" called Binder merrily, from upstairs.

I ground my teeth, took my staff in my right hand, and said to Michael, "Come on."

And then I took off down the hallway.

Chapter
Thirty-five

The hallway beyond the first security door ran for a bit less than a hundred feet, and I found the mental shields against my various pains fluttering as I put more demand on my body. I ground my teeth and got through it, while Michael moved with effortless, well, *grace* at my side, even steadying me once when I wobbled.

At the end of the hall was another security door with a hole scorched through the wall beside it—and again I was treated to the stench of burned Genoskwa hair.

I ducked and went through the hole with Michael right behind me, and found myself in a room that was walled on two sides with what at first glance looked like lockers and which I realized a second later were security-deposit boxes. Minimum security, I guessed, where people stored copies of their important paperwork and such, from the size of them.

The third wall was made of obdurate, unjointed steel, broken only by a large steel door with a relatively small, unobtrusive control panel in its center. The panel didn't look like cutting-edge tech to me. It was simply a keypad, a large combination wheel, and a small LED display.

Anna Valmont stood in front of the control panel with her tool roll splayed out on the floor beside her feet, all her equipment at the ready. She had what looked like a small flashlight in her hand. She was facing not the door, but Nicodemus.

The leader of the Denarians stood off to one side, his little automatic in his hand, pointing it steadily at Valmont. Deirdre stood on his right, and Grey on his left. The Genoskwa was a giant blur against the wall behind them and a stench in the air.

"I still don't see the problem," Nicodemus said.

"The problem," Valmont said, her eyes flicking nervously to me, "is that this *isn't the door from the plans you gave me.*"

"My information sources are impeccable," Nicodemus replied. "They assure me that the door I showed you was the one installed when the bank was built."

"Obviously, they aren't as smart as they think they are," Valmont replied tartly. "Marcone must have had the door changed out secretly after it was installed."

"Then open *this* door," Nicodemus said, and gestured with the gun. "Now."

"You don't get it," Valmont said. "With the blueprints and a day to plan, I might have been able to crack the door. Maybe. This one is another Fernucci, but it's a custom job, and it could be designed completely differently. Not only that, but *this* door . . ."

A horrible instinct hit me. "Hell's bells. It's wired, isn't it?"

Grey scowled at me. "How did you know that?"

Because my brother's girlfriend had seen Marcone defending one of his strongholds with her own eyes a few years before, against an angry Fomor sorcerer. He'd had the place rigged with mines and defensive strong points and booby traps. Thomas had told me about it. But all I said to Grey was, "How? I'm a freaking wizard, that's how."

Valmont gave me a grim nod, and jerked her head toward the hole in the wall where we'd entered. "We're lucky Ascher didn't set them off on the way in."

I padded over to the wall and examined it. At the edges of the scorched hole, I could see the melted plastic edges of shapes I recognized from previous horrible experiences—claymore antipersonnel mines. They'd been set into the wall, between the concrete and the drywall, facing into the room.

I swallowed. One claymore, when detonated, would spew hundreds of ball bearings out in a broad arc in front of it, a giant's shotgun. I counted eight of the devices, stacked vertically, one per linear foot. I think the things were about a foot across.

So. Assume Marcone wanted anyone who tried to force their way into his vault reduced to salsa. Assume he was perfectly well aware how hard a lot of supernatural beings were to hurt. How would he handle it?

Overkill, that's how.

I was guessing he'd installed one claymore mine per square foot of wall. Multiply that by, for simplicity's sake, three hundred ball bearings each, and you had a whole freaking *lot* of round pieces of metal waiting to tear us all to shreds. They would bounce around the steel walls of this room like BBs rattling around the inside of a tin can and render any physical body in it to churned meat sauce.

"Fun," I said. I turned to Nicodemus and said, "Looks like this party is over. You weren't sufficiently prepared."

"We aren't stopping now," Nicodemus said, staring at Valmont. "Open the vault, Miss Valmont."

"It would be stupid," Valmont said. "I think I could have done the first one. This is a door I know nothing about. Even if I do everything right, I could run into something that trips the circuit just because I don't know it's there."

"I'm going to give you three minutes to open the vault, Miss Valmont. After that, I'll kill you."

"Are you insane?" Valmont demanded.

"Hell's bells, man," I said. "Calm down. The target isn't going anywhere. You aren't getting any older. What's the rush?"

He bared his teeth. "Time is relative, Dresden. And, at the moment, it is running out. We open the vault, today. Either Miss Valmont does so or she dies."

"Or she sets off the mines and we *all* die?" I blurted. "Have you lost it?"

"Feel free to wait outside if you are frightened," he said calmly.

And I realized that I could. I could back out of the room and pull Michael with me. Valmont would have nowhere else to go, no other options, and I knew exactly what she would do, facing certain death—she'd blow the system in an attempt to take Nicodemus and Deirdre with her. Or maybe she would pull off a minor miracle and open the door, in which case we could proceed just as we had before. If she died, the raid was blown and Mab's obligation to Nicodemus was met or at least delayed—and if I got lucky, maybe it would put paid to a roomful of bad people at the same time. If Valmont survived, I was no worse off than before.

And all I had to do was throw a woman to the wolves. The math said it was the smart move.

"Math was never my best subject," I muttered. "Michael, get clear."

He ground his teeth, but Michael had worked with me long enough to trust me when things were tight—and we both knew that not even *Amoracchius* and the purest intentions in the world would save him from a blast like the one Marcone had rigged. He left.

"I'm not frightened," Grey said. "I want to make that perfectly clear." Then he also left the room.

"What are you doing, Dresden?" Nicodemus asked.

"Helping. Stop the shot clock and let us work," I said, and made sure the manacles were locked tight against my wrist as I strode over to Anna Valmont. "Okay," I told her. "Let's do this."

She widened her eyes at me. "What are you doing? Get back!"

"I'm helping you," I said. "I'm helping you open this door without blowing anyone to hell. Especially yourself. Also me."

She whirled the little flashlight up and shone it on the ground at my feet. "Stop!"

It was an ultraviolet light. I barely managed to stop my foot before it came down on a circle of vaguely Norse runes painted on the stone floor, invisible to normal light but picked out by Valmont's flashlight.

"Stars and stones," I breathed. "It's a ward."

She shone the light around the floor in front of the vault door. There were at least a dozen wards the size of dinner plates in the immediate area around it.

"That's why the door is different," I said. "They've got passive spells running all over the damned room."

"I didn't see the first one until I'd already trampled all over them," she said. "That suggests, to me, that I'm not the right sort of person to set them off."

"Give me the light again," I said, and she shone it at my feet. I bent over and peered down at the ward, examining it carefully. "Good call. These are built to react to a practitioner's aura. Not real strong—there's no threshold to base them on. But enough to put out a surge of magical energy."

"Enough to break a circuit, you think?"

"Definitely."

"So a practitioner walks on one of them and . . ." Valmont opened the fingers of her left hand all at once, an elegant gesture. "Boom."

The chatter of automatic gunfire came from upstairs— one of the suits had opened up with an Uzi. Valmont and I both flinched at the sudden sound.

"Christ," she breathed.

"We have no time," Nicodemus said. "Open the door, Miss Valmont."

She swallowed and looked at me.

"Shine the light at my feet, so I can see the way," I said.

She did, and I picked my way over the wards until I reached her side. "Okay," I said. "Three things. One, I'm not going to run off and leave you here alone. Two, I'm not going to let him shoot you. And three—you can do this."

"I don't know if I can," she said in a low whisper. "What if this door is more complex than the first one?"

"It can't be," I said.

"You don't know that."

"Yes, I do," I said. "Because of the way magic interacts with technology. Marcone's got all these low-grade wards spread out around the door. Whatever electronics or mechanics are inside it, the more complex they are, the faster the magic in this room would break them down and trip the circuit." I pointed a finger. "That door has got to be assembled out of simpler parts and far simpler electronics than the original. That's why it got installed secretly—not to stick an even meaner door on, but to hide the fact that the door has to be less complicated than the original."

Valmont looked at me for a moment, frowning. "Are you sure?"

"Yeah," I said. "I mean, you know. In theory."

"God, Dresden," she said. "What if you're wrong?"

"Well," I said, "if I am, neither one of us will ever know it. Because I'm not going anywhere."

She stared up at me uncertainly.

I put a hand on her shoulder and said, "This is what happened to the audacity of the woman who stole my coat and my car after I rescued her from certain doom? I remembered you with a little more attitude than that."

A spark of some kind of defiance, or amusement, or

maybe both, flickered in her eyes. "I don't remember it happening that way."

"Probable doom," I allowed, and felt myself grinning like a loon. "Highly possible doom. Look, Anna, you robbed the *Vatican* when you swiped the Shroud. How tough can it be to handle the pad of a schmuck gangster from Illinois?"

She took a slow, deep breath. "You make an excellent point," she said seriously, and bent to her tools.

She moved with swift, precise professionalism. She had the cover off the control panel in half a minute, and was getting into the wires behind it seconds later.

"You were right," she reported. "There are no chips or microcircuits at all."

"Can you open it?" I asked.

"If I don't make any mistakes. Yes. I think. Now hush."

More gunfire erupted from upstairs as she worked. It wasn't answered by anything I could hear, but I was pretty sure Binder's goons wouldn't be firing off their weapons for fun.

Grey slid back into the room and reported, conversationally, "They're using suppressed weapons. There are enough of them to make a great big mess of this entire operation, but so far they're just probing us."

"Heh," I said. "Probe."

"Wizard," Grey said, a trifle impatiently, "are you sure you want to keep pushing it like this?"

"Yeah," I said. "Think so."

"Grey, stand by," Nicodemus said. "Should Valmont open the vault, we'll need you to handle the scanner."

Grey grunted and said, "Guess I'd better put my game face on."

And once again, he seemed to quiver in place, a motion that I couldn't quite track with my eyes, and suddenly Grey was gone and poor Harvey was standing there, looking nervously through the scorched entry of the vault. More gunfire rang out and Grey-Harvey flinched, darting quick glances behind him.

Huh.

"Bloody hell," Valmont muttered, reaching for another tool. She started operating the combination lock, watching a bobbing needle on some kind of sensor as she did. "Impossible to work with all this jabber."

"I could make some white noise for you," I said helpfully, and followed by saying something like, "Kssssssssshhhhhhhhhhhhhh."

"Thank you, Dresden, for that additional distract—" Her eyes widened in sudden terror and she stopped breathing.

I felt my spine go rigid with anticipation. If those claymores went off, there was no way my duster was going to save me from that much flying metal. I clenched my teeth.

Valmont looked up at me, abruptly showed me a tigress's smile, and said, "Gotcha." Then she pushed a final button with a decisive stab, and the vault door made an ominous *clickety-clack* sound. She turned the handle, and the enormous door swung ponderously open. "Schmuck gangster from Illinois, indeed."

"Get that UV light on the wards again," I said.

"On it," Valmont said.

"Grey," Nicodemus said.

Grey-Harvey hopped rather nimbly through the wards as Valmont illuminated them, and went through the vault door.

I went with him, my senses alert to any other bits of magical mayhem that might be waiting for us inside Gentleman Johnnie Marcone's vault.

It was huge. Fifty feet wide. A hundred feet long. Barred doors that looked sufficient to keep out King Kong stood at intervals along the walls. Each of the barred doors had a steel plaque on it bearing a number and a name. The first one on the right read: LORD RAITH—00010001. The room behind it was piled with boxes of about the right size to hold large paintings, strong-box-style crates, and several pallets bearing bricks made of bundles of hundred-dollar bills, stacked up in four-foot cubes and wrapped in clear plastic.

The strong room on the other side of us had a plate that read: FERROVAX—00010002, and it was filled with row upon row of closed, fireproof safes.

And there were eleven more rooms on each side of the vault.

In between the barred doors were storage lockers, shelves loaded with precious artwork, and more of those giant cubes of money than I really wanted to start counting.

It was the fortune of a small nation. Maybe even a not-so-small nation.

And the only door in the place with a little computerized eye-scanning thing next to it was at the very, very far end of the vault, in the center of the rear wall—the Storage Cubby of the Underworld.

"Looks like that's it," I said.

For a second, Grey-Harvey said nothing. I looked at him. He was scanning the room, slowly.

"It's just money," I said. "Get your head in the game."

"I'm looking for guards and booby traps," he said.

I grunted. "Oh. Carry on."

"I shouldn't be here," Grey muttered, almost too quietly to be heard. "This is stupid. I'm going to get caught. I'm going to get caught. Someone will come for me. Those things will get me."

I gave him a somewhat fish-eyed look. "Uh," I said. "What?"

Grey blinked once and then looked at me. "Huh?"

"What were you talking about?" I said.

He frowned slightly. The frown turned into a grimace and he rubbed at his forehead. "Nothing."

"The hell it was," I said.

"I'm too Harvey right now," he said. "He doesn't like this situation very much."

"Uh," I said. "What do you mean, 'too Harvey'?"

"Shifting this deep isn't for chumps," he said. "It's nothing you need to worry about. Trust me."

"Why should I do that?"

His voice turned annoyed. "Because I'm a freaking shapeshifter and I'm the one who knows, that's why." He eyed me. "You'd better wait here. Manacles or not, those retina scanners are damned finicky."

"I'll stop short," I said, and started walking to the end of the vault. I didn't doubt that Grey was right about the scanners, but I'd have to be a lot more gullible than I was to let someone like him out of my sight if I could help it. I stopped thirty or forty feet short of the back wall, and Grey-Harvey sidled up to the panel. He lifted his fingers and tapped out a sequence of maybe a dozen or fifteen numbers into the keypad, swiftly, as if his fingers knew it by pure reflex. A panel rotated when he was done, and a little tube appeared. He leaned down and peered into it, and red light flashed out. He straightened, blinking, and a second later there was a quiet clack.

"Here goes nothing," he said, and turned the handle on the door to the strong room.

The door to the mortal vault of the God of the Underworld (labeled HADES—00000013) opened smoothly, soundlessly. It would have taken more muscle to get into Michael's fridge.

Grey turned to me, resuming his own shape, and his mouth twisted into a perfectly invincible smirk. "Damn, I'm good."

"Okay," I said. "Go get everybody else. I'll get the Way ready."

Grey turned to go and then paused, eyeing me.

"If I wanted to shut this thing down," I said, "I could have done it pretty much anytime in the past twenty minutes." I shifted to a maniacally indeterminate European accent and said, "We're going through."

"The Black Hole?" Grey asked, incredulously. "*Nobody* quotes *The Black Hole*, Dresden. Nobody even remembers that one."

"Hogwash. Ernest Borgnine, Anthony Perkins, and Roddy McDowall all in the same movie? Immortality."

"Roddy McDowall was just the voice of the robot."

"Yeah. And the robots were awesome."

"Cheap *Star Wars* knockoffs," Grey sneered.

"Not necessarily mutually exclusive," I said.

"I wasn't worried about you scrubbing the mission," he said. "I was thinking you might indulge yourself in a little Robin Hood action against this Marcone character."

"Doubt it would make him any angrier than he's already going to be," I said. "But ripping off *this* vault isn't the job."

Grey considered me for a moment and then nodded. "Right. I'll get the crew." He turned and jogged to the entrance to the vault—

—and was suddenly *pulled* out of the vault and into the security room beyond by an abrupt and severe force.

"Yeah, that can't be goo—," I started to say.

Before I could finish, Tessa in her mantis form blurred through the vault door, fantastic in her speed, terrifying in her strength, and slammed the door closed behind her. Her rear legs rotated the inside works of the door— meant to allow the door to be locked or unlocked from the inside—and the lock of the heavy vault door shut with a very final-sounding *clack*.

Suddenly, the only light came from some tiny floor lamps along either wall, and they gleamed madly from the mantis's thousands of eye facets.

"You," came her buzzing, two-layered voice, poisonous with hate. "This is *your* fault."

"What?" I said.

My hand went to the thorn manacles still on my wrist—and then froze. Michael and the others were outside, in the booby-trapped security room. If I started throwing magic around, even at this distance, I would almost certainly trip the antiwizard fail-safe Marcone had built into it.

"No matter," Tessa spat. "Your death will end the chain even more readily than the accountant's."

And then a furious Knight of the Blackened Denarius came hurtling toward me with insectile speed—and if I used a lick of magic to fight her, I'd blow my friends to Kingdom Come.

Chapter

Thirty-six

Tessa's wings blurred and she came at me, scythe-hook arms raised to strike.

The voice inside my head was screaming a high-pitched, girly scream of terror, and for a second I thought I was going to wet my pants. There wasn't any time to get cute, there wasn't any space to run, and without the super-strength of the Winter mantle, I was as good as dead.

Unless . . .

If Butters was right, then the strength I'd gained as the Winter Knight was something I'd had all along—latent and ready for an emergency. The only thing that had been holding me back was the natural inhibitors built into my body. Not only that, but I had another advantage—during the past year and a half or so, since I'd been dead and got better, I'd been training furiously. First, to get myself back on my feet and into shape to fight if I had to, and then because it had provided a necessary physical outlet for the pressures I was under.

The thing about training of any kind is that you get held back by an absolute limit—it freaking hurts. Little injuries mount up, robbing you of your drive, degrading the efficiency of whatever training you're into, creating imbalances and points of relative weakness.

But not me.

For the duration of my training, I'd been shielded from pain by the aegis of the Winter mantle. It wasn't just that it made me physically stronger—it also allowed me to train longer and harder and more thoroughly than I could possibly have done without it. I wasn't faster and stronger than I'd been before solely because I wore the Winter Knight's mantle—I'd also worked my ass off to do it.

I didn't have to *beat* Tessa. I just had to *survive* her. Anna Valmont would already be on the vault door, finessing it open again, and now that she'd done it once, I was pretty sure that her repeat performance would be even faster. How long had it taken her to take the door the first time? Four minutes? Five? I figured she'd do it in three. And then Michael would be through the door and this situation would change.

Three minutes. That was one round in a prizefighting ring. I just had to last one round.

Time to make something awesome happen, sans magic, all by myself.

As Tessa closed in, I flung my mostly empty duffel bag at her, faked to my right, and then darted to my left. Tessa bought the fake and committed, sliding past me on the smooth floor. I jumped up on top of a money cube and, without stopping my motion, bounded up again to the top shelf of a storage rack of artwork, got my feet planted, and turned with my staff raised over my head as she came blurring through the air toward me.

I let out a shout as I swung the heavy quarterstaff, giving it everything I had. I tagged her on the triangular head, hammering her hard enough to send the shock of the blow rattling through my shoulders. She might have been fast and psycho-angel strong, but she was also a bitty thing and even in her demonform she didn't have much mass. The blow killed her momentum completely and she plunged toward the floor.

But instead of dropping, she slammed her hooks into the metal shelf, their points piercing steel as if it had been cardboard, and she let out a shriek of fury as she started hauling herself up toward me.

I didn't like that idea. So I jumped on her face with both of my big stompy boots.

The impact tore the hooks free of the shelf and we both plunged to the floor. I came down on top, and the landing made my ankles scream with pain, and drove a gasping shriek from Tessa. I tried to convert the downward momentum into a roll and was only partly successful. I scrambled away on my hands and knees about a quarter of an instant before Tessa slammed a scythe down right where my groin had been. She'd landed on her back, and for an instant her limbs flailed in a very buglike fashion.

So I dropped my staff, grabbed one supporting strut of the steel shelving, and heaved.

The whole heavy storage rack and all its art came crashing down onto her head with a tremendous crash and a deafening sound of shattering statuary. I grabbed my staff and started backpedaling toward the entrance to Hades' strong room.

Tessa stayed down for maybe a second and a half. Then the shelves heaved and she threw them bodily away from her and scrambled back to her feet with another shriek of anger. She turned toward me and came leaping my way.

I stopped in my tracks, drew the big .500 out of my duster pocket, took careful aim, and waited until Tessa was too close to miss. I pulled the trigger when she was about six feet away.

The gun, in the confined space of the vault, sounded like a cannon, and the big bullet crashed into her thorax, smashing through her exoskeleton in a splash of ichor, and staggering her in her tracks. Behind her, a money cube suddenly exploded into flying Benjamins.

I took two or three steps back before she got moving again, and then I stopped and aimed once more, slamming another round into her. I stepped back and then fired a third round. Back again, and a fourth. After the fifth, my gun was empty and Tessa was still coming.

The bullets hadn't been enough to do more than slow her down, but they'd bought me what I needed most—time.

I stepped back into Hades' strong room and slammed the barred door closed just as Tessa came at me again. She hit the far side of the door with a violent impact and wrenched at it with her scythes but it had locked when it closed, and it held fast. She shrieked again and her scythes darted through the bars toward me. I reeled back in time to avoid perforation, and my shoulders hit the wall behind me.

"Hell's bells!" I blurted. "At least tell me *why*!"

The mantis's scythe-hooks latched onto two of the bars and began straining to tear them apart. Metal groaned and began to bend, and I suddenly felt one hell of a lot less clever. Tessa wasn't all that *big*, and it wouldn't take much of a bend in the bars to allow her into the strong room with me, without leaving an opening big enough for me to use to escape. If she opened them enough to come in, I was going to die a savagely messy death. Seconds ticked by in slow motion as the demon mantis quivered with physical strain and pure hatred.

"Why?" I demanded. My voice might have come out a little bit high-pitched. "What the *hell* are you doing screwing around with this mission?"

She didn't answer me. The bars groaned and slowly, slowly bent maybe an inch, but they'd been built extra thick, as if they'd been precisely intended to resist superhuman strength, which in all probability was exactly the case. Tessa threw back her insect's head and let out a screech that pressed viciously on my ears.

Halfway through, the mantis's head and face just *boiled* away, and the screech turned into a very human, utterly furious scream as Tessa's head appeared, both sets of her eyes wide and wild.

"I have *not* invested fifteen centuries to see it thrown *away*!" she shrieked.

I stared at her helplessly, my heart pounding furiously in my chest. I tried to think of something clever or engaging or disarming to say, but what came out was a helpless flick of my hands and the words "Psycho much?"

She focused on me, utterly furious and she spat several words that might have been an incantation of some kind, but her fury was too great to allow her to focus it into a spell. Instead, she just opened her mouth and *screamed* again, a scream that could never have come from a simple set of human lungs, one that went on and on and on, billowing out of her mouth along with particles of spittle, and then clots of something darker, and then of larger bits of matter that I realized, after a few seconds, had legs and were *wriggling*.

And then her scream turned into a gargle and she began vomiting a cloud, a *swarm* of flying insects that poured through the bars of the cage and came at me in an almost solid stream, slamming into me like water issuing from a high-pressure hose.

The impact drove the air from my lungs, and I couldn't suck it back in right away—which was just as well. The insects that hit my body clung on, roaches and beetles and crawling things that had no names, and swarmed up my neck toward my nose and mouth and ears as if guided by a malign will.

A few got into my gaping mouth before I clamped it shut and covered my nose and mouth with one hand. I chewed them to death and they crunched disgustingly and tasted of blood. The rest went for my eyes and ears and burrowed beneath my clothing to begin chewing at my skin.

I kept my cool for maybe twenty seconds, slapping them away from my head, getting a few strangled breaths in through my barely parted fingers, but then the insects got between my fingers and into my eyes and ears at almost the same time, and I let out a panicked scream. Burning agony spread over my body as the swarm chewed and chewed and chewed, and the last thing my stinging eyes saw was Tessa's body emptying like a deflating balloon as the insect swarm kept flooding out of it, and I had a horrified second to realize that she *was* in the strong room with me.

And then my mental shields against pain fluttered as panic began to settle in, and agony dropped me to my knees—putting me hip-deep in the focused malice of thousands and thousands of tiny mouths.

I dropped my hands desperately to fumble with the key to the thorn manacles, because without the use of magic I was going to die one of the more ugly deaths I'd ever considered, but my hands were one burning sheet of flame and I couldn't *find* the damned manacles and their keyholes under the layers and layers of swarming vermin, which seemed devilishly determined to keep them hidden from me.

Seconds later, the swarm filled my nostrils and started chewing at my lips, and forced me to close my eyes or lose them, and even then I could feel them chewing at the lids, ripping at the lashes.

I have been trained in mental disciplines most people could hardly imagine, much less duplicate. I have faced terrors of the same caliber without flinching. But not like this.

I lost it.

Thought fled. Pain came flooding through my shields. Terror and the urgent desire to *live* filled every thought, blind instinct taking over. I thrashed and crawled and writhed, trying to escape the swarm, but I might as well have been holding completely still for all the good it did me, and after time, the lack of air forced me to the floor on my side, curled up in a fetal position, just trying to defend my eyes and nose and mouth. Everything turned black and red.

And voices filled my ears. Thousands of whispering voices, hissing obscene, hateful things, vicious secrets, poisonous lies and horrible truths in half a hundred tongues all at once. I felt the pressure of those voices, coursing into my head like ice picks, gouging holes in my thoughts, in my emotions, and there was nothing, *nothing* I could do to stop them. I felt a scream building, one that would open my mouth, fill it with tiny, tearing bodies, and I knew that I couldn't stop it.

And then a broad hand slammed down onto the crown of my head, and a deep voice thundered, *"Lava quod est sordium!"*

Light burned through my closed eyelids, through the layers of insects covering them, and a furious heat spread down from the crown of my head, from that hand. It spread down, moving neither quickly nor slowly, and wherever it passed over my skin, as hot as scalding water in an industrial kitchen sink, the swarm abruptly vanished.

I opened my eyes to find Michael kneeling over me, *Amoracchius* in his left hand, his right resting on my head. His eyes were closed and his lips were moving, words of ritual Latin flowing from them in a steady stream.

Pure white fire spread down over my body, and I remembered when I had seen something similar once before—when vampires had attempted to manhandle Michael, many moons before, and had been scorched and scarred by the same fire. Now, as the light engulfed me, the swarm scattered, outer layers dropping away, while the slower inner layers were incinerated by the fire. It hurt—but the pain was a harsh, cleansing thing, somehow honest. It burned over me, and when the fire passed, I was free, and the swarm was scattering throughout the vault, pouring toward the tiny air vents spread throughout.

I looked up at Michael, gasping, and leaned my head forward. For a second, the pain and the fear still had me, and I couldn't make myself move. I lay there, simply shuddering.

His hand moved from my head to my shoulder, and he murmured, "Lord of Hosts, be with this good man and give him the strength to carry on."

I didn't feel anything mystic. There was no surge of magic or power, no flash of light. Just Michael's quiet, steady strength, and the sincerity of the faith in his voice.

Michael still thought I was a good man.

I clenched my jaw over the sobbing scream that was still threatening me, and pushed away the memory of those tiny, horrible words—the voice of Imariel, it must have been. I forced myself to breathe in a steady rhythm, despite the pain and the burning of my skin and my lungs, despite the stinging tears and tiny drops of blood in my eyes. And I put up the shields again, forcing the pain to a safe distance. They were shakier, and more of the pain leaked through than had been there before—but I did it.

Then I lifted my eyes to Michael and nodded.

He gave me a quick, fierce smile and stood up, then offered me his hand.

I took it and rose, looking past Michael to where Grey stood, melting back from Harvey's face to his own, one last time. He'd opened the door to Hades' vault again. Behind him, the rest of the crew, minus Binder, was approaching, while the huge, vague shape of the Genoskwa closed the door to the vault with a large, hollow boom of displaced air.

"She came through fast, during the firefight," Michael said to me. "There wasn't any way for me to stop her."

My throat burned and felt raw, but I croaked, "It worked out. Thanks."

"Always."

Nicodemus approached us with his expression entirely neutral, and eyed Michael.

"We needn't fear further interference from Tessa. It will take her time to pull herself together. How did you do that?" he demanded.

"I didn't," Michael said simply.

Nicodemus and Deirdre exchanged an uneasy glance.

"All of you, hear me," Michael said quietly. He turned and stood between them—Fallen angels and monsters and scoundrels and mortal fiends—and me. "You think your power is what shapes the world you walk in. But that is an illusion. Your choices shape your world. You think your power will protect you from the consequences of those choices. But you are wrong. You create your own rewards. There is a Judge. There is Justice in this world. And one day you *will* receive what you have earned. Choose carefully."

His voice resonated oddly in that space, the words not loud, but absolutely penetrating, touched with something more than mortal, with an awareness beyond that of simple space and time. He was, in that moment, a Messenger, and no one who heard him speak could doubt it.

Silence settled on the vault, and no one moved or spoke.

Nicodemus looked away from Michael and said calmly, "Dresden. Are you capable of opening the Way?"

I took a steadying breath, and looked around for the key to the manacles. I'd dropped it while being simultaneously eaten, smothered, and driven insane. Hell, I was lucky there hadn't been any anaphylactic shock involved.

Or, all things considered, maybe luck had nothing to do with it.

Michael spotted the key and picked it up. I held out my hand and he began unlocking the manacles.

"What did that mean?" I asked him in a whisper.

"You heard it as well as I did," he replied, with a small shrug. "I suppose it wasn't a message for us."

I looked slowly over the others as the manacles came off and thought that maybe it had been.

Uriel, I thought. *You sneaky bastard. But you weren't telling me anything I didn't already suspect.*

The thorn manacles fell away and the icy power of Winter suffused me again. The pain vanished. The raw, chewed skin became nothing. The exhaustion fell away and I drew a deep, cleansing breath.

Then I summoned my will, spun on my heel, slashed at the air with my staff, and called, *"Aparturum!"*

And with a surge of my will and power, and a sudden line of sullen red light in the air, I tore an opening into the Underworld.

Chapter

Thirty-seven

The lights blew out in showers of sparks and there was an instant, thunderous explosion behind us, and the closed door of the vault rang like an enormous bell. While the thick steel walls of the vault were impenetrable to the shot of the antipersonnel mines, I didn't want to think about how much metal had just rebounded from them and gone flying off at every angle imaginable, and I wondered if anyone had just died as a result.

There was a great grinding sound, as if some part of the building's structure had slowly collapsed, somewhere outside the vault, and in the dim red glow of the tear in the fabric of reality, I could barely make out the faces around me.

"Hell's bells," I said to Michael. "Binder? His prisoners?"

"I helped him move them," Michael said at once. "It's partly why it took me so long to get to you. Once we knew about the mines, we got everyone out of that hallway and back up to the first floor."

"Where there were only bullets flying around," Grey said, his voice dry.

I grimaced, but there'd been no help for it. Marcone had set up those mines, not me, and I just had to hope that the initial impact against the vault had robbed the explosively propelled projectiles of most of their strength.

Meanwhile, the torn-cloth ribbon of light in the air of the vault had spread, the Way to the Underworld opening before us, red light pouring into the strong room, and I could see scarlet flames dancing on the far side. The smell of sulfur wafted out of the Way. A moment later, there was a sudden, hot wind driving even more of the scent out of it, and pushing my hair back from my forehead.

As the flames danced and bowed with the wind, I could see a dark shape behind them—a wall rising up maybe forty yards away from us, with a clear arch shape beneath it. The arch was filled with brilliant fire, so dense that I could see nothing beyond it.

Nicodemus stepped up to stand beside me, staring into the Underworld. His dark eyes glittered with scarlet highlights.

"The Gate of Fire," he murmured. "Miss Ascher, if you please."

"Um," Hannah Ascher said. She swallowed. "No one said jack about me being the first one into the Underworld."

"I'm not sure anyone else could survive in there for more than a moment," Nicodemus said. "Dresden?"

I squinted at the inferno raging beyond the Way and said, "It's pretty tough to argue with fire. That's why wizards like to use it as a weapon. Heat that intense, I could keep it off me for maybe ten or twenty seconds—if you let me get a nap and a meal in before you asked me to deal with the next gate." I peered more closely. "Look there, in the archway. On the right wall, about five feet up."

Hannah Ascher stopped next to me, and squinted through the Way. "Is that a lever?"

"Looks like it," I said. "Walk through, pull the lever. Seems simple enough."

"A little too simple," she said, and started taking off her own thorn manacles.

"Sure," I said. "If you're immune to fire, it's a piece of cake." I blew out my breath. "I can make that sprint before my shields fail. I think. Assuming I don't trip and fall on anything. I can't see what the ground is like."

"Dammit," she said. "No. No, I guess this is where I earn my cut." She stared at the Way and dropped the two empty backpacks she carried over one shoulder. Then she took a short breath and stripped out of her black sweater in one smooth motion, revealing a black sports bra beneath.

"Wow," Grey said. "Nice."

She rolled her eyes and gave him a short look, then pressed the sweater into my hands. "Hold this for me."

"Okay," I said. "Why?"

Her boots and fatigue pants came off next, and Michael resolutely turned slightly to one side and studied an empty section of the strong room's wall. "Because my clothes wouldn't survive it, and I would rather not spend the entire rest of the trip without any clothes."

"I would," Grey said. "I would rather that."

"Grey," I said. "Stop it."

"We're wasting time," Nicodemus said.

Ascher met my eyes for a second, a fairly daring thing to do between two practitioners, and her cheeks flushed a little bit pink before she shucked out of her socks and underwear, motions quick and entirely without artifice. She pressed the rest of her clothes into my hands and said, "Don't do anything weird with them."

"I was going to shellac them into a dining set and serve a four-course meal in them," I said, "but if you're gonna get all squeamish about it, I guess I'll just hold them for you."

Ascher eyed me obliquely. "Did you just ask me out to dinner?"

I felt myself baring my teeth in a smile. Nothing much I like more than a woman with guts. "Tell you what. We both get out of this in one piece, I'll show you where to buy the best steak sandwich in town," I said. "Good luck."

She gave me a quick, nervous smile and turned to the Way. She stared at it for a couple of seconds, licked her lips once, twitched her hands in a couple of nervous little gestures, then clenched her jaw and strode through the Way, naked, into the fires of the Underworld.

Granted, I hadn't ever seen anyone with quite her degree of precision and power in pyromancy before, but even so, I cringed as she hit the first wall of flame. It surged up to meet her like it had an awareness of its own and was eager to devour her—and had about as much luck as a wave breaking on a stony shore. The fire wreathed her and recoiled, twisted into miniature cyclones that whipped her long dark hair this way and that. The wind from the flame roared and shifted, blowing hard enough to make her balance wobble. She put her hands out to either side of her, like someone walking on slippery ice, and proceeded slowly and carefully. I could see the way that focus and concentration made her spine straight and tense, and no, I was not staring at her ass. To any inappropriate degree.

I realized that Grey was standing beside me, watching her intently, his expression unreadable. He keyed in to my realization, even though neither of us looked at the other, except in our peripheral vision.

"Got to love a woman with guts," he said.

"You talk too much," I said.

"How is she doing that?" he asked. "I know the basics, but I've never seen anything quite like that."

"She's redirecting the energy," I said. "See how when the waves hit her, they bounce off, all swirly?"

He grunted.

"She's taking the heat and turning it into kinetic energy as it reaches her aura. It's impressive as hell."

"So far," Grey said. "But why do you say that?"

"Because it's *hard* to deal with that much heat, when you're immersed in it," I said. "She's not just stopping it at one point. She's dealing with it from every angle, and she's got to be doing the same enchantment about a dozen times at once to stop it all, in successive layers."

"And that's hard?"

"Tell you what," I said. "Why don't you go play Simon, Concentration, checkers, chess, solitaire, Monopoly, Sudoku, Clue, Risk, Axis and Allies, poker, and blackjack all at the same time, while counting to twenty thousand by prime numbers only, standing on one foot and balancing a Styrofoam cup of hot coffee on your head. And when you can do that, we'll start you with walking through a small campfire."

"I can play poker," Grey said seriously. "So she's gutsy *and* she's good."

"Yep."

"Good person to have on your team."

"Or a bad one to have on the other team," I said.

His eyes moved to me. They were an almost physical pressure. "Meaning?"

I shook my head and said, "Meaning nothing."

His eyes stayed on me for a second, and then he shrugged and looked at Hannah Ascher again. Who wouldn't?

She was almost all the way to the gate before the Salamander made its move.

From the thickest flame beneath the gateway, something that looked like a Komodo dragon made of material from the surface of a star came roaring forth. It moved with the same scuttling speed as a lizard, and Ascher only just managed to skitter to one side and avoid its first rush. The Salamander hissed out its displeasure in a blast-furnace roar, and the light around it grew even brighter and more intense. The flamestorm around Ascher intensified, and she staggered a few steps back, her face tight with concentration. The fire around her swirled and became thicker, a miniature hurricane spinning slowly around her, with her vulnerable flesh as the eye.

The Salamander roared again, and came for her.

"Dammit," I said.

Michael came to my side and said, "She's got no weapons."

"Can you get to her?" I asked my friend.

Michael shook his head, his eyes worried. "She isn't an innocent in danger. She chose this."

"Grey?"

"I can't help her in that," Grey said. "I wouldn't last any longer than you would."

I turned to look at Nicodemus and said, "Help her."

He eyed me once, and then nodded. Then he drew the sword from his side, narrowed his eyes, took two smooth steps and cast it in a throw.

Swords are not meant for such things. That said, flying pieces of metal with long, sharp edges and pointy ends are inherently dangerous, and Nicodemus had probably spent the idle afternoon, every few decades, throwing a sword around just for fun. After two thousand years of that, he knew exactly what he was doing.

The tumbling blade struck the Salamander on the snout, drawing a line of molten fire along its furnace-flesh and sending up a shower of scarlet sparks. It roared again, in surprised pain, and staggered a few steps to one side, then whirled toward the Way, lashing its tail. A blast of hot, sulfurous wind blew out, making my duster flap wildly and drawing tears from my eyes. Michael lifted a hand to shield his face, his white cloak billowing.

"The lever!" I screamed. "Go for the lever!"

I don't know if Ascher heard me or just reached the same conclusion I had. When the Salamander turned from her, she sprinted for the gateway and the lever in it. The Salamander saw her and whirled, snapping at her legs, but she was past it, quick and lithe. She flung herself at the lever and hauled down on it—letting out a scream of pain as she did so.

There was an enormous rushing sound, and a vast metallic grinding—and suddenly the flames of the entire room shifted down the spectrum in color and dropped lower. I got what was happening at once. That much fire needs an enormous amount of oxygen to supply it, and the lever had somehow reduced that supply.

The Salamander's flesh went from yellow-white to a deep orange within seconds, and it let out another roaring blast of heat from its mouth—and then retreated, much more slowly than it had moved a moment before, toward a low hole in one wall of the archway. Its fire and light filled the tunnel beyond the hole for a moment and then faded, and as it did, the flames all around the Gate of Fire withered away and flickered into scraps and remnants.

"Not yet!" called Ascher in a panting, tense voice, as Nicodemus stepped toward the Way. "Give it a couple of minutes to cool off!"

I waited about forty-five seconds and then muttered a spherical shield into life around me, channeling it through my staff. I would rather have had my old shield bracelet, but assembling a decent metalcrafting tool shop takes money and time, and I hadn't had time to rebuild much of either—and certainly not to the degree I'd been prepared back in my old lab at my apartment.

The spells I'd carved into the new staff were much the same as the ones in my old shield bracelet, if less efficient and less capable of tightly focusing power, but it was much better than I could have managed without any focus at all, and it was sufficient to protect me from harm as I crossed the still smoldering-hot ground.

Passing from the mortal world into the Nevernever is both more and less dramatic than you'd think. There's no real sensation to it, apart from a mild tingle as you pass through the Way itself, kind of a protracted shiver along your skin. But when I stepped into the Underworld, I *knew* that I had just crossed an unimaginable distance. My body felt slightly heavier, as if the gravity itself was different from that on Earth. The air was hot and tainted with sulfur and other minerals, and it felt utterly alien in my nose and mouth. The ground around me was all stone, covered in protruding chunks of what might have been still-glowing charcoal, and I could see the melted stumps of what must have been, at one point, stalagmites, their limestone now running like candle wax. Shattered, half-molten remnants of what must have been stalactites fallen from a ceiling out of sight in the darkness overhead were scattered around my line of vision.

Of course. We were in a cave. An unthinkably enormous cavern that stretched out of sight in the glowing light of the Way behind us and that was interrupted by a wall at least forty feet high and the archway set into it in front of us.

I crossed the ground rapidly to Ascher's side. My shield was good when it came to stopping fire, but it probably wasn't quite as good as a single one of the layers she'd held in place around her. "Hey," I said. "You all right?"

"I was sweating," she said, her face twisted with pain, and she lifted her hands to show me blisters bubbling up in a line along her palms where she had grabbed the lever. The lever itself still glowed red with heat that it hadn't yet lost. "Dammit. The sweat went into steam and screwed up the last few layers of protection."

"You just grabbed freaking red-hot metal with your bare hands and you've got nothing to show for it but blisters," I said. "Totally badass."

A smile fought its way through her expression of pain for a moment, and she said, "Yeah, it really kind of was, wasn't it? Was that a Salamander?"

"Pretty sure," I said.

"They're so much *bigger* than in those Xanth books."

"No kidding," I said. "Maybe Ha—our client got one some hormone treatments." I offered her the clothes I held cradled in my broken arm. "Shellac free."

She took them from me with another grimace of pain and said, "Thanks."

Grey came ambling up over the ground. If the temperature bothered him, he didn't show it. "Want a hand with those?"

Ascher arched an eyebrow at him. "From you? I think I'm a little smarter than that."

"You only say that because you think I'm only interested in you for your body."

"Yes, obviously."

"Totally unfair," Grey said, with a disarming smile. "I'm also interested in what you might elect to *do* with your body." He added, in a more sober voice, "You're going to have trouble with clasps and buttons with your fingers like that. I know."

Ascher squinted at him. She looked at me uncertainly, and then said to Grey, "Probably true."

She got dressed. Grey helped her, without doing anything untoward, and the rest of the crew joined us a moment later.

"Maybe I should have let you handle that one, Dresden," she said. "Traded you for the ice thing. Normally when some beastie comes at me, I use fire. Useless here."

"I'd never have gotten through when it turned up the heat," I said. "But if you'd like to handle my gate for me, I'm willing."

"Maybe I will," Ascher said with a cocky grin.

"Come," Nicodemus said. He'd picked up his sword. One of its edges was blackened and had been visibly dulled, steel bubbling up like the edges of a pancake when the griddle is too hot. "Defeating the Salamander has surely warned someone of our presence here. The less time wasted, the better."

And so all of us passed through the Gate of Fire, through a tunnel about thirty feet long that had me briefly worrying about the Murder Holes of Fire, but no threat materialized. We came out of the archway onto another broad expanse of stony cavern.

But this one was covered in ice.

The stalagmites and stalactites were all intact at this gate, and were in fact spread out in a suspiciously regular, almost geometric pattern for a couple of hundred yards, stretching between us and the next gate. They were covered in a thick sheath of old, old ice, which had universally come down from the stalactites to meet the rising stalagmites, forming great columns as thick as I was tall. The ice sparkled in the light cast by the last smoldering remains of the flames at the Gate of Fire, throwing back shimmering spectra of color. The floor, too, was covered in the same shimmering ice, starting about ten feet from the opening from the Gate of Fire. The air was dry and bitterly cold, and I saw Ascher draw a short breath and stop suddenly as it reached her.

I stared out at the glittering, frozen cathedral between us and the Gate of Ice and my palms began to sweat a little. I licked my lips and took a steadying breath as I regarded the passage in front of us.

Michael came to stand at my side and said, "It doesn't look too bad."

"Yeah," I said, "which worries me."

"Dresden," Nicodemus said. "The time has come for you to redeem Mab's word."

"Hold your demonic horses," I said, annoyed.

I put my hand forward for a moment, half closing my eyes, reaching out with my wizard's senses. The air was frigid, as bad as anything you'd find at the South Pole, but that wouldn't bother me much more than would a cold October evening back home. I sensed no enchantments, which meant little here in the Nevernever, where enchantment could just as easily be a part of the very fabric of reality, and thus no more remarkable or out of place than gravity or air in the mortal world.

I took several cautious steps forward, and put the toes of my left foot down on the edge of the icy floor.

And as if some vast machine had whirled to life, a block of ice the size of a small house plunged down from overhead and smashed onto the floor five feet in front of me, retaining its cut shape, its regular edges. No sooner had it settled than it whirled in place, flopped on its side, and a second house-sized block came rumbling out along the horizontal, sliding along the ice floor to smash into the first block. They parted for an instant, then slammed together again and shattered into dozens of smaller blocks that whirled off on their own, spinning into positions, slamming into one another with the speed and energy of high-speed traffic collisions, rearranging themselves into random, violent stacks every few seconds, each impact resounding through the vast space with enormous grinding crunches.

I stared at the field of gnashing, mashing ice-oliths in dismay, and saw more of the original huge blocks sliding out of the shadows to the side of the cavern, and falling down from overhead.

Dozens and dozens of them.

In seconds, there were thousands of blocks crunching and grinding and smashing away at one another over every foot of the space between me and the Gate of Ice. The air filled with the deafening sounds of impact, as if a glacier had come to life and begun to utter threats.

The smallest of the blocks, if they trapped me between them, would have smashed half of my body into tomato paste.

"Dresden," Ascher said, and swallowed. "Uh. I've decided that maybe you *should* handle this one."

Chapter

Thirty-eight

Giant, angry, crushy blocks of ice, check.

One deity of the ancient world about to be royally pissed off, check.

Pack of rampant bad guys with whom I was about to lose major value, big check.

First things first.

I whirled away from the Gate of Ice, pointed my staff at the distant glow of the Way standing open behind us, unleashed my will and thundered, *"Disperdorius!"*

Magic lanced from my staff, disruptive and hectic, a spear of greenish light wreathed with corkscrewing helixes of green-white energy. The dispersal spell smashed into the Way and tore it to shreds, closing the passage between the mortal world and the Underworld as thoroughly as dynamite brings down a tunnel.

And instantly, the Underworld was plunged into pitch-darkness, broken only by the few smoldering remnants from the Gate of Fire, visible only dimly, at the other end of the tunnel.

I heard several sharp indrawn breaths before I could

bring light from my staff and my mother's pentacle amulet with a murmur and a minor effort of will. Green and blue light, respectively, illuminated the area around me, and spread out for a remarkable distance, reflected endlessly by the Gate of Ice and its thousands of moving parts.

The light revealed Nicodemus's hard, narrow eyes. "Dresden," he snapped. "Explain yourself."

"Sure," I said. "See, the way I figure it, after I get you through this gate, I've got exactly zero utility to you people. It would be a great time for you to stick a knife in my back."

"That wasn't the plan," Nicodemus said.

"Yeah, you're such a Boy Scout, Nick," I said, "with the best of intentions. But for the sake of argument, let's say you weren't. Let's say you were a treacherous bastard who would enjoy seeing me dead. Let's say you realized that here, in the most secure portion of the Underworld, the demesne of a major Power, there'd be no way for Mab to directly observe what you do. Let's say your plan all along was to kill me and leave me here in the Underworld, maybe even try to pin the whole thing on me so that you don't have to worry about the client, later—you could just let him tangle with Mab, sit back on your evil ass, and laugh yourself sick over it."

Something ugly flickered far back in Nicodemus's eyes. I didn't know if I'd gotten every single little detail of his plan right, but I was sure I'd been in the ballpark.

"Maybe you can still pull it off," I said. "But if you do, you're going to have to find another ride. If I don't make it to the end of this, there's no one left to open the Way home—and we *all* stay down here."

His jaw tightened, but other than that, his expression didn't change.

"Christ, Dresden," Grey complained. "What if you get killed trying to run through that thing? How are we all supposed to get out of here then?"

It was a point that had bothered me, too, but I'd had few options to work with. Besides, given a choice between a psychotically dangerous, bone-crunching obstacle course or Nicodemus at my back with nothing to gain by keeping me alive, I knew damned well which was more likely to result in my death—and once Nicodemus took me out, there was no way he'd choose to leave my friends alive behind me as witnesses to his treachery.

"Well, golly, Goodman. Then I guess it looks like you'll all be well motivated to genuinely wish me good luck and think positive thoughts," I said. I turned to the hulking blur that was the Genoskwa. "Starting with you, big guy. Come on over. I need to get a better look at this thing."

A subterranean growl rumbled through the air, audible even over the grinding of the Gate of Ice.

"Hey," I said, spreading my hands. "Be that way if you want to. It's not like that attitude might get all of you trapped in the Underworld forever or anything. I hear, like, two or three whole people made it out of this place. Ever."

The Genoskwa rippled out from beneath his veil and stalked toward me. I'm pretty sure I only imagined that his footsteps shook the ground beneath my feet as he walked, and I had a sudden desire to flee with my arms out in front of me and my legs rotating in a circular blur.

But instead, I stood my ground, eyed the Genoskwa, and thrust out my jaw as it got closer.

Michael laid his hand on his sword and put himself between Anna Valmont and the rest of the group, his expression questioning. I gave my head a quick shake. If Michael drew *Amoracchius* in earnest against this crew, there would be a fight to the death and that's all there was to it. I didn't mind the thought of a fight, but I wanted better ground and better odds if I could get them.

"Nick," I said, without looking away from the Genoskwa, "run the numbers before your gorilla does something stupid."

I saw Nicodemus nod his head to one side, and Deirdre suddenly slipped between me and the Genoskwa, facing him, both palms lifted in a gesture of pacification.

"Stop," she said in a quiet voice. "The wizard is insufferable, but he's correct. We still need him."

The Genoskwa could have kicked Deirdre aside like an empty beer can, but instead he slowed, glowering down at her and then, more intensely, at me.

"Arrogant child," the Genoskwa rumbled. His eyes went to the Gate of Ice and then back toward the now-closed Way. "You think you're clever."

"I think I want to get home alive," I said, "and if I thought that you people would be willing to behave with something approaching sanity for five minutes, stuff like this wouldn't be necessary. Shut up and play the game, and don't come crying to me if you aren't winning. Lift me up. I need to get a look at the whole field if I can."

"Because that might help." He lifted one rubbery lip

away from his tusks and said to Deirdre, "Rather rot down here than help this one for two minutes." Then he turned his broad, shaggy back and padded away.

Deirdre turned toward me, her blade-hair rasping and slithering against itself, and shook her head with an expression of faint disgust. "You've won the round, boy. There's no point in doing a victory dance too."

"Still need the big guy to give me a lift," I insisted.

"Why?" she demanded.

I jerked a thumb at the Gate of Ice. "They're moving in a pattern. If I can see the whole field, if I can track the pattern, I can find a way through. But I can't see over the first row of blocks. So I need to get higher."

Deirdre stared at me steadily, both sets of eyes on mine, and I dropped my gaze away from hers hurriedly. The last thing I needed, at the moment, was to accidentally find myself in a soul gaze with a Fallen angel or a psychotic murderess with centuries of dark deeds behind her.

"Very well," she said. "I will lift you."

"How?" I asked.

Her hair suddenly burst into motion, striking down into the stone of the cavern floor and sending up bursts of sparks where the steely stuff bit deep into the rock. I would have jumped back from her if doing so wouldn't have put me far enough out onto the ice to get myself smashed flat. Then some more of the blades slithered down to the floor and lay flat, side by side, in several layers. It was like looking at a floor tile made from razor blades.

"Stand there," Deirdre said. Plenty of strands of her hair were still free and moving slightly. "I will lift you."

I arched an eyebrow at her. "You're kidding, right? What happens if you drop me? It'll be like I fell into a blender."

"Well, golly, Dresden," she said, deadpan, "then I guess it looks like you'll be well motivated to keep your balance and think positive thoughts."

"Heh," said Grey.

I glowered at him for a second and then said, "Fine," and stepped onto Deirdre's hair, keeping some bend in my knees.

The hair moved and she lifted me slowly, while other razor-blade strands rustled and rasped around me. There was something deliberate about the motion, as if it was taking all of her concentration to prevent herself from slicing me into confetti, and I decided that a comment about split ends and using some chain-saw oil for conditioner could go unspoken.

That's what I call diplomacy.

She got my feet up maybe ten feet off the ground, which was more than enough for me to be able to look over the entire two hundred yards. I lifted my staff, murmured a word, and willed more light to issue forth from it. The air was filled with droplets of water and tiny chips of ice, where the blocks were smashing into one another, creating a glittering haze over everything, but I could track the motion of the blocks well enough, and in the archway ahead, I could see another lever exactly like the one at the Gate of Fire.

Seemed pretty simple. Get through the grinders. Get to the lever. I scanned the place for some kind of ice-amander, but saw nothing. Nothing that I knew of would be able to survive all the abuse the grinders were dishing out, but that didn't mean that there wasn't something I didn't know about that could handle it just fine.

My imagination promptly treated me to an image of a viscous, blobby monster that could lie flat on the floor in perfect concealment, and be smashed between grinders with no particular trauma and that would melt my face off the second it touched me. Then my imagination showed me my skinless self, flailing around like a victim in a horror movie, getting blood everywhere—for about two seconds. Then I imagined two of the grinders smashing me to jelly that could be readily consumed by osmosis.

My imagination needs therapy.

I closed my eyes for a second and dismissed such flights of fancy. That wasn't what I needed right now. I needed to find the pattern in the movement between me and the gate, to determine the path I could take to get inside. I opened my eyes again and watched.

It took me several minutes to see where it began. The movement of the nearest blocks began to repeat itself after seventy-five seconds or so. The next row had a similar pattern, though it was happening on a separate cycle. As was the next, and the next, and the one after that.

I stood there watching the patterns for a good fifteen minutes, tracking them, focused, keeping track of every separate motion in my head, in much the same way you had to do with the most complex of spells, and realized that I could simplify the model for each row to a cog with one broken tooth. As long as I entered the row on the beat that the broken tooth was aligned with me, I could breeze through it. So it just became a matter of timing my run so that the openings lined up for me. Theoretically.

I watched for another ten minutes, until I was pretty sure I had it, and could see the patterns aligning to give me my string of openings.

"Harry?" Michael asked, finally.

I held up my hand to silence him, bouncing my hand slightly to help me keep track, following the pattern. The way through was going to open about . . . now.

I leapt down to the ground and started running.

I was five strides onto the ice, and through the opening in the first row of grinders, before I realized that I may have miscounted, and that if I had, I would have no opening through the next-to-last row.

There was no help for it. The opening behind me was already gone. I'd just have to adjust on the fly.

I kept moving forward, dashing ahead through a pair of house-sized grinders before they could crash together with me in the middle. I whipped to the diagonal for a couple of rows, and the air got colder and colder as I went ahead. I could stand at the heart of a cavern of ice deep within a glacier, naked and wet from the shower and not shiver, but *this* cold was beginning to get to me. My breath became a large plume, visible in the air, and the floating chips of ice gathered on my eyelashes, making me fear that if I blinked, they might freeze together.

On I went, going over a single smaller block like a hurdler, and the cold got deeper and deeper, and while the Winter Knight had nothing to fear from slipping on simple ice, the fine, powdery sleet coating the cavern floor from all the grinding impacts did not make things easy, even for me.

One hundred and eighty yards or so, and things went

relatively well. Then I found out that I had, indeed, miscounted.

I ran for the place where the opening in the row of spinning, randomly slamming grinders should have been, and realized about a step before I got there that it wasn't coming.

So I pointed my staff at the more battered-looking of the blocks in front of me, focused my will and shouted, *"Forzare!"*

Unseen force smashed into the block, sending it spinning wildly away from me. The block into which it had been about to smash went spinning after it, as if the two were attracted by mutual gravity. I followed in their wake, as they smashed into a couple of blocks in the next row, and ice shattered into a cloud of mist and flying chips. Something hit my stomach and something else hit my hand. A section of block came tumbling wildly toward me, and I bounded up into a rolling dive that took me a good six feet off the cavern floor, shouting, "Parkour!"

Then I was through the grinders and into the shelter of the archway.

The cold there was a living thing, something that abruptly doubled me over, my body beginning to shudder and tingle. It took everything I had to lift an arm, secure a hold on the lever with my bare fingers, and haul it steadily down.

There was a loud grinding sound, like ancient, ice-encrusted gears beginning to whir together, and an enormous thumping sound that reminded me of explosives going off at a safe distance. The horrible cold faded almost immediately to something merely Antarctic, and I sank to one knee and peered back the way I had come.

The blocks had ceased their motion, simply dropping to the ground wherever they were moving or spinning or crashing.

I was through.

I stood up and waved my still-lit staff left and right in a broad motion. Then I paused to take stock of myself.

My shirt was bloody and so was my right hand. I lifted my shirt to examine my abdomen and found a small wound there. It took me a minute, but I was able to get my fingers around the end of a splinter of ice approximately the size and shape of a small nail, and I withdrew it in a little squirt of steaming red blood. Ugly, but it hadn't gone all the way through the muscle and it couldn't have pierced my abdominal wall. Not dangerous. I checked my right hand. A similar shard of ice had pierced me, but it was smaller and the heat of my blood had evidently melted it away. It wasn't bad. I'd lost a couple of layers of skin to the frozen metal of the gate's deactivation lever. That was it.

But, man, I was glad I didn't have a mirror to look in right about now.

By the time the rest of the crew reached me, the air was merely wintry, and I was on my feet again, and I'd used a small fire spell to sear away the blood that was on the little shard of ice, along with the shard itself.

Michael approached me with his eyes wide and said, "Dear God in Heaven, Harry. That was amazing. I've never seen you move so quickly."

"Yeah," I said. "There aren't many perks to being the Winter Knight, but that's one of them."

"Did you shout 'Parkour'?" Michael asked.

"Well, sure," I said. "That was kinda Parkour-like."

Michael fought to keep a smile off his face. "Harry," he said, "I'm almost certain one doesn't *shout* 'Parkour.' I believe one is supposed to simply *do* Parkour."

"Do I criticize your Latin battle cries? No, never once."

"That is true," Michael said soberly. He nodded toward my belly. "Are you all right?"

"Flesh wound," I said. "I'll get some Bactine on it when we get back. Or let Charity drag out her bottle of iodine."

"She'd like that," Michael said, nodding.

"Ugh," Ascher said, stepping beneath the arch, her arms folded against her stomach. "I hate the cold."

"Wear looser clothes," Valmont suggested in a voice so dry that it defied anyone listening to find any snark in it. "Nice moves, Dresden."

"Thanks," I said. "I'm auditioning for the sequel to *Frogger* in a week."

Nicodemus, Grey, the Genoskwa, and Deirdre entered the archway together a moment later. Which was not even a little suspicious.

Michael turned to me with a quizzical expression on his face, and had begun to form a question when the Genoskwa lunged, powering toward me with ferocious speed, and simply seized me by the upper body, his thumbs pressing against my chest, his hands wrapping around my arms and pinning them at my side.

Michael swore and went for his sword, but Grey suddenly had Valmont by the hair, her head tilted back. Fin-

gers that ended in an eagle's talons pierced her throat
delicately, drawing beads of blood, and he said, "Easy
there, sir Knight. We don't want any needless bloodshed."

The Genoskwa leaned down to glower at me and rumbled, "Please. Struggle. I would *love* some needless
bloodshed."

"Nicodemus," Ascher said, her voice sharp. "What is
the meaning of this?"

Nicodemus walked up to the arch arm in arm with
Deirdre. "Because we have come to the Gate of Blood,
children," he said. He drew the Bedouin dagger from his
belt and its damascene blade glittered in the light of my
staff and amulet. "The time has come for one of you to
die."

Chapter

Thirty-nine

Michael's sword swept out of its sheath, and the silver-white fire of *Amoracchius* filled the archway. He said nothing. He didn't need to. He took the Sword in a two-handed grip and settled into a relaxed ready position.

Deirdre and Nicodemus immediately split apart, so that they forced Michael to divide his attention between them. She dropped into a fighting crouch, while Nicodemus narrowed his eyes and became very still. Grey regarded Michael impassively, while in his grasp, Anna Valmont turned completely pale and held very still. I felt the Genoskwa's summer-sausage fingers tighten painfully.

"Now, now, sir Knight," Nicodemus said, his voice almost a growl. "There's no need for this to devolve into general mayhem, is there?"

"I will not allow you to harm them," Michael said.

"Lower the Sword," Nicodemus said. "Or I will order Grey to kill Valmont."

"If you do that," Michael said calmly, "Dresden and I will fight to the death."

I felt my eyes get a little bit wider, and my voice might not have been as deep and steady as it usually was, but I managed to say, "Right. We'll fight you. Not each other. In case that wasn't clear."

"How assured is your victory?" Michael asked Nicodemus. "How many times has *Amoracchius* foiled your plans over the centuries?"

"You've never beaten me, Knight," Nicodemus said.

"Almighty God as my witness, and as He gives me grace," Michael said, "if you harm that woman, I will strike you down."

"Right," I said. "Me too."

Nicodemus gave me an impatient glance and turned his attention back to Michael. "You should have stayed in your little house, quietly retired," he said. "You didn't matter there. I didn't care about you any longer. If you begin a fight here, you will never see your family again."

Michael smiled faintly. "That is where you are wrong. With God's blessing, it will take a good many years. But I will see them again."

"Think where you *are*, sir Knight," Nicodemus said, his mouth quirking up into a mocking smile. "The Underworld is a prison for souls. Do you think yours is so great as to escape it?"

"I am not great," Michael said quietly. "But God is."

Nicodemus's smile was like something you'd see on a shark. "One of the great disappointments in killing a Knight is knowing that he or she does not suffer as a result. But you are in the Underworld, Christian. Here, I think, your eternity will be something entirely different than you have been promised."

"On the one hand, I have your word," Michael said. "On the other, I have my Father's. I think I know to which voice I should listen."

"This is the land of Death," Nicodemus said. "Death must be part of the offering to let us in. You have been so eager to lay down your life, sir Knight. Perhaps you will do so again, rather than forcing me to slay another."

Michael's eyes narrowed. "I don't think so," he said. "No force compels you but your own ambition, Nicodemus. You could choose to turn back—and I will not let you destroy a life to serve your purposes."

"Even if by doing so, you force me to denounce Dresden and his mistress?" Nicodemus asked. "You know the consequences of that, should Mab be shamed by his failure to keep her word—and you are here on *his*. Should you bring this mission to a halt, Dresden will have broken Mab's word. I imagine that his death will be a terrible one."

Michael was silent for a fairly awful moment.

"Michael, no," I said. "You're carrying enough of a burden already."

That made him look at me, his eyes troubled. We had already been standing on some fairly shifty moral ground, and it was only getting muckier as we went forward. Laying down one's life for a friend was pretty much *the* definition of a selfless act—but doing it so that a monster could get his hands on a supernatural weapon of tremendous power put it in an entirely different context, and not a flattering one. Especially not for a man carrying an archangel's grace around like so much priceless china.

"Wait," Hannah Ascher said, stepping forward, her

hands partly lifted, palms showing. "People, wait. This is not the time for us to turn on one another. We're close. Your precious cup, Nicodemus. Twenty million each for the rest of us. If you let this explode right now, none of us gets anything except trapped down here. And somehow I don't think our client will be a kind and gracious host, given what we've come here to do."

Nicodemus's eyes flicked to Ascher and back to Michael. He stared at the Knight for a long moment and then said, "Deirdre. Conference." He looked over his shoulder at Grey and the Genoskwa. "If they start to struggle, kill them."

He took a step back from Michael and then turned, walking calmly toward the other end of the archway. Deirdre went with him.

Ascher let out her breath in an explosive hiss. "What *is* it with you religious types?"

"Name like Hannah Ascher and you aren't Jewish?" I asked.

She sniffed. "That's different."

I snorted, tracking Nicodemus and Deirdre's movements. They went to the end of the tunnel, where there was another stretch of open cavern and a final stone wall. There was the impression of an archway carved into the stone, but no actual gate there. Shadows hung heavy over it. Nicodemus and his daughter stopped about five feet from the stone wall, and began speaking quietly.

I could feel the Genoskwa practically quivering with the desire to do violence. I knew that if I showed any sign of physical resistance, he'd start on me. Maybe he wouldn't kill me—not without having another way home—but he'd be happy to crack some ribs, rip off a couple of fingers, or maybe put out one of my eyes. If things got desperate enough, that might be a price I'd have to pay, but for the time being it made more sense to be still and keep my eyes open.

"Grey," I said, "I thought you were a pro."

"I am," Grey said calmly. "You knew something like this was coming, wizard." His fingers flexed gently on Valmont's throat, by way of demonstration. "Do you really want everyone to fall apart right now?"

I thought about it hard for a minute. "Not yet. Look, what I did, I did for insurance," I said, "but he's talking about killing one of us . . ."

Wait a minute.

If Nicodemus had chosen this moment to turn on us, against all reason, then why the hell was he bothering to negotiate anything? It hadn't made much sense to move against me in the first place, especially since he would need me to make good his escape. It made even less sense to start it and then hesitate. I knew him well enough to know that he wasn't a waffler. If Nicodemus decided someone needed killing, he killed them, and then he went on to the next chore on his list.

He was up to something. He had to be. But what?

Nicodemus was a liar, through and through.

This was theater. It had to be.

And I realized his plan in a flash of insight: He hadn't had Grey and the Genoskwa grab us because he'd been about to turn on us and kill us. He'd done it to force Michael to stay near us if he wanted to intervene—instead of intervening somewhere else.

Deirdre and Nicodemus stood close together, his hand on her arm. I saw the demonform young woman look up into his eyes, her expression fragile and uncertain, and I focused my thoughts exclusively on my hearing, Listening as hard as I could.

". . . wish there was another way," Nicodemus was saying quietly. "But you're the only one I can trust."

"I know, Father," Deirdre said. "It's all right."

"You will be safe from the Enemy here."

Deirdre lifted her chin, and her eyes were wet. "I have chosen my path. I regret nothing."

Nicodemus leaned over and kissed his daughter's forehead. "I am so proud of you."

A tear rolled down Deirdre's cheek as she smiled, and the demonform faded away, until a blade-thin girl remained, staring up at him. "I love you, Father."

Nicodemus's rough voice cracked a little. "I know," he said, very gently. "And that is the problem."

And he struck with the curved Bedouin dagger.

It was an angled thrust, up beneath the sternum and directly into the heart. Deirdre never broke eye contact with him, and never moved a muscle. The blade sank in to the hilt, and the only reaction she gave was a slight exhalation. Then she moved, leaning closer to Nicodemus, and kissed his mouth.

Then her legs buckled and she sank slowly down. Nicodemus went with her, down to his knees, and held her gently, the jeweled hilt of the dagger standing out sharply from her body.

"Mother of God," Michael breathed. "He just . . ."

Nicodemus held her for maybe two minutes, not moving. Then, very carefully, he laid the body down on the cavern floor. He withdrew the knife with equal care. He dipped two fingers into the wound, felt around for a moment, and then withdrew something small and covered with blood and gleaming. A silver coin. He cleaned his daughter's blood from it and from the dagger with a handkerchief. He pocketed the Coin, sheathed the knife, and rose, calmly, to walk back toward the rest of us. His face was as blank as the stone floor beneath his feet. Everyone stared at him in shock. Even Grey looked surprised.

"Mother of God, man," Michael breathed. "What have you done?"

Nicodemus stared at Michael with steady eyes and spoke with quiet contempt. "Did you think you were the only one in the world willing to die for what he believes, sir Knight?"

"But you . . ." Michael looked like he might be near tears himself. "She just *let* you do it. She was your *child*."

"Did your own precious God not ask the same of Abraham? Did he not permit Lucifer to destroy the children of Job? I, at least, have a *reason* for it." He gestured curtly at Grey and the Genoskwa and said, "Release them."

Grey let go of Valmont at once. The Genoskwa turned me loose only reluctantly, and gave me a little push as he did it that nearly knocked me to the ground.

Michael's mouth opened and closed. "I could have talked to her," he said.

"If he'd given you the chance," I said. "That was the whole point of the hostage drama. To make sure you were focused somewhere else."

Nicodemus stared at me coldly.

"He was worried that you might say something, Michael. That in the moments before she knew she was going to die, Deirdre's faith might have wavered. Particularly if someone like you was there to offer her an alternative."

Nicodemus inclined his head to me, very slightly. Then he said, "You have never beaten me, sir Knight. And you never will."

"You're insane," Michael said quietly, sadly.

Nicodemus had begun to turn away, but he paused.

"Perhaps," he said, his eyes distant. "Or perhaps I'm the only one who isn't."

Anna Valmont moved to my side and said quietly, "Look."

I looked.

Deirdre's corpse stirred.

No, that wasn't right. There was movement at the corpse, but the body wasn't moving. Instead, a faint, silvery glow seemed to begin radiating from it. Then there was motion, and the glow coalesced into a humanoid shape, which after a moment refined itself into a translucent silvery shade in the shape of Deirdre. She sat up from the corpse, separating herself from it, and rose to her feet. She turned and paused, frowning down at the body, and then lifted her own hand and stared at it.

Behind her, the same silvery glow that had surrounded the body began to suffuse the solid stone image of an archway carved in the next wall. It spread to the edges of the carving where a silvery translucent lever appeared, in the same place the lever had been on the previous two gates.

Deirdre's shade turned to look at her father. She smiled, sadly. Then she turned and drifted over to the lever. She wrapped ghostly hands around it and pulled it slowly down. The light in the stone intensified, becoming brighter and brighter, until there was a flash and it was gone, taking Deirdre's shade and the stone alike with it, leaving an open archway in their place.

Light poured from the archway.

Golden light.

"Ladies and gentlemen," Nicodemus said, his voice calm, "we have done it."

Chapter

Forty

I just stood there for a moment, still stunned at what Nicodemus had done.

I tried to think of what would have to happen to motivate me to do something like that to Maggie. And it just didn't click. There was nothing, nothing on earth I wouldn't do to protect my child.

But you were willing to cut her mother's throat, weren't you? said a bitter little voice inside me. *Are you any better?*

Yeah. I was better. What I'd done to Susan had been at least partly her choice, too, and we'd done it to save Maggie and by extension the tens or hundreds of thousands or millions of victims the Red Court would have claimed in the future.

Nicodemus had consigned his daughter to death for what? A room welling up with a golden glow that . . .

Okay.

I'm not what most people think of as a greedy sort of guy, but . . .

All of us rolled forward a few steps, toward that golden light. Even Michael.

"That's it," Anna Valmont said quietly.

Ascher swallowed, and let out a nervous little laugh. "What do you think is in there?"

"Fortune and glory, kid," I said. "Fortune and glory."

"Dresden, Ascher," Nicodemus said. "Check the way in for any further magical defenses. Valmont, watch for mechanical booby traps. The Genoskwa will accompany you and intercede should any guardian appear."

"I thought once we were through the three gates, we were in the clear," I said.

"My specific information, beyond here, is limited to inventory," Nicodemus said. "It is at this point that I had assumed the intervention of more mythic forces, if they were to be had."

"He's right," Valmont said. "You never assume you're in the clear until you've gotten the goods, gotten away, and gotten liquid."

"Michael," I said, "come with. Just in case there's anything big, bad, and smelly that tries to kill me."

The Genoskwa let out an almost absentminded growl. His beady eyes gleamed reflected golden light.

"Of course," Michael said. He carried *Amoracchius* at port arms, across the front of his body, grasping the blade lightly in one gloved hand with the other on the handle, rather than sheathing it.

"Grey," Nicodemus said, "watch the rear. If you see anything coming, warn us."

"Going to be hard to collect my loot from out here," Grey said.

"I'll spell you once I have the Grail."

Grey nodded, albeit reluctantly. "All right."

"Dresden," Nicodemus said.

I took point, with Ascher on my right hand and Valmont on my left. Michael and the Genoskwa followed, a pair of mismatched bookends, though I noted that the Genoskwa was not making threatening noises or gestures at the wielder of *Amoracchius*. The Swords have a way of inspiring that kind of wariness in true villains.

I shook my head and focused on the task at hand, moving forward slowly, my magical senses extended, searching for any hint of wards, spells, or energies or entities unknown. Beside me, I could feel Ascher doing the same thing, though my sense of her was that she was tuned in on a slightly different bandwidth than I was, magically speaking. She was hunting for more subtle traps, illusions, psychic land mines. She wouldn't be able to detect as many things as I would, but she would probably be better at spotting what she was looking for. Valmont had removed an old-style incandescent flashlight from her bag, one that was unlikely to fail in our presence unless some serious magical energy started flying. She shone it carefully, slowly on the ground and sweeping the walls ahead of us, watching for the shadows cast by trip wires, or pressure plates, or whatever other fiendish things she would probably know all about finding.

We crossed to the arch, one slow step at a time, and then into the tunnel. I strained my senses to their utmost.

Nothing.

And then we were in Hades' vault.

. . . it . . .

. . . uh . . .

Imagine Smaug's treasure hoard. Now imagine Smaug

with crippling levels of obsessive-compulsive disorder and fanatic good taste.

It's a pale description, and in no way a substitute for seeing it in person, but it's the best I can do, except to say that looking upon Hades' treasure vault made me feel like a dirty, grubby rat who had gnawed his way into the pantry. And my heart lurched into thunder. And I'm reasonably certain the pupils of my eyes vanished, to be replaced by dollar signs.

The light came primarily from the outstretched hands of two twenty-foot-tall golden statues in the center of the room. I found myself walking to one side, enough to see the details of each statue. Both consisted of the shapes of three women, standing back to back, in a triangle, their arms thrust outward and up, palms lifted to the ceiling. One of the women was an ancient crone. The next was a woman in the full bloom of her strength and maturity. The third was that of a young woman, recently matured out of childhood. The flames of one statue burned golden-green. The other statue's flames were an icy green-blue.

And just looking at that, my heart started beating faster all over again.

Because I'd met every single one of them. I recognized their faces.

"Is that Hecate?" Ascher murmured, staring up at the statues in awe. "The triple goddess of the crossroads, right?"

I swallowed. "Uh. It . . . Yes, it might be."

And it might also be Grannies Summer and Winter, Mab, Titania, Sarissa, and Molly Carpenter. But I didn't say anything about that.

I pulled my eyes down from the statues and forced myself to look around the rest of the vault.

The room was about the size of a football field. The walls were a parquet of platinum and gold triangles, stretching up out of sight overhead. The floor was a smooth surface of white marble shot through with veins of pure, gleaming silver. Corinthian columns supported rooftops straight from ancient Athens in scores of small, separate display areas around the vault. Some of them were raised as much as seven or eight feet off the floor, and had to be reached by stairs of more silver-shot marble. Others were sunken in descending rows in a curling bow that looked almost like a Greek amphitheater, if it had been built with box seating.

I looked at the nearest . . . shrine. Or display case. Or whatever they were.

The spaces between the columns had been filled with walls made from bricks of solid gold. Those were just the backdrop. The *backdrop*.

The nearest case was filled with paintings by Italian Renaissance masters, all working in the theme of divinity, showing images of saints and the Virgin and the Christ. Veneziano. Donatello. Botticelli. Raphael. Castagno. Michelangelo. Freaking da Vinci. Maybe fifty paintings in all, each displayed as meticulously as they might have been in the Louvre, in protected cases, with lights shining just so upon them from oddly shaped lanterns that might have been made from bronze and that put out no smoke whatsoever.

Surrounding the paintings, framing them, was a variety of topiary shapes—except instead of being made from living plants, I saw, after several glances, that they'd been made from emeralds. I couldn't tell how whatever crafts-man had shaped them had done it. Hell, I could barely tell that they weren't plants at all. A fountain poured wa-ter silently into a shining pool in the display's center, but then I saw that it wasn't water, but diamonds, tiny and shining, pouring out in streams that somehow gave the impression of liquid.

That fountain could have filled every backpack we'd brought with us, plus all the improvised containers we could manufacture from our clothes. Never mind the em-eralds. Never mind the tons of gold. Never mind the hundreds of millions of dollars in priceless art, paintings that had probably been written off as lost forever.

That was only one of the displays. And, I realized, as I swept my eyes slowly around me, it was one of the more modest ones.

"Okay," Ascher breathed, her eyes wide. "I don't know if I'm about to pass out or have an orgasm."

"Yeah," I croaked. "Me too."

Valmont shook off the awe of the place first. She strode over to the diamond-fountain, unzipped her back-pack, and held it beneath the spigot in a matter-of-fact gesture, filling it as if it were a bucket.

"Seriously?" Ascher asked her. "You aren't even going to shop?"

"Highest value for the weight," Valmont replied tightly. "And they're small enough to move easily. There's no point in taking something you can't sell when you get it back home."

"But there's so much," Ascher breathed.

"Ascher," I said. After a couple of seconds, I said, louder, "Hannah."

"Uh, yeah?"

"Go tell Nicodemus that it looks clear. Let's get our stuff and get gone."

"Right," she said. "Right. Gone." She turned and hurried from the room.

I turned to Michael and the Genoskwa and said, "I'm going to do a quick circuit of the room with Valmont and check for anything else, just in case. Don't wander anywhere until I give you the high sign."

Michael nodded slowly. There has never been a backpack made that was big enough for the Genoskwa. But he had several military-style duffel bags looped to a long piece of cargo strapping like you see used on diesel trailers on the highway.

"Come on, Anna," I said. "Let's check for more booby traps." I started walking. Valmont shouldered her pack and came after me. I lifted my staff as we went, pouring out more light, until Valmont had to squint against it, and we walked out of sight of the others. Our shadows faded to mere slips beneath the extreme illumination.

"What's with the light show?" she asked me.

"Trust me," I said quietly, and dropped my voice to a bare whisper, leaning down close to her ear. "When it starts, stay close to me. I'll protect you."

Her eyes widened and she gave me a quick nod without saying anything back.

I nodded my approval, then leaned my staff against another Corinthian column, putting enough effort of will into it to make the light continue issuing forth for a while. Then I put a finger against my lips, and beckoned Valmont to follow me.

I cut immediately through the displays to get to the amphitheater, and descended into it, heading for the stage, at the feet of the two enormous statues.

Valmont looked back at my brightly blazing staff in sudden understanding. *Look, everybody, Dresden and Valmont are right there, see? Nowhere near the heart of the collection.*

The amphitheater stage, in stark contrast to every other display in the vault, had no overwhelming riches, fantastic jewels, or precious metals. It was stark and bare, with a single block of silver-veined marble rising about four feet off the stage floor in its center.

And upon the marble sat five simple objects.

An ancient wooden placard, its paint so faded that the symbols could not be recognized.

A circlet woven from thorny branches.

A clay cup.

A folded cloth.

A knife with a wooden handle and a leaf-shaped blade.

Why take one priceless holy relic when you could take *five* of them?

And I knew exactly what relic Nicodemus truly wanted.

I turned to Anna and mouthed, "Check it."

She nodded and hunkered down to examine the block, moving cautiously around it. Meanwhile, I extended my senses toward them, feeling carefully for any enchantments that might be protecting them.

That was a mistake. There weren't any traps on the objects, but the collective aura of power around them seared my awareness as sharply as if I'd jammed a penny in an electrical outlet. I let out a hiss and leaned back, while my thoughts blazed with the energy focused upon those artifacts—a combined aura that made the thrumming power of a roused *Amoracchius* seem like a low-wattage lightbulb by comparison.

"My God," I breathed, before I could remember to remain silent. "These are *weapons*." I looked slowly around me. "This isn't a vault. It's an *armory*."

Anna Valmont did not respond.

In fact, she didn't move at all.

I stepped around the block and found her peering at its rear side, her expression focused in concentration. She was entirely frozen.

I then realized that the quality of the light had changed, and I looked up at the flames in the outstretched hands of the two Hecate statues. The flames had ceased flickering. They hadn't gone out—they'd simply frozen in place.

The hairs on the back of my neck didn't go up so much as they let out tiny, hirsute whimpers and started trembling as violently as the rest of me.

"You are, of course, correct," said a basso rumble of a voice from behind me. "This is an armory."

Slowly I turned.

A man in an entirely black suit stood on the amphitheater stage behind me. He was seven feet tall if he was an inch, with the proportions of a professional athlete and the noble features of a warrior king. His hair was dark and swept back from his face in a mane that fell to the base of his neck. His beard was equally black, though marked at the chin with a single streak of silver. His eyes . . .

I jerked my gaze away from those caverns of utter midnight before I could be drawn into them. My stomach twisted, and I suddenly had to fight not to throw up. Or fall down. Or start weeping.

"Wh—" I stammered. "Wh—wh— Are, uh, y-y-you—"

"In point of fact," he said, "it is *my* armory, mortal."

"I can explain," I blurted.

But before I could try, Hades, the Lord of the Underworld, Greek god of death, seized the front of my duster, and a cloud of black fire engulfed me.

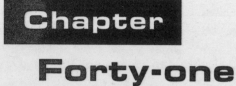

The black fire faded and left me standing half crouched down with my arms up around my head. It's possible that I was making a panicked noise, which I strangled abruptly when I realized that the fire had neither burned nor consumed nor otherwise harmed me in any way at all.

My heart beat very loudly in my ears, and I made myself control my breathing and stand up straight. The terror didn't fade so much as drop to manageable levels. After all, if I wasn't dead, it was because Hades didn't want me dead.

He did, however, apparently want to speak to me in a different room, because we were no longer in the vault.

I stood in a chamber that might have belonged to a Spartan king. The furnishings were few, and simple, but they were exquisitely crafted of nothing but the finest materials. A wooden panel, stained with fine smoke and time, framed a fireplace, and was carved with images of the gods and goddesses of Greece scattered about the slopes of Mount Olympus. Two large chairs of deep, polished red wood and rich black leather sat before the fire, with a low wooden table between them, polished to the same gleaming, deep red finish. On the table was a ceramic bottle. A simple, empty wineglass sat next to it.

I looked around the chamber. A bookcase stood against each wall, volumes neatly aligned, and the spines showed a dizzying variety of languages. There were no doors.

I wasn't alone.

Hades sat in one of the chairs in front of the fire, holding a second wineglass in one negligent hand. His dark eyes gleamed as he stared at the flames. The light was better in here than it had been out in the vault. I could see several dozen tiny objects moving in a steady circular orbit around his head, maybe eight or ten inches out from his skull. Each looked like a small, dark mass of shadow, trailing little tendrils of black and deep purple smoke or mist and . . .

Oh, Hell's bells. It was mordite. A substance so deadly that if it simply touched anything alive, it would all but disintegrate it on the spot, devouring its life energy like a tiny black hole. Hades was wearing a *crown* made of it.

On the floor next to Hades was a mass of fur and muscle. Lying flat on its belly, the beast's shoulders still came up over the arms of the chair, and its canine paws would have left prints the size of dinner plates. One of its heads was panting, the way any dog might do during a dream. The other two heads were snoring slightly. The dog's coat was sleek and black, except for a single blaze of silver-white fur that I could see on one side of its broad chest.

"Sir Harry," Hades rumbled. "Knight of Winter. Be welcome in my hall."

That made me blink. With that greeting, Hades had just offered me his hospitality. There are very few hard and fast rules in the supernatural world, but the roles of guest and host come very close to being holy concepts. It wasn't unheard of for a guest to betray his host, or vice versa, but horrible fates tended to follow those who did, and anything that managed to survive violating that custom would have its name blackened irreversibly.

Hades had just offered me his protection—and with it, the obligations of a good guest. Obligations like not *stealing* anything from his host, for example. I had to tread very carefully here. Bad Things Would Happen To Me if I dared to violate my guest-right. But I couldn't help but think that Bad Things Would Happen To Me even faster if I insulted a freaking Greek god by refusing his invitation.

I remember very little of my father, but one thing I do remember is him telling me always to be polite. It costs you nothing but breath, and can buy you as much as your life.

What, don't look at me like that. I'm only a wiseass to monsters.

And people who really need it.

And when it suits me to be so.

Oh yeah. I was going to have to watch my step very, very carefully here.

"Thank you, Lord Hades," I said, after a pause. My voice quavered only a little.

He nodded without looking away from the fire, and

moved his free hand in a languid gesture toward the other chair. "Please, join me."

I moved gingerly and sat down slowly in the chair.

Hades gave me a brief smile. He poured wine from the ceramic bottle into the other glass, and I took it with a nod of thanks. I took a sip. I'm not really a wine guy, but this tasted like expensive stuff, dark and rich. "I . . . ," I began, then thought better of it and shut my mouth.

Hades' eyes shifted to me and his head tilted slightly. He nodded.

"I feel that I should ask you about the passage of time," I said. "It is possible that time-sensitive events are occurring without your knowledge as we speak."

"Very little in the lives of you or your companions has occurred without my knowledge for the past several days," Hades replied.

I got that sinking feeling that reminded me of all the times I got called in front of the principal's desk in junior high. "You, uh. You know?"

He gave me a very mildly long-suffering look.

"Right," I said quietly. "It's your realm. Of course you know."

"Just so," he said. "That was fairly well-done at the Gate of Ice, by the way. Relatively few who attempt it take the time to watch first."

"Um," I said. "Thank you?"

He smiled, briefly. "Do not concern yourself with time. It currently passes very, very slowly for your companions at the vault, as compared to here."

"Oh," I said. "Okay. That's good."

He nodded. He took a sip of wine, directed his gaze

back upon the fire and trailed the fingers of one hand down over the nearest head of the dog sleeping beside his chair. "I am not what the current age of man would call a 'people person,'" he said, frowning. "I have never been terribly social. If I had the skill, I would say words to you that would put you at ease and assure you that you are in no immediate peril of my wrath."

"Your actions have already done so," I said.

The wispiest shade of a smile line touched the corners of his eyes. "Ah. You have a certain amount of perception, then."

"I used to think so," I said. "Then I started getting older and realized how clueless I am."

"The beginning of wisdom, or so Socrates would have it," Hades said. "He says so every time we have brunch."

"Wow," I said. "Socrates is, uh, down here?"

Hades arched an eyebrow. He lifted his free hand, palm up.

"Right," I said. "Sorry. Um. Do you mind if I ask . . . ?"

"His fate, in the Underworld?" Hades said.

I nodded.

Hades' mouth ticked up at one corner. "People question him."

The dog took note that it was no longer being petted, and the nearest head lifted up to nudge itself beneath Hades' hand again. The Lord of the Underworld absentmindedly went back to petting it, like any man might with his dog.

The second head opened one eye and looked at me from beneath a shaggy canine brow. Then it yawned and went back to sleep.

I sipped some more wine, feeling a little off-balance, and asked, "Why did you, um, intervene in the . . . the intrusion, just now?"

Hades considered the question for a while before he said, "Perhaps I did so to thwart you and punish you. Do not villains do such things?"

"Except you aren't a villain," I said.

Dark, dark eyes turned to me. The fire popped and crackled.

"Granted, I'm basing that on the classical tales," I said. "Which could be so much folklore, or which could have left out a lot of details or wandered off the truth in that much time. But you aren't the Greek version of the Devil."

"You'd hardly think so from the television," Hades said mildly.

"TV rarely does the original stories justice," I said. "But the stories bear out that you might not be such an awful person. I mean, your brothers got up to all kinds of shenanigans. Like, utterly dysfunctional shenanigans. Turning into a bull and seducing a virgin? How jaded do you have to be for *that* to sound like fun?"

"Careful," Hades said, very, very gently. "I do not deny anything you say—but they are, after all, family."

"Yeah, uh, right," I said. "Well. My point is that they each had a sphere of responsibility of their own, and yet they seemed to spend a lot of time maybe neglecting that responsibility—which is not my place to judge, sure, but such a judgment might not be without supporting evidence."

Hades flicked a few fingers in acknowledgment of my statement.

"But the thing is, there are no stories about you doing that. The others could sometimes show capricious temper and did some pretty painful things to people. You didn't. You had a reputation for justice, and never for cruelty. Except for that . . . that thing with your wife, maybe."

Fire reflected very brightly in his dark eyes. "How I stole Persephone, you mean?"

"Did you?" I asked.

And regretted it almost immediately. For a second, I wanted very badly to know a spell that would let me melt through the floor in a quivering puddle of please-don't-kill-me.

Hades stared at me for a long, intense period of silence and then breathed out something that might have been an extremely refined snort from his nose and sipped more wine. "She came of her own will. Her mother failed to cope. Empty-nest syndrome."

I leaned forward, fascinated despite myself. "Seriously? And . . . the pomegranate seeds thing?"

"Something of a political fiction," Hades said. "Hecate's idea, and my brother ran with it. As a compromise, no one came away from it happy."

"That's supposedly the mark of a good compromise," I said.

Hades grimaced and said, "It was necessary at the time."

"The stories don't record it quite that way," I said. "I seem to recall Hecate leading Demeter in search of Persephone."

That comment won a flash of white, white teeth. "That much is certainly true. Hecate led Demeter around. And around and around. It was her wedding present to us."

I blinked slowly at that notion. "A honeymoon free of your mother-in-law."

"Worth more than gold or jewels," Hades said. "But as I said, I've never been the most social of my family. I never asked the muses to inspire tales of me, or visited my worshipers with revelations of the truth—what few I had, anyway. Honestly, I rarely saw the point of mortals worshiping me. They were going to come to my realm sooner or later, regardless of what they did. Did they think it would win them leniency in judging their shades?" He shook his head. "That isn't how I operate."

I regarded him seriously for a moment, frowning, thinking. "You didn't answer my question."

"Words are not my strong suit," he said. "Did you ask the best question?"

I sat back in the chair, swirling the wine a little.

Hades had known we were coming, and we'd gotten in anyway. He'd known who I was. And there was, quite obviously, some kind of connection between Hades and the Queens of Faerie. I sipped at the wine. Add all that together and . . .

I nearly choked on the mouthful as I swallowed.

That won a brief but genuine smile from my host. "Ah," he said. "Dawn."

"You *let* Nicodemus find out about this place," I said.

"And?"

"Mab. This is Mab's play, isn't it?"

"Why would she do such a thing?" Hades asked me, mock reproof in his voice.

"Weapons," I said. "The war with the Outsiders. Mab wants more weapons. Why just get revenge when she can throw in a shopping trip at the same time?"

Hades sipped wine, his eyes glittering.

I stared at him, suddenly feeling horrified. "Wait. Are you telling me that I'm *supposed* to take those things out of here?"

"A much better question," Hades noted. "My armory exists to contain weapons of terrible power during times when they are not needed. I collect them and keep them to prevent their power from being abused in quieter times."

"But why lock them away where anyone with enough resources can get them?" I asked.

"To prevent anyone without the skill or the commitment to use them well from having them," he said. "It is not my task to keep them from all of mortal kind—only from the incompetents."

Then I got it, and understanding made the bottom of my stomach drop out. "This hasn't been a heist at all," I said. "This whole mess . . . it was an *audition*?"

"Another good question. But not the most relevant one."

I pursed my lips, and tried to cudgel my brain into working. It seemed too simple, but hell, why not take the direct route? "What *is* the most relevant question, then?"

Hades settled back into his chair. "Why would I, Hades, take such a personal interest in you, Harry Dresden?"

Hell's bells. I was pretty sure I didn't like the way that sounded, at all. "Okay," I said. "Why would you?"

He reached out a hand to the middle head of the dog

and scratched it beneath the chin. One of the beast's rear legs began to thump rapidly against the floor. It sounded like something you'd hear coming from inside a machine shop. "Do you know my dog's name?"

"Cerberus," I said promptly. "But everyone knows that."

"Do you know what it means?"

I opened my mouth and closed it again. I shook my head.

"It is from an ancient word, *kerberos*. It means 'spotted.'"

I blinked. "You're a genuine Greek god. You're the Lord of the Underworld. And . . . you named your dog *Spot*?"

"Who's a good dog?" Hades said, scratching the third head behind the ears, and making the beast's mouth drop open in a doggy grin. "Spot is. Yes, he is."

I couldn't help it. I laughed.

Hades' eyebrows went up. He didn't quite smile, but he nonetheless managed to look pleased. "A rare enough sound in my kingdom." He nodded. "I am a guardian of an underground realm filled with terrible power, the warden of a nation-prison of shades. I am charged with protecting it, maintaining it, and seeing to it that it is used properly. I am misunderstood by most, feared by most, hated by many. I do my duty as I think best, regardless of anyone's opinion but my own, and though my peers have neglected their charges or focused upon inconsequential trivialities in the face of larger problems, it does not change that duty—even when it causes me great pain. And I have a very large, and very good dog . . ."

Spot's tail thumped the side of Hades' chair like some enormous padded baseball bat.

". . . whom other people sometimes consider fearsome." He turned to me, put his wineglass down, and regarded me frankly. "I believe," he said, "that we have a great many things in common." He rose and stood before me. Then he extended his right arm. "You are here because I wanted to take a moment to shake your hand and wish you luck."

I stood up, feeling a little off-balance, and offered my hand. His handshake was . . .

You can't shake hands with a mountain. You can't shake hands with an earthquake. You can't shake hands with the awful silence and absolute darkness at the bottom of the sea.

But if you could, it might come close to what it was like to trade grips with the Lord of the Underworld, and to receive his blessing.

"Wish me luck?" I breathed, when I could breathe properly again. "You aren't going to help?"

"It is not my place," Hades said. "I wish you good fortune, and will hope that you triumph. But even if we yet lived in the age where my will could guide the course of destiny, it is not for the Lord of Death to take sides in this struggle. The fate of the weapons you have found must be decided by those who found them."

"But you've already helped me," I said. "Just by pointing out what was going on."

Hades didn't smile, but the corner of his eyes wrinkled. "All I did was ask you a few questions. Are you ready?"

"I have one more question," I said.

"Mortals generally do."

"What will happen to Deirdre?"

Hades drew in his breath. His face became expression-less. For a long moment, I thought he wasn't going to answer, but then he said, "Relatively few new shades come into my realm these days. Foremost amongst them are those who perish in the gates—particularly at the Gate of Blood. She will remain in my keeping."

"The things she's done," I said quietly. "The people she's hurt. And she gets to skate justice?"

My host's eyes became hard, flat, like pieces of coal.

"This is my realm," he said, and there was a note in his voice like the grinding of tectonic plates.

Behind him, Spot let out a warning growl. Magnified by three throats and rumbling in that huge chest, it sounded like machinery in a slaughterhouse.

I didn't answer. At least I had enough brains to pull my foot out of my mouth and stop talking. I bowed my head, as meekly as I knew how.

Hades' voice smoothed out again, and at a gesture of his hand, Spot quieted down. "Should you survive the hour, consider your classics again, Sir Harry. And revisit the question in your thoughts."

I nodded, and thought of others in the Underworld. Tantalus. Sisyphus. Vultures tearing out livers, water that could be carried only in sieves, and ever-spinning wheels of fire, punishments tailored specifically to the soul in question.

I didn't know what was going to happen to Deirdre—but she wasn't going to get off light.

"I understand," I said quietly.

Hades nodded. "You will return to the same moment in which I slowed time," he said, "and in the same position. Are you prepared?"

I drew a slow, deep breath. "I guess I'd better be."

His eyes flickered and he gave me a brief nod, maybe of approval.

Then black fire swallowed me again.

Chapter
 Forty-two

"If there's any kind of device built into this thing, I can't see it," Valmont reported in a near whisper, and rose from behind the altar.

I looked around a bit wildly, my eyes taking a second or three to adjust to the dimmer light. I was, just as Hades had said, right back where I'd been a few objective fractions of a second before.

Five artifacts. Mab had promised Nicodemus that I would help him recover the Grail. She hadn't said a damned thing about any of the others. So that meant that there were four things I could keep away from him, right here, right now. Nick hadn't seen them yet, so he couldn't know for certain that they were here. I had to recover them if I could, but keep them away from him at all costs. That meant getting them out of sight and splitting them up as best I could.

But it meant more than that. It meant winning the game Mab had set up for me.

Or, now that I thought about it, the game Mab had *rigged* for me. Mab had arranged to give me a target I couldn't miss if I tried. It wasn't a very appetizing target, but not every job I'd ever done was clean and enjoyable.

I knew how to win the game to Mab's satisfaction. The trick was going to be both winning the game and *surviving* it.

Mentally, I went over those cards that I'd been holding close to my chest.

Yeah. If I played them properly, I thought I had a winning hand.

"Right," I said quietly. I stepped up to the altar and started seizing holy objects. The placard. The crown.

"Take these," I said in a whisper, passing them to Valmont. "Get out of sight. Stow them in your pack if you can. Hide them somewhere else if you can't."

Valmont stared at me with her eyes wide. "Why?"

"They can't be allowed to fall into the wrong hands," I said.

"Dresden," she said, "I'm in this for the money, and revenge if I get a chance at it. I'm not here for a cause."

I clenched my jaw for a second, and then regarded her frankly. "Anna," I said, "when have I ever done wrong by you? I need your help. Who do you trust more to get you out of here? Nicodemus? Or me?"

She stared at me hard for only a fraction of a second before she gave me a curt nod, and took them. She started stuffing them into her pack. She hadn't filled even half of it with diamonds, and was able to slide them in. "Hey, is that the Shroud?"

"This one looks older and shabbier than the one you stole from the Church," I said, rolling up the old cloth and stuffing it into my duster's pocket. It was thin stuff, terribly thin, and made a smaller bundle than you'd think. "Hell, maybe that investigative panel was right. Maybe the Church does have a knockoff."

"But I thought that one had power?" she asked.

"It did, but not like this." My fingers still tingled from touching the cloth. "Besides, we're talking about the power of faith, here," I said. "Enough people believe that the fake is really the Shroud, maybe that's enough to make it powerful all by itself."

"Seems like a cheat."

"Don't knock it," I said.

Her head snapped up, and her eyes widened. "Dresden," Anna hissed.

I heard footsteps approaching a couple of seconds later. My heart thudded in my chest. I managed to get the knife and slip it up the sleeve of my duster, then quietly slid the cup into the exact center of the altar. Even that brief contact was like touching a live wire. Tingles flew up my arm and set every hair of my body on end.

I fought to suppress a full-body shudder, and about half a second later, Nicodemus appeared, trailing Michael, Hannah Ascher, and the Genoskwa. Ascher carried my staff in one hand, the lights of its runes gradually growing dimmer. She looked tired but smug, wearing one backpack that sagged with wealth and lugging a second like a too-heavy carry-on bag at the airport.

"There," Michael said when he spotted me. He looked relieved, and he hadn't, as far as I could tell, picked up anything. "Thank God."

I waved a hand at the group, using the gesture to let

the knife fall a little deeper into my sleeve. "Over here. Found it."

They all came down to the stage with me. Nicodemus's eyes were narrow with suspicion as he walked. "Dresden. You've found the Grail?"

"I just had Valmont check this altar for traps, and she says it's clear," I said, not quite lying. "I just got done examining it myself."

"Why did you leave your staff back there?" Nicodemus asked, his rough voice harsh. "A distraction?"

"Figured you guys could use it as a waypoint to find us," I lied blatantly. I stepped aside with a little Vanna White gesture, revealing the cup, and said, "Ta-da."

Nicodemus stared at me hard for a second, then at the cup on the marble altar. I could see the wheels spinning in his head as he thought. Michael's eyes went to it as well, widening.

"That's it?" Michael asked. "That's really it?"

"Thing makes my teeth buzz, it's so powerful," I said. "Yeah, I think that's it." I looked at Nicodemus and said, "You've got your damned cup. Let's pack up, get Grey his share, and get the hell out of here."

Nicodemus walked a slow circle around the altar, examining it. His shadow twisted and writhed with eagerness where it fell on the floor around him. I took a step to one side to avoid letting it fall on me, because ick.

"I know you've been aching to have your hands on my staff," I said to Ascher, as Nicodemus examined the altar for himself. I held out my hand. "But I'd rather be the one fondling my tool. Wizards are weird like that."

"Wow," she said, and flashed me a grin, her face

flushed, excited. "You left me nowhere to go with that one. I have nothing to add."

"I'm just that good," I said.

She tossed the staff back to me, imprecisely, and I fumbled it for a second and nearly dropped it. I had a hell of a time both catching it in my right hand and keeping my left arm bent enough to keep the knife from slipping out of my sleeve.

And the brass hilt of the knife clicked against the aluminum splint still on my left arm.

Nicodemus looked up sharply at the sound.

His eyes stayed on me, dark and opaque for a moment.

"Miss Valmont," he said quietly. "Go back to the entrance. Stand watch there and tell Grey he's free to collect his share."

Valmont hesitated, looking at me.

She was a liability here. If I could get her clear, it would be harder for Nicodemus to use her against me. Also, the more I could spread these artifacts out, the better.

I nodded, and Valmont vanished silently toward the entrance to the vault.

Michael came to stand next to me, and abruptly tilted his head, looking up at the statues. "Harry," he asked, "does that statue look like Molly to you?"

Oh, crap. I so didn't need this kind of thing distracting either of us right now.

"Pffffft," I said. "What? No. That's absurd. Maybe a little. Some people might think so. She's got, uh, one of those faces."

He pursed his lips and eyed me.

"Would you get your head in the game?" I said.

"Trapped in the Underworld, possible epic Greek men-
ace all around us? Focus, please."

Michael eyed me.

Dammit, I so didn't need this right now. Anna had, by
now, gotten well out of the way. For the next few moments, Grey might be distracted with collecting his share,
leaving Nick and the Genoskwa against me and Michael.

I'd take that fight.

But where would Hannah Ascher come down? Whichever side she chose would have the advantage, and that
was that. Ascher liked me, on the one hand. But on the
other, Nicodemus had saved her life against the Salamander, and she had signed on to be a part of his crew, not
mine. If she held to Binder's mercenary code, she'd back
Nick's play and not mine. I racked my brains for anything
I could do to get her to come down on my side, at this
point. But I had nothing.

Man.

Maybe I shouldn't have rejected her advances. Especially not if she'd already been feeling the rejection from
Binder. Maybe that would have made a serious difference.

On the other hand, who knows? It had been a while
for me. Maybe that would have hurt my chances even
more.

Something nagged at the back of my brain, an instinct
that was attached to Ascher but too vague to make any
sense out of.

The moment was passing, when Nicodemus was at the
height of his tension and uncertainty. If I didn't hurry, I
was going to lose it. Time to start pushing.

"Would you hurry it up?" I said to Nicodemus. "I

don't want to get eaten by a three-headed dog or maybe bump into the shade of Medusa because you went into gloat-mode like every Evil Overlord shouldn't. I told you we already checked it."

"If you don't mind," Nicodemus said, going back to his examination, "I'm going to make certain for myself."

"Oh, for Pete's sake, you can't be serious," I said. "Mab is a tricksy bitch, but she's good to her word. She gave you her word that I would help you secure the cup and bring it back as long as you didn't get up to any shenanigans, and that's what I'm going to do. It's safe. Stick a needle in my eye."

Nicodemus continued in his slow circle.

"You get all cautious now?" I asked him. And I shifted my staff into the crook of my left arm and plucked up the Grail.

Nicodemus's hand went to his sword, and his eyes narrowed, but I just held it speculatively, bouncing it in my hand. "See? No traps. It's not an Indiana Jones movie, man."

Nicodemus remained there, frozen—but his shadow exploded back across the amphitheater stage and climbed halfway up the rear arch of the seating, its edges flaring out wildly, like a monstrous cobra. As tells go, that seemed like a pretty damned big one.

My stomach turned as I began to speak, but I didn't let that show in my voice. "This is what you came for, right?" I said quietly. "What your daughter died to give you. Hey, if I dropped it, do you think it would break?"

"Dresden," Nicodemus said. There was no silk in his voice now—only rasp.

"Gravity seems a little higher here," I said. "You notice? Maybe exactly high enough to break something like this if it fell. And then she'd have died for nothing."

"Give me the Grail," he said, his voice a whisper. "Now."

"Sure. Come get it," I said.

He started stalking around the altar toward me, and I casually mirrored him, keeping it between us. "Deirdre talked to me about your relationship yesterday," I said. "Did you know that?"

He swallowed. His shadow shifted, surging toward me, spreading out in a large circle around us. The light from the upraised hands of the two triple statues grew a little dimmer. It was like suddenly being enfolded in enormous, shadowy wings.

"She went on about the centuries you two had spent together," I said carelessly. "About how there was no word for how close you two had become because no mortal could possibly understand. Hell, I guess that's true. Because you threw her away like she was so much trash. I don't have a word that seems sufficient to cover a father who would do that."

At that, Nicodemus went still again. "Give me the Grail," he whispered. "And shut your ignorant mouth."

"You said she was the only one you trusted, back where you murdered her," I continued in a conversational tone, putting a little emphasis on the verbs. "Call me crazy, but it seems to me that it's going to be a long, cold, empty place for you for the next few millennia. I mean, talk about having an empty nest. That Coin in your pocket must feel pretty heavy right about now."

Nicodemus began to breathe faster.

He was thousands of years old. He was a villain who had forgotten more victims than the most wildly successful serial killer ever claimed. I had no doubt that he'd killed men for much less reason than I was currently offering him. He was skilled in every form of the infliction of damage and death that the world had to offer. He was the most personally dangerous foe I'd ever faced.

But somewhere, deep inside the monster, was something that was still almost human. Something that could feel loss. Something that could feel pain.

And because of that, he was furious.

And he was beginning to lose control.

This, I thought, *is just about your best plan ever, Harry.*

"That must have been really difficult for someone so used to wielding power," I said. "To realize that as a result of the life you'd led, there was no one who would willingly come with you, willingly let you slaughter them, willingly pull that lever for you after you had. I'll bet you chewed that problem for years, trying to crack it. Did it hurt when you realized what you were going to have to give up?"

Nicodemus's chest started heaving, and his eyes got wider.

In my peripheral vision, I could see Michael standing with his sword at port arms, his eyes cast slightly to one side, focused on nothing. The Genoskwa loomed behind him. I saw Michael ripple the fingers of his right hand into a fighting grip on *Amoracchius*, and take a slow, centering breath.

"The funny part is that bit about her being protected

from Hell," I said. "You brought her *here* and expected that she wouldn't get her sentence? Have you *read* Greek mythology? Do you *know* the kinds of things Hades sentences people to endure? At least Hell is, by all reports, more or less nondiscriminatory. Down here, they get *personal*. Did you just try to give her a comforting lie at the last minute? Just to make sure she pulled the lever?"

Nicodemus's sword sprang into his hand. "Give me the Grail or I'm going to kill you."

Hell's bells. I was hurting him.

I considered the Grail and felt bad for what I was doing, and I didn't hesitate or slow down for a second. There are weapons that have nothing to do with steel or explosions or vast arcane power, and I used mine. "Do you remember?" I asked in a very quiet voice. "The first time you saw her? The first time she looked at you? Do you remember that change? That shift, when the whole universe suddenly tilted? Do you remember looking at her and knowing that you would never, ever be quite the same person? Do you think the cup will do that for you?"

I flicked him the Grail, sending it in a smooth arc through the air.

His eyes widened in surprise, but he caught it adroitly, his whole body shuddering as its power washed over him.

I watched him, his face, his posture, and put every ounce of scorn I had into my voice. "I don't know how you said it back in the day, but I'll bet you anything her first word was 'Dada.'"

Something snapped.

His chest stopped heaving.

A single tear appeared.

And he said, in an utterly flat, utterly dead voice, "Kill them."

And that ended the game, right there.

I win?

Chapter

Forty-three

With those words, Nicodemus broke his pact with Mab and freed me of any obligation to keep helping him secure the Grail. I had fulfilled every ounce of her promise to him, or at least to well within the obligation as Mab would see it. Hell, I had actually *given* him the Grail. And if he couldn't take a little harsh truth, as Mab would see it, then that was Nicodemus's problem, not hers.

Well. Nicodemus's problem—and mine. The big downside of the plan to infuriate an emotionally traumatized psychopath into trying to kill me was part two, where the lunatic actually did it.

As spots for a fight went, this was better than most. It was limited to as few people and as few environmental factors as possible. If I'd waited until we were back in Chicago, Nick would have had a virtually unlimited number of civilians to harm and possible hostages to seize. Not only that, but *I* would have had a virtually unlimited number of collaterals to damage, and I didn't imagine that any fight with the head of the Denarians was going to be something I wanted to finesse. Additionally, if we'd duked it out in Chicago, I would have had to worry about whose side Binder would throw in on, not to mention a possible strike team of Denarian squires standing by in the wings, and on top of all of that I was pretty sure that Marcone's troubleshooters would be trying to murder us all.

Here, in the Underworld, I could take the gloves off. The fight would be clean, or as clean as such things got, and I wouldn't have to worry about innocents being harmed.

Just, you know, Michael and me.

I could think abstract thoughts about the decisions leading up to the fight in the back of my head all I wanted, because the real fight happened almost too fast for any thinking to get involved.

The Genoskwa lunged toward me, making a foolish mistake—he should have gone after Michael.

The Knight of the Cross pivoted on the balls of his feet, and *Amoracchius* blazed into furious light. He didn't move with blinding speed. Michael's attack was all about timing, and his timing was pretty much perfect. As the Genoskwa thundered past him, Michael whirled, cloak flying out, and struck a spinning blow that started at the level of his ankles and swept up until he was holding *Amoracchius* over his head in both hands. On the way, the Sword cut a line of light into the back of one of the Genoskwa's thick, hairy knees.

I heard the suddenly parted tendons, thicker than heavy ropes, snap like bowstrings, and the Genoskwa's leg melted out from underneath it in the middle of its stride.

At the same moment, Nicodemus flung both his arms forward, and a terrible, smothering darkness came slamming down upon me.

I'd had two possible responses to his first attack in mind—and they had to be responses, not assaults of my own. When all this was over, I wanted there to be absolutely no question in Mab's mind that he had turned on me, not the other way around. He might have come at me with his sword—it was how he normally preferred to do business, in every case that I had seen. A shield would have held him off, at least for a time.

Or, in his rage, he might unleash the full malice of Anduriel upon me. Which he had done.

This was not a normal circumstance for Nicodemus.

I'd prepared the proper defense.

"Lumios!" I shouted, as the darkness closed in, and I poured my will into the same light spell I'd used earlier—only I added a measure of soulfire into the mix.

The light leapt forth in a sphere and exploded into sparks as it collided with something that simply *devoured* it, swallowing it into nothingness as it streamed forth. The effect was damned odd-looking, from the inside. Light poured forth to be enveloped by a slithering blackness all around me, something that recoiled from the sparks and then came surging back in their wake with frenzied agitation—but the darkness could reach no closer than just beyond the reach of my arm.

I heard Nicodemus shout something in a language I didn't understand, and the Genoskwa let out a howl of furious pain. Something heavy made the ground quiver beneath my feet, and there was an enormous crashing sound.

Michael's voice rang out like a silver trumpet, calling, *"In nomine Dei! Lux et veritas!"*

Steel rang on steel, and I realized that I hadn't figured the numbers right after all. It wasn't Nick and the Genoskwa versus me and Michael. It was Nick, the Genoskwa, and *Anduriel* versus me and Michael. And I had the last two as my dance partners.

The Genoskwa let out a roar, and I knew it was coming right at me. I couldn't move without stepping into that smothering blackness, and that seemed like a horrible idea, so instead I folded my arms across my chest, and muttered, "Let's see you ground *this*, ugly." Then I called upon Winter, and cried out, *"Arctispinae!"*

I expanded my arms out explosively, and as I did, slivers of Winter cold froze the water in the air into hundreds of spines of needle-pointed ice that exploded out from me, into the darkness and beyond. No magic attached itself to the spines of ice once they had been formed—they simply became sharp, hurtling pieces of solid matter. I was betting that whatever power the Genoskwa had to negate the effects of directly applied magic, it still had to follow the laws of magic as I understood them.

The bet paid off. The Genoskwa let out another ear-shattering roar of pain from no more than seven or eight feet away.

I used the sound as a point of reference and whirled my staff in a swooping arc, its green-silver soulfire-infused light driving back the substance of the Fallen angel still trying to compress in upon me. My will gathered more Winter ice around the end of the staff in an irregular globe the size of my head and harder than stone, and I aimed at the source of the sound and cried, *"Forzare!"*

A lance of pure kinetic energy flung the hailstone from the end of my staff and out through the darkness like a cannonball, and it hit something with an enormous and meaty-sounding *thunk* of obdurate ice against muscle-dense flesh. I must have gotten him in the breadbasket, because instead of roaring, the Genoskwa let out a windy, seething sound.

Steel rang on steel again, and I heard workboots pound the marble, coming near me. Michael shouted, *"Omnia vincit amor!"* and the blinding white fire of *Amoracchius* shattered the darkness around me as if it had been a dry and dusty eggshell.

My vision returned. Nicodemus was coming along in Michael's wake, blade in hand, but as Anduriel was shattered, he screamed and staggered, falling to one knee, and only managed that because he threw out his left arm to support himself.

Not far away, the Genoskwa was rising from where he had fallen. The hailstone I'd conjured had apparently knocked him backward over the marble block in the center of the stage, and one side of his rib cage looked distorted. The creature crouched on three limbs, his leg dragging, and bared his teeth at me in a silent snarl, yellowed tusks showing.

"Enough, Nicodemus!" Michael thundered, and his voice rang from the marble and the riches of the vault. "Enough!"

The sheer volume and force in his voice staggered me. I found myself standing back to back with him so that I could keep the Genoskwa in sight.

"Has today not been enough for you?" Michael said, his voice dropping to something almost like a plea. "In the name of God, man, have your eyes not yet been opened?"

"Michael," I growled, low, between clenched teeth. "What are you doing?"

"My job," he answered me, just as quietly. "Nicodemus Archleone," he said, his tone gentle, directed back toward the fallen Denarian. "Look at yourself. Look at your fury. Look at your pain. Look where they have *led* you, man. Your own *child*."

From where he had fallen, Nicodemus looked up at Michael, and I saw something I had never seen on his face before.

Weariness. Strain. Uncertainty.

"This is what it has taken, Nicodemus," Michael said quietly. "This journey into the darkness of greed and ambition. You stand amongst untold, unimaginable wealth, and you have lost the only thing that really matters because of them. Because of the lies and the schemes of the Fallen."

Nicodemus did not move.

Neither did the Genoskwa. But I gathered another hailstone-cannonball onto the end of my staff, just to be sure I was ready if he did.

Michael lowered his sword, the wrathful fire of *Amoracchius* becoming something less fierce, less hot. "It is not too late. Don't you see what has happened here?

What has been arranged, all the pieces that have been moved to bring you to the only place where your eyes might be opened. Where you might have a chance— perhaps your very last chance—to turn aside from the path you have walked for so long. A path that has caused you and those close to you and the world around you nothing but heartache and misery."

"Is that what you believe this is?" Nicodemus said in a wooden, uninflected tone. "My chance at redemption?"

"It isn't a matter of belief," Michael said. "I need look no further than the evidence of my eyes and mind. It's why I took up the Sword in the first place. To save you, and those like you, who have been used by the Fallen. It's why I have been given the grace to take up arms again, this very night—in time to offer you a chance."

"For forgiveness?" Nicodemus spat.

"For hope," Michael said. "For a new beginning. For peace." He swallowed and said, "I can't imagine anything happening to my daughter. No father should have to see his child die." Michael's voice stayed steady, quiet, and sincere. "As different as we are, as much separated in time and faith, you are still a human being. You are still my brother. And I am very sorry for your pain. Please. Let me help you."

Nicodemus shuddered and dropped his eyes.

I blinked several times.

And for a second, I thought Michael was going to pull it off.

Then Nicodemus shook his head and let out a low and quiet laugh. He stood up again, and as he did, his shadow seemed to accrete beneath him, gathering darkness from all around the room and drawing it into a nebulous pool at his feet.

"Choirboy," he said, contempt in his tone. "You think you know about commitment. About faith. But yours is as a child's daydream beside mine."

"Don't do this," Michael said, his tone almost pleading. "Please don't let them win."

"Let *them* win?" Nicodemus said. "I do not dance to the Fallen's tune, Knight. We may move together, but I play the music. I set the beat. For nearly two thousand years have I followed my path, through every treacherous bend and twist, through every temptation to turn aside, and after centuries of effort and study and planning and victory, they follow *my* leadership. Not the other way around. Turn aside from my path? I have *blazed* it through ages of humanity, through centuries of war and plague and madness and havoc and devotion. I *am* my path, and it is me. There is no turning aside."

The shadow at his feet seemed to darken as he spoke, to throb in time with his voice, and I shuddered at the sight, at the pride in his bearing, the clarity in his eyes, and the absolute, serene certainty in his voice.

Lucifer must have looked *exactly* like that, right before things went to Hell.

I was still standing back to back with Michael, and I felt his shoulders slump in disappointment. But there was nothing of remorse or weakness in his voice as his sword swept back up to guard position. "Despite all you have given in their service, you stand alone before *Amoracchius* now. I am truly sorry for your soul, brother—but this time, you will answer for what you have done."

"Alone," Nicodemus all but purred. "Do you think I am alone?"

He gave us his hungry shark-smile, and my stomach went into free fall.

Behind the stone block the Genoskwa smiled as well, and that would have been a hideous thing to see if a second set of glowing green eyes hadn't opened above the cavernous gleam of the Genoskwa's beady orbs, along with a faintly glowing, swirling sigil in the center of his forehead—and made the sight truly nightmarish. Even as I watched, curling ram's horns erupted from the Genoskwa's skull, and the already enormous creature began to swell, growing in mass, his patchy fur thickening, an extra set of limbs swelling out from his sides. Within a heartbeat or three, the shape of a creature like some enormous bear of a forgotten epoch, except for the extra legs, eyes, and the horns, stood where the Genoskwa had been. Tons of it.

"Ursiel," I breathed. A Fallen angel so powerful that it had taken all three Knights of the Cross together to take him out the last time he'd appeared. And this time he wasn't powered by the skinny husk of an insane gold miner, either. "Oh, crap."

"It gets better," said another voice.

I looked past where Ursiel and the Genoskwa stood, to find Hannah Ascher mounting the steps to the top of the stage. She'd shed her packs, and walking with a lazy, deliberate sensuality, she stretched her arms overhead as she reached the stage, and her clothing just . . . dissolved, like so much smoke, into a clinging, purplish mist that drifted around her in spiraling tendrils—not so much for modesty as for accent, yet for the most part, covering her most delicate parts with the same coyness as a fan dancer's feathers. She smiled, slowly, and a second set of glowing purple eyes opened above her own, as a glowing sigil, vaguely suggestive of an hourglass appeared on her forehead.

I knew the symbol.

It had been etched in my flesh for years.

"Lasciel," I whispered.

"Hello, lover," said a throaty, playful voice that was not quite Hannah Ascher's own. "You have no idea how much I've missed you."

I leaned my head back to Michael a little and said, "You and I definitely need to have a talk with the Church about what the word 'safekeeping' means."

Michael glanced at me with a faint frown, to let me know that this was not the time.

Lasciel laughed, musically, the sound of it pure pleasure on the ears. "Oh, Harry," she said. "Did you really think that it's possible to pick up corruption in a nice clean handkerchief and lock it away in a box? No, of course not. Forces such as we cannot be contained by mortals, my lover. We are a part of you all."

Michael leaned his head back a little toward me and asked, "Lover?"

I twitched one shoulder in answer and said, "It's complicated."

"Oh dear."

I turned to Lasciel and said, "Hey, Hannah. Take it from someone who knows. You really don't want to be doing what you're doing."

Ascher's human eyes narrowed. "Oh, sure," she said,

in her own voice. "Because the high road is just so awesome. Wardens of the White Council have been trying to kill me for most of my adult life because when I was seventeen years old I defended myself against three men who tried to rape me."

"I'm not defending them," I said. "But you killed people with magic, Hannah. You broke the First Law."

"Like you haven't," she snarled. "You hypocrite."

"Hey, whoa," I said. "Hold on there. Me and Lasciel have some history, but even if we've been on different sides of the law, you and I don't have a personal quarrel."

"The hell we don't," she said. "After a few years on the run, I got in with the Fellowship of St. Giles. You remember them, right? Bunch of folks who fought the Red Court? They gave me training, safe places to live. Hell, I lived on the *beach* in Belize for six years. I had a life. Friends. I even fought the good fight."

"Yay?" I said, trying not to sound as baffled as I felt. "What's that got to do with me?"

"Everything!" she screamed, and the purple mist around her was suddenly suffused with sullen, glowing flame.

I swallowed, despite myself.

"When you destroyed the Red Court, you killed most of the Fellowship with it. All the half vampires more than a few decades old just *withered* away in front of our eyes. People who had given me trust. Respect. My *friends.*" She shook her head. "And, you arrogant son of a bitch, I'll bet you never gave them a thought before you did it, did you?"

"If I'd known it was going to happen," I said, "I'd

have done it anyway." Because if I hadn't, Maggie wouldn't have survived the night.

"The world fell apart after that," Ascher spat. "The finances, the coordination, the communication. I was on the street. If Binder hadn't found me . . ." She shook her head.

"Yeah, Binder and his Rule Number One," I said. "He doesn't know about what you've done, does he?"

She narrowed her eyes and her voice became a degree hotter. "Nicodemus and Lasciel and the other Denarians have treated me with *respect*," she said. "They've talked to me. Trusted me. Worked with me. Made me *rich*. When one side treats you like a sad freak and a hunted animal and the other treats you like an equal, it gets really easy to decide where you stand."

Hard to argue with that. But I tried. "Doesn't mean you have to run everything exactly the way he wants you to do it," I said.

She let out a harsh laugh. "But I *do* want to do it," she said. "I've been looking *forward* to it. Every time you looked at me, flirted with me, spoke with me."

"As have I," said Lasciel's voice, from the same mouth. "No one's ever turned me down before, Harry. Not once. And to think that I *liked* you."

"We wouldn't have worked out, babe," I said.

"Perhaps," she said. "Perhaps not. In any case, be assured that I may have one of the few accurate perspectives in the universe when I say that 'Heaven has no rage like love to hatred turned, nor Hell a fury like a woman scorned.'"

Ah. So that's what my subconscious had been trying

to warn me about. That Lasciel was right there in front of me, and itching for payback.

"Meaning what?" I asked her.

"Meaning that since a whisper in your ear that should have killed you seems to have failed, I intend to skip the subtlety, rip your head apart, and collect our child. She's far too valuable a resource to be allowed to die with you."

My eyes widened. "You, uh, you know about that."

"Child?" Michael said, baffled.

"*Complicated,*" I said through clenched teeth.

Well. At least now I knew which side Ascher was taking.

"I'd tell you to give me the knife, Dresden," Nicodemus said, still smiling. "But unlike your friend, I don't do second chances. And you won't have any need for it in a moment."

Ursiel made a sound that I normally only associate with tractor-trailer rigs, and which might have been a hungry growl. Then he stepped over the four-foot block with no particular difficulty and padded in near silence to my left. Lasciel took up station a bit to my right, with Nicodemus making the third point of a lopsided triangle surrounding us.

This day was going bad a little more rapidly than I had anticipated. It had, in fact, sprayed gravel on the windshield of my worst-case scenario as it went rocketing past.

And then footsteps sounded, and Grey sauntered into the amphitheater, casually carrying Anna Valmont's pack over one shoulder.

There was blood on it, and on Grey's fingers.

"Ah, Grey," Nicodemus said. He was enjoying getting

a little of his own back after the theater I'd thrown into his face. "And?"

"Valmont's dead, as ordered," Grey said calmly. He surveyed the scene on the stage as he approached, his eyes lingering on Lasciel appreciatively. "We about done here?"

"A few final details to tie up," Nicodemus said. "Have you considered my offer?"

"The Coin thing?" Grey asked. He shrugged and glanced at Lasciel again. "It's got possibilities. I've got questions. Let's finish the job and talk about them over dinner."

"Excellent," Nicodemus said. "Would you mind?"

I tracked Grey, staring hard at him as he took up position at the fourth corner of the square centered on me and Michael, watching him as he set the pack of diamonds and artifacts to one side and cracked his knuckles, smiling.

"I never pretended to be anything but a villain," he said to me, as if baffled by my glare. "Should have seen this one coming, wizard."

"You really killed her?" I asked.

"No particular reason not to. It was quick."

"You are a treacherous son of a bitch," I said.

He rolled his eyes. "Maybe you should have been the one to hire me, then."

His response made me grind my teeth.

There weren't going to be any temptations offered this time, no bargains to think twice about, and no cavalry was about to ride over the horizon. Nicodemus meant to kill us.

Michael and I could not win this fight.

I heard him take a deep breath and murmur a low, steady prayer. He set his feet and raised his sword to the high guard.

I gripped my staff mostly in my right hand, holding it across my body with a few fingers of my damaged left arm, and called forth my will and Winter, readying for a hopeless battle.

Lasciel turned her hands palms up, and searing points of violet light appeared in them. Waves of heat shimmered around Hannah Ascher's body.

Anduriel seethed up around Nicodemus like a dark cloak made from a breaking wave, foaming around the slender man as he raised his sword and started forward.

Ursiel let out a subsonic rumble that shook my chest, and the Genoskwa's beady eyes stared hate from the face of the prehistoric demon-bear.

Grey tensed and crouched slightly, his bland features relaxed and amused.

And I stopped being able to fight back the maniac's grin that had been struggling to get loose as I played my hole card and said, "Game over, man. Game over."

Chapter
Forty-four

A good con doesn't just happen.

It's all about the setup.

Let's rewind.

Set the Wayback Machine for three mornings ago, just after walking out of that first meeting with Nicodemus and Deirdre at the Hard Rock, while riding away in the limo with Mab.

I told her who I wanted to see.

For a moment, she didn't react. Her eyes were locked somewhere beyond the roof of the limo, her head tracking slowly, as if she could still see Nicodemus and Deirdre in their suite. There was no expression on her face, absolutely none—but the interior of the car had dropped several degrees in temperature, purely from the intensity of whatever she wasn't showing.

"You grow in wisdom, my Knight," she said a moment later, turning her head back to face the front. "Slowly, perhaps, but you grow. He is the logical person to consult in this matter. I have already arranged a meeting."

"Oh," I said, and idly fingered the earring, unused to the sensation of something metallic there. "Good."

"Stop playing with that," Mab said. "The less attention you draw to it, the better."

I scowled and futzed with it a little more, just to show her that I could, but she was right. As things stood, it might be seen as a simple fashion statement. If Nicodemus realized that by taking the earring away, he could all but incapacitate me, things could go downhill rapidly once we finally came to grips.

So I dropped my hands and schooled myself mentally the rest of the way to the meeting, focusing on accepting the new sensation and dismissing it from my thoughts entirely.

I started playing with it again as the limo stopped, and Mab sighed.

McAnally's pub is the best of the watering holes in Chicago that serve the supernatural community. It's a basement bar, like Cheers, but there the resemblance ends. It's all decorated in stained and polished wood, with clunky electric ceiling fans from the thirties whirling lazily overhead. The ceiling isn't very high, so they whirl away just a few inches over my head, and I remind myself not to do the bunny hop every time I come through the door.

Normally, Mac's does a brisk trade, but today there was a sign on the door that read: CLOSED FOR PRIVATE PARTY. A second sign hung inside the door, a wooden one, into which the words ACCORDED NEUTRAL TERRITORY had been neatly burned. It meant that the establishment was officially neutral ground under the guidelines of the Unseelie Accords, what amounted to the Geneva Convention of the supernatural world. Mab had written the Accords, and their signatories defied them at peril of the antipathy of the supernatural establishment and, worse, her personal displeasure.

One corner of the sign was scorched and cracked, which had happened in a battle with Outsiders, who weren't very civic-minded.

Mac, bald, lean, and silent, stood behind the bar in his usual crisp white shirt and spotless apron. When Mab entered, he put down the rag he was using to polish the wooden bar, and bowed at the waist, somehow giving the gesture an accent of courtesy rather than obeisance.

"Barkeep," Mab replied, and inclined her head considerably more deeply than she had to Nicodemus a few minutes before. "May your patrons be prosperous and honest."

Mac, as a rule, rarely uttered multi-syllables. Today, he said, "May your scales always return to balance."

Her mouth quirked at the corner and she said, "Flatterer."

He smiled and nodded to me. "Harry."

"Mac. I haven't had good food in months. Though, uh, I'm a little short on funds. I will gladly pay you Tuesday for a sandwich and a beer today."

He nodded.

"Thanks."

Mab turned to the table nearest the door and gave me a look. It took me a beat to realize what she wanted, and to pull out a chair for her. She sniffed and sat down, folded her hands in her lap, and stared at nothing in particular, dismissing the rest of us from her world as thoroughly as if she had entered a locked room.

My contact was waiting for me at a table in the back corner, and I walked over to join him. He was a big man by every definition of the word, tall and strong and solid, with a barrel for a chest and a smaller keg of a belly to go with it. His hair and beard were white and silver, though the rosy smoothness of his cheeks belied any indication of old age, and his eyes were blue and bright. He wore a chain-mail shirt and hunting leathers, and a long, hooded red coat trimmed in white fur hung from the back of the chair beside him. A simple, worn-looking broadsword hung at his side, and a large, lumpy leather sack sat on the floor beside him, as natural there as a mail carrier with his bag.

"Sir Knight," he said.

"You're here as Kringle, seriously?" I asked him.

Kringle winked at me. "The Winter Knight called for me in his official capacity as an agent of the Winter Court. Mab has the right to summon Kringle. If she'd called for Vadderung, I'd have told her to get in line."

Donar Vadderung was the name of the CEO of Monoc Securities, a corporate security interest that provided information and highly skilled specialists to those with a great deal of money. Vadderung had access to more information than anyone I knew, except maybe the Senior Council of the White Council of Wizardry—only he was a hell of a lot smarter about using it. He was also, I was reasonably certain, *Odin*. The Odin. Or if he wasn't, he could do an awfully good impersonation. Oh, and also, he was Santa Claus.

Vadderung is a complicated guy.

"But you and Kringle are the same person," I said.

"Legally speaking, Kringle and Vadderung are two entirely different people who simply happen to reside in the same body," he replied.

"That's just a fiction," I said, "a little game of protocol."

"Little games of protocol are how one shows respect, especially to those with whom one does not get along famously well. It can be tedious, but generally is less trouble than a duel would be."

Mac set a couple of his homebrewed beers down on the bar. I rounded them up and returned to the table, putting both bottles out in the middle. Kringle chose one, nodded to the chair across from him, and I sat.

"To start with, I'm going to assume you know everything I do," I said.

His eyes wrinkled at the corners as he took a drink. "That seems wise."

I nodded and sipped my own. Wow. Mac's beer is an excellent argument that there is a God, and that furthermore, He wants us to be happy. I savored it for a couple of seconds and then wrenched my mind back to business. "I want to float some thoughts at you and see if you think they're sound."

"By all means."

"First," I said, "Nicodemus is after something powerful. I don't know what it is, but I do know that if I can get him to *tell* us what he's after, it's going to be a lie. He'd never let anyone know his true goal if he could help it."

"I concur," Kringle said.

I nodded. "He'll assemble a crew. Some of them will be his people, and some of them will be outside specialists, but I'm pretty sure at least one of them is going to be a plant—they'll look all independent but they'll have one of those Coins on them and one of the Fallen whispering in their ears."

"I would consider that a high probability," Kringle said.

"Third," I said, "he's going to betray me at some point along the line. He's proactive, and obsessed with control, so he'll be the one who wants to stick the knife in first. He knows the limits Mab has placed on me, so he'll want to do it after I've gotten him to wherever he wants to go, but before we finish the job, to guarantee him the first blow."

"Also sound reasoning," Kringle said.

"Dammit," I said. "I had hoped I was wrong about something. If I'm to follow Mab's rules, my options are limited."

Kringle's eyes went to the slender figure at the table by the door. "May I offer you a word of advice, based purely upon my knowledge of the Queen's nature?"

"Sure."

"Mab moves in mysterious ways," he said, looking back at me with a grin. "Nasty, unexpected, devious, patient, and mysterious ways. I don't think she'd throw away a piece as valuable as you on a lost cause. Look for an opening, a weakness. It will be there."

"Have you seen this guy in action?" I asked. "Nicodemus Archleone is . . . He's better than me. Smart, dangerous, ruthless, and experienced. All by himself, he'd be bad enough. I've never even seen him go to his bench. All the other Denarians whip out their Fallen buddies left and right, but Nicodemus, as far as I can tell, mostly uses his to chauffeur him around. I've got no idea what Anduriel can do, because Nick has never had to fall back on him."

"Perhaps that's because Nicodemus understands just as well as you do where true power comes from," Kringle said.

I arched an eyebrow at that. "Knowledge," I said. I thought about it, putting pieces together. "Wait. You're telling me that he doesn't use Anduriel in fights because Anduriel isn't a fighter."

"Any of the Fallen are absolutely deadly in battle," Kringle said severely, "even hampered as they are. But the Master of Shadows doesn't prefer to operate that way, no."

Nicodemus's control over the gang of superpowered lunatics was starting to make more sense now. "Master of Shadows. That's an old, old phrase for a spy master."

"Exactly," Kringle said. "Nicodemus knows very nearly as much as I do. Anduriel has the potential to hear anything uttered within reach of any living being's shadow, and sometimes to look out from it and see."

My eyes widened and I looked down at my own shadow on the table.

"No," Kringle said. "That's why Mab remains here, to secure this conversation against Anduriel. But you must exercise extreme discretion for the duration of this scenario. There are places Anduriel cannot reach—your friend Carpenter's home, for example, or your island, now that you have awakened it. And the Fallen must know to pay attention to a given shadow, or else it's all just a haze of background noise—but you can safely assume that Anduriel will be listening very carefully to your shadow during this entire operation. Anything you say, Nicodemus will know. Even writing something down could be compromised."

"Hell's bells," I said. If that was the case, communicating with my friends would just get them set up for a trap. Man, no wonder Nicodemus was always a few steps ahead of everyone else. "I'm . . . going to have to play the cards really damned close to my chest, then."

"If I were you, I'd hold them about three inches behind my sternum, just to be sure," Kringle said.

I swigged beer and drummed my fingers on the table. "Yeah," I said. "Okay. Good to know. But it's not enough. I need another advantage."

"I never find having too many advantages any particular burden."

"What would be perfect is a plant of my own," I said. "Someone Nicodemus doesn't see coming. But to work that angle, I'd have to know who he was getting together, someone he already planned to have in place."

Kringle took on the air of a professor prompting a stumbling protégé. "How could you work with this theoretical person, without the ability to speak with him, to coordinate your efforts?"

"Hide it in plain sight," I said, "disguised as something else. Code."

"Interesting. Go on."

"Uh . . . ," I said. "He'd be taking his cues from me, so mostly he'd be the one asking me questions. Tell him to refer to me as 'wizard' just before he asks a question relating to the situation at hand. The first word of my response would be the answer. Then we could make the actual conversation sound like something else entirely. We play along until it's time for me to make my move. Then I use the phrase 'game over' and we hit them."

Kringle took a pull of his beer. "Not bad. Not perfect, but then, it never is." He set his bottle aside and reached down into the sack by his foot. He rummaged for a moment and then produced a large envelope, which he offered to me.

I regarded it carefully. Gifts have an awful lot of baggage attached to them among the Fae, and both Kringle and I were members of the Winter Court. "I didn't get you anything," I said.

He waved his other hand negligently. "Consider it a belated holiday gift, free of obligation. That island is a tough delivery."

"Prove it," I said. "Say 'ho, ho, ho.' "

"Ho, ho, ho," he replied genially.

I grinned and took the envelope. I opened it and found a photo and a brief description inside.

"Who is this?"

"A covert operative, a mercenary," Kringle replied. "One of the best."

"I've never heard of him."

He arched an eyebrow. "Because he's covert?"

I bobbed my head a bit in admission of the point. "Why am I looking at his picture?"

"There are four operatives who could play one role Nicodemus needs filled in this venture," he said. "Two of them are currently under contract elsewhere, and the third is presently detained. That leaves Nicodemus only one option, and I know he won't exercise it until the last possible moment—and he's not far away."

"You think if I get to him first, I can hire him?"

"If I make the introduction and we establish your communication protocol under Mab's aegis? Yes."

"But if he's a mercenary, he can by definition be bought. What's to stop Nicodemus from outbidding me?"

Kringle sat back in his seat at that, considering the question. Then he said, "If you buy this man, he stays bought. It's who he is."

I arched an eyebrow. "You're asking me to trust a stranger's professional integrity?"

"I wouldn't do that," Kringle said. "I'm asking you to trust mine."

I exhaled, slowly. I took a long pull of beer.

"Well, hell," I said. "What's the world coming to if you can't trust Santa Claus?" I leaned forward, peering at the printed summary and said, "So let's meet with Goodman Grey."

Chapter

Forty-five

I hadn't quite finished the "r" sound in "game over" before Grey had crossed forty feet of intervening space and was on top of Ursiel and the Genoskwa.

One second, Grey was standing there, looking smug and anticipatory. The next, there was a blur in the air and then a *creature* was clawing its way up Ursiel's back. It was about the size and vaguely the shape of a gorilla, but the head on its shoulders might have belonged to some kind of hideous werewolf-bulldog hybrid, and grotesquely elongated claws tipped its hands. Its weird golden eyes were Grey's. Before Ursiel could realize that he was under attack, the Grey-creature was astride its ursine back, fangs sinking into the huge hump of muscle there, oversized jaws locked into place. The huge bear-thing reared up onto its hind legs, only for Grey to reach around to its head with gorilla-length arms and sink nine-inch claws like daggers into its eyes.

Ursiel and the Genoskwa let out an ear-tearing roar of agony.

I whirled the heavy end of my staff toward Nicodemus

and snarled, *"Forzare!"* The hailstone flew at him like a bullet, but though the shock of Grey's betrayal was still evident on his face, Nicodemus's superb reflexes were still in fine operating order, and he dropped into a lateral roll, dodging the missile.

Michael shouted, "Harry!" and hauled me to one side an instant before an orb of absolutely searing white heat appeared precisely where my head had been. The blast coming off of it was so intense that it singed the hair on that side of my head. I turned my head to see Ascher and Lasciel lifting her other hand, preparing to hurl a second sphere at me.

"You get Nick," I panted.

"Seems fair," Michael said.

In the background, Ursiel continued to roar and thrash. I couldn't see how it was going for Grey, but Ursiel crashed off of the stage and into a display featuring at least a dozen statues of various saints and holy figures, reducing them to rubble and scattering fabulously valuable gems in every direction.

The second sphere came flying at me and I countered by lifting my staff and shouting, *"Defendarius!"* A broad wall of force shimmered into being in front of me, and the sphere smashed against it and exploded into a cloud of flame that spread out along its length and breadth, as if seeking a way around it. The heat was viciously intense, and enough of it would have burned through the shield—but it was a question of volume. Ascher had struck at me with pinpoint precision and intensity. I'd countered her with raw power, using a shield big enough to spread the heat over a wide enough area to keep it from burning through.

Ascher let out a snarl of frustration and hurled another sphere. Her thinking was obvious—if she could keep pouring fire onto me and force me to hold up shield after shield against it, eventually she could either burn through it or exhaust my ability to keep holding it up. I'd have taken that fight against a lot of practitioners: There are relatively few wizards on the White Council who can stay with me in terms of pure magical horsepower. But while there are plenty of wizards who could wear themselves out pounding on my shields, I had a pretty solid intuition that Ascher could keep throwing fire until I was a gasping heap on the ground, especially with Lasciel's knowledge and experience backing her up. Worse, Lasciel knew me, inside and out.

Or at least, she had *known* me. So it was time to use a few tricks I'd developed since we'd parted ways.

In the past, I'd worn rings designed to store a little excess kinetic energy every time I moved my arm. Then I could let loose the saved energy all in one place to pretty devastating effect when I really needed to do it. I hadn't had the resources I needed to make new rings, but I'd carved the same spell in my new wizard's staff.

Seventy-seven times.

It wasn't as handy as my layered rings had been—instead of being broken up into multiple units, the energy of the spell was all stored in one reservoir, so I only had the one shot.

But it was a doozy.

So as another white-hot sphere splashed into flame against my shield, I whirled the butt end of the staff where the energy storage spells were carved toward

Ascher, focused my concentration on the shield, braced my feet, and shouted, *"Arietius!"*

The staff bucked in my hands like a living thing and shoved my shoes several inches across the floor as the stored energy unleashed itself and drove into the rear of my shield. For a second, I worried about the staff shattering—I had never tried it with this much stored energy before, and there was always the chance that I had exceeded the design tolerance of the spell at some point. If I had, I would be the center of my own spectacular and splintery explosion. But my work was good and the staff functioned perfectly. I held the structure of the shield together and let the energy from the staff drive it forward, toward Ascher, and suddenly a large, obdurate, and extremely solid invisible wall was rushing at her like an oncoming freight train, shedding a trail of fire in its wake.

I had never lowered the shield, and my actions had been obscured by all the fire chewing away at it—so Ascher recognized the danger a second too late, and that was where her inexperience showed. She might have real power and a gift with fire, but in a fight there's no time to think your way through spells and counterspells. Either you've done your homework or you haven't, and despite the advantage of having Lasciel in her corner, Ascher wasn't ready for something like this. She was focused entirely on offense, not on protecting herself as well, and couldn't come up with a counter in time.

The wall hit her with about the same force as an oncoming garbage truck, and blew her right out of the veil of purple mist that clung to her naked form. She flew back off the stage in a windmill of flailing limbs, and crashed into a display of particularly fine ecclesiastical robes and garments, most of which burst into flame as the sheath of shimmering heat around her body brushed against them.

As that happened, the light in the great vault changed. The fire in the hands of the two triple statues flared into large, dangerous-looking scarlet bonfires, painting everything in shades of sudden blood. I shot a glance up at the statues, and their *mouths* were moving. No voices were coming out, but the damned things were *talking* and a raw instinct told me what had happened. The wanton destruction of part of the collection had set off some kind of alarm.

And we were all standing, more or less, in one enormous prison for the shades of the dead.

Michael and Nicodemus, meanwhile, were engaged in a furious exchange of blows. *Amoracchius* glowed like a beacon, and its humming power filled the air. Nicodemus's shadow danced and threatened and obscured his form as he moved like some oily and poisonous liquid, sword flickering—but I had seen all of that before.

I had never seen Michael going all out.

Michael was a big guy, built broad and strong, and the contrast between him and Nicodemus was striking. There's an old truism in fighting that says a good big man will beat a good small man. The advantage gained from having superior height, reach, and greater physical mass and power is undeniable, and for the first time, I saw Michael using it all.

Blow after blow rained down on Nicodemus, a furious attack, and the smaller man had no choice but to give way before the assault, driven step by step backward before the onslaught of the Knight of the Sword. His lighter blade managed to flick out once, then twice, but each time Michael twisted his body to catch the blow on his mail, trusting the armor Charity had forged for him to protect him—and it did. He kept coming forward, and none of his blows was aimed to wound or incapacitate. *Amoracchius* swept down at Nicodemus's head, his throat, his belly, his heart, and any one of the strikes could have delivered a mortal wound.

I flicked a glance toward where Ascher was, for all I knew, on fire. I thought about going over and making sure she stayed down and it made me feel sick enough that I decided I wasn't quite that far gone yet. Besides, dangerous as she was, she didn't hold a candle to Nicodemus. Michael had him on the ropes. This was our chance to put that monster away.

Michael drove Nicodemus to the edge of the stage, until the Denarian had to twist with a snarl and dive off to the ground below. He tucked into a roll and came back up again, neat as an acrobat.

And I tagged him with another hailstone before he could turn around and see it coming.

I hadn't had time to get together as much ice as I'd used on the first two, but the hailstone that hit him was the size of a very large apple and moving considerably faster than a major-league fastball. It didn't break when it hit. Nicodemus did. There was a wet thump of impact when it hit him in the left side, below the ribs, and he went up onto his toes in reaction, his body drawing to one side in a bow of pain. Then he staggered to one side and fell to a knee.

Michael took two steps and leapt from the stage, Sword grasped over his head, and brought it down on Nicodemus like a headsman's ax. No demonic power or Fallen angel could save Nicodemus from that blow, delivered by that man, with that Sword.

Nick saved himself with pure nerve.

As *Amoracchius* swept down, Nicodemus, his face twisted in pain, lifted not his sword to block Michael's—but the Holy Grail.

Michael let out a cry and twisted at the hips, pulling his blade to one side, and the blow swept past Nicodemus without touching him. Michael landed off-balance and fell into a heavy roll. From the ground, Nicodemus thrust his slender blade at Michael's back, and sank the tip into the back of one of his thighs. Michael cried out in pain, and came up to his feet heavily, favoring his wounded leg.

Nicodemus rose, his dark eyes glittering, holding his left arm in close to his ribs, where the hailstone had hit him, favoring that side, and moving stiffly. He turned to make sure he could see both me and Michael, and had visible trouble shifting his weight. He was hurt.

But not nearly hurt enough to suit me.

I called another hailstone to my staff. I raised it and aimed.

Nicodemus lifted the Grail again, a small smile on his face as he held it between me and him as a hostage. "Careful, Dresden," he said. "Are you willing to accept such a loss?"

"Yep," I said, and snarled, *"Forzare!"* again, sending another hailstone at him.

Nicodemus's eyes widened, but he turned his body to shield the Grail, and the hailstone struck him in the right shoulder blade. He let out another breathless cry—and then sudden blackness engulfed him and a tide of shadow swept him away.

"Michael," I said, and hurried to my friend's side.

Michael's eyes were busy, roaming left and right, looking for Nicodemus. He turned so that I could see the wound. It was a thrust, narrow but deep. There wasn't an inordinate amount of blood staining the leg of his jeans, and I didn't think it had gone into the artery.

"What happened there?" I asked. "Is he gone?"

"I'm . . . I'm not sure . . . ," Michael said. "I've never seen him forced to run before."

"We should finish him."

"Agreed," Michael said. "How? He just flew away."

"Gimme a minute," I said, and felt myself baring my teeth in a grin. "How does the leg feel?"

"I've had worse," Michael said, his voice strained. He shifted his weight, testing the leg, and made a hissing sound—but it supported his weight. "Only a flesh wound."

"Yeah," I said. " 'Tis but a scratch. Come on, ya pansy."

He blinked and looked at me. "Pansy?"

"Oh," I said. "You weren't quoting the movie. Sorry."

"Movie?"

"Holy Grail?"

"Nicodemus still has it."

I sighed. "Never mind."

From the other side of the amphitheater, there was a roar of collapsing stone, and I looked up in time to see a couple of sets of Corinthian columns falling, to the accompaniment of Ursiel's furious roars.

"So," Michael said, "to be clear, Grey is on our side?"

"Yeah. I hired him before this started."

"But he killed Miss Valmont!"

"No, he didn't," I said. "He lied to Nicodemus. She must be outside the vault somewhere, waiting for us."

Michael looked nonplussed. "Oh. Still. I don't care for the man."

"Hey, we're alive right now."

"True," he said. He drew a deep breath. "And if he's kept faith with you, we should help him."

Just then, Ursiel went up on its hind legs. Grey was still in that same monstrous form, and still hanging on. The Genoskwa's physical eyes were a bloody ruin, but Ursiel's glowing green orbs were furious and bright. The giant bear-thing roared, a sound guaranteed to haunt my nightmares, should I live long enough to have any, and toppled over backward, into another Corinthian column, attempting to smash Grey upon it. They went down with another huge crash and a spray of glittering gems. The sound of the impact was . . . just freaking *huge*. The kind of noise you associate with the demolition of buildings, not with a brawl.

I swallowed. "Yeah. I guess we sh—"

I paused, as cold that had nothing to do with the movement of molecules crawled up my spine.

I knew the feeling. I'd gotten the sensation before,

when surrounded by hostile specters, back when I'd been mostly dead. It was a creepy, thoroughly nasty sensation that gathered around them like body heat.

Which might not be a big deal in the physical world. Specters often could not interact with the material realm, or could do so only in specific and limited ways. But we weren't in the physical world. This was the Nevernever, the Underworld, and down here spiritual forms would be every bit as real and as deadly as physical foes—actually, much more so.

In fact, given how many truly horrible monsters the various Greek heroes had slain, Hades might have a very, very nasty crew of guardians indeed. The guy might, in fact, be the only one in the universe who could actually give the order "Release the kraken." But why would they be coming toward us? I mean, the guy had wished me well. Sure, he hadn't interfered, but . . .

I looked up at the moving lips on the statues and winced. "Oh, crap."

"What?" Michael asked.

"I think we've tripped some kind of automatic fail-safe," I said. "I think there's a load of dangerous spirits on their way toward us right now."

"Then we should leave."

"Posthaste. Let's go get Grey and boogie."

We both turned and started moving toward Grey—Michael's best speed was a trot—but I hadn't gotten a dozen steps before a cry of pure fury rose up behind me.

"Dresden!" howled Lasciel through Ascher's mouth. I looked back to see a form rising up from the small inferno consuming the garment display, violet glowing eyes blazing. She planted her feet and seemed to inhale—and the flames all around her suddenly burned low, and blazed the same ugly shade of purple as her eyes. The smell of brimstone filled the air.

"Oh, *crap*," I breathed.

And then a lance of pure Hellfire roared toward me.

Chapter
Forty-six

There was no time to think. I ran on instinct.

I couldn't shield a blast of flame infused with Hellfire, the demonic version of soulfire. Hellfire enormously increased the destructive potential of magic. When Lasciel's shadow had been inside me, I'd used it. If I'd had my last shield bracelet, I might have parried most of it, but even that wouldn't have been enough to stop it cold.

Couldn't counter it with Winter. If I flung ice out to stop the fire, they would form steam, and the Hellfire would flow right into *that*, and continue on its way. Same result, only I'd be steam-cooked instead of roasted.

Once or twice in my life, I'd been able to open a Way in front of me, fast enough to divert an incoming attack away from me, into the Nevernever or out into somewhere else in the mortal world. But from here, in the secured vault, there was no way I was going to be able to open a Way—not until I got back out beyond the first gate again.

Fire was hard enough to deal with. Infuse it with Hellfire and it was almost unstoppable.

So I didn't even try to stop it.

Instead, I redirected it.

As the strike hurtled toward me, I lifted my staff in my right hand, whirling it back and forth in front of my body in a figure-eight spin, and sent my will racing out through the staff, infused with soulfire to counter the Fallen angel's Hellfire, shouting, *"Ventas cyclis!"*

A howling, whirling torrent of wind whipped out of my staff, spiraling tightly in on itself as the Hellfire reached it. There was a flash of light, a thunderous detonation, and the sharp scent of ozone as the two diametrically opposed energies met and warred. The spinning vortex of wind caught the violet fire and bent it up toward the distant ceiling of the vault, slewing back and forth, a gushing geyser of unearthly flame.

The effort to control that wind was tremendous, but even though the fire came within a few feet, the rush of air moving away from me prevented the thermal bloom from cooking me where I stood. My defense carried the entire power of the strike to the roof of the cavern, where it splashed and danced and rolled out in vast circular waves.

It was actually damned beautiful.

Ascher let out a short snarl of frustration as the last of the strike flashed upward. I released the wind spell but kept my staff spinning slowly, ready to counter a second time if I had to do it. Ascher had plenty of anger still raging in her, and she drew on it to gather more fire into her hands.

"Don't do it, Hannah," I called. "You aren't going to beat me. You haven't got what you need."

"You cocky son of a bitch," she said. "I've got everything I need to handle *you*, Warden. God, I was a fool to think you were any different than the rest of them."

"Here's the difference," I said. "Back down. Walk away. I'll let you."

She actually let out a brief, incredulous laugh. "There is no *end* to the ego of the White Council, is there?" she asked. "You think you can pick and choose who is going to live and die. Decide all the rules that everyone else is going to live by."

"The rules are there for a *reason*, Hannah," I said. "And somewhere deep down, you know that. But this isn't about the Laws of Magic or the White Council. It's about you and me and whether or not you walk out of this vault alive." I tried to soften my voice, to sound less frightened and angry. "That thing inside you is pushing your emotions. Manipulating you. She can show you illusions so real that you can't tell the difference without resorting to your Sight. Did she tell you that?"

Ascher stared at me without saying anything. I wasn't sure she'd heard me.

Hell. If Lasciel was inside Ascher's head, twisting her perceptions with illusion right now, she might *not* have heard me.

"You can't have had her Coin for long. A couple of weeks? A month? Am I right?"

"Don't pretend you know me," she spat.

"You're right," I said. "I don't know you. But I know Lasciel. I had that Coin once upon a time. I had her inside my head for *years*. I know what she's like, the way she can twist things."

"She doesn't," Ascher said. "Not with me. She's given me power, knowledge. She's taught me more about magic in the last few weeks than any wizard did in my whole lifetime."

I shook my head. "Fire magic is all about passion, Hannah. And I know you must have a lot of rage built up. But you've got to think your way past that. She hasn't made you stronger. She's just built up your anger to fuel your fire. Nothing comes free."

Ascher let out a bitter laugh. "You're scared, Dresden. Admit it. I've got access to power that makes me dangerous and you're afraid of what I can do."

And, right there, she showed me the fundamental difference between us.

I loved magic for its own sake. She didn't.

The Art can be a lot of work, and it can sometimes be tedious, and sometimes even painful, but at the end of the day, I love it. I love the focus of it, the discipline, the balance. I love working with the energy and exploring what can be done with it. I love the gathering tension of a spell, and the almost painful clarity of focus required to concentrate that tension into an effect. I love the practice of it as well as the theory, the research, experimenting with new spells, teaching others about magic. I love laying down spells on my various pieces of magical gear, and most of all, I love it when I can use my talents to make a difference in the world, even when it's only a small one.

Ascher . . . enjoyed blowing stuff up and burning things down. She was good at it. But she didn't love her talent for the miracle it was.

She merely loved what she could do with it.

And that had led her here, to a place where she had tremendous power, but not the right frame of mind to understand the consequences and permutations of using it—or at least not where she needed it, deep in her bones. To wield power like she currently possessed, she needed to understand it on the level of gut instinct, having assimilated the Art so entirely that the whole reality of using it came to her without conscious thought.

It was why virtually every time she'd used magic in the past few days, it had been to destroy something, or else to protect her own hide from the immediate consequences of her own power. It was why she hadn't put in the practice she needed to go up against someone with a broad range of skills. It was why she had focused exclusively on attacking me, to the neglect of her own defenses a few moments before. It was why she'd said yes to the Fallen angel who was now driving her emotions berserk.

And it was also why she hadn't thought through the consequences of unleashing that much elemental destruction in a large but ultimately enclosed area.

Ascher had talent, but she hadn't had the training, the practice, or the mind-set she needed to beat a pro.

"I'm scared," I told her. "I'm scared for you. You've had a bad road, Hannah, and I'm sorry as hell it's happened to you. Please, just walk. Please."

Her eyes narrowed, her face reddened, and she said, words clipped, "Condescending bastard. Save your pity for yourself."

And then with a cry she sent another lance of Hellfire at me, redoubled in strength.

Again, I caught it with a conjured cyclone infused with

soulfire, though the effort was even more tremendous. Again I sent it spiraling up toward the ceiling—but this time I sent it all to one spot.

Even before the last of the Hellfire had smashed into the ceiling, I dropped to one knee, lifted my staff, and extended the strongest shield I could project, putting it between me and Ascher. It was a calculated bit of distraction on my part, giving her something she wasn't psychologically equipped to ignore.

She screamed at me, her eyes furious, gathering more fire in her hands, seeing only a passive target, weakened and fallen to one knee, one she could smash to bits with a third and final strike—but I saw Lasciel's glowing eyes widen in sudden dismay and understanding as the Fallen reached her own comprehension of consequences a few portions of a second too late to do any good.

An instant later, several hundred tons of molten and red-hot rock, chewed from the earth above us by Ascher's own Hellfire-infused strike, came crashing down on top of her.

The noise was terrible. The destruction was appalling. Glowing hot stones bounced from my shield and then began to pile up against it, pushing at me and physically forcing me back across the ground. The pileup shoved me a good twenty feet across the amphitheater floor, with Michael hobbling frantically along a couple of feet ahead of me, crouching to take advantage of the protection of my shield.

After a few seconds, the falling stone became less violent and random, and I dropped my shield with a gasp of effort. I stayed right where I was, down on one knee, and bent forward at the waist, struggling to catch my breath, exhausted from the efforts of the past few moments. The vault was spinning around and around, too. When had it started doing that?

The air had gone thick with dust and heat and the smell of brimstone. Half of the freaking amphitheater had been buried by fallen stone. One of the enormous statues was covered to the thighs.

And Hannah Ascher and Lasciel were gone.

A few last stones fell, clattering over the mess, bouncing. I noted, dimly, that their arches didn't look the way they should have. Gravity was indeed something heavier here than in the physical world. It was so heavy, in fact, that I thought I might just close my eyes and stay on the floor.

"Harry," Michael breathed.

"Sorry about that, Hannah," I heard myself mutter. "I'm sorry."

Michael put his hand on my shoulder. "Harry? Are you all right?"

I shook my head, and gestured weakly at the fallen rock with one hand. "Hell's bells, Michael. That wasn't even a fight. It was just murder. She wasn't a monster. She just made a bad call. She let that thing inside her and . . . it just pushed her buttons. Drove her."

"It's what they do," Michael said quietly.

"Could have been me over there . . . There but for the grace of God goes Harry Dresden."

Michael limped around to stand in front of me, slapped me lightly on the cheek, and said, "We don't have time for this. Reflect later. We'll talk about it later. Get up."

The blow didn't hurt, but it did startle me a little, and make me shake my head. The immediate exhaustion of slinging that much power around began to fade, and I shrugged off the lethargy that went with it. The ugly, prickling cold was still coming closer.

"Harry," Michael said, "are you with me?"

"Headache," I muttered. And then I realized what that meant. Mab's earring burned like a tiny frozen star in my ear, and my head was beginning to pound anyway.

I was running out of time. And unless I could get everyone back to the first gate and open the Way back to Chicago, it was running out for everyone else as well. I planted my staff and pushed myself to my feet. I felt creaky and heavy and tired, and I couldn't afford to let that matter.

Everything snapped back into focus, and I swiped at something hot and wet in my eyes. "Okay," I said. "Okay. Let's get Grey and get the hell out of here."

Just then, something that looked vague and lean, and had huge batlike wings, streaked through the air toward us from the far side of the amphitheater. One of its wings faltered, and it tumbled out of the air, hit the marble floor, and started bouncing. The form rolled several times, and when it stopped, Grey was lying there looking dazed. The lower half of his face, as well as his hands and forearms, were soaked with scarlet blood.

"Michael," I said.

We moved together, getting Grey onto his feet between us, and started back toward the entrance to the vault, skirting the hellish heat coming off of the rubble. "Grey," I said, "what happened?"

"He got smart and shifted down," Grey said. "My

jaws slipped. But something got in his eyes, and I disengaged before he could reverse the hold on me."

From somewhere behind us came the Genoskwa's furious roar and the crash of another column falling. Then another roar, pained, that grew deeper in register as the Genoskwa assumed Ursiel's demonform again and rose up onto his hind legs, coming into sight of us. Doing so put his head damned near twenty feet off the ground, and though we were most of the way up the amphitheater stairs, Ursiel's glowing eyes and the Genoskwa's ruined and bloody eye sockets were level with my own. The demon-bear opened his jaws and roared in fury.

"He looks pissed," I squeaked.

"Certainly hope so," Grey said, slurring the words a little. He was only barely supporting his own weight, and his eyes still looked vague. "Gimme sec, be fine."

Ursiel dropped back down to all sixes and started toward us. He was limping on the leg Michael had cut, but it wasn't just flopping loosely the way it should have been. Hell's bells, he recovered fast.

"Valmont," I said to Grey. "Where is she?"

"Sent her back to the first gate," Grey said, "with your magic artif . . . art . . . toys."

"That's it," I said to Michael. "You're hurt. Grey's scrambled. Get him back to the first gate and do it as fast as you can."

Michael clenched his jaws. "You can't fight Ursiel alone, Harry. You can't win."

"Don't need to fight him," I said. "Just need to buy you two some time to get clear. Trust me. I'll be right behind you."

Michael closed his eyes for a second and then gave me a quick nod and shouldered Grey's weight more thoroughly. "God be with you, my friend."

"I'll take whatever help I can get," I said, and stopped at the top of the amphitheater stairs, while Michael half carried Grey back out the way we'd come.

My head pounded. I shook the sheathed knife out of my sleeve and dropped it into the duster pocket with my overgrown revolver, then checked the Shroud to make sure it was secure.

From the far rear of the vault, I heard something let out an eerily windy-sounding cry, and the sensation of cold around me grew more and more intense, gaining an element of irrational, psychic terror to go with it. An instant later, other cries echoed the first, and the sensation of unthinking panic swelled. My heart sped up to a frantic pace and my limbs felt shaky and weak.

The shades were coming.

Ursiel let out another furious roar and then the twenty-foot horned bear the size of a main battle tank broke into a lumbering run as it came up the stairs toward me, fangs bared, intent upon mayhem.

And rather than turning to flee like a sane person, I brandished my staff in one hand, flew him the bird with the other, and screamed, "Hey, Yogi! Here I am! Come get some!"

Forty-seven

Ursiel was too big to fight.

Look, people go on and on about how size isn't everything, and how the bigger they are, the harder they fall, but the people who say that probably haven't ever faced down a charging demon-bear so big it should have been on a drive-in movie screen. As a defensive adaptation, sheer size is a winner. It's a fact. Ask an elephant.

But.

As a *hunting* adaptation, size is only good when the things you're hunting are also enormously huge. Successful predators aren't necessarily bigger than the things they take down—they're better armed, and just big enough to get the job done if they do it right. Too much bulk and nimble prey can escape, leaving the hunter less able to handle a broad range of targets.

Grey had done something brilliant, in blinding the Genoskwa: He'd forced it to rely upon Ursiel's eyes. That meant, apparently, that he had to stay in that giant bear form to do it. If the Genoskwa had been able to pursue me in his natural form, he would have caught me and torn me apart in short order—I'd seen him move. The bear might have been an irresistible mass of muscle, claws, and fangs, but I'd had a little experience with very, very large creatures on the move, and I'd learned one important fact about them.

They didn't corner well.

Ursiel closed in and went into a little bounce, a motion as close to a pounce as something that size could manage, and I darted to one side. Harry Dresden, wizard, might have bought the farm right there. But Sir Harry, the Winter Knight, dodged the smashing paws and snapping jaws by a tiny margin, hopped back several yards, and shouted, *"Olé! Toro!"*

Ursiel roared again, but its head swung around toward the retreating forms of Michael and Grey. Ursiel was no tactical genius, from what I'd seen of it, but both it and the Genoskwa were predators—and Michael and Grey were wounded and vulnerable. It could catch them and dispatch them easily and then hunt me down at its leisure, like a cat dealing with so many troublesome mice.

So I lifted my staff, pointed it at the demon-bear, and shouted, *"Fuego!"*

The blast of fire I sent at him wasn't much. I didn't feel like passing out from exhaustion at the moment, and both the Genoskwa and Ursiel had displayed a troublesome resistance to my magic. That wasn't the point. The mini-blast of flame struck the bear in the side of the nose, and while it didn't sear the flesh, it singed some hairs and I bet it stung like hell.

The bear's head whipped back toward me and it rolled a step forward. Then the glowing eyes brightened and it swung again toward the wounded men, now leaving the vault. The conflict of wills going on between the Genoskwa and the Fallen angel was all but visible.

"Jeez," I drawled, in the most annoying tone I possibly could. "You suck, Gen. I'll bet you anything River Shoulders wouldn't be all torn and conflicted right now."

That got it done.

The great bear whirled back to me and lunged into instant, savage motion, and again I skittered out of the way a couple inches ahead of being ground into paste. I darted a few more yards to one side, putting one of the displays between us. It didn't bother to go around—it just crashed straight through, spraying gold and jewels everywhere, and I damned near got my head redecorated with a falling marble column. I slipped, recovered my footing, and kept moving, forcing the huge bear to keep turning laterally if it wanted to pursue me.

It went like that for a subjective century and a half, and maybe thirty objective seconds. Several suits of armor were crushed and scattered when a flashing, enormous paw shattered the marble column holding up the roof of their display area. Half a dozen pieces of art that might have been Fabergé eggs in delicate golden cages were smashed flat when a sledgehammer blow missed me by an inch. At one point, I picked up a cut diamond the size of my fist, screamed, "Get rocked!" and flung it at Ursiel's nose before darting behind another exhibit, this one of rare sacred texts, featuring half a dozen Gutenberg Bibles as the centerpiece.

And then something scary happened.

The roaring stopped.

I froze in place, instantly. Everything got quiet, except for the rushing sound of the flames in the hands of the giant statues, and a rising tide of moaning, terrifying wails coming steadily and unnervingly closer from the rear of the vault.

Something made a metallic clinking sound. Like, maybe the sound a great big foot would make as its blind owner accidentally kicked a fallen gem into something made of precious metal.

Oh, crap.

I looked around, and realized that there was rubble scattered over every inch of floor around me for fifty feet in every direction. I had forgotten that Ursiel's bestial nature was not the only one I had to deal with. The Genoskwa's intellect had been at work behind it, too, and I'd been had.

The Genoskwa had been trying to catch and kill me, sure—but he had also been intentionally covering the floor around us with detritus so that there would be no way in hell I could move without making noise.

Then he wouldn't *need* eyes to catch me and kill me.

"Little wizard," rumbled the Genoskwa's voice. It had a weirdly modulated quality to it. It was coming from behind a veil, maybe, and I couldn't isolate the direction of its origin. "Going to twist your head off your skinny neck. Going to enjoy it."

I had some material I could have thrown back at him, but I didn't dare speak. I would have sounded terrified, anyway. The howls and the eerie presence of the shades continued to grow closer and more intense, and my heart was pounding hard enough to shake my chest. I held my feet perfectly still and tried to turn my head without rustling my clothing at all, scanning for the Genoskwa. I couldn't see him, but his voice was close.

I knew I would only get one chance to move. If I didn't do it right, he would run me down and do exactly what he said he'd do, and a weird little fluttery sensation went slithering through my neck at the thought of it. I had to know where he was.

"Take off your head like a cap, little wizard," the Genoskwa rumbled, pausing to listen between each sentence. "Drink your blood. Like a bottle of pop."

That image was so vivid that I nearly let out a nervous giggle. I caught it just in time and closed my eyes, listening as hard as I could. I could hear small, faint sounds. Crunching rubble. Weight shifting atop a pile of spilled gems. But it all had the same distorted tone as the Genoskwa's voice, impossible to localize.

Stop behaving like a prey animal, Harry, and use your brain.

Right.

The Genoskwa couldn't hear me and couldn't know exactly where I was—but sooner or later, if I held still, he'd find me. If I muttered the word to a spell to veil my own movement, he'd hear that, too. My pounding head was already under enough pressure that I didn't dare try to use magic without a verbal utterance. I could do it, but the psychic feedback was devastating and the last thing I needed was to slip up and take myself out for him. Even using my magical senses might give me away—the Genoskwa was something of a practitioner himself, and might well be able to feel me extending my aura to detect energy around me.

The shades came closer, and the air in the vault had grown uncomfortably warm with the heat from the melted rock. The heated air around it was rising, and that updraft was what was fanning the fires in the hands of the statues, making them growl quietly.

Draft.

Air brushed across the fine hairs on the back of my hand, flowing gently past me from the exterior of the vault and in toward the hot stone more or less in the center of the huge chamber.

Don't think like a human, Harry. Think like a predator. Ignore sight. Forget hearing. Where would a predator go when stalking his prey?

Downwind.

The Genoskwa would be moving downwind of me, locating me through my scent. It wasn't the same as knowing where he was, but for my purposes it was close enough.

Assuming, of course, that my reasoning was correct. If it wasn't, I was about to trap myself with him and become Harry Dresden, human beverage.

I didn't have much energy left in me for spells, but I had to chance it.

So I called upon Winter, focused my will through my staff, and shouted, *"Glacivallare!"*

Icy cold rolled out of the staff and solidified into a wall of ice maybe twenty feet long and a foot thick, curved slightly toward me. I prayed that the Genoskwa was on the other side of it, turned, and sprinted, my life depending upon it.

I hadn't gone twenty feet when something hit the wall and shattered it with a crash. I flashed a quick look back over my shoulder to see the Genoskwa as a large, humanoid blur behind a veil that had faltered as tiny flecks of ice landed on the Genoskwa and melted to water. The veil shimmered and fell, and he didn't bother trying to restore it. He recovered his balance after almost a whole half second, and came after me, coming along the ground in a rush, using his huge arms as well as his legs to run.

If Michael hadn't lamed him, the Genoskwa could have claimed his five-cent deposit for my corpse. But though he was on the mend, he still wasn't moving at full speed, and I was able to stay a couple of steps ahead of him. His stench filled my nose, and his huge breathing was terrifying as he came along behind me, tracking me by the frantic sound of my running feet and labored breath.

I couldn't fight this guy.

But that didn't mean that I couldn't kill him.

We flew out of the vault, and out past the Gate of Blood, and I poured it on, committing all of my reserves to the effort. I called light to my staff as I sprinted down the tunnel that emerged at the Gate of Ice, and as I went by it, I drew upon the power of the Winter mantle to slam the iron lever back up to the ON position and snap it off at the base in the same savage motion.

And then I plunged out into the two-hundred-yard-long killing field as the house-sized blocks of ice began to fall and shatter and slide and flip and smash together like some kind of enormous, demented garbage disposal unit.

"Parkour!" I screamed, dropping to a slide that took me just under a horizontally flying block of ice as big as a freight car, then popping back up to keep running.

"Parkour!" I shouted again, bounding up onto a small block and diving over several more, ducking and weaving between them, the Genoskwa hot on my tail, casting frantically quick glances back at him, watching him close the distance inch by inch, his huge body moving with an utterly unfair amount of agility as he handled the obstacles better than I could have, even without his eyes.

And then the cold started to get to him.

It wasn't much at first. He lost a step on me. But then in the next row of grinders, one of them clipped his monstrous shoulder. He recovered his balance and kept moving, and we were nearly through the field when I played dirty.

I jumped over a pair of low grinders, and turned in midair, just enough to point a finger back at the ground behind me and snap, *"Infriga!"*

I didn't use a lot of power. Barely a whisper, really— just enough to coat a ten-foot patch of cavern floor with smooth Winter ice.

And his foot slipped.

It wasn't a big slip. But his cold-dulled reflexes weren't up to catching him and his balance wavered. Not much— he was, after all, running on all fours. But enough. It staggered him as he came after me, slowing his pace again.

Suddenly, there was a ten-foot wall of grinders in front of me, each individual block spinning and smashing and flipping at unpredictable intervals, and I let out a scream and leapt *over* it completely, high-jump style. My shoulders brushed the top of the wall, treating me to a dandy view of another house-sized block falling straight at me from the darkness overhead, and then I bounced off the top of the wall and tumbled into the clear.

The Genoskwa grabbed the top of the wall and vaulted it easily, his huge hairy form moving with effortless power. He'd somehow anticipated its presence. He must have heard my shout and jump, and maybe the way I'd gone over it at the top. Or maybe Ursiel was helping him through his sightless chase, the way Lasciel had once helped guide me in total darkness.

But neither the Genoskwa nor the Fallen angel sensed what was plummeting soundlessly toward them.

A block of ice the size of a building came down like the hammer of God Almighty, and crushed the Genoskwa like a beer can.

I rolled to a stop and flopped on the stone cavern floor, utterly exhausted, breathing like a steam engine. But I had enough energy to turn my head to the gruesome remains being tossed about like a rag doll among the last row of grinders.

"Parkour," I panted. "Bitch."

Then I just breathed for a minute.

Footsteps approached a moment later, and I felt hands hauling me up. Michael had sheathed *Amoracchius* again, and he steadied me as I rose. Grey stood and watched the grinders grind for a moment before he shook his head and said, "Yuck."

"Right?" I said.

Anna Valmont shuddered, her face pale, and turned to me. "Are you all right, Harry?"

"Nothing two months asleep in a good bed won't cure," I said.

A chorus of moaning wails suddenly came toward us, as though the shades that had begun flooding the vault had reached some kind of critical mass and were now surging forward. I still hadn't seen them, and I didn't want to see them. I had this vague image of the scrubbing bubbles of undeadness from that *Lord of the Rings* movie in my brain, and I was sure that would serve fine for imagining the threat drawing quickly nearer.

"What was that?" Anna asked.

"Bouncers," I said. "We don't want to be around when they get here. Let's get clear of the first gate, people."

And we did, hurrying down the tunnel to the location of the original Way. I took a deep breath and steadied myself for what I hoped would be the last serious effort of the day.

"Michael," I said.

"Yes?"

"I figure Nicodemus had Lasciel and Ascher as his backup Way home," I said. Ascher had been throwing Hellfire around. With a couple of weeks' training from a good teacher, say a Fallen angel who could provide her with images and communicate directly in thought, she might have enough talent to learn how to manage a Way—but probably not from inside several hundred tons of molten rock. "Maybe the Genoskwa could have done it. But they're out. That leaves one way for him to get back."

Michael grunted and drew his sword, and Grey frowned and looked warier than he had a moment before.

"We're not in much shape for a fight, Harry," Michael said.

"Neither is he," I said. "Eyes open. Get through the Way as quick as we can, and I'll zip it closed behind us. Nick can find his own way home." Then I focused my will, drew a line in the air with my staff, and said, *"Aparturum."*

Once more, a line of light split the air and widened, and from where I stood, I could see the inside of the vault back at Marcone's bank.

I leaned heavily on my staff, and felt fairly proud of myself for not falling over and going to sleep right there.

"Michael," I said. "Go."

Michael drew his sword and went through first, his eyes wary for any danger.

"Anna," I said.

Valmont went through, still carrying her backpack, I noted. It was one of the identical ones that Nicodemus had provided for everyone and that I had ignored. Grey had used a duplicate as his decoy, back at the amphitheater.

"My God," Grey said, looking at me. "You didn't get any loot? How the hell are you going to pay me?"

"Think of something," I said.

Grey smirked. "I know we're in a hurry, but there's something you need to realize."

"What?"

"No one got Binder's share," he said. "We're all worn pretty ragged—and he's got an army of demons he can jump us with. Food for thought." Then he went through the Way.

"Oh," I said. "Crap."

I just wanted to go have a nice lie-down somewhere. Why was nothing ever simple?

I stepped through the Way and back into the mortal world, and almost instantly I felt better, lighter, more free. Gravity change. I wrenched my head back into the moment, because I had to focus. Nicodemus might be rushing the Way even now—as might a few million furious shades. I didn't think Hades would allow his prisoners to come flooding into the mortal world, but on the other hand, you never know with those types.

At least wrecking the weaving of a spell was easier work than creating it.

"Michael," I said. "Cover me."

He came to my side, Sword in hand. I turned to the Way, tired to my bones, lifted my staff and muttered, *"Disperd—"*

And a black shadow hurtled through the Way, hitting me like a truck.

I was watching for trouble and ready. Michael was ready. Either we were both wearier than we realized, or the shadow moved with such speed that neither of us had a chance to react. Or both.

The impact spun me around in a circle and dumped me on the ground with my everything hurting and my elbows tangled with my scapulae.

I jerked my head up blearily, raising my arms in a de-

fensive gesture, to see that the streak of shadow had
whooshed to the far end of Marcone's vault, to its main
door.

Nicodemus rose up out of the swirl of shadow. He
looked pale and awful, his eyes sunken with pain, but he
held himself straight. His sword was sheathed again, and
he still carried the Holy Grail negligently in one hand.
Moving with obvious stiffness and pain, he twisted a handle that opened the main door of the vault from the inside. The door swung open when he pushed.

Then he looked directly at me and quite calmly
snapped the handle off at its base.

"Dresden," Nicodemus said. There was something furious and horrible in his eyes—I could see it, even from
there. "From one father to another," he called. "Well
played."

I felt my eyes widen. "Stop him!" I blurted and flung
myself to my feet.

Michael started running. Grey blurred toward the far
end of the vault, moving at speeds one normally associates with low-flying aircraft.

None of us got there in time to stop Nicodemus from
letting out a harsh, bitter laugh, and slamming the huge
door closed.

I ran to the other end of the vault anyway, or mostly
ran, breathing hard. Anna Valmont stayed beside me, still
carrying her tool roll.

"God!" I said. I tried what was left of the handle, but
couldn't get a grip on it. The vault door had locked, shut-
ting us in. I slammed a shoulder against the door, but it
wasn't moving, and I wasn't sure I could have blasted it

open even if I'd been fresh. "Michael, did you hear what he *said*?"

"I heard," Michael said grimly.

"How could he know?"

"You told him," Michael replied quietly. "When you taunted him about Deirdre. You said things only another father would know to say."

I let out a groan, because Michael was right. Once Nicodemus had realized that I was a father, it was not too much of a stretch to identify the dark-haired, dark-eyed little girl who had suddenly appeared at Michael's house, a place that I knew damned well Nicodemus would surveil, even if he couldn't use his pet shadow to do it. And she had appeared there immediately after my insane assault on the Red Court and my apparent death, to boot. It wasn't hard to figure.

Nicodemus might not be able to walk onto Michael's property—but he had an entire dysfunctional posse of squires with assault rifles and shotguns who could, and he was filled with the pain of losing his daughter.

Maggie was there. So were Michael's children. So was a defenseless archangel.

"He's going to your house," I breathed. "He's going after our families."

Chapter

Forty-eight

"Get back," Anna Valmont said sharply, and knelt to flick her tool roll open on the ground in front of the broken handle. "Dresden, get out of my way."

I moved aside and said, "Hurry, hurry, hurry."

She started jerking tools out of the roll. "I know."

"Hurry."

"I *know*."

"Can't you just cut it open?"

"It's a vault door, Dresden, not a bicycle chain," Valmont snapped. She gave Michael an exasperated look and jerked her head toward me.

Michael looked like he wanted to tell her to hurry, too, but he said, "Let her work, Harry."

"Won't be long," she promised.

"Dammit," I said, dancing from one foot to the next.

"Dresden?" Grey asked.

"What?"

A chorus of moaning wails echoed through the vault as if from a great distance.

Grey pursed his lips. "Should that Way be standing open like that?"

I whipped my head around and stared at the Way. The only light on the other side came from the Way itself, but that was just enough for me to see a huge figure step to the Way. Its hairy kneecap was level with my sternum. Then it knelt down, and a huge, ugly humanoid face with a mono-brow and one enormous eye in the center of its forehead peered hungrily at me.

I gripped my staff and drew together my will. "Just *once* I want something go according to plan," I snarled. *"Disperdorius."*

Energy left me in a dizzying wave, and the outline of the Way folded in on itself and vanished, taking the cyclops with it. I turned from the collapsing Way back to the vault door, even before the light show had finished playing out.

There was a little *phunt* sound, followed by a hissing, and I turned to find Valmont holding a miniature welding torch of some kind, hooked to a pair of little tanks by rubber hoses. She passed a steel-shafted screwdriver to Grey and said, "I need an L-shape."

Grey grunted, took the thing in both hands, and narrowed his eyes. Then, with an abrupt movement and a blur in the shape of his forearms, he bent the screwdriver's shaft to a right angle.

"Slide it inside the socket where he broke it off, here, and hold it," she said.

Grey did. Valmont slid a strip of metal of some kind into the hole, held a little square of dark plastic up to protect her vision from the brilliant light of the torch, and sparks started to fly up from the door. She worked on it for about five hundred years that probably fit inside a couple of minutes, and then the torch started running out of fuel and faltered.

"Hold it still," she said. "Okay, let go."

Grey released the screwdriver's handle, which now stuck out of the original fitting in approximately the same attitude as the original handle.

"Do it. Let's go," I said.

"No," Valmont snapped. "These materials aren't proper and I'm none too sanguine about that braze. We've got to let it cool or you'll only break it off, and I haven't the fuel for a second try. Sixty seconds."

"Dammit," I said, pacing back and forth. "Okay, when we get out, I'm heading for the house as fast as I can get there. Michael, I want you to get to a phone and—"

"I'm going with you," Michael said.

I turned to face him and said in a brutally flat, practical tone, "Your leg is hurt. You'll slow me down."

His jaw clenched. A muscle twitched. But he nodded.

"And you'll need to help the others get clear of the bank. Hopefully without getting shot to pieces on the way. Get clear, find a phone and warn Charity. Maybe she'll have time to get them to the panic room."

"He'll burn the house down around them," Michael said quietly.

"Like hell he will," I said. "Follow along as quick as you can."

He nodded. Then, silently, he offered me the hilt of *Amoracchius*.

"Can't take that from you," I said.

"It's not mine, Harry," he said. "I just kept it for a while."

I put my fingers on the hilt, and then shook my head and pushed it back toward him. The Sword had tremendous power—but it had to be used with equally tremendous care, and I had neither the background nor the disposition for it. "Murphy knew she shouldn't have been using *Fidelacchius*, but last night she drew it anyway and now it's gone. I'm no genius. But I learn eventually."

Michael smiled at me a little. "You're a good man, Harry. But you're making the same mistake Nicodemus always has—and the same one Karrin did."

"What mistake?"

"You all think the critical word in the phrase 'Sword of Faith' is 'sword.'"

I frowned at him.

"The world always thinks that the destruction of a physical vessel is victory," he said quietly. "But the Savior was more than merely cells and tissue and chemical compounds—and *Fidelacchius* is more than wood and steel."

"It's gone, Michael," I said quietly. "Sometimes the bad guys win one."

"Sometimes they seem to. But only for a time."

"How can you know that?"

"I can't know," he said, his face lighting with a sudden smile. "That's why they call it faith, Harry. You'll see."

Grey, I noticed, was staring at Michael intently.

"Time," Valmont said. She reached up and braced the shaft of the screwdriver with her fingers. Then, very gently, she turned the handle.

The vault door let out a heavy click, and swung open.

"Let's get moving," I said.

"Assuming Binder lets us," Grey added.

We pushed out of the vault and into the secure room, and found the place absolutely wrecked. The exterior of the vault had been pocked with dents half an inch deep. More dents and smears covered the security boxes on the other two walls. The wall that had contained the mines was simply gone, bared to the concrete beneath, and that had been chewed and mangled by ricocheting ball bearings, some of which were still visible, buried in the wall. The floor was covered in gravel and debris.

Also, thirty of Binder's goons were in formation around the vault door, covering every possible angle. They were all pointing Uzis at us.

"Whoa!" I said, gripping my staff. "Binder, wait!"

"Move another inch and you're slurry!" came Binder's voice from the hallway outside the security room. By some minor miracle, the door was still on its hinges, and the little mercenary was staying out of sight behind it. "Where's Hannah?"

My first instinct was to say Binder's partner was coming along right behind us, but something told me that would be a bad idea. So I swallowed and said, "Dead."

There was a moment of silence. Then Binder's voice came back, roughened. "What happened?"

"She forgot Rule Number One," I said. "She took one of the Coins. I didn't have a choice."

"Didn't have a choice. You White Council boys say that a lot," Binder said in a very mild tone that sounded infinitely more frightening than a harsh one would have been. "Nicodemus says your crew betrayed us, killed

Deirdre, Hannah, and the big monkey, and that you're keeping all the loot."

"He told you some of the truth," I said. "But he's lying about who tried to stick the knife in first. We played it straight. He turned on us."

Part of Binder's face appeared from behind the door, and he grunted. Then he jerked his chin at Michael and said, "Sir Knight, is that what happened?"

"Your partner took the Coin of Lasciel," Michael said firmly. "Nicodemus murdered his own daughter to open the Gate of Blood. Once we were inside, he ordered Miss Ascher and the Genoskwa to turn on the rest of us. We fought. They lost."

Binder squinted at Grey, a disapproving scowl coming over his features. "You turned your coat, then?"

"Dresden contracted me before Nicodemus did. I did what he hired me to do."

Binder lifted an eyebrow. "Ah. That explains it."

Grey shrugged.

"Hannah," Binder said, his eye going back to me. "You killed her?"

"I did," I said. "I offered to let her back down. She wouldn't. I'm sorry. She was too strong to handle any other way."

Binder spat a quiet, vicious oath, and looked away. "Stupid kid. Not a bad partner. But not a scrap of sense."

"Just curious," Grey said. "You going to shoot us or what?"

"Eh?" Binder said. Then he glanced at the goons, and they lowered their weapons and began filing back out. "Ah, no, the lads ran out of ammunition at least twenty minutes ago. It was hand-to-hand after that, but then the coppers started to arrive and Marcone's people backed off to think about things for a bit."

"More like to get the Einherjaren as backup," I muttered. Binder's goons were formidable, but they weren't going to be able to stand up to a crew of genuine Norsemen with a dozen centuries of experience each, who hadn't been impressed by death the first time around. "What's the status out there?"

Binder's eyes seemed to glaze over for a moment. Then he reported, "A dozen patrol cars have blocked off the area. Some fire trucks are here. Parts of the building above us are on fire. There're a million more vehicles on the way, one presumes, but the streets are one big sheet of ice, and for now the cops are just covering the exits. The weather's turned foul. There's a heavy fog coming off the Lake."

"Ice and fog," I said. "I like it."

"Sun's not up yet," Binder said. "And some evil, handsome old bloke hexed all the streetlights and spotlights out. We get out of here now, we might do it in one piece."

"What happened to Nicodemus?" Michael asked.

"He flew out," Binder spat. "Told me you'd killed Hannah and left me to rot."

I grunted.

"The bit about the money," Binder asked. "How true is that?"

"We've got one backpack," Valmont said quietly. "Small stones, easy to move. We'll have to split it once we're all clear."

I blinked and looked at her.

She gave me a calm, indecipherable look. "All for one," she said. "I want out of this, too."

She was right. I was nearing the end of my rope. Binder looked exhausted as well. If we just ran out the door all willy-nilly, pure chance would decide our fates. Dark or not, foggy or not, Chicago patrol cops were heavily armed, and given the gunfire and explosions and so forth, they had to think that this was some kind of terrorist attack in progress. They'd shoot first, and second, and third and fourth, and ask questions to fill the time while they reloaded.

Some buckshot through the skull would not improve my response time to the attack on the Carpenter house— and I owed Valmont and Michael a lot more than to let them get shot whilst fleeing the scene of a crime. More than anything, I wanted to be moving toward Michael's home—but to do that, I had to get us out of the building in one piece first. The only way to do that was to work together.

"Binder," I said. "Nicodemus screwed us all. But I'm offering you a new deal, right here, a mutual survival pact. We split the pack evenly between the five of us once we're out of here. They aren't red ones, but twenty percent of them are yours if you sign on with us to get us all the hell out of here."

"Your word on it?"

"My word," I said.

"Dunno," Binder said. "Seeing as how you didn't follow through on that promise to kill me if you saw me here again . . ."

I glowered.

"Sir Knight?" Binder asked. "Will you give your word?"

"You have it," Michael said.

"Are you in or not?" I asked.

Binder regarded Michael for a moment, then nodded once. "'Course I'm in. What choice do I have?"

"Everyone else?"

There was a general murmur of agreement.

"Right, then, listen up," I said, feeling the urge to go sprinting after Nicodemus in every fiber of my body. But I used my head. First things first. Get out of the death trap we were in—then save Maggie from hers. "Here's the plan."

Chapter

Forty-nine

The plan didn't take long to put into effect.

Binder's goons poured out of all sides of the bank building in a howling horde, crashing through windows and sprinting through doorways. They ran straight into gunfire from two dozen patrol cars surrounding the place. Binder's goons died hard, but die they did, after taking several rounds each. They leapt onto cars. They waved their arms threateningly. They brandished their empty Uzis with malicious intent.

But they didn't actually hurt anybody. Binder's share was forfeit if they had. And when they went down, they splattered back into the ectoplasm they'd been formed from in the first place—a clear, gelatinous goo that would rapidly evaporate, leaving nothing behind but empty Uzis and confusion.

Most of the goons went out the west side of the building. Our little crew went out several seconds behind them, covered in my best veil—which is to say, looking slightly blurrier and more translucent than we would have normally appeared.

Veils aren't really my thing, all right? Especially not covering that many people all at once.

In that light, in that weather, in the howling confusion of an apparent assault by demons of corporate dress code, my paltry veil was enough. I took the lead, Michael brought up the rear, and we all held hands in a chain, like a group of schoolchildren traveling from one place to another. We had to—the veil would only have covered me, otherwise.

Outside the ring of police cars was a perimeter of other emergency vehicles—fire trucks and ambulances and the like, parked on whatever uneven slew they had managed on the ice. The press had begun to arrive, while an insufficient number of other cops tried to cordon off the block around the Capristi Building. Every single person there was straining to see through the fog, to get an idea of what was happening during the howling chaos of the attack and the subsequent hail of gunfire. I kept the veil around us as we hobbled through the confusion at Michael's best pace. It didn't stop people from noticing that someone was hurrying by, but at least it would prevent anyone from identifying us.

Michael's bad leg lasted for another block and then he dropped out of the chain, gasping, to stumble to a halt and lean against a building.

Once his grip was broken, my veil faltered and fell apart, and the five of us flickered fully back into sight.

"Right," I said. "You three keep moving, fast as you can, before Marcone's people twig to what's going on. Find a phone soonest."

"We should split up as quick as may be," Binder said.

He looked pale and shaken. He'd been born in an age before the invention of cardio, and he'd been summoning demons all night.

Valmont added a firm, silent nod to Binder's opinion.

"When you're doing crime, listen to the crime pros," I said. "Take your share and give Michael what's left."

"God go with you, Harry," Michael said.

"Grey," I said, "with me."

And I turned, called upon Winter, and started running.

It took several seconds for Grey to catch up with me, but he did so easily enough. Then he let out an impatient sound and said, "Try not to clench up."

"What?" I blurted.

"Parkour," he said impatiently. And he caught me by the waist and flung me into the air.

I went up, flailing my arms and legs, and looked down to see something that was basically impossible.

Grey smoothly dropped to all fours, blurred, and suddenly there was a large, long-legged grey horse running beneath me, and I came down on his back. I managed to angle it to minimize the, ah, critical impact zone, catching most of my weight on my thighs, but doing so nearly sent me tumbling off, and I had to flail pretty wildly to hang on.

I did it, though, and set myself. I hadn't ridden a horse since my days on Ebenezar's farm down in the Ozarks, but I'd done it every day down there, and the muscle memory was still in place. Riding a running horse bareback isn't easy when you're feeling a little croggled from seeing someone completely ignore the laws of physics and magic as you know them.

Shapeshifting I could deal with, but Grey had done something more significant than that—he'd altered his freaking mass. Rearranging a body with magic, sure, I basically knew how that worked. You just moved things around, but the mass always remained the same. Granted, I'd seen Ursiel shift into his bear form and add oodles of mass, so I knew it could be done somehow, but I'd figured that was maybe a Fallen angel thing. Though that didn't make sense, either. I'd seen Listens-to-Wind reduce his mass pretty significantly in a shapeshifting war with a naagloshii, but I'd figured he had managed to make some materials denser and heavier, crowding the same mass into a smaller area.

Grey hadn't just made himself bigger. He'd made himself seven or eight *times* bigger, and done it as quick as blinking. My pounding head was making it hard for the thoughts to get through, but I got my staff tucked under my arm so that I could hold on to the horse's mane with the fingers of my good hand, and realized that I was babbling them aloud.

"Oh," I heard myself realize, "ectoplasm. You bring in the mass the same way Binder's goons make some for themselves."

Grey snorted, as if I had stated the very obvious.

And then he shook his head and started *running*.

When I'm running with Winter on me, I can move pretty fast, as fast as any human being can manage, and I can do it longer. Call it twenty-five or thirty miles an hour. A Thoroughbred horse runs a race at about thirty-five. Quarter horses have been clocked at fifty-five miles an hour or so, over short distances.

Grey started moving at quarter-horse speed, maybe faster, and he didn't stop. I just tried to hang on.

The ice storm had brought Chicago to a relative standstill, but there were still some cars out moving, a few people on the sidewalks. Grey had to weave through them, as none of them was fast enough to get out of the way by their own volition. By the time they could see Grey moving toward them through the fog, it was too late for them to avoid him, and there was very little I could do but hang on and try not to fall off. At the pace Grey was moving, a tumble would be more like a car wreck than anything else, only I wouldn't have the protection of, you know, a *car* around me when it happened. The experience gave me a new appreciation for Karrin and her Harley—except that her Harley didn't freaking jump over mailboxes, pedestrians, and one of those itty-bitty electric cars when they got in its way.

I noticed, somewhere along the line, that Grey was as subject as anyone else to the slippery ice on the streets and sidewalks of the town. At some points, he was more skating than running, though he seemed to handle it all with remarkable grace.

If it wouldn't have reduced my odds of surviving the ride, I'd have closed my eyes.

We were moving in the right direction, and it didn't occur to me until we were nearly there that I'd never told Grey where to find Michael's house.

By the time we got there, Grey was breathing like a steam engine, and the hide beneath me was coated with sweat and lather and burning hot. His wide-flared nostrils were flecked with blood. As remarkable as he was, moving that much mass that quickly for that long apparently had a metabolic cost that not even Grey could escape. We thundered past Karrin's little SUV—still stuck where she'd crashed it yesterday evening—and it was as he tried to turn down Michael's street that Grey's agility met his exhaustion and faltered.

He hit a patch of ice, and we went sideways toward the house on the corner.

I felt his weight leave the ground and we started to tumble in midair. It was going to be an ugly one. Most of a ton of horse and about two hundred and fifty pounds of wizard were going to bounce along the frozen earth together and smash into a building, and there wasn't a whole hell of a lot I could do about it.

Except that it didn't happen that way.

As we tumbled, the horse blurred, and suddenly Grey was back, along with a great, slobbering heap of steaming ectoplasm. He grabbed me in midair, pulling my shoulders back hard against his torso, and when we first hit the ground, his body cushioned the shock of impact, taking it on his back instead of on my skull. We bounced and it hurt, spun wildly once, and then slammed into the side of the house about a quarter of a second after all the ectoplasmic goo. Again, Grey took the impact on his body, sparing mine, and I heard bones snapping as he did. Between him, some thick bushes at the base of the house, and the cushion of slime, I came to a bone-jarring but nonfatal halt.

I pushed myself up and checked on Grey. He was lying in a heap, his eyes closed, his nose and mouth bloody, but still breathing. His chest was grotesquely misshapen, but even as I watched, he inhaled and a couple of ribs seemed to expand back toward a more natural shape. Hell's bells, that guy could take a beating. And that was *me* saying that.

"The things . . . I do . . . ," he rasped, "for . . . Rent money."

I lifted my head, blearily, to see the big unmarked vans Nicodemus had used for transport at the start of the job turn the corner at the other end of the street and lumber slowly toward Michael's house.

Grey had gotten me there in time, if only barely.

Of course, now that I was here, the question was what I was going to do about it.

I stood up, calling my veil about myself again. It might not accomplish much, but at least it didn't take a lot of energy to do it, and I started moving quietly toward the enemy. The Winter Knight's feet were absolutely soundless on the ice.

My head was killing me, a steady pounding. My arm, ditto, even through the insulation offered by the Winter mantle. Fatigue and hard use had tied knots in my back, and I didn't know how many more spells I could pull off before I fell over—if any.

So why, I asked myself, was I walking toward the vans, preparing for a fight?

I blamed the Winter mantle, which continually pushed at my inner predator, egging me on to fight, hunt, and kill my way to a solution. There was a time and a place for that kind of thing, but as I watched the vans begin to slow carefully on the icy streets, my sanity told me that it wasn't here or now. I might be able to drop an explosive fire spell on the vans, but explosions are hardly ever as neat and as thorough as the people who create them hope for—and the effort might just drop me unconscious onto the sleet-coated ground. I could lie there senseless while the survivors murdered my daughter.

Too many variables. Why duke it out with the bad guys when maybe I could grab the Carpenters and Maggie and slip out ahead of them?

So instead of starting a rumble, I kept the veil up and sprinted around the house on the corner, and started leaping fences, moving through backyards to the Carpenter house. I came up to the back door and tried the doorknob. It didn't move, and I risked a light rap on the glass of the storm door. "Charity!" I said in a hushed, urgent tone. "Charity, it's me!"

I checked the corners of the house, in case the squires had deployed people on foot, to move through the backyards the way I had. And when I looked back to the storm door, the heavy security door beyond it had been opened and, the twin barrels of a coach gun gaped in front of my eyes.

I dropped my veil in a hurry and held up my hands. I think I said something clever, like "Glurk!"

Charity lowered the shotgun, her blue eyes wide. She was wearing pajamas and one of her handmade tactical coats over them—a layer of titanium mail between two multilayered coats of antiballistic fabric. She had what looked like a Colt Model 1911 in a holster on her hip. "Harry!" she said, and hurriedly opened the storm door.

I hurried in and said, "They're coming."

"Michael just called," she said, nodding, and shut the

security door behind me, throwing multiple bolts closed as she did.

"Where are the kids?"

"Upstairs, in the panic room."

"We've got to get them out," I said.

"Too late," said a voice from the front room. "They're here."

I padded forward intently, and found Waldo Butters crouching by the front windows, staring out. He was wearing his Batman vest with all its magical gadgets, and holding a pump-action shotgun carefully, as if he knew how to use it, but only just.

In the doorway to the kitchen stood Uriel. He was wearing an apron. There was what appeared to be pancake flour staining his shirt. Instead of looking dangerous and absolute, the way an archangel should, he looked slender and a little tired and vulnerable. He didn't have a gun, but he stood holding a long kitchen knife in competent hands, and there was a quiet balance to his body that would have warned me that he might be dangerous if I hadn't known him.

Mouse sat next to Uriel, looking extremely serious. His tail thumped twice against the vulnerable archangel's legs as he saw me.

"Da . . . ," Charity began, when she saw Uriel. "Darn it," she continued, her voice annoyed. "You're supposed to be upstairs with the children."

"I was fighting wars when this planet was nothing but expanding gasses," Uriel said.

"You also didn't leak and die if someone poked a hole in you," I said.

The angel frowned. "I can help."

"Help what?" I asked him, drawing the monster revolver from my duster pocket. "Slice up bananas for pancakes? This is a gunfight."

"Harry," Butters said urgently.

"Ennghk," I said in frustration, and went to Butters. "Mouse, stay with him, boy."

"Woof," Mouse said seriously. That was obviously the mutt's plan, but I read somewhere that a good commander never gives an order he knows won't be obeyed. It therefore stood to reason that he might as well give orders that he knows will be obeyed whenever possible.

"Kill the lights," I said to Charity.

She nodded. Most of the lights were already out, but a few night-lights that could double as detachable flashlights glowed in power outlets here and there. She went around detaching them, and the interior of the home became darker than the predawn winter light outside.

I moved to Butters's side and peered out through the translucent drapes while I reloaded my big revolver. I could dimly see squires unloading from the two vans, now parked in front of the house. They carried shotguns and rifles, as they had before.

"Nine," Butters said quietly, counting gunmen. "Ten. Eleven. Jesus."

"Keep counting," I said. "It might matter."

Butters nodded. "Fourteen. Fifteen. Sixteen? Sixteen."

"Stay down," I told everyone. "Stay away from the windows. Don't let them know anything."

Someone moved through the dark and crouched quietly next to me. "I called the police already," Charity said.

"They're responding to a big emergency," I replied. "Be a while before they get here." I noted two pairs of gunmen splitting off from the others, heading around either side of the house. "They're going around."

"I'll take the back," Charity said.

"You know how to use guns, too, huh?" I asked her.

I saw her teeth gleam in the dimness. "I like hammers and axes better. We'll know in a minute."

"Luck," I said, and she vanished back into the rear of the house.

Michael's house had been fortified the same way mine had been, with heavy-duty security doors that would resist anything short of breaching charges or the determined use of a ram. With anything like a little luck, they might try the doors, find them tough, and waste some time figuring it out.

But Nicodemus didn't leave room for luck in his plans. Eight men started carefully toward the front door over the lawn. Two of them were carrying small charges of plastic explosives. Of course, he'd already scoped the place out. Or maybe he just planned to blow the door off its hinges even if it was made of painted paper.

Dammit, I wasn't a soldier. I didn't have training in the whole tactical thing. But if it was me, and I wanted to get inside a house where I expected at least a little bit of fight, it might be smart to go in from two directions at once. Maybe I'd have most of my guys coming from the front, and just a few from the back, to reduce the chances of them massacring one another by mistake. For that matter, maybe I'd just put a few guys on the back door to plug anyone who tried to run away.

Of course, the whole point of breaching a room is to do it when you aren't expected. And they were. That gave us at least a little advantage, right?

Sure it did.

"They're going to blow the door," I said to Butters. "And maybe toss in a few flashbangs, and then they'll roll in here and start shooting. Get over there behind the couch and wait for them. Soon as that door opens, start shooting through it."

Butters swallowed, and nodded in a jerky motion. His face was pale and beaded with cold sweat. "Right." He crawled over to the couch.

Meanwhile, I went to the wall beside the staircase that went upstairs. When the door blew, it would slam open, or if it got taken off the hinges, fly back onto the staircase. I would crouch beside the staircase, where most of my body would be hidden except for my gun arm and my head. I got into position and put the gun down on the floor where I could find it easily.

Then I waited.

Ten seconds later, there was a sound like a huge hammer hitting a flat rock, and a sensation like standing in surf and being hit in the chest with a wave, only less substantial. The door flew open. I could barely get the air out of my chest, but I flicked my hand at the door and muttered, *"Ventas servitas."*

A gust of powerful wind hit the doorway from my side just as several small objects tumbled in from the other side, and they fell back to the porch with dull thumps before there was a wash of light and sound that would have obliterated my vision if I hadn't already shielded my eyes with my hand. A couple of wordless cries of confusion went up from the squires outside, and exhaustion from the effort made my vision narrow to a tunnel. I saw someone move in the doorway, and then Butters opened up with the shotgun.

I grabbed my pistol, aimed it at the doorway, and fired two rounds as quickly as I could aim them. A man was knocked down, and while I'd like to claim credit for being an awesome gunslinger, odds were better that it was Butters and his shotgun who were responsible.

There wasn't time for anything more than that. Fanatics they might be, but they weren't stupid. It took them less than a couple of seconds to clear away from the porch and our lines of fire. Even the guy who went down scrabbled away, leaving a smear of blood behind him as he did.

I stopped shooting, frustrated at the lack of targets, but Butters kept pumping shell after shell into the empty doorway. He didn't stop until the shotgun clicked on an empty chamber three or four times.

I darted a look at him, to find him staring at the doorway, trembling visibly, his face pale as a sheet.

"Dude," I said. "Reload."

He stared at me with goggle-eyes for a second, then jerked his head in a nod and started fumbling at one of his pockets. I waited until he had the shotgun reloaded and said, "Cover the door. I'm going to check on Charity."

"Right," he said.

I turned and paced toward the back of the house, trying to remember where the walls were so that I didn't walk into them—and as I rounded the corner nearly walked into a squire with a shotgun.

No time to think. I swept my staff from left to right, knocking it against the shotgun. The weakened grip of my left hand didn't give me a lot of leverage, but when fire and thunder bloomed from the barrel, instead of dying I reeled in sudden agony at the pain of the sound so near my eardrum, so it was enough. The squire knocked the staff from my weak grip with a slash of the shotgun's barrel.

I shot him twice in the stomach with my big revolver.

He let out a gasp and went down, and I kicked the shotgun out of his hands as he fell.

Behind him, his partner drew a bead on me with an assault carbine and had me dead to rights. Terror spiked through me. I tried to fling myself away, knowing as I did that it wouldn't do me any good.

Uriel melted out of the shadows behind the second squire with his kitchen knife, and opened both of the squire's big arteries and his windpipe with a single slice. The man collapsed, and Uriel rode him to the floor, pinning the assault rifle down with one hand for a few seconds, until the squire stopped struggling.

He looked up at me, his expression sickened.

I stared at the two squires. They'd come in the back.

Charity.

By the time I got to the back door, it was standing open, one side of it twisted and blackened with the force of the breaching charge that had opened it. Charity's shotgun lay on the floor, a couple of expended flashbangs next to it. There was a smear of blood in a trail leading to the door and out into the ice.

Charity was gone.

It wasn't hard to figure. The bad guys had blown the back door, only she hadn't had a wizard there to stop the flashbangs. They'd sailed in, stunned her, and she'd been taken before she could fire a shot.

I saw a flash of movement outside the door, and leapt back as another shotgun roared. The squire missed me, but not by much, and a section of drywall the size of my fist vanished from the wall behind where I'd been.

"Harry!" Butters howled.

I hurried back to the front of the house to find Butters staring out through the curtains, his expression twisted up in horror.

Nicodemus was standing on the sidewalk outside the Carpenter house, his shadow writhing.

Tessa stood beside him in human form, wearing black trousers and a black shirt. Her expression was distant, haunted. She looked awful, thin and wasted away, like those movies of people rescued from concentration camps, but her eyes burned with some dark emotion that the word *hate* didn't begin to cover.

As I watched, two squires half dragged, half carried Charity over to him. They dumped her on the sidewalk in front of Nicodemus. She seemed stunned. Her leg was covered in blood. The armored coat was chewed and torn over her wounded thigh, where most of the shotgun pellets had been caught and stopped.

Nicodemus seized a handful of Charity's hair and dragged her faceup, to where she could see her house.

My heart twisted and rage filled me. I knew what he was doing. Nicodemus planned to leave a message for Michael. It wasn't enough for Nicodemus simply to kill the Knight's children—not when he could kill them and leave Charity's corpse behind in such a fashion as to make clear that she had been forced to watch them die, first.

"Watch, Mrs. Carpenter," Tessa hissed. "Watch."

Nicodemus turned his head toward three squires, who were standing by with bottles of vodka fitted into Molotov cocktails with bits of cloth. The bottles were already lit.

His gravelly voice came out low and hard. "Burn it down."

Chapter

Fifty

I stepped up to the door with my staff in hand just as the three men hurled the bottles of vodka, pointed the staff, and snarled, *"Infriga!"*

Icy air screamed. The bottles soared up toward the house and hit the roof with a number of dull *thunks*, then came rattling back down to fall to the lawn, glass cracking, their contents frozen solid.

A number of things happened, all at once.

Tessa let out a hellish screech. She lifted a hand toward me, gathering power in her palm, but as she released it, Nicodemus seized her arm and directed the blast straight up into the air.

Squires started shooting at me. A bullet smacked into my duster over my left lung and hit me like a fist, spinning me to one side.

Mouse hurtled toward the rear of the house.

And, as I fell, Mab's earring burst, the two pieces flying out of my ear in different directions and bouncing off the walls of the entry hall, and all the pain in the universe came crashing down on me at the same time.

Dimly, I heard Butters calling my name. Bullets hit the entry hall and the doorway and darted past me in spiteful, hissing whispers to thwack into the stairs behind me. I lay there in a stupor of pain, and another round hit my duster again, and then Butters was hauling me out of the doorway by main force.

I tried to care about other things that were happening, but mostly I was trying to work up enough energy to curl up into a defensive fetal position—and failing.

"Harry!" Butters screamed, propping me up. "Harry, get up! They're coming back!"

"Burn it!" Tessa shrieked. "Burn them! Burn them all!"

"Harry!" Butters howled. "*Do* something!"

I didn't have enough left in me to contort my face.

"Oh, God," Butters said. "OhGodohGodohGod . . ."

And that was when I saw Waldo Butters choose to be a hero.

He looked up the stairs, toward where the children were hidden. Then he looked out toward the men outside. Then he hardened his jaw.

And with businesslike motions, he stripped me out of my leather duster. He put it on. The sleeves were too long and it was grotesquely oversized, but I had to admit that he got a lot more coverage out of the thing than I ever did.

"Bob," he said.

Glowing lights surged up out of one of the pouches on his Batman vest, dancing nervously in the slowly growing light of dawn. "Yeah, boss?"

"We're going in."

"Uh . . ."

"If anything happens to me," he said, "I want you to head back to the skull. Tell Andi everything you saw. Tell her I said to get you to someone responsible. And tell her that I said that I loved her. Okay?"

"Boss," Bob said, his voice subdued. "You sure about this?"

"There's nobody else here," Butters said quietly. "Harry's down. Charity's been captured. We can't risk Uriel's demise. And if we wait for help, they'll burn the kids to death while we wring our hands."

"But . . . you aren't up for this. You can't possibly beat them."

"Gotta try," Butters said.

"You'll die trying," Bob said. "And it won't make any difference."

"I've got to believe that it will," he said. "Maybe I can slow them down until some real help gets here."

"Oh," Bob said, his voice very small.

"You ready?" Butters asked. "Can you access the duster?"

"Sure. I tutored Harry on these spells."

"Keep the bullets off me for as long as you can," Butters said.

"Got it," Bob said. "Let's give 'em hell, boss."

"That's the spirit," Butters said. He took a deep breath, and then put his hand on my shoulder and said, "Don't worry, Harry. You've done enough. I got this."

I wanted to scream at Butters not to go, not to throw his life away—to go get the kids and try to run. It would have been just as hopeless, but he might not realize that.

And at least they'd die with bullets in them instead of being burned to death. But I couldn't move, or think or do anything else. The pain was simply too great. It wasn't a headache now. It was a worldache. I didn't have a broken arm anymore—I didn't have a body at all. I just had pain.

But I started crying as Waldo Butters stood up, rolled the sleeves of my duster up until his hands could reach out of them, grabbed a couple of things from his vest, flung something on the floor of the porch and went out the door.

The first globe he'd hurled down released a sudden, brief cloud of opaque smoke that went roiling out in all directions, and guns began firing outside.

No, dammit.

No.

I couldn't let things end like this. Butters was a friend, and too good a man to let die while I lay on the floor unable to go to his aid.

I fought to rise, but my arms and legs couldn't hear me through the pain. Again, I struggled, throwing up every mental shield I could against the agony, and this time I managed to shift my weight, and fall heavily onto my side. My cheek lay on the floor and I found myself staring along it, down the hall toward the back of the house, past the dining room where I'd struggled with the squires who invaded . . . and where the remnants of *Fidelacchius* had been carefully set on the dining room table.

The table had been jarred in the fight. The broken hilt of the Sword of Faith had fallen and rolled toward the front of the house. It was only a few feet away from me.

Could it be?

When the Knights of the Blackened Denarius set out to wreak harm, the Swords were there to oppose them. The Sword of Faith was no more. But that did not mean that the power that guided the Swords could not find another means of expressing itself. I'd seen Charity Carpenter rely upon her faith when Molly was in danger before. How much deeper would it be now, with her home and family in peril?

Maybe Michael was right about the Sword. If he was, there was still a chance.

And I had to believe that. People I loved were going to die. I had to believe that there was hope.

Hope lets you do things you would otherwise never be able to do, gives strength when everything is darkest. In that moment, maybe it helped me—because I forced my nerve endings to respond and dragged myself toward the hilt of the Sword, clenching my teeth in sheer defiance of the agony supplanting my existence. It felt like it took forever before my fingers settled on the wooden grip of the Sword, but by the time I finally reached it, and turned back to the door, Butters had only at that moment reached the front gate. My duster whirled and swirled around him like a living thing, orange light playing along the normally invisible black runes I'd tattooed into the leather, the mantle flaring up wildly like a cobra's hood.

Half a dozen squires stood stupefied and confused in dissipating clouds of memory mist, and of the others who were moving, only one had a clean shot at Butters. But the little guy's hand pointed and an orange flicker danced out, a thin line wrapping around the barrel of the gunman's weapon and holding fast. Butters heaved, shouting, and hauled the rifle out of the man's hands. The cord released the gun in a glitter of orange light and slithered back up Butters's sleeve.

And then, before any of the scrambling gunmen could get a clear shot at him, Butters hurdled the Carpenters' little fence and smashed into Tessa in a tackle that, if not exactly physically impressive, was dynamic as hell.

The impact tore the pint-sized Tessa loose from Charity, and the emaciated Denarian let out a furious squall and went down under Butters's weight.

Nicodemus drew his sword and thrust it at Butters's back, but the flying folds of my leather duster slapped the blade aside. Butters wasn't much of a fighter, but he was game. He screamed and slammed his head down into Tessa's.

Then she lifted her hand and shouted something, and there was a crash of sound, a flash of light.

Butters flew off of her and landed six feet away, sprawled and dazed on the icy street. I could see blood running from one of his ears. He made a vague, spreading gesture with one hand, and Bob's trail of campfire sparks emerged from the duster and soared away in the general direction of Butters's apartment.

"What was *that*?" Tessa demanded, her tone furious as she came back to her feet.

"A detail," Nicodemus said, his tone harsh. "Stupid, but brave, little man. Nice try." He stepped over to Butters and raised his sword. Butters clenched his jaw and raised his hand in a hopeless defensive gesture. He knew what was coming—what had to come. But though his face was ghostly white, his eyes were steady, unflinching.

He'd made his choice, and he would accept the consequences of his actions.

And for that moment, everyone out there was looking at Nicodemus and Butters—and no one was looking at Michael Carpenter's wife.

Hope gave me a last burst of strength.

"Charity!" I croaked.

Her head snapped around toward me, and she blinked in my direction.

I threw the broken hilt of *Fidelacchius* as hard as I could.

There are moments in your life that, when you look back at them, you realize were perfect. A hundred million things had to happen, to all come together at the same time, for such moments to come into existence—so many things that it beggars imagination to think that they could possibly have happened by random chance.

This was one of them.

The broken hilt of the Sword tumbled in a perfect arc. It flew up, soared down, and cleared the little fence in the front yard by maybe an inch. The rotation of its length was as precise as a juggler's throw, setting the hilt to tumble directly into Charity's palm.

But she bobbled it, and missed the grab.

The wooden hilt with its lonely, harmless little fragment of the Sword's blade bounced off the icy sidewalk and up into the air. It tumbled several more times, clipped Nicodemus's shoulder . . .

. . . and landed directly in Waldo Butters's upraised hand.

His fingers closed around the grip of the broken Sword of Faith, and if I hadn't seen it with my own eyes, I would scarcely have believed what happened.

There was a flash of light.

There was a sound like a howl of holy trumpets backed up by the voices of an entire choir.

And suddenly a shaft of blinding silver-white light three feet long sprang from the broken hilt of *Fidelacchius* and shone in the first golden light of that day's dawn, humming with the full power of the Sword, only louder now, more melodic, and *physically* audible.

Nicodemus's sword was already falling, and when it met the blade of light, there was a shriek of protesting metal, a flash of sparks, and he reeled back three quick steps, staring at his own weapon in incomprehension.

Fidelacchius had sheared it off as neatly as if it had been paper instead of steel. The severed end of Nicodemus's sword glowed white-hot.

"Ah," said a voice next to me, in a tone of intense satisfaction, and I jerked a quick glance up to see Uriel crouching next to me, his teeth showing, his eyes glittering.

Butters came to his feet, and his jaw hung open. He stared at the humming blade in his hands for a second and then suddenly his teeth showed in a joyous smile that was no less fierce for being so.

And his eyes locked on Nicodemus.

Suddenly, there was an incoherent scream from behind one of the vans, and the vehicle rocked, as if something enormous had smashed against it. A second later, Mouse stepped out from behind the van, where its bulk was shielding him from the immediate aim of the slowly recovering squires. The Foo dog's head was low, his body crouched and tensed, hackles raised, gleaming, sharp, freshly bloodied teeth bared. He was no more than a few feet from Nicodemus's back, and at his appearance, Anduriel's shadow form went berserk, flickering and twisting in a dozen directions at once, like a panicked animal running to the ends of its tether.

"Nice try?" Butters said. "Mister, where I come from, *there is no try.*"

And he lifted the Sword to a guard position and charged, coat flaring dramatically, impossibly.

Mouse let out a great, coughing roar of a bark and flung himself forward, silver-blue light gathering in his fur and around his mane and jaws.

I saw the fury and the rage and bafflement in Nicodemus's face as the newly minted Sir Butters came toward him, and I saw something else there, too.

Fear.

The furious light of the Sword of Faith renewed filled him with terror.

He let out a cry of frustration and leapt into the air, where Anduriel's shadow gathered around him in a sudden blob of fluid darkness, and then streaked away, up into the dawn-lit fog, and was gone.

Butters whirled at once, toward Tessa, but the other Denarian had already fled into the fog, leaving behind a frustrated cry that turned into her demonform's brassy shriek as it faded.

Butters, with Mouse at his side, turned to face the squires who still remained. The nearest one, I saw, was Jordan, who clutched his shotgun in white-knuckled hands, his expression bewildered.

In fact, as I looked around, I saw the same expression on the faces of every squire there. Utter confusion, as if they'd just beheld something that they knew damned well was impossible. They'd just seen their unbeatable lord and master humbled and forced to flee by a pipsqueak of a Knight who wore black-rimmed spectacles and might have weighed a hundred and twenty pounds soaking wet.

"It's over," Butters said. *Fidelacchius*'s ominous hum gave his voice a certain terrifying punctuation. "We make an end of it, right here. It's *over*, guys."

Jordan, his eyes welling with tears, dropped his arms to his side, abruptly, limply, like an exhausted child. His weapon tumbled to the ground. And, over the next few seconds, the others did exactly the same.

The Sword of Faith, I thought, cuts both ways.

I realized my cheek was back against the floor a moment later, and dully noted that my eyes had stopped working at some point. They were open, but they weren't showing me any images. Maybe that's what they meant by the phrase "lazy eye." Hah. I'm hysterical when I'm dying.

I heard a sound then—a distant howl of northern wind, rapidly growing louder in pitch and volume.

"Easy, Harry," said Uriel's voice in the blackness. "Molly's here. Easy."

And then I went away.

Chapter

Fifty-one

I woke up in bed. There was a colorful cartoon pony on the ceiling above me.

My body ached. I mean it ached to no end. Just breathing felt like a motion that stretched sore muscles. I was hideously thirsty and ravenous, and considering the complaints from my bladder, I'd been down for a while.

I looked around without moving my head. I was in Maggie's room. Judging from the amber sunshine coming in through the window and covering one wall, it was evening. I wondered if it was the same day. Maggie's raised bed towered over me, and I realized that I was on a mattress laid on the floor of her room. Something heavy was on one of my feet, and it had gone to sleep. I moved my head enough to see what it was, and wished I hadn't done that. My skull pounded like a little man was slamming it with a hammer.

I winced and focused my eyes through the discomfort. Mouse slept on the floor beside the bed, and his massive chin rested on my ankle. His ears were twitching, though his eyes were closed, his breathing steady.

"Hey," I croaked. "Gonna lose my foot, you keep that up. Fall right off."

Mouse snorted and lifted his head. He blinked blearily for a second, as any reasonable person does upon waking, and then dropped his mouth open in a doggy grin. His tail started wagging, and he rose so that he could walk to my head and start giving me slobbery dog kisses while making little happy sounds.

"Ack!" I said. I waved my hands without any real enthusiasm, and settled for scratching him under the chin and behind the ears while he greeted me. "Easy there, superdog," I said. "I think I exfoliated a couple of licks ago."

Mouse made a happy chuffing sound, tail still wagging. Then he turned and padded out of the bedroom.

A moment later, he returned, and Molly followed him in.

She made an impression walking into the room. I was used to Molly in old jeans and sandals and a faded T-shirt. Now she wore slacks and a deep blue blouse that looked like they'd been hand-tailored to fit. Her hair, which I had seen in every improbable shade and configuration imaginable, was now long and straight and the color of moonlight on corn silk. She still looked a shade too angular and thin. Her eyes had been haunted and strained the last time I'd seen her in the flesh. Now they had a few added wrinkles at the corners, maybe, and a gravity I hadn't seen in them before—but they were steady and calm.

Without a word, she knelt down beside me and gave me a hard hug around the neck.

"Ack," I said again, but I was smiling. Again. It made all the muscles in my body twinge, but I moved one arm and patted her hair. "Hey, grasshopper."

"I'm so sorry," she said. Her arms tightened a little. "I'm so sorry I didn't get here sooner."

"Hey, it all worked out," I said. "I'm okay."

"Of course you're okay," she said, and despite the bravado in her words, I thought she might have been sniffling. "I was the one working on you."

"Look," I said. "The parasite. It isn't some kind of hostile entity—"

She nodded, her hair rubbing against mine. "I know. I know. The guy in black told me all about it while I was in there."

"Is the spirit all right?" I asked.

She released me from her hug/choke hold and nodded at me, smiling, her eyes suspiciously wet. "Of course, the first thing you want to know is if someone else is all right." She reached across me and picked up something from the floor near my head, where I hadn't been able to see. It was the wooden skull I'd carved for Bob.

"It was a tough delivery," Molly said. "She's very tired."

I grunted, lifted my hand, and took the wooden skull in my fingers.

Immediately, tiny flickers of greenish light appeared in the eye sockets, and the little spirit made a soft, confused sound.

"Shhh," I said. "It's me. Get some rest. We'll talk later."

"Oh," said the little spirit. "Hi. Good." And the flickers of light vanished again with a small, weary *pop*.

"You know," Molly said, smiling, "it's traditional to

have a home of your own if you're going to keep adopting strays."

I tucked the wooden skull into the crook of my arm and said, "Home is where, when you go there and tell people to get out, they have to leave."

She grinned, smoothed some hair back from my forehead, and said, "I'm glad to see that you're feeling more like yourself."

I smiled at her a little. "Makes two of us," I said. "How you holding up?"

Her eyes glittered. "It's . . . been really interesting. It all looks very, very different from the inside."

"Usually how it works," I said. "Tell me about it?"

"Can't, literally," she said cheerfully and waved an airy hand. "Faerie mystique and all that."

"Figures. You like it?"

"Not always," she said without rancor. "But . . . it's necessary work. Worth doing."

"Yet you didn't tell your folks about it."

For the first time, Molly's calm slipped a little. Her cheeks turned a little pink. "I . . . Yeah, I haven't quite gotten around to that yet." Her eyes widened suddenly. "Oh, God, you didn't . . ."

"No," I said. "Skated past it just in time. Though I think I might have given your father the impression that we, uh . . . you know."

A small, choked laugh, a sound equal parts mirth and absolute horror burst out of her mouth. "Oh. Oh, *God. That's* what those looks were about." She shook her head.

"You should tell them," I said.

"I will," she said, with a little too much instant assurance. "You know. When I find a way to bring it up." She bit her lower lip, maybe unconsciously, and said, "You, uh . . . you'll let me do that, right?"

"If that's your choice, I'll respect it. You aren't really my apprentice anymore, Molls."

She stared at me for a second after I said that, and I saw hurt and realization alike flicker through her features. Then she nodded and said quietly, "I guess I'm not, am I?"

I made another major effort and patted her hand. "Things change," I said. "Nothing to feel sad about."

"No," she said. She squeezed my fingers back for a second and forced a smile. "Of course not."

"Mab been around?" I asked.

She shook her head. "She knows I'm going to want to talk to her about sidetracking me. But she's in town. I can feel that much. Why?"

"Because I'm going to want to talk to her too."

One hour, one shower, and one barrage of painkillers later, I was dressed and able to shamble down the stairs under my own power, just after sundown. Mouse followed me carefully. Molly didn't *quite* hover around like a Secret Service agent prepared to throw herself into the way of a bullet if necessary, but only just.

"You know what's weird?" I said, as I got to the first floor.

"What?" Molly asked.

"The lack of cops," I said. "There should be cops everywhere. And police tape. And handcuffs." I raised my wrists. "Right here."

"Yeah," Molly said. "I noticed that too."

I looked at her and arched an eyebrow. "Was this you?"

She shook her head. "I wouldn't really know how to go about bribing the authorities. And I'm not sure Mab understands the concept."

The first floor of the Carpenter house had always been something of a riot in progress, even in calm times. Tonight was no exception.

"Run!" screamed a young woman with curly blond hair, who was dressed in a school uniform, was a shade taller than Molly, and who probably caused neck injuries when turning the heads of the boys in her school. She fled past the bottom of the stairs, firing one of those toy soft-dart guns behind her. As she ran past, she waved a hand at me, flashed me a grin, and said, "Hi, Bill!"

"Hell's bells," I said, feeling somewhat bewildered. "Was that Amanda?"

"She still wears the uniforms," Molly said, shaking her head. "I mean, even *after* school. Freak."

"Rargh!" roared a young man, whose voice warbled between a high tenor and a low baritone. He was lanky with youth, with Michael's darker hair and grey eyes, and was running after Amanda half bent over at the waist, with his hands pressed up against his chest as if mimicking relatively tiny dinosaur claws. I recognized "little" Harry immediately. He looked like he was big for his age, developing early, and already starting to fill out through the shoulders, and his hands and feet looked almost comically too large for the rest of him.

Maggie was riding astride his back, clinging with her

legs, with one arm wrapped around his neck. She'd have been choking him if she wasn't on the small end of the bell curve herself. She clutched a toy dart gun in her free hand, and sent a few darts winging aimlessly around the room, giggling.

"Dinosaur Cowgirl wins again!" she declared proudly, as Harry ran by.

A moment later, another blond girl came through, calmly picking up fallen darts. She was older than Harry, but younger than Amanda, and shorter than any of the other Carpenters. She smiled at me and said, "Hey, Harry."

"Hope," I said, smiling.

"Hobbit," she corrected me, winking. "Molly, Mom says to tell you that our guests need to get going."

Maggie, her steed, and her prey went running by in the other direction with the roles reversed, with my daughter shrieking, "No one can catch Dinosaur Cowgirl! Get her, Mouse!"

Mouse's tail started wagging furiously and he bounced in place, then whipped his head around to look at me.

"Go play," I told him.

He bounded off after them.

I watched them rampage off in the other direction for a moment. I sensed Molly's eyes on me.

"Man," I said quietly. "Is . . . is it like this for her all the time?"

"There are crazymaking moments too," Molly said quietly, in the tone of someone delivering a caveat. "But . . . mostly, yeah. Mom and Dad have some pretty strong opinions but . . . they know how to do family."

I blinked my eyes quickly several times. "When I was a kid . . ." I stopped talking before I started crying, and smiled after them. When I was a kid in the foster system, I would have given a hand and an eye to be a part of something like this. I took a steadying breath and said, "Your family has given my daughter a home."

"She's a pretty cool kid," Molly said. "I mean, as Jawas go, she's more or less awesome. She makes it easy to love her. Go on. They're waiting for you."

We went into the kitchen, where Charity was sitting at the kitchen table. Her eyes were a little glazed over with prescription painkillers, but she looked alert, with her wounded leg propped up and pillowed on another chair. Michael sat in the chair next to her, his own freshly wounded leg mirroring hers on a chair of its own, and the pair of them were holding hands, a matched set.

Michael's cane, I noted, was back. It rested within arm's reach.

Binder and Valmont sat at the table across from them, and everyone was drinking from steaming mugs. There were five brand-new locking metal cash boxes from an office supply store sitting side by side on the table.

Binder was in the middle of a story of some kind, gesticulating with both thick-fingered hands. "So I looked at her and said, 'That's not my pen, love.'"

Michael blinked and then turned bright pink, while Charity threw back her head and let out a rolling belly laugh. Anna Valmont smiled, and sipped at her tea. She was the first to notice that I had come in, and her face brightened, for a moment, into a genuine smile. "Dresden."

Binder glanced over his shoulder and said, "About bloody time, mate. You look a right mess."

"Yeah, but I feel like an utter disaster," I said, and limped to the table. "Where's Grey?"

"He won't come in the yard," Michael said.

I arched an eyebrow and looked at him. "Hngh."

Michael spread his hands. "He said he'd be around and that you would take him his pay."

"Said he didn't want a share of the stones," Binder said in a tone of utter disbelief. "That he had his pay coming from you."

I lifted my eyebrows. "Huh."

"There's professional," Binder said, "and then there's just bloody odd."

"Not everyone is motivated solely by money," Valmont said, smiling into her tea.

"And how much more sensible a world it would be if they were," Binder said.

"I've divided the stones by weight," Valmont said. "Each box is the same. Everyone else should pick theirs and I'll take whichever one is left."

"Sensible, professional," Binder said in a tone of approval. "Dresden?"

"Sure," I said. I tapped a box and picked it up. It was heavy. Diamonds are, after all, rocks.

Binder claimed one. Michael frowned thoughtfully.

"Michael?" I asked him.

"I'm . . . not sure I can accept—"

Charity, very firmly, picked up one of the boxes and put it on her lap. "We have at least twenty-three more child-years of college education to finance," she said.

"And what if there are grandchildren one day, after that? And have you considered the good we might do with the money?"

Michael opened his mouth, frowned, and then closed it again. "But what do we know about selling diamonds?"

"Anna assures me it's perfectly simple."

"Fairly," Valmont said. "Especially if you do so quietly, over time. I'll walk you through it."

"Oh," Michael said.

"And we have an extra," Valmont said, "since Grey didn't want a share."

"Here's a brainstorm," Binder said. "Give it to me."

"Why on earth would I do that?" Valmont said.

"Because I'll take it to Marcone and bribe him with it to not kill us all, after we wrecked his perfectly nice bank," Binder said. "Walking away rich is all very well, but I want to live to spend it."

"Give it to me," I said. "I'll take care of it."

"Harry?" Michael asked.

"I know Marcone," I said. "He knows me. I'll use it to keep him off of all of us. You have my word."

Michael exhaled through his nose. Then he nodded and said, "Good enough for me. Miss Valmont?"

Anna considered me and then nodded once. "Agreed."

"Better you than me, mate," Binder chimed in. "Just you try to get some kind of warning to us if he kills you when you go to talk to him."

"I'll bear it in mind," I said, and took a second box. Valmont claimed the last one.

We were all quiet for a moment.

Then Binder rose and said, "Ladies, gents, what a treat

it's been scraping out of a mess by the skin of our teeth with you. Godspeed." And he headed for the door.

Valmont rose, too, smiling quietly. She came over to me and gave me a hug.

I eyed her. Then I made a bit of a show of checking my pockets for missing items.

That made her laugh, and she hugged me again, a little longer. Then she stood up on tiptoe to kiss my cheek and said, "I left your things in the closet of the room you were sleeping in."

I nodded, very slightly.

She withdrew then, smiled at Charity, and said, "Give me three days. Then call me at the number I gave you."

"I will," Charity said. "Thank you."

Anna smiled at her, nodded to Michael, and left.

Michael idly unlocked his box and opened it. Light spilled off of the diamonds heaped inside.

"My, my, my," Michael said.

Charity picked up a stone carefully and shook her head, bemused. "My, my, my."

"Watch my loot for me?" I asked. "I need to go speak to Grey."

I found Grey standing on the sidewalk outside the house, leaning against the streetlight with his arms folded over his chest and his head bowed. He looked up as I came out of the house and shuffled down the front walk to the gate.

"Dresden," he said.

"Grey. You really came through for me."

"What you hired me to do," Grey said, as if I might be a bit thick.

"I guess I did, didn't I?" I said. "You could have bailed. You could have taken Nick's money."

He looked at me as if I had begun speaking in tongues.

"Guess Vadderung was right about you."

Something not quite a smile touched Grey's mouth. "Heh," he said. "He's one who would know, isn't he?"

"So how come you won't come in the yard?" I asked, stepping through the broken gate to join him.

Grey stared at me, his eyes opaque. He turned his head to the Carpenters' home, and looked up and around the yard, as if noting the position of invisible sentries. Then he looked back at me.

And his body language shifted, relaxing slightly. His eyes flickered and changed, from brown orbs with that odd golden sheen to them to something brighter gold, almost yellow, the color spreading too wide for human eyes, the pupils slit vertically like a cat's. I had seen eyes exactly like them once before.

My heart leapt up into my throat and I slammed the gate shut. "Hell's bells," I stammered. "A naagloshii? You're a freaking naagloshii?"

Grey's eyes narrowed and changed back to mostly human brown again. He was silent for a moment, and then said, "You didn't choose to be the son of Margaret LeFay. You didn't choose the legacy she left you with her blood. And she was a piece of work, kid. I knew her."

I frowned at him, and said nothing.

"I didn't choose my father, either," Grey said. "And he was a piece of work, too. But I do choose how I live my life. So pay up."

I nodded, slowly, and said, "What's it going to cost me?"

He told me.

"What?" I said. "That much?"

"Cash only," he said. "Now."

"I don't have that much on me," I said.

He snorted and said, "I believe you. We going to have a problem?"

"No," I said. "I'll go get it."

"Sure," he said, and bowed his head again, as if prepared to wait from now until Judgment Day.

And I shambled back into the house, went in to Michael and asked, "Can you loan me a dollar?"

I watched Grey depart, walking down the sidewalk, turning the corner, and continuing on his way. The day had warmed up enough to melt the ice, and the evening was misty, cool, and humid. The streets gleamed. It was very quiet. For a moment, I stood there alone.

"If you have a minute," I said to the air.

Uriel suddenly stood next to me.

"Look at you," I said. "Got your jet plane back."

"Undamaged," he said. "Michael is a good man."

"Best I know," I said. "Would you really have nuked Grey if he'd come in the yard?"

Uriel considered the statement for a moment. Then he said, "Let's just say that I'm relieved that he didn't make the attempt. It would have been awkward."

"I think I'm starting to see the picture now," I said. "Who was really moving this whole mess."

"I thought you might," he said.

"But I don't get your role in it," I said. "What was your angle?"

"Redemption," he said.

"For Nicodemus?" I asked him. "You risked that much—your grace, the Sword, Michael, me—for that clown?"

"Not only for him," Uriel said.

I thought about that for a second and then said, "Jordan."

"And the other squires, yes," Uriel said.

"Why?" I asked. "They made their choices, too, didn't they?"

Uriel seemed to consider the question for a moment. "Some men fall from grace," he said slowly. "Some are pushed."

I grunted. Then I said, "Butters."

Uriel smiled.

"When Cassius Snakeboy was about to gut me, I remember thinking that no Knight of the Cross was going to show up and save me."

"Cassius was a former Knight of the Blackened Denarius," Uriel said. "It seems appropriate that he should be countered by an incipient Knight of the Cross. Don't you think?"

"And the Sword breaking?" I asked. "Did you plan that, too?"

"I don't plan anything," Uriel said. "I don't really do anything. Not unless one of the Fallen crosses the line."

"No? What is your job, then?"

"I make it possible for mortals to make a choice," he said. "Ms. Murphy chose to act in a way that would shatter the Sword. Mr. Butters chose to act with a selflessness and courage that proved him worthy to be a true Knight.

And you chose to believe that a ruined, broken sword could make a difference. The sum of those acts created a Sword that is, in some ways, greater than what was broken."

"I didn't choose for it to do *that*," I said. "Seriously. There might be some kind of copyright infringement going on here."

Uriel smiled again. "I must admit," he said, "I never foresaw that particular form of faith being expressed under my purview."

"Belief in a freaking movie?" I asked him.

"Belief in a story," Uriel said, "of good confronting evil, of light overcoming darkness, of love transcending hate." He tilted his head. "Isn't that where all faith begins?"

I grunted and thought about it. "Huh."

Uriel smiled.

"Lot of *Star Wars* fans out there," I noted. "Maybe more *Star Wars* fans than Catholics."

"I liked the music," he said.

I took the extra box of diamonds and went to see Marcone.

Molly came with me, but I didn't need her intuition to know who I would find there. When we got there, she looked at the building and said, "That bitch."

"Yeah," I said.

I knocked at the door of the Brighter Future Society. It was a small but genuine castle that Marcone had paid to move to Chicago. It was not lost on me that he had erected the damned thing on the lot formerly occupied by the boardinghouse whose basement I'd rented for years. Jerk.

The door opened and a man the height and width of a drawbridge glowered down at me. He had long hair, a mad bomber's beard, and enough muscle to feed a thousand hungry vultures.

"Your name is Skaldi Skheldson," I said. "You know who I am. I'm here to see Marcone and his guest."

Skaldi frowned. Skaldi's frown would have been intimidating if I hadn't spent the past few days hanging out with the Genoskwa.

I bobbed an eyebrow at him and said, "Well?"

The frown became a scowl. But he stepped aside and let me in. I said, "Thanks," and headed for the conference room. I knew right where it was. I'd visited when I was a mostly dead ghost. Skaldi hurried to keep up with me. The fact that I already knew where I was going appeared to leave him a little unsettled.

Wizard.

We passed several other Einherjaren as I walked through the building, and opened the door to the conference room without knocking.

Mab was inside, seated at one end of the table, her expression distant and implacable, her back ramrod-straight. Her dress and her hair were both pitch-black, as were her eyes, all the way across her sclera. She was here, then, in her aspect of Judgment.

People *die* when Mab shows up in black. The last time I'd seen her in that outfit, two Faerie Queens had bled out onto the soil of Demonreach.

Seated at her right hand, wearing a charcoal-grey suit,

was Gentleman Johnnie Marcone, Baron of Chicago under the Unseelie Accords—and made so, at least in part, by my own signature. There might have been slightly more silver at his temples than the last time I'd seen him, but it only made him look more distinguished. Otherwise, he looked exactly as he always did: calm, alert, impeccably groomed, and as merciful as a lawn mower's blade.

"You could have told me from the beginning," I said to Mab.

She regarded me with flat black eyes and tilted her head, a curiously birdlike gesture.

"You were balancing the scales with Nicodemus," I said. "But it was never about paying back a favor. And it wasn't about foiling his scheme. This was full-scale political vengeance."

Very, very slowly, Mab lifted her hands and placed them flat on the table in front of her. Her nails were black and looked sharp enough to slice silk.

"You set Nicodemus up from the very beginning," I said. "You, Hades, and Marcone."

Marcone tilted his head from one side to the other and said nothing.

"It's the only thing that makes sense," I said. "Why you sent Molly away—because she'd have known you were up to something. Why the plans to Marcone's vault were available. Why the bodies got cleaned up, and why the cops didn't crawl all over this thing when it was done. Hell, they're probably spinning the shoot-out and the explosions as some kind of terrorist attack. And I'll bet you anything that the squires found themselves offered a new job, now that their demigod has fallen from grace. Right?"

A ghost of a smile haunted Marcone's lips.

"Nicodemus violated your Accords," I said to Mab. "He kidnapped Marcone. He abducted the emissary appointed under the Accords. This was your payback. You arranged for him to get the details about Hades' vault." I turned to Marcone. "You *built* your vault specifically to create the link so that a Way could be opened there. All so you could set Nicodemus up, years after he wronged you both." I met Mab's unwavering gaze and said, "And you dealt him the worst pain you could imagine. You took away his daughter. No, you did even worse—you made him do it himself."

Neither of them said anything.

But Mab's raven black nails sank a fraction of an inch into the wood of the table, and her void black eyes glittered.

"Now he's lost his lieutenant," I continued. "He's lost his squires. When word gets out of his treachery, he'll lose his name. No one will want to work with him. No one will deal with him. From where you're standing, you've done worse than kill him. You've wounded him, strangled his power, and left him to suffer."

A long moment of silence passed.

I turned to Marcone. "And what did you get out of it? You got to build the vault, and to secure the clientele who use it. My money says that Hades was your first depositor. That when he made that gesture of trust in you, others followed his example—and that now you're holding in trust a treasure trove like none in the supernatural world. And if you got a little payback on Nicodemus as a side effect of that, you didn't mind it at all. And you'll have plenty of money to pay to have him hounded down, now that he's been weakened."

Marcone's eyes, the exact green shade of old dollar bills, focused pleasantly on me. Still, he said nothing.

Then Mab finally spoke, her voice sepulchral. "Do you have a point, my Knight?"

"I wanted you to know that I knew," I said. Then I turned to Marcone. "There were people involved in the robbery. People who aren't otherwise involved in this affair."

"People who violated my territory, nonetheless," Marcone said quietly.

"While helping you get your vengeance," I said. "Go after Nicodemus as hard as you want. Leave the rest of them out of it. They took nothing from you."

"They took the life of one of my employees," Marcone said.

"The woman who did that is dead already," I said. And I tossed the cash box onto the conference table. It landed with an impressive thump.

Mab frowned.

Marcone raised his eyebrows briefly. "And what is this?"

"It's weregild," I said. "You know the word?"

"Salic Code," he replied, instantly. "Blood money."

"That's right," I said. "That's for your dead employee's family. Take care of them with it. And leave my people out of it. It ends here."

Marcone considered the box and then me. "And if I should disagree with your terms?"

"Then you and I are going to have a serious problem,"

I said. I turned to Mab and added, "Right here. Right now."

Mab's eyes widened.

If I threw down on Marcone, any number of things could happen—but one of them would certainly be a major disgrace for Mab. She was a guest under Marcone's roof. For her Knight and instrument to betray that trust would utterly destroy her name in the world—and what's more, she knew it.

"Come, now, Baron," Molly said, her voice smooth, soothing. "Consider how much you have gained. You are in the process of destroying the man who truly wronged you. What does it matter if his hirelings go about their business? After all, you might need their services yourself, one day. The offer is a reasonable one." And on those last words, she reached over to the cash box, unlocked it, and opened it.

Marcone's expression rarely showed much—but his eyes widened, if only for an instant, as he saw the stones.

I stared at Marcone without blinking or looking away.

Marcone looked up from the diamonds and returned the stare for a long time.

I put my hands on the table, leaned in close to his face, and said, "Just you remember who pulled your ass out of the fire when those maniacs grabbed you. You owe me."

Marcone considered that for a moment. Then he said quietly, "You did so as a favor to Mab. Not to me." He reached out and smoothly closed the cash box, then drew it to his side of the table and squared it with the table's edge. His voice was almost silken—but there was a blade hidden within the folds of it. "However, the fact that

there is a debt remains—and I would not see Mab's name
suffer any childish diminishment when she has kept such
excellent faith with me. I accept your offer, Dresden. This
balances our account. Do you understand my meaning?"

I understood it, all right. It meant that the next time I
crossed him, he would feel perfectly free to waste me.

Which was fine. The feeling was pretty much mutual.

Mab was far too contained to give any reaction to the
resolution of the situation, beyond a very, very small nod
to Marcone. But she regarded me with a look of displeasure that promised me a reckoning later. Molly got the
same glare.

I doubt that my former apprentice looked any more
chagrined than I did.

". . . the point of having a squadron of angels around the
place if they aren't going to *do* anything to protect it,"
Molly said, exasperated.

We were walking up to Karrin's room in the hospital.
Visiting hours were almost over, but I didn't want the day
to go by before I'd seen her.

"Any kind of supernatural threat, they'd have been all
over it," I said. "Nick obviously knew that, too. That's
why he sent purely vanilla mortals in, with purely mortal
weaponry."

Molly scowled. "It's a pretty darned huge loophole.
That's all I'm saying."

"So do something about it," I said.

"I already have," she said. "The house is being
watched now. And I'm buying the place for sale down the
street."

"You can afford that?" I asked. "Mab pays that well?"

"The account balance I have now has eight zeroes in it," Molly said. "I could buy the neighborhood if I wanted. There will be someone keeping an eye on my parents' place twenty-four seven in case anyone tries the same thing again."

"Unseelie bodyguards." I grunted. "Not sure they're going to like that."

"They don't have to like it," Molly said. "In fact, they don't even have to know about it."

"I'm sensing a pattern here, Molly."

She gave me a quick glance, and for a second, I could see the worry in her eyes. "Harry . . . if you hadn't been there today . . ." She swallowed. "They're my family. I have to do whatever I can to protect them."

I walked for a few steps, thinking, and said, "Yeah. You do."

She smiled faintly as Karrin's room came into sight and her steps slowed. "You go ahead. I've got some things to arrange. I'll be back later tonight."

"Cool," I said, and offered her my closed fist.

She shook her head and said, "Not very respectful of you, sir Knight."

I waggled my fist and said, "Come on. You know you want it."

That drew a quick, merry laugh from her. She bumped my fist with hers, and turned away—and as she walked away from me, I saw her pull a cell phone out of her pocket and turn it on.

That stopped me in my tracks.

Cell phones were some of the technology that was absolutely the most sensitive to the unbalanced fields of energy around a mortal wizard. When one of us got near a powered-up cell phone, it was likely to kick the bucket right there.

Inhuman practitioners, on the other hand, had no problem with that effect whatsoever.

And I suddenly felt very afraid for Molly.

She was hiding a lot of things from her parents. And now I had to wonder how many things she might be hiding from me.

More things to keep an eye on in the future.

I traded a greeting with Rawlins and walked into Karrin's room, to find Butters sitting in the chair by her bed, his feet on the seat, his butt on the back, waving his hands animatedly as he spoke. ". . . and I looked at him and said, 'Mister, where I come from, *there is no try.*' And I went straight at him, and the evil son of a bitch *bailed.*"

Karrin looked like she'd been beaten with rubber hoses after a double triathlon, but she was sitting up, and if she looked a little bleary, she also looked composed. One of her arms had been wrapped up and immobilized in a sling fixed to her body. Her hair was a lank mess, and she had an IV line running to her unwounded arm. "You are telling me lie after lie, Waldo Butters," she said. She turned to me and her smile widened. "Hey, Harry. You look terrible."

"I'm in good company," I said, and put my hand on her head for a second, grinning.

"Tell her," Butters said. "Harry, you were there, right? Tell her." He blinked. "Oh, God, you were pretty out of it. Don't tell me you don't remember."

"I remember," I said. "Butters went full-on Jedi Knight on us. Sword. *Vomm. Vroom, krsoom, kazark, skreeow.*"

Karrin gave me a suspicious glance, and looked back and forth between us. "You can't be serious."

"Got it with you?" I asked Butters.

"Are you kidding?" he said, grinning. "I may never put it down again."

"So show her," I said.

"You think that's . . . you know. Okay? To show it off like that?"

"You aren't showing off," I said. "You're confirming her faith."

Butters screwed up his face and then said, "Yeah. I guess that's okay, then." He reached into his coat and produced the hilt of *Fidelacchius*. The moment he drew it from his coat, the blade of light hissed out to its full length, banishing shadows from the room and humming with power.

Karrin's eyes widened. "Mary, Mother of God," she said. "And . . . he just *ran*?"

"Not right away," I said. "He took a swing at Butters here, first. And that thing sliced through Nick's sword like it was made of pasta."

"Yeah," Butters said. "Seemed to catch him totally off guard. And even if he'd still had a sword, I don't think it would have helped him much. I mean, *lightsaber*. Actually, it was kinda unfair."

"That guy's earned it," I said.

"Butters," Karrin said, shaking her head. "That's . . . that's really amazing. I'm so proud of you."

If Butters could have floated up off the floor, Karrin's

words would have made him do so. "Yeah, I . . . Thanks, Murph."

Murph.

Well, look at you, Butters. One of the boys.

"Well deserved," she said. "But . . ." Her face turned grim. "You don't have to keep it if you don't want to, you know."

Butters frowned and moved to return the handle to his coat. The blade vanished seemingly of its own accord. "Why wouldn't I keep it?"

"Lot of responsibility, bearing one of those," Karrin said.

"Lot of travel, too," I said, just as seriously.

"Bad guys," Karrin noted.

"Hopeless situations you'll be expected to overcome," I said.

"Monsters, ghosts, ghouls, vampires," Karrin said.

"And all the Knights of the Blackened Denarius will want to stuff you and mount you on the wall," I said, my voice harder. "Butters, you took Nicodemus by surprise on what was probably the worst day he's had in a couple of thousand years, when his only backup was a woman twisty enough to marry him, who had spent the past two days trying to derail his plans. He retreated because he was facing a new and unknown threat and it was the smart thing to do. Next time you see him, he won't be running away. He'll be planning to kill you."

Butters looked at me uncertainly. "Do . . . do you guys not think I can do it?"

I stared at him, expression suitably grave. Karrin too.

"Michael and Charity said they'd train me," he said

seriously. "And Michael said he'd show me how to work out and eat right and help me figure out what the Sword can do. I mean . . . I know I'm just a little guy but"—he took a deep breath—"I can *do* something. Make a difference. Help people. That's a chance a lot of people never get. I want it."

Karrin glanced at me and asked, "What do you think?"

I winked at her, and we both grinned as I said, "He'll do. I mean, he routed Nicodemus Archleone and all. I guess that's something."

"Yeah," Karrin said. "That's something."

Butters grinned in relief. "Oh," he said. "There is one thing I . . . I sort of have an issue with."

"What's that?" I asked.

He spread his hands and said, "A *Jewish* Knight of the Cross?"

Karrin burst out into something suspiciously like giggles. Later, she would swear that it had been the drugs.

Butters left Karrin and me alone a little while later. We had a few minutes until some polite nurse would be along to kick me out.

"You're going to have to take care of yourself," Karrin said quietly. "Over the next few weeks. Rest. Give yourself a chance to heal. Keep the wound on your leg clean. Get to a doctor and get that arm into a proper cast. I know you can't feel it, but it's important that—"

I stood, leaned over the bed, and kissed her on the mouth.

Her words dissolved into a soft sound that vibrated against my lips. Then her good arm slid around my neck, and there wasn't any sound at all. It was a long kiss. A slow one. A good one. I didn't draw away until it came to its end. I didn't open my eyes for a moment after.

". . . oh . . . ," she said in a small voice. Her hand slid down my arm to lie upon mine.

"We do crazy things for love," I said quietly, and turned my hand over, fingers curling around hers.

She swallowed. Her cheeks were flushed with color. She lowered her eyes.

"I want you to rest and get better, too," I said. "We have some things to do."

"Like what?" she asked.

I felt myself smile. There might have been something merrily wolfish in it. "Things I've only dreamed about."

"Oh," she breathed. Her blue eyes glittered. "That." She tilted her head. "That was . . . was me?"

"That was you," I said. "Seems fair. It was your bed."

Her hand tightened on mine and her face broke into an open grin. I lifted her hand and kissed her fingers, one at a time.

"I am on so many drugs right now," she said.

I grinned. She wasn't really talking about her IV.

The nurse came in while we were kissing again. She cleared her throat pointedly. Two or three times. I let her. The kiss wasn't finished yet. The nurse went out in the hallway to complain to Rawlins, who appeared to listen politely.

Karrin ended the kiss with another little laugh.

And she didn't even know I'd slipped her half of my diamonds in a couple of knotted-off socks when she wasn't looking.

*   *   *

By about ten that night, I was back at the Carpenters' house. The evening had turned unseasonably gentle, even if it was a little muggy. I was sitting on the porch with Michael, in one of a pair of rocking chairs that he had made himself. Both of us had a bottle of Mac's Pale Ale in hand, having already emptied the pair of bottles at our feet.

Maggie was sitting with her legs across my lap. She'd fallen asleep with her head against my chest half an hour before, and I wouldn't have disturbed her for the world. Or a third beer. Mouse dozed at my feet, delighted to be able to take up a station close to both of the people he most wanted to slobber on.

"So Karrin's surgery was successful? She's going to recover?" Michael asked.

"Probably not ever to where she was," I said. "But the doctors told her she could get to ninety percent."

"That's wonderful," Michael said. I saw him glance down at his bad leg, propped up on a kitchen chair Molly had brought out for the purpose. I could practically hear him wondering what it would have been like to get back to fifty percent. At least Nicodemus had stabbed him in the leg that was already messed up.

"What was it like?" I asked him. "Getting out into the fight again?"

"Terrifying," he said, smiling. "And for a little while . . . like being *young* again. Full of energy and expectation. It was amazing."

"Any regrets?" I asked.

"None," he said. Then he frowned. "One."

"Yeah," I said. "Nick got away with the Grail."

He nodded, his face darkening with worry.

"Hey, we went four for five on the artifact score-board," I said. "That's not bad."

"I'm not sure this is a score that can be tallied," he said.

"What do you think he'll do with it?"

Michael shrugged and took a thoughtful sip of beer. "The Grail is the most powerful symbol of God's love and sorrow on the face of the earth, Harry. I don't see how he could use it to do harm—but if Nicodemus sac-rificed so much to acquire it, I suspect that he does."

"I figure the Grail was a secondary goal," I said. "He really wanted something else."

The knife was still in the pocket of my duster, now draped over the back of my chair in deference to the eve-ning's warmth.

Michael glanced at my coat and then nodded. "What will you do with the other four?"

"Research them. Learn about them until I can see when and how they should be used."

"And until then?"

"Store them someplace safe." I figured the deepest tunnels of Demonreach should do.

He nodded and regarded his bottle. "Did you ever once consider giving them back to the Church?"

"All things considered," I said, "nope."

He grimaced and nodded. And after a very long si-lence he said, "I fear you may be right."

That made me look at him sharply.

"The Coins we captured should not have been able to escape from storage so quickly or easily," he said slowly. "Which suggests . . ."

"That someone in the Church facilitated their recirculation," I said.

"I fear corruption," Michael said simply.

I thought of the state of affairs in the White Council, and Molly's cell phone, and shuddered. "Yeah," I said. "Lot of that going around."

"Then you'll understand this." Michael leaned his head back and called, "Hank!"

A moment later, little Harry appeared at the door. He was carrying *Amoracchius* in his arms, scabbard, baldric, and all. He passed them off to Michael, who ruffled the boy's hair and sent him back inside.

"Here," Michael said simply, and leaned the Sword against the side of my chair. "When you store the artifacts, take that as well. You're its keeper again."

I frowned. "Because I did such an amazing job the last time around?"

"Actually," Michael said, "you did an excellent job. You defended the Swords from those who would try to claim them, and you issued them to people who used them well."

"Murphy didn't," I said quietly. "I mean, I know it worked out in the end—but my judgment was obviously in error."

"But you didn't call her to be a true Knight," Michael said. "You entrusted her with the Sword for one purpose—to help you save your little girl from Chichén Itzá. She appointed herself the Swords' keeper after you apparently died. And this morning, you gave the Sword of Faith to the right person at the right time."

"That was an accident."

"I don't believe in accidents," Michael said. "Not where the Swords are concerned."

"Suppose I don't want it."

"It's your choice, of course," Michael said. "That's sort of the point. But Uriel asked me to pass it to you. And I trust you."

I sighed. Maggie's limp, warm little body was emitting a barrage of some kind of subatomic particle that was making me drowsy. Probably sleepeons. Mouse snored a little, generating his own sleepeon field. The gentle night wasn't helping things, either. Nor was my battered body.

I had a surplus of burdens already.

"The thing is," I said quietly, "the Swords' keeper needs clear judgment more than anything else. And I'm not sure I have it anymore."

"Why not?" Michael asked.

"Because of the Winter mantle. Because of Mab. If I take the Sword, bad things could happen down the line."

"Of course they could," Michael said. "But I don't believe for a second that they would happen because you chose to make them happen."

"That's what I mean," I said. "What if . . . what if Mab gets to me, eventually?" I waved my hand. "Stars and stones, I just spent the weekend working with Denarians on behalf of freaking Marcone. I've had this job for . . . what? A couple of years? What will I be like five years from now? Or ten? Or a hundred and fifty?"

"I don't believe that for a second," Michael said. "I know you."

"I'm not sure I do anymore," I said, "and it scares the hell out of me. What happens if she docs it? What happens if she turns me into her personal monster? What is she going to do with me then?"

"Oh, Harry," Michael said. "You're asking exactly the wrong question, my friend."

"What do you mean?" I asked.

He looked at me, his face serious, even worried. "What is she going to do with you if she *can't*?"

A fluttery fear went through my belly at the thought. Silence fell. The night was dark and quiet and misty. Somewhere, out there in it, Mab was moving, planning. Part of her plans, the dark, bloody, violent parts, included me.

Maggie was warm and soft beside my heart. Mouse stirred for a moment, and shifted until his big shaggy head was lying on my foot before going back to sleep. Behind me, the Carpenter household was settling into the quiet, stable energy of a home going through a familiar pattern. Bedtime.

Sometimes you realize you're standing at a crossroads. That there are two paths stretching out ahead of you, and you have to pick one of them.

Without a word, I took *Amoracchius* and settled it where I could reach it easily when it was time to stand up.